The Sleeping Phoenix: Part III
DELIVERANCE

A Transformational

Science-Fiction Fantasy

Epic Journey

ishKiia Paige

First paperback edition August 2022

Book design by ishKiia Paige
Illustrations by ishKiia Paige

ISBN 978-1-956297-10-2 (paperback)
ISBN 978-1-956297-11-9 (hardback - laminate)
ISBN 978-1-956297-12-6 (hardback - jacket)
ISBN 978-1-956297-13-3 (ebook)
ISBN 978-1-956297-14-0 (audiobook)

Narration for the audiobook are done by:
Graham Mack and ishKiia Paige

Dedication

I dedicate this book to Graham Mack, my narrator for The Sleeping Phoenix Series. Narrators are extremely under-appreciated, under-paid, very easily criticized, yet the single most critical thing in an audio production. So, I wanted to make sure he got a little public appreciation.

He would say it was my writing, and that all he did was to interpret the words. But his narration in books 1 and 2 helped me become a much better author.

Hearing his voices in my head as I wrote this book helped to make sure that I wrote the book well for the readers, but also for the audiobook listeners.

—His contribution didn't stop there—

Book three will be the first one that is narrated by both him and myself. When I started getting into the narration industry, he was a priceless mentor for me, and still is.

I could never express my depth of gratitude and appreciation for his gift of narration and mentorship.

The fun part of all of this is that he won't know about this dedication until he narrates it. I really have an evil grin on my face right now.

Thank you for narrating yourself into my life, dear friend. Sending much love and support to you and your wife's continued happiness and abundance.

Much respect, ishKiia.

Epigraph

> "
>
> Hopelessness in our lives,
> in any situation...
> is just an accidental mislabeling
> of a doorway of exponential potential;
> and with it,
> comes the opportunity to see it — we only need
> to open the door and walk through.
> "
>
> ~ishKiia Paige

Foreward

by Dr. Jennifer Meyer

Like most of us avid readers and adventurers, I'm grateful when a debut author refreshes the market with something... new or quirky in some way, especially in the genre of sci-fi.

ishKiia Paige does just that with her debut sequential series, The Sleeping Phoenix.

Deliverance, the third book, continues the saga of multi-dimensional adventure set both in space and on Earth with plenty of that satisfying mix of gaming, tech, quantum, and the in-depth characters that bring you along for the ride.

As a natural health coach and author, I also expand the physical into metaphysical with a touch of humor and how to use quantum in our own health. This is evident in my urology book, Piss to Bliss.

ishKiia does this too within fiction by entertaining us and giving us keys to our own health and journey as a human playing on this Earth. Zreyas, the little blue dude, makes me chuckle, and it's a pleasure watching him grow, and learning from him.

ishKiia and I share a love of metaphysics with the touch of whimsical and fantasy. Her wealth of knowledge in such matters comes across brilliantly in her books, but she doesn't stop there. Her passion drives her to share this epic story with many, so she has now trained as a voice actor for those who prefer listening to reading.

She brings some of her characters to life in this book as a co-narrator in a way that only she can as their creator. If you allow it to take you deeply on the journey, this series could show you much about yourself and how to succeed at life in a very entertaining way.

Now that, to me, is a bargain and even a new genre she is a founder of, transformational science fiction. And I crave new genres. After all, who wants to fit in a box?

Happy reading,

Jennifer

TABLE OF CONTENTS

Deliverance – Part III of The Sleeping Phoenix

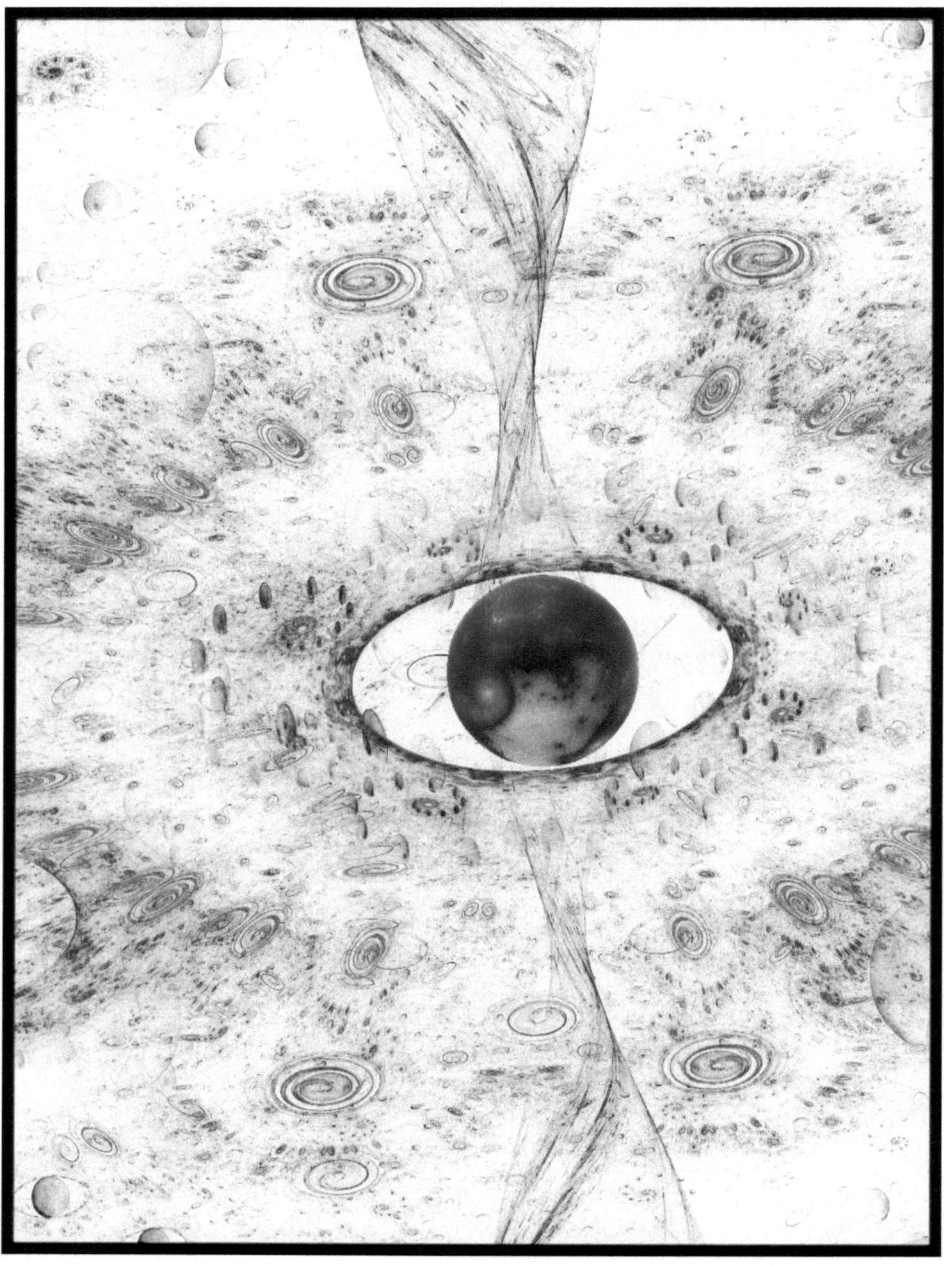

1 Countdown

Rtu

This is an Aqum Interruption:
— Reminding you —
We are the challenge node that Zreyas of the Atra named
Aqum.
Current Place: Quantum ship named The Potential, i.e. Tap.
Relational Time: Just after leaving Tarq.
Recent Event: killing nagodara and the fight
against the Dark One inside Zreyas' Body.
— End of Transmission —

Rtu said with a wide, joyful grin, accentuated by his large dark freckles, "Little buddy, the balances have changed and shifted, so if you will have us longer, I would like to help as much as I can. It will be more in an incarnate capacity to keep things balanced rather than full visage help. It might not seem like much, but Rhom and I have vast knowledge with two extra pairs of arms and legs." Rtu chuckled with an infectious radiant joy in his expression, "And legs and arms can be helpful! We also have the challenge to work together on too. I'll even throw in a few laughs."

"I would pheno-mi-like to have you two with us longer! I'm not sure we would make it without you, honestly. It's great that things turned out better in that area, at least."

"My boy, it will help us too," added Rhom. "We are up against something bigger than us. We feel just as helpless as you probably do. And we need to talk about what happened more before we forget. That Dark One is using ways of war never used before in history, and we need to understand them as soon as possible."

"I agree," Rtu said, shaking his head. "Trying to keep you and the others alive during that Dark One attack inside your body was *not* a pleasant experience. Also, depending on the balances of the challenge itself, we might increase or decrease our visagely-mojo utilization here, depending on what the Dark One is doing outside of that challenge."

"Yeah, that ticking-LFO cheats, and only follows the rules of the challenge as a coincidence.

Rhom then added, "That low-frequency quantum-using visage is blurring the lines between the two."

"Blurred? That mag shitting LFO doesn't have lines!" Zreyas blurted out with heat.

Rtu chuckled, "I agree with Zreyas on that one."

The level-headed Rhom then continued. "We got word from Aqum that the emperor tried to stop the challenge.

"Oo-oh?" Zreyas leaned forward, feeling the excitement rise.

Rhom held up a finger. "But... the Dark One stopped his request at the last confirmation at terrible expense to the emperor. He might have led in fear, but in the end, he tried to do the right thing."

"Ticking-hell."

Rtu propped his face up on his hand. "I actually feel bad for the dethroned emperor. He might not be dead yet, but he has been challenged, and killed, in a different way."

"At least he ended up not being -all- magshit, but he still deserved that." Zreyas had no sympathy for his old leader and pushed away that empathy that wanted to creep in.

All the crew exchanged gasps and head shakes. Several of them said versions of 'he deserved it.'

Rhom nodded. "I understand all of your sentiments. This whole thing has hurt a lot of souls and nature. This is *way* beyond a hunt for you now. And it also factors into the challenge rules. It's all very overwhelming and different for us, too. So, my boy, you and your new crew give us comfort in a difficult time, too."

Zreyas noticed his mind shift to something he needed to take care of. "Before I forget it though," said Zreyas, holding up a finger. "It's important for me to take care of this, so it is not on my mind constantly. Tap, do we have a room for our four-legged friends they can call home?"

"No, Captain, but I can easily make one."

"They are just as important as we are. I might not know the little one very well yet, but she is a miracle I would like to help grow and nurture in a good direction. She is as much a part of our family as we are. Where is Switch?"

"Right here, Captain," he said as he stepped through the crowd.

"Until we have a conversation after at least two varSas, I want her checked several times a week for the taint and Dark One. I don't have reason to mistrust her, but I know now what the Dark One can do."

Zreyas scanned the common room. Every Janquar had an interested expression. Every little thing seemed to excite them. He could relate to that. "So, let's get down to the unpleasant experience. First, I want to put something in place so if it ever happens again, where Tap is shrinking and dying, the shell of a real physical ship gets deployed, otherwise we will need to plan for another ship that we can adjust Tap to. I can't live with wiping everyone out in one swipe, if we can help it, over something like that."

Tap's hologram changed colors to a bright yellow, almost as if she was changing emotions. "Yes, Captain, I agree. I think I know how, but I need Master Rhom's help, if he is willing."

Rhom nodded. "That is a grand idea, my boy. I understand what you want. Tap, it is possible for you to do. Let me show you." A hologram of schematics appeared in the center of the room. It changed from plan to plan at lightning speed, way too fast for Zreyas to comprehend.

Rhom spoke to Tap. "Put that condition and trigger there," as he pointed to a still schematic, "and you will become a physical ship of your design with your intelligence duplicated as the A.I. If you survive, go here..."

All that science, for the not-quite-so-science Zrey, made his eyes glaze over and seemed to fade in the background. That was way over his head.

He looked around, and Silence and the new cub came into his view. "Hello, Silence, and hello to you, little one! You have grown already!"

"Yes, Mother, she has grown with the nourishment that Switch and Master Rtu have given her."

Rtu smiled. "The younger they are, the faster they grow on the outside. But she will be a large one. Probably about the size Silence will be as an adult, but without the wings, obviously."

The cub watched Zreyas standing on the table as he climbed up the leg of a Janquar. The poor Janquar winced as the claws pierced his clothes and into his skin, but Zreyas figured he didn't want to scare her, or... she scared him. Zreyas knew Janquar were not accustomed to animals living around them. They killed everything, so this was a fresh experience for them all. And truthfully, new for him, too.

"Do you know what species this one is, Freckles?"

"It is unique," said Rtu. "It has the genes of a feline, but incubated with darkness *and* your light. We don't know how she will mature."

Zreyas said thoughtfully, "I'm sure its experiences of being in a demented form, not of her design, was horrible, much less staying in the same body as the Dark One. It's why I feel a little bad for the emperor that really doesn't exist anymore. I have a very difficult and dark side that I learned to work *with* for good aims. I hope to help her with that if she has that issue. She may not, though."

"Don't worry, little buddy, she has no taint of the Dark One or the demons. In fact, she is resistant to those low frequencies, oddly enough. But she *does* like you!"

Just as Rtu said that, the big pawed feline pounced on him playfully. Without thinking about it, as soon as Zreyas fell off balance under her pounce, he Q-leaped to right himself, causing the cub to land with nothing under it.

Zreyas leaped down on top of it and started scratching behind its ears. He stood and watched the cub roll over on its back, holding its front paws out to the side and up, claws spread as if frozen in place.

Zreyas noticed it had no bits between its legs as he scratched her belly. "So you are definitely female. I will rub your belly, but I'm not falling for that trick of pouncing on you when you are in that position."

The cub purred and blinked sleepily as he rubbed her stomach. When Zreyas stopped, she rolled over and stood. She walked up to Zreyas, and he noticed that the cub's back height was just about high stomach height to him.

Rhom had measured him in the medical wing earlier and Zreyas was not quite forty-five and a half centimeters tall. He had grown again, though they weren't sure if it was because of the flying fight or the inner fight with the Dark One that did it. But they surmised it was likely the flying situation, since he had a very large energy experience. It seemed to be a pattern.

"You need a name, but nothing is coming to me right now. I would like to get to know you better first if that is okay."

The cub walked up and rubbed her body up against Zreyas, almost knocking him over.

"You are stocky and solid for your kind, I think. Are you made of iron?"

Rtu laughed. "I noticed that too. I think depending on the energy she grows up in, it will change. She seems to be influenced by what is around her, just like all of us. And by the way, before we tried to kill you as instructed, that cub stood over you and growled. She was not having any part of letting us do that. I had to subdue her and have a little talk with her on a visagely-mojo level. I sent her images of what was going on so she would understand your sacrifice."

"My boy, we have established a plan now. I apologize."

Zreyas looked at the cub with a smile, then turned toward Rhom. "No, don't apologize, I feel better now. And it was critical to make sure you all were safe in case something like that ever happened again. Plus, I got to pet our new member of the crew."

Cree spoke up. "Thank you, Captain. That was scary watching what happened to you and... Everyone. We weren't afraid of dying, we were afraid of living without you, Tap, Master Rhom, and Master Rtu. We just found you."

Zreyas' heart sank a bit as he reflected on losing Tracker to Tap shrinking. He was glad he had renamed him Everyone. In hindsight he figured it might be a little confusing for others in the future, but he didn't care.

Then he looked at Rhom and Rtu suspiciously, realizing Cree knew far more than he should have.

"Don't look at us, my boy, we weren't the ones that showed them what was going on," raising an eyebrow toward Tap.

Zreyas lifted his own eyebrow. "Uh-huh! Ta-a-ap."

Tap's hologram turned orange with static waves of blue running across it. "Captain, it was my duty to show that you weren't dead, so they didn't give up. They thought you were, and they tried to do what you told them to do. As all of it happened, I showed them everything. The only thing they didn't get was your thoughts, so they didn't get to see your strategy and way of thinking."

"Little buddy, you did it though... your peace killed the small part of the Dark One in you. That peace and love you shine when you are in that state... nothing dark can survive it. Well, I shouldn't say dark, I really mean low frequency. We should change its name to Low One!"

"The big D.O. Or the Low Frequency One," said Zreyas. Ever since Rtu had snuck and given him the ability to read, he had been thinking of plays on words and spellings. It was like a new world to him. "The LFO."

Zreyas had everyone laughing and throwing in their versions. Then he sobered and got back to business. He felt a little creepy doing that because of the subject-matter, but things had to get done.

"So the peace killed it. I'm ticking-glad that the big LFO had a chunk taken out of him."

"Yes, and when we knew it was gone, we stopped trying to shove you out of the dimension," said Cree.

Zreyas asked suspiciously, "How did you know it was gone for sure?"

"Tap expanded again," said Cree.

A loud alarm went off, making everyone flinch.

"Warning, Captain. Incoming! I'm pulling it up on screen now."

Tap pulled up a hologram and an image of the stars appeared with a huge glowing black thick mist with red veins shooting through, and it was hurling toward them at an alarming speed.

"Estimated time of impact is one minute, thirty-two seconds and it is following us. I have tried changing directions. This is not natural, Captain."

Zreyas said, "The big ticking-LFO strikes again! He was in our dimensional space. He knows where we are now. Get me to the control room. I'm lost in this place still. Rhom and Rtu, can you teach Tap how to create a new dimension for herself?"

Without asking, Cree scooped him up and sprinted out of the room and through a corridor as he shoved him up on his shoulder.

"Rhom and Tap, I don't care how you do it, but change our dimensional coordinates in the quantum as soon as you can or we will dodge these for the rest of our lives with no chance. This happened to Tulyata."

He could hear Rhom and Rtu running behind him, conversing as they ran. Then Rhom confirmed, "We can do it, but we can't right now. We have to wait till this situation passes."

"Mother, we are with you. Do not doubt your skills," he heard somewhere distant behind him.

Everyone knew more about this ship already than he did. "Tap, how long till impact?"

"Fifty-three, fifty-two."

"Two large rooms away, Captain," said Cree.

After what seemed like forever, they entered the command room.

Zreyas Q-leaped over to the command center. It adjusted to his frame and height immediately. "Remind me how to do this? Or did you even tell me before?"

No one said a thing, not even Tap.

"Ticking-hell, I'm on my own again on this."

"We can't help you, little buddy. We don't understand it. Trust yourself, you figured things out before, and we all know you will do it again. You are a wizard at strategy and the quantum."

Zreyas looked over at Rtu, who was smiling with an expression of pride and confidence. *He doesn't even look stressed.*

"Thirty-one, thirty, twenty-nine..."

"Mother, I will sing my song for you. It will help you remember," Silence coaxed.

Rtu snickered and chuckled, despite the desperate situation. Zreyas wanted to punch him but couldn't help but do a one-ha laugh.

The air of support and Rtu's humor at such a time made him feel at ease and more focused. Zreyas didn't feel overwhelmed at all. He felt calm, then he heard Silence's song and felt the resonance. He coached himself—*Remember the fracture day. You made it through and it was still the best day of your life, and you didn't even know it. Today will be the same kind of day. Just watch and manifest the solution. Remember the quietness you felt while you were at war? Remember the crevasse and how it brought you through to more potential.*

As Zreyas focused, he heard his own song harmonize with Silence. He smiled. Even though the Low Frequency One used the quantum, he knew they would make it because he saw them at gate forty, the gate of deliverance that Rhom had spoken of. Their deliverance already happened, and he put it out there in the quantum space, shielded from the ticking-LFO by his and Silence's song.

The countdown Tap was giving him faded from his ears and the last number he heard was the echo of one... one... one...

2 Consent

ꊸꊸꊸ *Zreyas* ꊸꊸꊸ

(Somewhere in quantum space.)

— Can you hear me, Captain? We did a quantum jump, but something is wrong.

Nope, not really, Zreyas communicated mentally.

— If you don't hear me, how can you respond to me?

I don't know that either, but I understand you. It's weird.

— Agreed, Captain. It seems I'm learning just like you are.

I thought you did a lot of test drives with Rhom?

— This is different, Captain. We… semi- merged… when you came to me.

Wasn't it the other way around?

— I think it is a matter of perspective, Captain.

You have a point. I'm not sure I'm in my body anymore, either. We might be stuck in the quantum. I know this feeling. Is my crew safe? Did we die or get blown up? It feels like we are in the quantum but I don't see energy signatures like I normally do in a Q-leap.

— I see you. But the crew's bodies, including yours, are in the quantum in a special containment space for each of you. Similar to an ancient technology of a cryopod. It's how the technology of the ship works to keep everyone intact as an individual while doing quantum jumps.

Zreyas considered this. *What's a cryopod?*

— There are many forms of it, Captain. But on Earth, where Ayya is, a little past her current time-line, they have chambers where they froze them into an ice state to suspend their body's functions. Then they would thaw them out and attempt to resuscitate them.

Eww, but don't bodies swell when frozen?

— Yes.

"I need to change the subject. Something about this gnaws at me like a mag-bug would a living person. So do you know how we operate independently, like when we are — "Oh, never mind. Can you be you, now that I am me, and try to not be so scattered?"

— No, Captain. Ha!

'That's the Tap I know! So now that I know the crew and my family are okay, let's check if that ticking-LFO is still following us."

— And that is the captain, *I* know! It is still following us, but your song is dispersing you so it can't track you in the normal way.

Zreyas thought and whispered, "Why does that seem familiar? Disperse... disperse."

— Captain, it's because you have a memory of it. It happened to you, but in the opposite direction. But I'm not sure how to pull it up for you. I'm still learning.

It's okay, Tap. **Zreyas mumbled,** *opposite direction...* **Then it hit him.** *"The dying dimension! I don't know what it is, but that brief time in the dying dimension still comes back to be a lesson for me so many times. I'm fortunate and feeling the gratefuls for that."*

— I know what you learned, Captain. But I need to learn to be a friend more than... a computer. So, I will listen to the boring, slow chatter.

Zreyas felt himself virtually blink as if he was anchored in his body. *"Uh, I guess I should give you the thankings for that but I don't think I will this time, Tap. I'm not sure I know why though."*

— It's okay, Captain. I don't need your thanks.

"Uh, Tap?"

— What do you want *now*, Captain?

"To know what the ticking-hell is wrong with you?"

— What is wrong with me is you are slow at figuring out what your memory is, and now I can't tell you because I don't want to say because something is happening, and it's all your fault!

If Zreyas had eyes, they would have narrowed. Then he realized what was going on.

"That ticking-LFO... okay, Tap, don't talk, just let me think. I need to figure out why he is affecting you, but not me. And if it is affecting you, then it is affecting my crew."

Zreyas thought back to the dying dimension when he, Rhom, and the light warriors were falling through the sky after his jump into the fracture. Though he was getting better at it, he still wasn't familiar with a lot of science. Maybe he could at least figure out enough of it so he could get them out of this mess.

"Okay, Tap. Rhom said that it dispersed us throughout the dimension, similar to how you confirmed what the song did to me. Tap, does the song affect you the same way?"

— Hell ticking-no, Captain!

"Are you being attacked by the LFO?"

— What the ticking-hell do you think, Captain? You can go—

"I got it, I got it. Ticking-mag-shitting pain in the—"

— 1 1 1 1

Zreyas knew that signature... that signature wasn't Tap, that was from the quantum experience before. As realization and information from what he had learned bounced around in his mind, he sent thoughts out to whoever sent the signature. *Sending you the thankings for the reminder. It s not any different from the Q-leap experience, is it?*

— 1 1 1 1

"Just to make sure, this is the same... person who I interacted with that day I saw the balances in the quantum leap, right?"

— 1 1 1... 1 1 1 1

He knew that was who he thought to be Tulyata now because she gave the time in the tick-tock room of 1:11. *Giving you the thankings for the verification.*

He started thinking out-loud drawing out his words. *"I'm not sure how my song affects me and why it isn't... wait... oooh. O-oh! Tap, I'm giving you the aplop-o-gies! I know what it is now! I didn't even know what I was doing when I started singing my song, or at least what I -forgot- to do. Hold on, Tap!"*

Zreyas thought about his song. He was actually surprised he was still emitting it because he hadn't thought about it consciously, but sure enough, there it was.

He concentrated on seeing the song's vibrations and frequencies. It wasn't long before they appeared all around him.

"Tap, hang on. I'm working on it. Do you consent for me to watch and work with you in the quantum space?"

— No way!—yy—es—aptain

Zreyas knew something was impeding Tap's speech now, and he considered it for a moment while feeling every sensation possible that panic could make him feel. But then the idea came to wait and watch. *"This might not come out right. I'm still learning words, as you know, but I'm going to listen to the real you, Tap—The extension of me not being affected by the ticking-LFO. I know you are in there, Tap, and I'm going to listen to the one who you normally are, not the words."*

He calmed himself as much as he could in this mess. He was approaching something far ahead, assuming it was gate forty, and felt an overwhelming feeling he was alone. Zreyas had a gut feeling he had better halt the approach, so he imagined himself stopping. Sure enough, he did, and was relieved because he didn't want to think about too many things at once with Tap in danger.

Zreyas watched the vibrations, waves of frequencies, and the colors of his song. Then he paid attention to Tap and her signature, much like the 1 1 1 1 signature taught him indirectly.

Tap wasn't being influenced by his song because she never gave him permission to affect her. She wasn't just his potential and part of him, she was now incarnated as an individual.

"Ticking-hell." He concentrated on shielding his mind with his song, the way he had done it before, then said to her, *"Okay Tap, it is just you and me. Let s do this together. Even though we are a part of each other, they incarnated you as an individual. And because of that, we have to treat you as if we were separate in certain situations, I think.*

That ticking bandhula has your location because your dimension was discovered and we can t fix it until you are safe. Let s get you out of danger. Just believe and think yes, and that will be enough."

Zreyas knew this whole song thing was really new to him, but there were no other options in his mind. He and his whole new family of choice were in trouble. One of them had already perished, and he wasn't about to let another one die by not taking action.

Inaction was the biggest killer of anything. Rtu had taught him that. Even conscious waiting for a reason was action, but now was not the time for that. This was not a fun and wondrous first flight experience, but ticking-hell, he was going to make it a significant first flight that was worthwhile. He had to. All their lives were on the line.

Thinking of closing his eyes made him feel better, and he concentrated on the song that gave him so much peace inside. It's probably the only reason he hadn't frozen in panic.

He wanted to push his song's signature into Tap's using his developed Janquarian warlike training, but he couldn't do that this time.

He reached out to the Tap he knew and extended a thought of an invitation to the uninfluenced by his song. Zreyas did not know what he was doing, but he did it anyway. He had felt his potential through various activities before all this happened, and he could tell it was dwindling.

Come on Tap, remember how to laugh. Laugh at the ticking-LFO. If nothing else, it will make us both feel better. I m inviting you to listen to my song and feel it. Zreyas paid attention to the signatures and felt his song, then opened his sight and watched.

At first, he thought nothing was happening because the outer edges of her frequencies were still shrinking slowly. But then he saw the edges of his song frequencies gaining small pushes like ocean waves might gently do on the shore.

That s it, Tap, it s working! We can do this! Let me shelter you. It will hide more and more of you as you let it in. Remember, we are as one; we are just different parts of each other. See, I m already hidden from that... well, you know who. Let s not think about that bandhula, let s think about us and how we first met, the gifts you finally got to give me, and working together on Tarq to free the blue Janquar.

Zreyas stopped talking and strengthened his song, but not forcefully. Tap needed time to integrate it gently. He knew the sneaky ways of that sick visage. Keeping his mind and thoughts shielded, he concentrated on inviting her to integrate again.

He realized she was trying to protect him. *Tap, stop trying to defend me. I m okay, but you are not. You did great in protecting me, but now it s time for me to help you or we are all lost. Don t let him take you from yourself.*

He concentrated on the peace he got from his song. The vibrations of that peace made him radiate more of it. He thought about Tap's safety so it would extend to where he touched Tap in order to hide her, too.

Zreyas opened his sight again and noticed veins of frequencies were growing through her. It wasn't invading her. She was accepting it and the comfort she got from it was visible. The longer his song went, the more hidden she became.

I'm here, Tap. We are going to be okay.

— 'es, -tain

His heart wanted to fly hearing those words... well, partial words. But he knew she was strong and not letting herself give in to the automatic responses. It just wasn't her way. *Oh, Tap, giving to you the thankings for not giving in. You are important to us for many reasons, not just because you are a pheno-mi-tastic ship. The whole multiverse needs what you have to give!*

Zreyas noticed changes as the veins of his song ran through her, hiding those parts that had shrunk. They grew until it eventually hid all of her.

— 'ank you, Cap-'n

"*Live, my new friend. You are doing so great... we are doing it together.*" Zreyas' joy seemed to magnify his song. The more it did, the more he and Tap pushed their outer edges of potential further out. *Keep going Tap, we are doing it. We must get past where your original range was or he will find us. Let s show him we aren t as easy to conquer as he thinks.*

He wasn't sure of that, but he had to say what was workable in his mind with all his heart, or Tap would notice his fear, and that meant they would likely fail since they were dealing with the quantum. He had learned that possibility was an actual thing, no matter how obscure it sounded, and that was what he was putting all his bets on.

Zreyas concentrated on his song and chose not to see what was going on so he wouldn't make a judgment on it, because it would affect it. Instead, he turned off his sight. How he did that, he didn't know, but he would take the time to figure that out later. He concentrated on what he thought was possible, how Tap had healed and even grown, and how his new family and crew were okay and thriving.

If he hadn't been in the quantum, he would have thought he had dozed off because it startled him awake.

— Captain, I'm okay. Wake the ticking-hell up!

Oh no, he thought, she is still under the influence of the—

— I'm kidding Captain! Ha! We are hidden and sitting near gate forty, and everything is okay.

"Are you actually using voice inflection and sarcasm?"

— Yes, Captain, but I'll try to curb myself a little on that.

Zreyas checked the song, then Tap, and sure enough, they had been camouflaged. "Tap, we need to change your dimension."

— Agreed, Captain. But I wanted to wait for you so we could do it together in case something happened to me in the future. I have now made it possible for you to do it, too. I can change it back if you wish.

"No, no, that is pheno' that you did. So let's do this."

Zreyas spent the next short bit of time having Tap walk him through, doing the dimension change with her. He didn't quite grab it and utterly failed to get it. But the dimension had changed, and they were safe. Both seemed to sigh in relief.

— We can practice regularly until you get it down, Captain.

"Yes, that will be a must, I think. It would make my mind rest at ease a bit more, for all our sakes."

— Yes, Captain. I agree. I want to take some time to breathe if that is okay.

"No, that sounds good to me. I think I coul—"

— Thank you, Captain. That was a nice rest.

"But..."

— Yes, Captain?

Zreyas chuckled. *"Shall we stop the quantum jump and let our friends and family breathe real breath again?"*

— Of course, Captain!

3 Jump-Hurl

When Zreyas came out of the ship's quantum jump, he felt nauseous, but not like the first time he jumped. He opened the container in his station and breathed in the medicine that Rtu had given him and immediately felt it begin to subside.

That is when he heard many grunts and sickening hurl noises. Everyone in the bridge area was on the ground throwing up their stomach contents except himself, Rhom, and Rtu.

"Oops, guess I better share," he said as Rtu nodded at him.

"I got an extra too. I'll help you, Captain."

"Giving you the thankings for that, Freckles. This will not smell good or look pretty, though."

"Not to worry, Captain. I'm taking care of the part that hits the floor and walls, here and in the rest of the ship."

Rhom shook his head. "That bad, huh?"

"Yes, Master Rhom. It's that bad. But there are some that have even spouted out the other-r... well, spouted."

"Tap, I want to speak to everyone, is that possible?"

"Yes, Captain, say anything you want and they will hear you now. I have the intercom on."

"This is Captain Zreyas. Welcome to your first quantum jump after-hurl. Don't worry, help is coming and Tap is cleaning up after you, so be sure to vomit on the floor for now." As he continued talking, he went to Cree, who was not doing well. "Master Rtu and I will come around with a jug of medicine. If you are an engineering or medical staff member, you will be a priority because we are working on something now to get everyone some help faster. In addition, so that we don't have to explain it every time, inhale the fumes. We are working on getting this integrated into Tap's systems, so there will be stations to go to if you are new to jumping. Till then, we do it the slow way."

"I can do that, Captain. I have put it on our list to get done."

"I'll help her now, my boy. There isn't much I can do for the moment and I might as well help Tap. We will need this system again soon," said Rhom, as he stepped over Cree to get to another station on the bridge.

Then he looked at his brother. "Rtu, can you get Engineer Right cured and up to speed so he can also take part in this project while we do it? It will be good training."

"I'm on it, brother!" came a faint yell from down the hall.

Rhom met a new hologram of Tap with an engineering insignia on the upper left chest area of her shirt. It had small and large gears rotating and the word 'Engineering' under it.

Zreyas lifted his eyebrows with a grin as he thought about how Tap was really enjoying the creative part of customizing herself. First it was the colors of her mood, and now this. As he worked to help, he told Tap, "Nice touch of the role insignia on the shirt of your hologram, Tap. It will be phen-o-mi' for many reasons."

— Thank you, Captain. I'm finding it is fun, and it's easy for crew members to identify who to ask for help.

Great idea! Zreyas thought about his four-legged friends and thought he would ask Tap privately about that so he wouldn't be on the intercom. *Tap, how do I turn on and off the intercom?*

— Captain, just say intercom on or intercom off. Once our connection is more comfortable, I can imagine all you would need to do is think about it as proficient as you are working with the quantum.

Intercom off. "Tap, how are Silence and the cub doing?"

"They are doing great, Captain. Silence is singing a song to help the men calm down, and the cub is trying to do the same, but it is coming out with little growls."

Zreyas asked Cree if he was okay. After getting a nod, and a breathy confirmation, Cree went to Kry to help him. He wanted to laugh at what Tap told him, but he didn't want it to be misinterpreted.

I would love to see the cub do that, Tap. Record it. I bet it's funny. But right now, I need to concentrate on the ones that are sick.

— Happy to do that, Captain.

Kry looked at him as he sat up. "Thank you, Captain. I think that is the first thing I want to learn to make as a doctor."

Rhom called out, "Come on over, Kry, we are working on that right now!"

Zreyas grinned as he watched Kry get up a little wobbly with a look of determination. "Anything to help with that mag-shitting jump sickness."

He then went to help Switch, and Zreyas thought he was probably the worst of them so far. "Switch, my friend. I am sending you the aplop-o-gies for the whole unexpected sickness. It happened to me just as bad, too. Breathe in deep. Trust me, you will want to give it the celebration embrace. Just don't take it—I'll hold it here as long as you need."

Switch hurled up more bile and then gave Zreyas a look that screamed skept-i-lation and leaned over to sniff the fumes over the jug. Was that the right word? He shrugged figuring it was one now.

The more Cree smelled it, the deeper his whiff got. He let out a groan of relief and started inhaling it again with enthusiasm.

While he held the jug for Switch he said, "Monitor what is going on outside the ship, Tap."

"Yes, Captain. Already on it. So far, it's only us and the big looming gate up there with long furry eel-like creatures swishing around it, but we are monitoring them, too."

Not really paying much attention to Tap, he tried to help Switch sit up as much as he could, being his size. "Cree, are you well enough now to help Switch? I think he needs to go to the medical place."

"Yes, Captain. Be right there." Cree sloshed and wavered up to his feet and walked over to Switch, falling a little hard down on his knees as he reached for Switch to help him sit up.

"While you are there, I think you might want to stay there with him for both your sakes."

"Yes, Captain, good idea." Cree and Switch helped each other get up and start the walk back down the hall, trying to step over bodies.

Zreyas spent the next hour making his way through the room and down the hall, helping his crew with the jump sickness.

"Captain, Master Rhom, Kry, and I have created the

system you wanted to create for having jump sickness. We made them useful for other types too, but we don't have it set up yet to connect to those medications."

Zreyas q-leaped back to the three on the bridge.

"There are stations next to the lavatories throughout the ship. When they walk in, they will get a dose of what it is they need, depending on the sickness."

"What is a lavatory?" asked Zreyas.

"Do you remember what Tulyata made for you in the wall in her dimension when you had to eliminate? It has several names for it; lavatory, bathroom, latrine, loo, etc."

"Ah, yes, we had another word for it, but I think 'bathroom' sounds better, but loo is easy and short, hmm."

"We also have shower rooms, Captain. They are near the quarters. And you have a private bathroom and shower room."

Zreyas nodded. "Sending you the thankings, Tap, for making it nice for all of us."

Rhom smiled and gestured toward his captain station. "All you need to do, my boy, is put your jug back in the place you had it before. It will replicate the chemistry and put it into tanks to disperse. In the future, when we get low, we will need to make the medicine by hand. But by then, Kry and his team will have learned how to make it."

Zreyas Q-leaped over to his station and put the jug back into its holder, then it sealed itself in. *Intercom on.* "Tap, Master Rhom, Right, and Kry have created stations that will disperse the medicine you need to calm your stomachs down. The stations are beside all bathrooms. The stations should be operational now. Nice work everyone. Zreyas, out." *Intercom off.* Zreyas plopped down in his chair, relieved.

Then he winced as he heard faint echoes of the words, 'Thank Zreyas' will.'

Before he could react, Rhom said, "Can I have a word with you, my boy?"

Suddenly distracted and eager to learn what he might want to talk to him about, he said, *Intercom on.* "Everyone but the Masters and Tap, clear the bridge. There is much to do and we need to assess what is going on as well. Report to your assigned officers if you have them. If you don't yet, assemble in the common room and wait for orders and start cleaning and doing what needs to be done. Be ready to help. Tap will come get you when she needs extra hands as well. Captain Zreyas out." *Intercom off.*

Zreyas looked at Rhom and waited for him while he just breathed. "I didn't think to warn them about the jump sickness."

"There wasn't enough time, Little Buddy. Don't worry about things that won't help now," said Rtu, happily sitting down.

"Would you like to hear some of my thoughts on what just happened?" Rhom asked.

Eager to see what he might have done wrong, he replied, "Yes, I would."

Rhom sat down in a station chair and turned toward him. "Honestly, I think you handled the situation perfectly, my boy. I can't think of anything that was not good."

Zreyas sighed in relief and put a hand to his chest. Just as he was about to say something, Rhom held a hand up. He knew then he was about to get a cracked off chunk of truth about something.

"Oh, here it comes, little buddy," said Rtu with a laugh.

Rhom grinned slightly. "It was what you were *about* to do that I wanted to talk to you about."

Zreyas considered what that might be. Then it hit him.

"Oh, when I winced and was about to tell them to stop saying things that were treating me like a visage."

"Don't be so hard on them about their references, my boy. Technically, they are thanking correctly. It was your will that put all this into place. You don't have to be a visage to be thanked reverently like that. Let them get oriented and over the shock of being saved, respected, and valued."

Rtu leaned forward eagerly. "Yeah, little buddy. He isn't saying that you are supposed to act like a visage or don't take credit that is due. Right now, you are still up in the air and out of their reach in a lot of their eyes. But, like the artisan, he has gotten to know you a bit and treats you with respect and loyalty, but still treats you as a respected captain, not a visage."

"Agreed, my boy. He's a little more grounded with knowing you. The others are in awe of the stories and what wonderful things you did in outlandish circumstances. So, they don't really know you yet. Give them time. They will settle down and have a more grounded perspective of you."

"We aren't saying to not say something if they go a little too far, but 'Zreyas' will' is technically correct if you are the one that made things happen. There are too many changes going on to get tripped up over a little thing like that. Gratefulness is a high frequency, no matter who and what you are grateful for."

Zreyas messaged his temples with his thumb and middle finger as he contemplated what they had just said. "But is that how they are meaning it?"

"Does it matter?" asked Rhom.

"Well, yeah... I don't know. I just don't feel comfortable with it. I don't want to mislead them."

"Are you?"

"No."

"Then what are you afraid of, my boy?" asked Rhom.

Zreyas thought and considered the question. He knew Rhom wasn't trying to manipulate him. His friend was just trying to help him.

He finally said, "I'm afraid of being that statue of pure hate, or a commander like my father. That is what I'm afraid of, but I don't see how that has anything to do with not feeling comfortable about my crew using the words, 'Zreyas' will'."

"Are you sure about that in your case?"

"It sounds so much like... you know what? I really don't know what you are getting at."

"What are you focusing on most?" asked Rtu.

Zreyas thought about the subject itself, making sure he got nothing else mixed up in it. "I guess I'm mostly not wanting to be like my commander or my old culture."

"So that is what you will..." Rhom held out a hand and stopped the sentence purposefully for him to fill in the blank.

He realized what they were trying to get at. "Ticking-hell." He rubbed his face, feeling so tired and overwhelmed. "I am attracting it by focusing on it all the time, making my battle against it even harder."

Both of his friends nodded.

Rtu gently asked, "What is the better tactical solution, little buddy?"

He knew Rtu was helping him use his own way of thinking to work this out and was grateful for that. Since it had been the base lesson for so many things for him, he thought about his Q-leaps as his exhaustion really set in.

Zreyas wasn't really sure if the visages knew what happened during the jump, but it was likely they did. He knew they wouldn't push him past what he could handle, so he tried to focus. Thinking about his Q-leap experiences from when he started doing them to the present time. He realized it was all about what he wanted to achieve and where he wanted to be. The one time he didn't focus on those things, he almost died.

When he looked up at his two friends and teachers, they were smiling already, but he said what they already knew he would say. "I want to focus on what I want to run toward, not run from. I don't want to be perfect, I just want to be a good leader, enjoy my life as chaotic as it is, and help us get us out of this mess with the ticking mag-shit LFO. Sometimes I just feel... overwhelmed."

"And that's okay," said Rhom. "Every bit of that is perfect to run to. But be aware of your limitations and take care of your body."

"Little buddy, your body needs some rest. You have us here. Why don't you go have a good long sleep while we watch things? We are in a good holding pattern and hidden, along with the gate. If there are issues, we will call on you."

"And Captain, your quarters are double hidden within another layer of a dimension."

He could tell Tap was trying to ease his mind. "I'm giving command to the twins while I rest. Giving you the thankings to you both for everything." He was really feeling the exhaustion now.

And out of the blue, he thought of Aaru, and how he missed him. He hadn't had time to even sit down and enjoy peace in a long while. They were right.

"Where are my quarters?"

"I'll show you, Captain."

"Don't worry, my boy, we will do a lot of training and organizing for you so we can be ready for what is ahead and get everyone settled," said Rhom.

4 Never the Same

As he followed Tap's hologram, he should have known where they were since he had access to the ship plans, but that's how exhausted he was. He remembered little about the walk there, either.

When they arrived at the door, Tap told him to just think about opening the door and she would comply with his order. But no one could enter unless he opened it for them. When he opened the door, there was a short entrance corridor, then another entrance. He supposed it was to show where the double nested dimensions started and ended.

— Captain, I tried my best to make your room what you would want, but you can change it anyway you like. I know you are tired, so I can tell you about your room as you take all your armor and clothing off. I suggest you do that, so you can have a good long sleep without being uncomfortable when waking up.

"Tap, I might be so tired I won't remember it all, but that is a good idea."

As he took off his armor, Tap showed him the general features of the room, including a desk console where he could pull up anything he wanted, as if he was at his command station. There was also a physical or mental button he could push that would switch it to a desk for personal use.

Zreyas didn't know why, but he immediately switched it to the personal use station. He thought maybe it might be something that would help him feel like a normal person with a life other than war and leading.

"You can redesign it as you wish, of course, Captain." To Zreyas, Tap's voice sounded sleepy and soft now, though not a whisper. It was soothing, not official. "If you would like me to teach you things like how to write or take up art, we can do that here."

She paused a moment, then said, "Captain, many species like to put up what they call pictures, also called photographs, up on the walls or sitting on flat surfaces that are usually of people, places, and activities of people they love. Would you like to do that now to help you get more comfortable here?"

As Zreyas took the last part of his armor off, he asked her, "How do we get those pictures?"

"Since we are part of each other and I am quantum based, all you have to do is think about a person, place, or activity in your mind and I can create one for you, Captain. I've already made two for you so that you can see how it works. There is one at the head of your bed and one on your desk. I turned them down for now, but you can sit them up or throw them away if you like when you are ready. There is a console next to your personal station that will print them, frames and all. You can even design the frames. It is a kind of art."

"Thankings to you, Tap. I'm sending the gratefuls for many things—like you, Rhom, Rtu and the crew. Maybe I will want their pictures." Zreyas took his vest off and laid it down beside the armor on a table next to a door leading into another room. He wondered if that led out of his room another way.

Tap sensed his question and said, "Captain, that room is where you can wash your body in a pool of warm water or have it shower over you. You can also do your incarnate eliminations there too."

As tired as he was his curiosity gave him the energy to have one more adventure before sleep, and he definitely could use a bath and do some of that eliminating. After he got the tour and Tap got a large warm pool of water ready for him, he used the steps down into it, hardly believing such a large pool of indoor water could be so inviting. He typically liked the cold water of the sea or ponds.

After Tap explained all the controls of the room while he sat down in the water, leaning his head back against the edge of the pool. Everything got quiet between them. He could tell his mind was slowing down, and it felt good to just... be. He let his mind sort things as they came and went.

It wasn't long and he started smelling scents wafting about the room. It was as if his memories were ghosts visiting him in the steamy room. First, he smelled the first flowers he had ever smelled in is life just after a war. He didn't know what they were, but since they were purple, he always associated the color purple with that scent. Then it left and he smelled another scent enter his nostrils; it was the scent of how Aaru smelled when he was young when he had to coax him out of a corner or entertaining the blue when he should have been practicing his fighting.

Then he smelled the sea, and as nice as all this was, he still missed the shores of Tarq. "Do you ever have feelings of loss or joy by yourself without being attached to me,

Tap?"

"Yes, Captain, I did. But I don't anymore."

"What did you miss?"

"You, before you came, Captain. Now you are here, so I don't miss you anymore."

"Interesting. You experienced the opposite of me. You missed me before I came, and I missed Aaru after he left. I also miss Tarq and my little cave. Even though parts of it were terrible, I had some good joys there."

"Like what, Captain?"

He was aware she knew, but he realized Tap wanted to be a friend, too. She was wise, like Rhom, with the right time to hold back what she knew for the benefit of communication and relationships. Zreyas smiled at how fortunate he was.

"Like my little cave, more because I would hear the haunting noises it would make in the wind. I felt protected there even though it was open. Listening to the waves and breeze work together to meet my ears. Swimming. But I also have good memories of who used to be called Tracker and Artisan, and the good times we had on our little clay trip."

For the next hour or more, he closed his eyes and told her about all the things he loved about Tarq and his experiences there. And how he didn't have the stress of leadership. He relished the freedom to just be himself with a single purpose, surviving, and how it made him realize his potential, like swimming with his eyes sealed.

"Why do you miss all that, Captain? It's vivid in your mind and body."

He thought a minute about what she said. "It's still with me, yes. But as an incarnate, memories fade and details are lost over time. I really don't want to go back there. I just don't want to forget them, I guess."

"They don't have to disappear, now that I'm here, Captain."

Zreyas heard the ocean waves fade in. He smelled salty air and felt a slight breeze. He opened his eyes and all around him was Tarq from the point of view of sitting on the rocks with the clay pots after Tracker and Artisan had left. Though their names were Everyone and Tracker now, they would always be Tracker and Artisan in his heart, because that is who he knew them as in the beginning.

He knew then that even if he went back to Tarq, things would never be the same. Zreyas wasn't sure if Tap really meant to help him learn that or not, but it turned out that way.

Zreyas stood and felt gentle swells in the water. A door opened on the floor near the edge of the pool and a cloth rose up, folded. Before he left the water, there was something he wanted to do. He took in a deep breath and closed his eyes and lowered himself into the water, where he just floated.

It was the one place he felt alone. He knew he wasn't, but it was as close as he could get. The water swelled around him and he felt lulled and at peace. When it was time to breathe, he put his feet under him and slowly rose out of the water.

Walking to the edge, he started drying off and realized his eyes were open already. Not really wanting to talk yet, he asked, *Tap, did you help my eyes with the water?*

"Yes, Captain," Tap said softly.

Zreyas nodded, reaching out to her to give the thankings, not really wanting to know the details, but knew he would in the future. But for now, he didn't care. As soon as he walked toward the door, he saw a place open in the wall by the doorway.

Even though he had seen nothing like it before, he

knew from his connection with Tap that it was where he was supposed to put his dirty clothing, so he threw the towel in and walked into his room. His entire room was an emulation of his home on Tarq. He froze in amazement that his walk from the bathing room to the bedroom was just like him walking from the rock plateau to his cave.

"This is pheno-mi-tastic, Tap!"

"I'm glad you like it, Captain. You can manipulate and change it anytime you like... I just gave you the idea of potential."

He walked over to his bed and laid down. As he looked up, he saw the sunset poking through the top holes, giving the surrounding area that surreal look. "Tap?"

"Yes, Captain?"

"I'm glad you waited for me."

"Me too, Captain. You are more than I expected, and I knew you were wonder-full even then."

"I'm feeling glad that you see it. Will you remind me when I need it?"

"Yes, Captain. There will be times you do. There might be times I will need you to tell me the same thing."

"Good trade."

"Yes, Captain."

Something wouldn't let Zreyas sleep yet. His mind seemed to loft between subject to subject, letting each one go. They didn't seem to hold his attention. Finally, he asked, "Tap, what about these photo-tafs?"

"The photograph I made you, Captain, is just above your head, face down. It's in a frame that will adjust to being prompted up or mounted to a wall by a special device, though you can't see it."

Zreyas lazily reached up over his head and felt the shelf, slightly turning his head to the side and up. When he saw it, he grabbed it and turned to look up. As his hand brought the photograph over his head. He felt like his heart would stop and his breath froze a few seconds.

"Captain, if I may, there is a story behind this that you don't know about yet."

"I know this story Tap, but how did you get this photograph? Were you there? Did Aaru take this somehow? I know this time and place."

"I know, Captain."

Zreyas looked at the picture. But it was in Aaru's perspective of looking back at Zreyas after putting on the helmet he found while he was looting the trader spoils that day. Tap explained that there was an event that she concealed from him so he would not break and go dark from grief.

"I apologize, Captain, but I was still not bound by the rules of incarnates without you being joined with me yet. I could have called you forth twenty-four hundred years ago, but I felt it needed to happen, so I waited for you to be born this time and captured the event. Every possibility I would try to emulate resulted in you joining with the Low Frequency One. Otherwise, I wouldn't have interfered. I hope you forgive me, Captain. I think you are ready to live it now. It might even give you peace after it settles."

"Well, until I live this said memory, I have no way of knowing if I should be angry with you or glad. But for now, I am sending you the thankings for not letting me become like that thing. How do I relive it?"

"Captain, thank you for not getting angry with me, yet. I think you will understand why it might have driven you mad. There is another photograph above your head on the other side."

Zreyas reached up over his head on the other side of his body and felt for the picture. Apprehensive, he grabbed it and pulled it over his head and held it.

It was another picture like the other one, but from *his* perspective this time. He was looking at Aaru that same day and moment. Aaru had that odd helmet on and wearing the biggest smile he had ever seen on him. It was *exactly* like that day.

He swallowed, feeling his chest swell and crack. His eyes moistened but didn't seal. Zreyas assumed that whatever Tap did for him in the bathing room was happening again.

"When you are ready, Captain, just touch the edges of the frames together and the memory of the dying dimension will be returned to you."

Zreyas swallowed hard, trying to keep the lump in his throat down. He realized he really didn't have the chance to put Aaru to rest in his heart, and he had no intention of doing it. He didn't want to forget him. But the more he thought about it, he figured that was why she made the pictures.

"Will I go mad when I relive this memory?"

"I'm unsure, Captain. But I know you, and it is of my opinion that you are strong and will process it and come out stronger."

"If I go mad and dark? What will happen to the others?"

"If you do, and it is your wish, I can bury this dimension in a place that you will hurt no one."

Zreyas thought about what that ticking piece of mag-shit did to so many, and he felt the weight of it all on and inside his chest. "That is my wish. Any time I go low frequency *and* stay, I *order* you to do that!"

"Yes, Captain," Tap said soothingly and gentle.

It was almost like she sounded sad. "Tap, are you okay?"

"I'm not sure, Captain. I'm learning feelings too, and I don't want you to hurt, and I feel your chest cracking. But I'm here with you, going through it. We are alone together because we are really one, yet you don't have to be lonely because I will always be with you until the day you tell me you want to part forever. Then I will die and leave you be."

The thought of that horrified him. "Tap, I don't want you to die or leave. I think those feelings fall into something like a word Rhom talked about in that dying dimension, called compassion, though I'm only starting to understand it. I have a long way to go."

Tap said nothing.

"Well, no time like the present." Zreyas held the two pictures in front of him as he looked up. He took a breath and put the edges together.

Flashes of light and blurred events shot into him, then this awareness shifted into the memory.

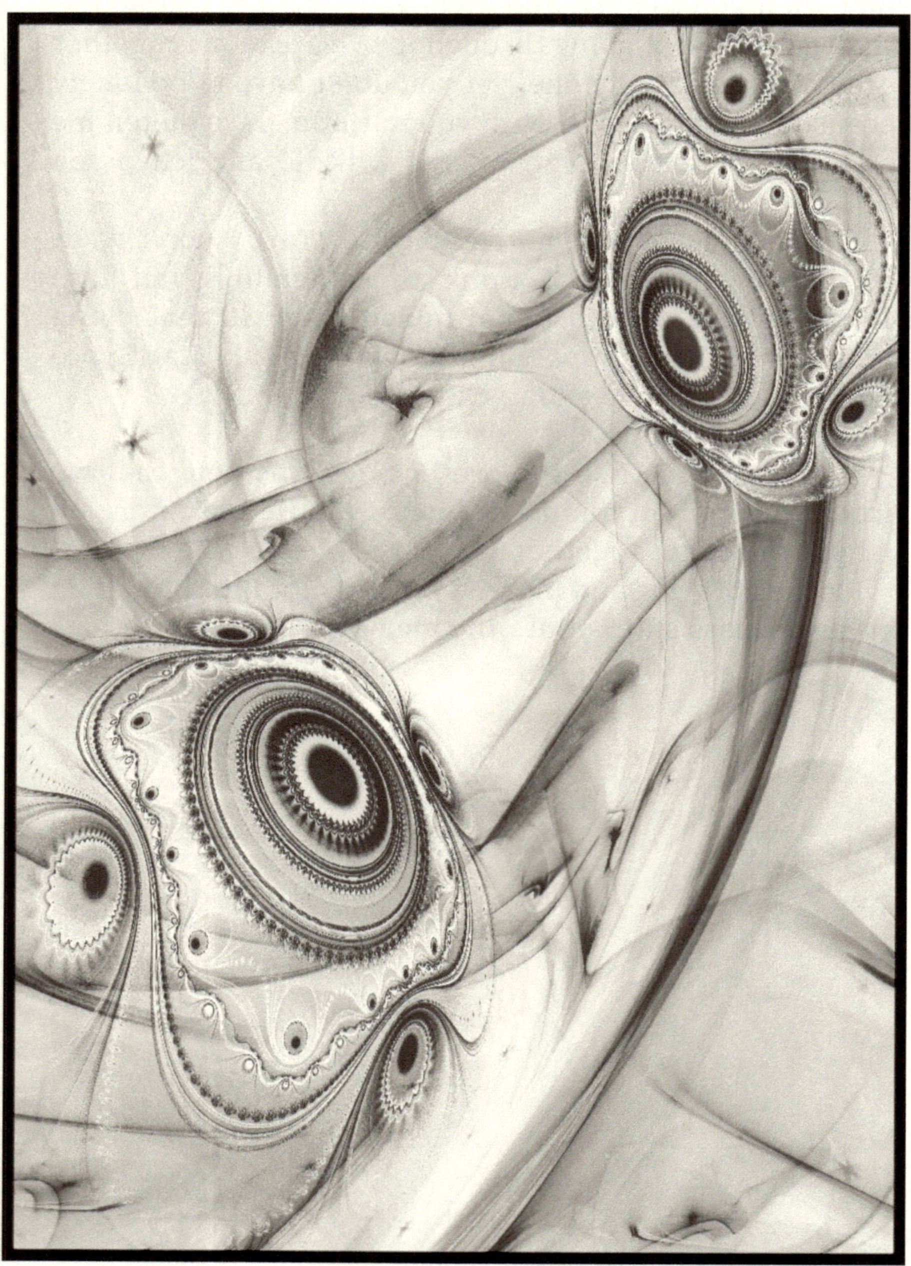

5 Switching Places

(Revealing the Memory)

"There is something you need to see, my boy," Rhom said as he scratched just above his right ear. "I'm not sure I even understand why. I'm just like any other person in an incarnation with limits. It feels like it will seem very difficult, and it will make or break you. After you told me the story of Aaru killing the trader family and finding the armor, I got intuitive guidance from the stars."

"There is so much ticking-shit going on right now, old man, and I don't understand most about what you do or talk about. Why should I trust you? Aaru will be dead soon, and I don't understand this Ayya of yours. I only have your word on this. I don't even understand most of the words you use! They sound suspicious to me."

Rhom held his hands up gently with a warding gesture. "I know, my boy, it sounds crazy to even me. But if it will make you feel better, I can promise you two things; one, it will help you understand Aaru better and that will help you in the future, and two, I offer to tie my hands to make sure you are safe and the light warriors will do the same if you like. All I know is, this is important for all of us."

Zreyas grunted. So far, he had never seen the old man go against his word. He also felt like he was sincere. "Old man, I would feel hostility from you if you wanted to hurt me. I would consider it a fun fight to take on light warriors, so no need to tie. If you attack and I die, then I have no worries. If I win, then I have one last kill before I die in this dimension. See, I don't care anymore. Aaru is all but dead from this life."

Rhom sighed. "I understand."

"You do?"

"I do, my boy. I'm in the same boat as you are, sailing the same seas. We might do it with different points of view, but we are doing it together."

Zreyas grunted, not wanting to listen to this mag-shit, but he couldn't help but notice the old man had a point. He relaxed a little more and breathed out unconsciously and decided right then to do what this old man instructed because he wanted to understand everything he could about Aaru.

"What do you want me to do, old man?"

Rhom sighed before saying, "Close your eyes and put yourself into Aaru's life. Remember his life as if you were him. Play it out in your mind from the time he came out of the tunnel you spoke about."

Zreyas growled, not seeing how this would help, but he did as instructed. He put himself in his place. *I want to understand you, brother—*.

— I know.

Zreyas jerked and opened his eyes. The voice seemed to come through crevices of his mind, soft and scratchy.

Rhom smiled gently. "It's okay. He is talking to you. Trust the experience, because it is coming from within you and him, not me."

Zreyas looked down at Aaru to find he was already looking at him. He blinked slowly, as if in confirmation. So, Zreyas closed his eyes again and let himself trust.

Aaru's confirmation was just too coincidental. He placed himself into Aaru's shoes and imagined what it might have been like to be him. After a while, it started turning into experiences as if he was really there.

Some of it was so weird he couldn't help but get restless and open his eyes. Following Rhom's direction, Zreyas slipped into an altered state of mind. He could no longer differentiate himself from Aaru. Yet, he understood he was having the experience of living *as* Aaru.

He realized that Aaru's life had always been scary. Every time he stood up for the inner belief that nagged at him about purpose, it took all the courage he could muster to do it. He shook inside at the fear of being tortured or killed.

Zreyas observed he no longer felt like himself, only as Aaru. Then he lost himself entirely to being Aaru.

He turned around to look at Zreyas. Aaru's feelings crept in again of not wanting to disappoint him, and feeling the forbidden emotions and admiration.

Aaru had this urge to run up and wrap his arms around his big brother. But if he did, he knew the commander would kill him, and possibly Zreyas. As he looked at his brother, his heart felt warm and full.

The shock of this made Zreyas slightly separate himself from the experience and Aaru again. He finally understood what love was, because he felt the same way, but had never understood it as anything but a fight from many angles. So, he never revealed it.

He now comprehended Aaru's fear of losing Zreyas because he was not what everyone thought he should be.

Aaru felt the effects of unworthiness on such a deep level that Zreyas wasn't sure he could take living as Aaru anymore. It was a pain he was not used to, but he stayed with it.

He felt Aaru walk his path every moment true to himself, and Zreyas experienced how free he was in it, even with the fear. Flashes of all different parts of Aaru's life came flooding in with all the emotions and struggles of each one. His life was colorful, despite all the torture inflicted by their culture. Then a memory hit Zreyas so hard he almost lost control of himself.

His most favorite memory of Aaru was the day he found that armor.

Aaru was casually plundering for items. He intentionally took his time... just so he could stay with Zreyas, alone, with no one else around, for longer. Aaru turned back to look at Zreyas, and gently cocked his head as he decided he was more his father than a brother, but he didn't dare tell him that. He was the best father anyone could ever have, and he pitied the rest of the Nation.

Zreyas about lost it. He tried to pull out of the experience but couldn't.

He felt himself live as Aaru. He didn't think about the items like Zreyas thought he had. Aaru didn't care about them and bathed in the time with his big brother. Zreyas heard him think, *He's my father, and I want to make him proud. But I have to do things my way from now on, even though it will probably kill me.*

That was too much for Zreyas. He started growling and worked himself up into a roar as he lived Aaru's experience.

Aaru loved the armor because it reminded him of that day. It gave him peace to think about how he got to enjoy time with Zreyas with a brief rest from being judged or threatened. He started using it as a way to calm himself down when he was afraid.

Zreyas realized just how much strength it took to live like that. He could have fit in and be someone else to make things easy. Aaru was stronger than all the Janquar.

Opening his eyes suddenly, Zreyas felt the liquid flowing down his face. He looked down at his little brother and heard another scratchy, soft voice come through those crevices again in his head.

— I love you, Zrey. No matter what happens, it will not stop. Ayya teaches me about being limitless, so I know I can tell you this with a truth that you can rely on. I will always be with you.

"No, no, no, I was part of what everyone did to you! I should be the one to die." Zreyas punched the wall so hard his entire arm went through into the tick-tock room. Then he had an idea. "Old man, can you use me to give Aaru back his life? I will switch places with him."

Rhom sighed with tears in his eyes and shook his head.

Zreyas came out of his memory with the full impact of what he had contributed to when he had lived with the Janquar. His chest hurt so badly he knew it would bust any time. He held the pictures to his chest and rolled to his side.

Tap said nothing, but he felt her there. He was glad she didn't because he knew he would snap at her. Right now, all he could think about was his brother and all he wasted by not paying attention to the little things. His silence was Aaru's enemy. For the first time in his life, he imagined holding his little brother in his arms.

But he knew it wasn't the same because all the guilt and grief was ripping him apart inside. He understood now why Tap stole this memory from him temporarily. It felt like cheating the balances to him. But he also knew that there were no balances anymore until the new age came in, whatever that meant.

Something inside him raged at losing his brother and it blew away any thoughts he was having in trying to stay rational. It was like a blow to the chest that was fatal.

He had raised Aaru from the very beginning, because no one wanted him. He was his father and Aaru was his son.

The flashbacks of memories replayed over and over. When he thought about holding the little one every time he watched another thing happen to Aaru, he felt the hot waves and stings of tears rip through his eyes.

The blind rage and grief cracked his chest wide open and he let out the first explosive cry in his life. After the rage exploded, it gave way to the all-encompassing loss that seemed to rip the life out of every tiny part of his body tissue. He felt the most hopeless he had ever felt in his life, and he knew he was about to die from it all.

Time left him, what was around him left him, and he didn't even feel his body anymore. He felt all that existed of himself was pain and the chasm of loss. The emptiness consumed him.

௳௳௳ *Rhom* ௳௳௳

Standing at the window in the command room looking out toward gate forty, his brother put his arm around him and squeezed him close a few times.

"I feel him too, bro, but I know your heart is breaking," said Rtu with immense compassion.

As tears started streaming from his eyes, Rhom said, "It's so hard to feel him go through that."

"That it is, dear brother, that it is. When it comes to the heart of an incarnate, all bets are off during these difficult times."

"At least he made the connection of understanding their actual relationship. The worst grief in the world is losing a child. Let's hope he can weather the storm. His species was not built for processing this kind of thing."

"I'm watching him closely, dear brother, don't you worry," Rtu said as he patted his belly. "I'm doing what I can to help him grow, and I'm just glad Tap, in her infinite wisdom, held that one back. What might have happened, I don't even want to think about."

"I'm not sure I could take losing that boy, Rtu. I trust your... what you call mojo. Take any of my elements to help if you need them. We *must* make sure he does it, though, but there is no harm in helping replenish what he needs."

Rhom sighed. "Well, we best get to work. Who knows when he will come out of that room, if he does at all? It's too early to tell, but I'm going to start the training and get the crew sorted."

Rtu pointed at the gate with all the swimming oddities around it. "That is a little... disturbing. I didn't create those... whatever they are. What do you think about them?"

"We need Tap's talents and diagnostics to get the specific information, but I think we have run into evidence that another set of twins, or at least someone else that can do what we do, actually exists. I see their energy and they have a higher frequency, but there is something... odd about it."

Rtu nodded and put his hands behind his back. "Agreed, and they obviously don't need the same kinds of atmosphere to thrive. But what attracted them to the gate,

I wonder?"

"I don't know, but I sure don't feel very visage-ly right now with as little as I know." Scratching his head over his right ear, he said, "I'm actually confused. But all we can do is the same things as we have been doing. I've decided I'm putting all worries aside, because I trust Zreyas will be okay. We have a crew that just signed up and we are going to need them sharp and educated."

"Yes. We will do everything we can without Tap first, then we might have to call on her. I can tell she is worried and focusing on just being there for my little buddy. She's silent though, very silent." Rtu rubbed his full cheeks with his palm, then asked as he pointed toward the gate. "Do you feel those frequencies and energies radiating from that gate? They are natural."

Rhom turned back around to look at the gate and nodded. "I noticed that. When I built the gate structure for the ship to use, I felt it then. Those frequencies, coupled with taking us out of this system to our new home, is why I called it the gate of Deliverance. Now that it has been here longer, I feel it more, and it's like ghosts of energies. It feels tribal, yet I feel the need to be alone when I'm near it. It's really odd. That species coming here confirms it— they are now calling it home."

"It is attracting whatever species that is there to it, so it must be powerful. Either way, I am looking forward to getting out of this galaxy. It's just like its name's meaning and I'm tired of it."

"Proioxis?"

"Yeah, there is a reason I named it that."

Rhom scratched just above his ear as he tried to remember its meaning as he watched the eel-like species swim around as if deep space was like water. "I wasn't privy to the meaning of what you named it, or was I?"

Rtu nodded. "It was when you were Viduri, I told you, but 'overwhelmed' is the term for your state of mind at the time to put it mildly, so I'm not surprised you don't remember it. It means onrush pursuit in battle. And I'm getting a little tired of all of us being pursued for a battle. Now that the Janquar are here along with the big LFO, as Zreyas calls it, it's like the whole air about this galaxy is built from ego, pursuing, and dominating. I don't know how Zreyas lived like that, given his true nature."

"I know you know this, but it's an extra cautionary tale about how badly we can let ourselves be conditioned into something we aren't by nature. It doesn't have to be just ego either." Rhom looked closer at the creatures swimming so gracefully in space. "Wa-ait a minute... I think I read something about that species at one point."

Rtu almost pressed his face up against the glass, trying to see better. "I'm going to cheat a little and enhance my vision."

"I think I might bend the rules a little on that myself, dear brother. If I'm correct, this is an old species before *our* time."

"We really need Mother during this time for many reasons... like this one. She would know." Rtu turned toward him with a hopeful expression. "That reminds me, did you ever—"

"No, brother. We have had no time to address that. Zrey said she was in the quantum, and something in my gut says he is correct."

"I think he is, too. Plus, he talked about how he felt her signature in that quantum jump on Earth he almost died in. Oh, I remember, he said he would never forget that cocktail of frequencies that made that signature. Knowing you, you will figure out how to—"

"I already have." As Rtu was about to ask about it, he

lifted a hand and said, "but we are going to have to enlist Zreyas' aid to get both his and Tap's help to do that."

"Oooh, and that isn't exactly going to happen soon with all that is going on." Rtu turned and leaned his back on the window. "But just in case, you should at least ask him about it so he can keep it in mind. I think this is going to be important or she wouldn't have bothered leaving the message."

"I agree. I'm going to have to call in a favor to Tap and see if she will allow me to have a lab I can work from on the ship. Anyway, we need to give him some alone time, and it just might be awhile. I wonder if this gate is influencing the intensity of Zreyas' processing of so many things." Rhom sighed thinking about Zrey and what he was going through. "Well, no matter."

"We must trust them, so let's get to work, shall we?" said Rtu.

Rhom tried his best to put on a smile.

Rtu lifted his hands and animated them as if he was his words were being acted out. "How about you take the engineers, and I'll take Switch and Cree to help them learn about the fur balls. After we get that started, then we can tag-team on the medical stuff after that. What do you say?"

Then Rhom smiled at his brother seeing the changes in him. It was like seeing glimpses of his past brother that figuratively died somewhere along the way. "Sounds like a plan, my brother. Sounds like a *great* plan."

6 Good Spaces

Ayya

She hugged her bear after making her bed. Then she whispered to it. She had always pretended it was the little toy she lost that day her father threw into the woods. Then it had helped save her from the fire. She never understood how he just showed up, but it was nice to know that even if she couldn't see him, she could pretend to talk to him.

Ayya whispered to it. "It's my birthday today, and Momma is having a party for me. But Daddy will be here too. Wish me luck!" She put the bear back down on her pillow, the only doll or stuffed animal she had. She just didn't enjoy playing with them.

On the way out of the room, she picked up her letter with the entry form and cereal box tops in them. She was sending it out for a toy gun that shot propellers so its owner could watch them float down.

When she got to the mailbox and put the letter in, she heard a static-y, but friendly, female voice say, "Happy Birthday, Ayya!"

Turning around to see who it was, the early sun

blasted her face, but she automatically said, "Thank you very much, ma'am. How are you today?"

Ayya held her hands up, trying to shield her eyes from the sun, but she couldn't see anyone.

"I'm doing good, Ayya. I'm enjoying the morning while I watch my two sons play 'save the world'. But I just wanted to let you know you are not alone and I am celebrating your birthday by trying something new. It's a nice day, don't you think?"

"Yes, ma'am. Thank you, ma'am. That is nice of you." Ayya tried once more to see who was talking to her, but had no luck.

She ran to the door and as she opened it, she turned around to see who had been there. No one was up or down the street. Ayya thought to herself, *I'm not saying anything to Momma—I already get in trouble enough for 'making up stories'.* Coming inside, she shut the door and walked to the kitchen, shaking her head. *Nope... I'm not telling her about that one.*

When Ayya approached her mother, she turned and smiled at her. "I'm glad you asked for cheesecake instead of a regular cake. It's my favorite too. Ms. Josephine made a cake for you for your party. Don't forget to thank her when you see her."

"Oh, she is coming too, Momma?" Ayya asked, lightly bouncing on her feet.

Her mother put a spoon into the sink. "She said she couldn't come today, sweetie, but she would make up for it when she could get back. She said that a family member was sick and not doing well so there was a lot to be done to help out."

"Aww, I hope they feel better soon, mm-hmm."

"Look at the cake she made you!" Her momma pointed at the counter to the left of the stove. "It's your favorite, too! She thought it was hilarious when I told her you didn't like chocolate cake but loved German Chocolate Cake. Did you ever tell her what your favorite cake was?"

Ayya thought a moment as she looked at the enormous cake in the shape of a large tree that had little gold sparkles in it that seemed to move when they glittered. "N-no ma'am, I don't think I ever did."

"Well, she said she thought she knew just how to make it so you could be extra happy when you ate it." Lanna sighed and leaned up against the counter, holding her stomach.

Ayya approached her and gently kissed her side. "I'm sorry you are hurting, Momma. Can I help you?"

Her mother patted her back and said, a little breathy, "Thank you, sweetie, I'm healing. It's just going to take time, is all. That is why I brought the stool in. Can you slide it over for me? That would be a big help."

"Yes, ma'am. I'm happy to help you." Ayya went over and grabbed the stool that would have been awkward to carry for her, due to size, but it was easy for her to slide over to her mother.

Her mother smiled at her warmly, and it made Ayya want to jump for joy inside.

Ayya couldn't help but worry and hesitated, but she asked anyway. "Momma, are you sure we should have this party? I don't want you to die because of me."

"Oh, I will not die on you, I promise. I'm just really sore from all the stitches. Now go ask your daddy if he needs any help with the grill and food outside. I'll be fine."

"Can I please stay here with you? Where's Katie? I can help with her, at least."

"She's outside with Charlie in the backyard. But go ask your dad if he has anything he needs from inside."

"Yes, ma'am, I lo-ove youuuu!" She bolted out of the door and down the back steps to the patio.

Her father was messing around at the grill and talking to the neighbor across the fence. She ran to him and waited for the break in conversation so she wouldn't interrupt. The neighbor across the fence saw her and smiled and said hello and excused himself to finish his yard work.

He whirled around to face her like she had done something wrong by being there, so she quickly said, "Momma would like to know if you need anything from inside. I can get it for you."

"No, you'll just create another disaster, just like you did on that business trip I had to take you on. Get away from me." Her father turned away from her and started scraping the grill down.

Ayya looked down and said, "Yes, sir." Then she heard a growl inside her again as she turned around. *Oh no, not today, please, not today. For once, I just want to have a good fun day without getting into some sort of trouble.*

She started looking for Katie and she came waddling around the hedges in her diaper. Sure enough, there was her duck, Charlie walking behind her, quacking. *Charlie is my miracle duck, sort of like you, Aaru. It was a gift. He saved Katie from going into the road once. He kept getting in her way till Momma could run to get her.*

She lined up behind Charlie and started singing a song for Katie. She always liked it when she sang to her. It seemed to make her toddle faster. She loved watching Charlie follow her.

Katie headed toward the back part of the half acre yard. The further back they got toward the yard into the trees, she felt Aaru's growl again. *Aaru, please don't cause trouble today. Please, I beg you. It's my birthday.*

Ayya played with Katie until the guests arrived. She tried to route Katie back toward the house, bribing her with the thought of a piece of cake. When that didn't work, she said cookie.

That word she understood. Katie squealed and started walking faster, with Charlie quacking along behind her.

Something caught her eye on the other side of the fence in the woods, but when she turned to face it, nothing was there. Aaru growled. Ayya felt herself tense up and couldn't help but feel like the day was going to be disastrous.

All the guests her age were boys, since there were only two girls in her neighborhood, and they were out of town. The only other girls she knew of were in the next neighborhood over, and they were bullies, and all about making people pay them to walk through their 'turf'. She was glad they were all boys because she was looking forward to playing tag football.

ಐಐಐ *Rhom* ಐಐಐ

"Confound it! Something is very odd here, Rtu. Look at this... we can't help! The time line is all red."

Rtu hurried toward the console and watched what Rhom was pointing to. He finally said, "My brother, I've concluded that there is something felonious about this challenge."

"You are just now coming to that conclusion? I don't know... maybe there is a good thing that is keeping us from helping. All we can do is watch and learn, albeit it feels a little helpless, but I'm just glad Tap agreed to let us put this challenge node into the ship!"

"It was quite smart of her to triple nest Zreyas' dimension and put an entrance to the challenge node room between the first and second ones. Now we can access it with one door and Zrey can access it without having to come out into the main part of the ship if needed. That will keep accidental entrances."

"I hadn't thought about the easy access for our little buddy without having to go into the main part of the ship. Well, the way Silence and the cub guard that door, even if it wasn't keyed to certain people, it would be impossible to go through," said Rtu with a chuckle.

Rhom laughed, then added, "We might want to talk to Tap about making that area at the front of the door almost like a small foyer and put their quarters on each side of his door. It would make me feel safer, too. Somehow, I would take their defense over dimension nesting any day."

Both twins laughed, then they sobered and looked at the screen.

Rhom rewound the time-line to let Rtu watch, but he caught something else that was a little off. "Interesting. Look at this. Here is Ayya, going out to put her letter in the mail. She turns around quick to talk to someone, then it all blanks out in fractals like what we see in the quantum. It skips and starts again as she walks up to the door. Something or someone has altered the time-line."

Rtu nodded in agreement, then added, "And from that point on, the time-line is red and we can't enter to help. I guess whatever it is they set in motion has to play out on all levels."

"Well, it is playing out now, and the past is short on the rollback. It's like the past is coming toward us on this console." Rhom turned around and asked Aqum, "Is this past rollback thing happening now going to be permanent? Otherwise, how are we going to help in the future?"

—The request to answer your questions has been approved, Visage Rhom. — We inform you with bright words of optimism. — You will help in the future.

Both of them sighed in relief.

Rhom considered, scratching just over his ear. "So, what is causing this interruption?"

—We are saying the answer with inflections of bright happiness — good spaces.

Both visages looked at each other with questioning expressions, mouthing the silent echo of Aqum's two-word response.

"Do you know what Aqum is talking about?" asked Rtu.

Rhom shook his head, as confused as Rtu was. "We are visages. We should be able to access this stuff. Now that I think about it, Tulyata was having problems accessing things before she left us."

"That is true! I'm just glad I made Ayya that cake before all this happened. I put a little visagely-mojo on it too, to help her wake up a little more. It was fun. I actually baked it myself!"

Rhom watched Rtu brighten and glow at how much joy he got from that. He couldn't help but smile at him. "I'm glad you found a hobby that you really enjoy."

"Du-ude! Me too! That firehouse incarnation corrupted me into the wonderful finger-licking deliciousness of baking and cooking. Though, admittedly, if it wasn't for someone like Ayya, I might not enjoy it as much. I tried doing it for myself, and it was good, but it didn't have that... lu-uv sparkle fun."

Rhom chuckled and said as he pointed, "Well, I think it worked. Look at her when she sees it."

The two watched the scene unfold in the kitchen with her mother. Then they watched the conversation she had with her father.

Rhom's fury rose and he felt the water part of him almost boil.

"By all the visages, it's a good thing that Mother didn't see this," Rtu said, shaking his head. "That would have set her off, and honestly, it sets me off too."

Rhom felt the heat in his face at his own anger. "I'm actually angry. If we had not seen the events before today, I wouldn't have gotten the reference."

"I'm going to have to steal some expletives from my little buddy. That ticking—" He sighed, then said more calmly, "That is why I don't like getting involved with incarnates directly. I can love at a distance without getting into the things that make me angry."

Rhom knew it was not Rtu's first experience with anything having to do with incarnations directly, but it had definitely been a long time.

Just as Rhom started saying words of comfort to his brother, Rtu stopped him with a warding wave of his hand.

"I can't believe he took her on a business trip and did that to her. Aaru is rising in her and waking up in defense, and let me tell you, brother, he... is... *pissed.*"

Rtu was pacing the floor, and he had never seen his brother like this before. Rhom knew this was serious. But he needed to let him rant so that he could think things through. His frustration was through the roof right now. He figured it was the first time his brother truly felt powerless.

After approximately fifteen minutes, he finally got

his chance to ask a question to help his brother check himself. Rhom asked quickly, but with calmness. "Do you want to rant some more to help you feel better?"

Rtu paused his pacing. "Hmm. Yes." And he did. He talked about all that he had watched that even Rhom had not seen.

It shocked Rhom what came out of his brother's mouth concerning the events. He realized Rtu was just as invested in Ayya as he was. Since he met Zrey, Rtu had changed and grown. He always had a heart, but Rhom was in awe at how deep his heart went, and how strong he was.

Rtu finally stopped and sighed.

"Do you feel better now?"

"Yes! More satisfied now that I got that off my chest. But, I'm still angry... now I know what my little buddy feels like when his anger simmers." Rtu laughed sardonically.

Rhom raised his eyebrow. "Would you like to tell me about what happened on this business trip so we can deal with the present event going on more effectively?"

"Yes, I would. You need to know."

"Then let's pop over to your dimension. We can be in your environment so we are not affected by time. Time is much slower here, but we need to make sure we miss nothing. I won't want to take a chance that it won't rewind far enough back to see what happens."

"Agreed, brother! I will update you on several other things too, and I'll remake the dimension just in case, then pull you in. I'm getting paranoid."

7 Oh No! - Oh Yes!

Rhom

Landing in the challenge node room, Rhom didn't feel like going through the portal to Earth yet to start another segment of life again as Paul.

As he walked over to one couch, he sat down and asked his brother, "Ayya seems to get a belt or a smack at least once a week, if not more. And he is so sneaky about it all. I understand that is really that awful commander bringing in the past with him, not to mention the Dark One's influence, but how can people be so blind not to see him and what he is doing, Rtu? This is your realm more than mine."

"He actually might have been okay had he not had that Dark One's influence. He wouldn't have been a teddy bear, but he wouldn't have been so extremely abusive. Honestly, he has not had a fair incarnation. It's another reason I'm upset about the whole matter... there is no real pure soul there anymore."

"Now that..." said Rhom, "is something I have seen

for a while now, the soul part. And you are right, he hasn't had a fair incarnation, and neither has Ayya nor Lanna, for that matter."

"We are a little behind schedule on waking her up, but I have hope." Rtu got an odd expression on his face, then said, "Uh oh, look." Rtu pointed toward the enormous screen. "Three boys were hiding behind trees, one holding a white duck."

"They have duplicated Charlie the duck. Okay, I'm going to watch this from there. We can communicate as things happen. I know I can't do anything to change things, but it makes me feel better I am with her."

"Good idea. I think you should view this from *her* point of view so you can see how the elders are doing, too, but mostly... Aaru. You haven't done that since she was a toddler, if I remember correctly. A *lot* has changed. I am getting a little nervous."

Rhom looked at his brother, feeling a confirmation of things he had been seeing, but too distracted to get oriented on. He still wasn't himself since he came back from his Viduri Seer incarnation. His brother was a lot more grounded in humanity and their designs. Species were only beginning to grow into the aether realms of awareness.

But there was one thing he knew. Ever since Rtu had dealt with his guilt and inaction, he seemed larger than life and his power had grown exponentially. One day soon, he would have to do the same. *But now is not the time*, he told himself.

Rhom closed his eyes. "I'm heading to her now, brother."

"Du-ude, I got your back, bro!"

Rhom chuckled at his brother's lingo as he got settled into Ayya's awareness. The first thing he checked on was the elders that he had spoken with before. Dhi, the elder of the mind, seemed strong... way stronger than he should have been. He sent his Vidurian greeting so that it would seem familiar to him. Treta, the elder of spiritual connection, seemed distant, but there. It made sense.

Ayya had been living in survival mode most all her life. Vesana, the elder of automatic tasks and survival, was horrendously busy, and she barely acknowledged him. And Gulloo, the elder of alchemy and emotion, was not himself at all. He was distant and a little on the grumpy side, and... fear laced everything about him. *Oh, this is not good, brother, not good at all. The elders are all out of balance.*

— Keep looking brother. You will see more in time. You know something is about to happen or we could influence things.

As Ayya followed her duck, Charlie, and sister back toward the house slowly, he looked further. He checked on Aaru. The boy seemed strong but quiet. Rtu said nothing, so he watched.

> Ayya howled in laughter when she watched Charlie use his bill to grab hold of Katie's diaper and pull.
>
> It made Kat giggle, arch her back, and wobble, and it made Ayya laugh more.
>
> The grills were smoking and all the adult men were standing around talking it up. Charlie was trying his best to hinder Katie's forward motion.

Rhom moved from Ayya's mind to Charlie's.
— Good idea, bro.
When he reached his mind, it startled him. The duck

wasn't a male. It was a female. Rhom chuckled to himself as he paid attention.

Charlie turned to look back. He saw Ayya, and he felt the affection that the duck had for her. It was deep and yet different from anything he had accustomed to working with, at least he thought.

Rhom's past was still fuzzy from the lack of adjusting back into visage-hood.

Charlie's mind didn't seem to get in the way. It was pure, and he decided he was going to revisit that whole thing again soon.

The boys on the other side of the fence were stalking down along the tree line when one boy threw a white duck over the fence.

Rhom realized ducks saw things more on an energetic level than higher-level sentients did because a lot of mental crap didn't get in the way. He felt the static danger Charlie felt through her protective nature.

Charlie pulled at Katie's diaper again, finally causing her to fall, then nuzzled her face and neck with soft quacks up Katie's ribs and chest.

Katie laughed hard with that infectious baby laughter.

Despite the situation, Rhom felt himself chuckle just as he heard Ayya yell to her mother that Charlie was doing it again.

Lanna turned to watch. She laughed.

But in Charlie's snuggles and nudges, she kept looking back at the boys on the other side of the fence.

Rhom adjusted more to the duck's awareness and sight, almost enjoying himself in all the antics. Then, when Charlie looked back again, he saw what Charlie had been seeing and feeling. He realized Charlie was trying to protect the girls by slowing them down. Those boys were from the challenge and definitely had the telltale energy of that... team.

One of them put their hands together and rubbed them as he said something to the others.

Rtu, we got serious problems and there is nothing we can do about it, but watch.

Rhom moved from Charlie to Ayya again and watched her friends come out the back door of the house. Ayya ran toward them, totally forgetting about Charlie and Katie.

— Rhom, this is a test. Do you remember what you just saw when you were with Charlie?

That perplexed Rhom. He thought hard as she watched Ayya reach the back patio. Charlie had apparently followed her and walked around the bushes to the concrete patio to look for morsels. Honestly, I remember nothing but fun and a little instinctive apprehension.

— I thought so. Don't worry about it. I got it. It wouldn't do you any good for me to tell you. You might influence Ayya somehow.

Wise, brother, wise.

It wasn't long, and Ayya was playing red-rover with the kids.

For Rhom, it was fun to enjoy a child's life while she was having a great time.

Rhom felt the elders within Ayya. They seemed weaker within her, but lifted in the fun as well. That made Rhom's heart soar.

Then a resounding aura thrummed through Ayya that almost caused him to leave her. It reminded him of... *Oh no, Rtu.*

— That is what I wanted you to see. And before you ask, yes, that is Aaru. Just watch and learn as much as you can.

Rhom felt all the sensations of it as Aaru thrummed

again. He watched the more sagely Elders shrink and weaken, Treta, Gulloo, and even Vesana seemed to weaken. And while Dhi strengthened, her brain seemed to weaken, changing Ayya's whole point of view.

Ayya's vision even changed. It went from crisp, bright, and clear, to having an almost graphical vignette appearance. Things seemed more blurred. Her whole body changed when that negative low frequency filled her.

Then Rhom watched as he heard and experienced her emotions. Her body tightened as she talked to Aaru.

> *Aaru, please don't do this. It's my birthday, and I don't want you to continually complain and ruin my day just because my daddy is around. Just shut up!*
>
> She looked over at her father as she held arms with her teammates to hold the other team back from breaking through their line.
>
> The grills were smoking and all the adult men were standing around while they drank and had their cigarettes."
>
> *See Aaru, there is nothing wrong.*

So, she is very aware of Aaru!
— Yes, bro, very much so.
It sounds like he has been a pain in her side by the way she talked to him.
— Maybe, but he is also her warning signal. When he warns her,

her wisdom shrinks. Something is wrong.

Lanna came out of the house holding sashes while she navigated the couple of steps down, being careful to not overdo. "Time to play Ayya's favorite game, kids!"

All the kids cheered the word, "Football!"

She held up two sets of sashes in each hand. One side was red with a yellow stripe and the other side was blue with a green strip.

Rhom felt the amazement and gratefulness that radiated through Ayya's chest and she almost cried in appreciation.

Lanna helped the kids put the sashes on while sitting down on the patio chair.

Ayya stood in line to get hers put on, too. When it was her turn, her mother asked if she was having a good time, to which she replied, "I'm having the best day of my life, Momma! Thank you for everything."

She reached down and kissed her mother and gave her a big hug. She felt the tears come just a little, but wiped them real quick before letting her go.

Ayya ran back out to the large yard, and they all started picking teams. When they got their teams established, they turned their sashes out to their appropriate color. She turned hers, blue side out.

"Ayya, come here!" her father yelled. "I got a secret play for you since you are the birthday girl!"

Ayya turned to face him. And the first thing she heard was a low thrumming growl inside. *Shut up. He's being nice.*

She ran over to her father, feeling excited that her daddy was being nice. This made her day the best day she could have ever had for the rest of her life in her mind.

Her father motioned her away from the rest of the men like he had a secret with a big smile. That was rare. She wasn't sure she had ever seen him smile that big before.

She followed him over, and as soon as she got there, he grabbed her arm with such strength it was all she could do not to yelp. Her breath caught, and she tried to raise her shoulder to lessen the pain, but it didn't work.

He turned her so no one could see their faces by bending down over her. "If you embarrass me with crappy play, you will get the belt like you never got it before. And you can say goodbye to your skateboard. Do you hear me?" His face had menace all in his expression.

"Yes, Daddy. I understand, sir."

"Now get out there and make me proud, for a change." He stood up, clapping with a smiling face like there had been no hostility as he turned around for all to see.

Rhom was shocked and grew livid at what he just witnessed. The pain radiated through and up her arm from his grip, yet no one mentioned the redness and hand print. It was like she had an illusion on her arm or something.

Do people not see what he is doing? Can they not see her arm and that there is something extremely wrong?

— Brother, it's the age. And the man has a design of charisma, so he can do a lot of things in front of people and somehow make it look like he as an angel. Remember the story we talked about with him beating the boy with his cast till he crushed his face at the prep school?

Surely people can feel that frequency of something just not feeling right though, brother.

— Look at her mother. When Ayya was born, she would have. But look at her now… really look at her. Why do you think she is sick?

She isn't living her life according to her design and purpose. She is living his life, too afraid to make the changes she needs to make. I'm afraid my incarnation as a Viduri didn't give me these kinds of extremes to experience.

— And though he has a highly charismatic design, the downside is that if he doesn't live by his design properly, he can feel pressure so strong that he can be violent and manipulative, and still get away with it. And with that Commander Rittak influence within him, along with the Dark One, he really has little chance of living his designed life he signed up for originally.

When it comes to humans, I know very little compared to you, brother. That commander is starting a ripple effect that will hurt many that are precious to us.

— We really can't blame it on the commander, either, because Ayya's father is making his own choices. No matter what lives people live beforehand, they always have the strength and inner tools to get past the old stuff. He has a strongly defined ego with energetic connections that jumpstart festering because of how he was born. With the way he is drinking, he will only get worse because it negatively affects the normally beautiful open chest center. And when he gets to a certain frequency, that commander is really going to have a heyday.

The implications of that, with what we are trying to do, are mind-boggling. The fracture event and the Dark One doomed Ayya to walk this path, and we are not making good headway in helping her awaken to get out of it because she is so stressed out and in survival mode. She can't even feel genuine joy for long to get balanced again, much less awaken. I saw what Aaru's growl did to her, too. That said growl has weakened all of her awakening mechanisms.

— Let's hope we underestimate Ayya and she shows us up. We view her as someone pure and helpless. Maybe if we hold space for her to pick the right times for her to stand up tall, she will keep some semblance of who she really is.

Good idea, because I got nothing else up my sleeve.

"Hey there boys!" called Ayya's father.

Ayya turned around in the direction her father was looking, and she saw two boys on the other side of the fence.

Both of them were at least a head taller than she was, and something wasn't quite right about them.

She knew all the kids in her neighborhood and all the others that surrounded hers, and she had never seen them.

They were pressing their foreheads against the chain-link fence, wrapping their fingers around the wires, staring at her.

"Did you boys want to play?" Ayya's father shouted. "It's Ayya's birthday and you wouldn't want to pass up a chance to play some football, would you?"

The boys shook their heads, then one of them said, "We'll play if we can be on the same team *and* on the red side. We like red." The kid grinned a very odd grin.

"Sure, we can arrange that!" her father agreed. "Come around the corner and open the gate. We will make room for you!"

Oh, no!

— Oh, yes.

Where did the other boy go?

He heard nothing from Rtu and figured he was checking on a few things. Judging from the silence, it told him enough. Ayya was in trouble... again.

Well, he, though limited in Ayya's view, would not leave her. So he calmed himself, checked in on the elders, who now seemed to have recovered a little from Aaru's thrums.

Rhom realized he had been quite uptight and that being here with Ayya, feeling everything she was feeling, was conditioning him to a certain degree, too. It was part of his design to have that happen temporarily with those around him so that he could see perspectives clearer, then incorporate those experiences to help others. This was all science of their multiverse, and it was one thing he loved about it.

Her father followed Ayya as she ran back to her teammates. He took one boy from the other team and put him on Ayya's because their team was short one member, anyway. He put the two strangers on the opposite team to even it up.

"There, now the teams are even," said her father as he looked pointedly down at Ayya with a sideways grin.

And there it was again... that black mist coming in and out of her father's eyes. Her body stiffened. It happened a lot lately. It surprised her she didn't hear Aaru. She figured everything would be okay.

Then one of her teammates grabbed her

arm and turned her around. "So what secret play did your dad give you?" he asked excitedly. "We are going to need it as big as those bums are."

"He didn't have a play, he lied. He just wanted to wish me luck, sorry."

Looking up at the large boys on the other team, the same friend said, "But you are good at coming up with plays. Let's use one of yours."

Just as he finished saying those words, Aaru thrummed inside her again. But she would not yell at him this time. She knew why he was warning her because she saw the black inky mist sliding in and out of their eyes.

Rhom used the newly learned cuss word, which he now enhanced, that worked for this kind of situation and said, *"Ticking-bloody-hell."*

8 Guilt

Keep calm, Ayya, keep calm, **she said to herself.** *Just play. What can they do that badly in front of so many people? Nothing right? At least if something happens, the adults will see it this time, Aaru.*

The first several plays went well, and she ran the ball in for another score. She had a couple of bruises already, but she didn't mind those kinds of bruises. She loved football.

Her team mate kicked to the other side and eventually turned the ball over again by scoring. Her teammates had more stockiness to them, so they always gave her the ball to run. Somehow, she could dodge and twist easier than the others lately.

Ayya looked at her father but he wasn't smiling. He just stood there with a straight face. She cocked her head and smiled. He was okay with her now. That was about as good as he would ever get with her, she guessed because she wasn't a boy since he seemed to throw it in her face a lot. She had short hair, wore pants, and played sports, so it confused her why she wasn't a boy yet. Then she realized her talk with Ms. Josephine got cut short recently, and she didn't get to ask more questions about things like that.

— Survive at all costs. You are not alone, **said the female voice** she had heard this morning. It seemed to come from everywhere.

Ayya didn't know who that was. She sounded stern and serious, but kind.

Her teammate covered her after she made a mistake. Two things happened—She thought about Ms. Josephine's cake, as she automatically looked at her angry faced father. Then she thought about when her father got angry at her and called her a blood crotch recently. She hadn't known what that meant, so she asked Ms. Josephine, who she now called Ms. J a lot. She had smiled at her and went to the kitchen and they made some tea. Then they had sat down at the kitchen table together with a piece of warm pie, then explained what it meant. Just as they had gotten the term explained and understood, her father came in and gave Ms. Josephine orders to go do some wash for him.

As she turned around to celebrate the score with her teammates, she thought about how she felt relief to know why he was always angry with her, at least one reason. Either way, it was something she couldn't help or change that she knew of.

Ayya thought about how she missed Ms. J and her talks now that her momma was home as she took possession of the ball. Ms. J had said that she had a grown-up maturely about the important things, even though she was a silly kid in other less important things. She loved Ms. J's hugs. They always seemed to make her feel better. Then she thought about the birthday cake and the vision of it felt like it charged her up and couldn't help but smile as she ran fast around a large but slow inky-eyed opponent. Ayya felt ultra-focused as she imagined the cake.

"Okay, five more minutes and then it's dinner time!" one of the adults called out.

The team caught the ball in the end-zone, but ran it anyway. She knew why he did. They hadn't scored yet, so there was extra motivation to score with only five minutes left. Ayya didn't blame him, she would have done the same thing.

Their team tackled him, and the next play was starting. Ayya was covering a boy that was going out for a pass, still on the high of thinking about Ms. Josephine's hugs. She really didn't feel like she was playing football anymore, but she focused.

The ball was high and not well thrown, so she ran for it. Just before her friend caught it, Ayya ran in front of him, blocked his view and caught it. "Sorry Trev, I'll explain later." He was her best friend at the time and lived two doors down.

Hugging the ball, she started running right for the two boys trying to steam-wall her.

— Go, go, go! Survive, and pay attention.

Ayya busted right through between the two. When she looked back, she saw both of the enraged boys running after her. Sliding, inky-black mist filled and spilled around their eyes. She focused on running as fast as she could and figured if they squished her in a tackle, at least she broke through them.

She set her sight ahead and really poured on as much speed as she could. Though she never really was a fast runner, she felt fast now since it had more motivation. There was something about getting squished by two inky-eyed bullies that didn't appeal to her.

As she bolted toward the end zone, a boy on the other team started running toward her from the right trying to cut her off. Unlike the others, he was fast. Then she noticed something that caused her to immediately panic.

An inky-eyed white duck had tackled Katie and was pecking at her head trying to get to her eyes from the looks of it. Luckily, her face was against the ground, likely thinking it was Charlie. Though she was giggling, it transitioned into a cry. She knew then it wasn't playing nice like Charlie normally did. Was that her duck gone bad?

Confirmation came as she saw Charlie coming off the patio, running faster than she had ever seen him run. Then, just as the boy was going to side tackle Ayya, she said, "Here!" and handed off the ball to him and kept running. Charlie reached Katie before she did, with raised wings, honking with a screechy tone, already fighting the inky-eyed boy.

Ayya reached the white duck with inky eyes and used both hands to grab its neck. As he took two more steps with it, the duck bit her wrists, but that didn't stop her from gripping it harder and throwing its body against the fence. Aaru thrummed within her but not in a warning way as she felt the neck pop. Almost feeling a quiet dance start inside her, Ayya spun around one more time and threw it again against the fence.

It was all surreal as she immediately went for Katie, swooped her up, comforted her with words, hugged, and bounced her gently. Katie started giggling through the tears, though she had trickles of blood dripping down the back of her neck and high on her cheek. It almost got to her eyes.

Ayya wanted to cry but Katie was such a focus it kept her from doing it.

Katie wiggled, wanting to get down and play with Charlie. Just as she put her back down, Ayya heard a scream.

— Survive.

Ayya jerked her head toward the scream just in time to get knocked to the ground by the two bullies that had been playing on the other team. She watched a third inky-eyed boy bash her mother to the ground off her chair. She felt herself reach for her momma as they both hit the ground hard. Hot tears spilled watching her mother hit her head on the patio. "Momma!"

Before she could get up to punch the two that had tackled her, they were already climbing the fence. Ayya staggered to her feet as she watched all the adults running toward her mother—all but her father, who was standing there with his arms crossed, staring at Ayya.

She was shocked and couldn't believe what she was seeing. Ayya tripped, trying not to step on Charlie, who was nuzzling Katie affectionately. She hit the ground again and couldn't help but let the emotion of everything that was happening come up.

Tears streamed as she rolled to her stomach to get up. An anger rose inside her, and it was not Aaru's. But Aaru seemed to help once he realized she was angry. It was almost like he panicked and went defensive.

— Survive.

Her father ignored her mother and stormed right toward Ayya. "You are one demented and sick kid, he ground out. "So, you want to be a duck killer?"

Ayya looked over at her mother, surrounded by all the adults, trying to tend to her and get her up.

Her father picked her up and threw her against the fence. "Now you will know what it might feel like, you little murderer!"

Just before Ayya's head hit the top bar of the fence, she watched Trev's horrified face. She couldn't feel any emotion other than feeling sorry for Trevor. Then her head hit the bar. She bounced off the fence and hit the ground.

Ayya looked up just in time to see a glimmer of a horrified and surprised look on her father's face, which was confusing. Then inky mist started sliding in and out of his eyes again.

"Go to your room and don't come back out!" Then her father turned and walked toward where her mother was being tended to.

Trev walked over to help Ayya get up. As he did, he whispered, "I'm sorry, Ayya."

Ayya grunted and barely whispered with hardly any breath, "Thank you for being my friend."

"Leave the murderer alone, boy!"

Trevor's dad shouted back at her father to stop yelling at his son for doing a decent thing. Then he turned around to Trev and said, "Let's go, son. Did you give Ayya her present?"

"Yes, sir. And I'm coming!" Then he turned around and whispered to her, "I hid it in your closet in the usual place. I'll use the hose to message you."

Ayya nodded and started the walk over to her mother to make sure she was okay. There was blood on the cement and a knot on her head. She almost panicked till her mother said to her, "It's okay sweetie, my stitches just broke loose. I'll be okay. Head into your room and I'll let you know when I get back from the doctor."

"Don't talk to her, Lanna!" her father barked.

Her mother looked up toward her father, clearly angry. "I'll talk to my daughter if I damn well please! She has done nothing wrong. And I watched the whole thing with Katie and Charlie."

Ayya remembered Katie and went back to her, picked her up slowly and walked up the stairs and into the house. *There! Whoever you are, I survived*, she thought bitterly. *Are you happy?*

— Yes, you did good, Ayya. You saved your sister. It is a good day. The voice waned with the next words and she almost couldn't hear it when the voice said, — and Ayya, there *will* be better days.

ᄁᄁᄁ *Rhom* ᄁᄁᄁ

Rtu, is that you talking to her?

— No. But it appears we have someone on our side at least. It's probably best you come back now, brother. Though she doesn't know you are there, you influence her with that 'company-is-here' vibe. I mean, you are a visage. She might need time alone to process. You got to see what I thought you should see so you could help her more. You still haven't had time to fully integrate yet.

That s obvious to me now. I feel like I have been through this trauma.

— You have. That was the point of you doing this. Come out, you are a little too integrated right now, brother.

> As Ayya looked out of her bedroom window, she stared at the duck she had just killed.

Rhom felt the guilt assail her as she leaned her head forward to touch the glass.

I love you, little phoenix, said Rhom. As he left her, Rhom felt empty and heartbroken.

When he arrived back at the challenge room node, he gasped for breath, even though he really didn't need to take one. He was a visage. It puzzled him.

"Welcome back, Rhom," said Rtu cheerfully. "That was quite the ride you had with Ayya."

Rhom nodded as he sat down hard and watched the screen in the trauma's aftermath, dazed.

Then Rtu said, with sadness in his words, "It's hard, isn't it... seeing and experiencing them suffer?" Rtu paused a moment as he held his chest. "It's why I have learned to... do what I do to stay up and be happy... genuinely. Without experiencing things like what you had to experience today, I wouldn't have learned how to do it."

As Rhom looked at Ayya on the screen, he thought about Zreyas, too. He realized he felt the same way about him, as he went through things like what he was going through now. But he got bits and pieces of it as things happened.

With Ayya, it was like a huge dump of tragic dismay all at once. And feeling her guilt over the duck. Well, he knew that guilt very well from his Vidurian incarnation. The pain of his guilt still plagued him. Maybe that was why he was having issues re-integrating into his visage-hood.

His brother came over and sat beside him, put an arm around him, and pulled him close.

Rhom understood more now what his brother dealt with while he was away in his incarnation, adding to the mix of emotions. He couldn't help it. He laid his head on his brother's chest and let his tears go.

To Rtu's credit, he didn't joke, he never said a word, and he held him as the whole place slowly filled with water.

௰௰௰ *Ayya* ௰௰௰

Ayya must have fallen asleep on her arm because the next thing she knew, she was hearing her mother's voice.

"Ayya, I'm back from the doctor and your father wants to see you in the dining room."

She tried to smile, and said, "Okay, Momma, thank you. Are you okay?"

"Yes, sweetie, I'm fine. It's just going to take longer to heal is all."

"I'm sorry that the boy did that to you."

"I'm not sure why he did that," she said as she scrunched her face up in the confusion of it all. "It was really weird."

Ayya felt bad. "I think it is my fault, Momma, even though I don't know how. The other two boys were trying to hurt me, and their duck was hurting Katie."

"I saw that, and that was when the other boy came to me. It's not your fault." She stiffly bent over and kissed her forehead. "Don't worry about me. Worry about yourself right now with having to go see your father. He really has a good heart in there. So, pretend he does and maybe things will turn out okay. We can hope."

Ayya looked up at her mother doubtfully. "Okay, Momma. I'll hope for your sake."

"And I'll hope for yours. Have we got a deal?"

She smiled at her mother and said, "Yes, ma'am!"

Her mother hugged her, and she went on her way and headed down the hall. Something made her stop and turn around to see her mother wiping her eyes walking into her bedroom.

I think Ms. Angel Queen is gone now, Aaru.

— Be careful, Ayya.

Shut up! I already know everything is a disaster! I don t want to know things ahead of time. It s a curse. Try saying nice things or helping me out if you want to meddle, she thought testily. As she got to the entrance hall, she stopped when she heard the voice's next words, her fists tightened and sweaty.

— You have had many successes. You have had many that have helped you. Many would give almost anything to have the help you have gotten. Stop acting like a whiny, spoiled bully, Ayya. It is your choice. You are meant for great things, or… evil things. Here is a question for you. Would you like to be like your mother, your father, or better than both? The choice is yours.

"Pfft." Ayya wiped her palms on her pants and she realized she hadn't even cleaned the blood off her, or changed her clothes. She did not know who that was, and she didn't care anymore. She wished that the voice hadn't even said happy birthday that morning. All she knew was she felt her anger rise and Aaru seemed to magnify it with his low and steady, quiet growl.

She walked through the living room, and the anger fueling the defiance and determination was the only thing keeping her from running out the door and never coming back.

Ayya rounded the corner to see into the dining room and there her father sat, blood-shot eyes turning to meet hers. He was grey with drunk. She didn't know why he looked grey, but he did to her. He gave her that look that he does when he wasn't being seen by anyone.

Ayya stood straight and defiant. She was sick of him and his tricks.

Then he pulled one of his best manipulative tricks she knew him for. In a different tone, much different from his eyes and expression, he said loud enough for her mother to hear, "That behavior is not acceptable. You didn't hurt yourself, you staged that because you didn't make the touchdown. You are a spoiled little kid." Then he really poured it on. "I want you to grow up to be respectable and something you can be proud of."

For her mother's sake, she said, "Yes, Daddy." She knew her mother was in the kitchen right next to them, and so did he.

"Lanna, go rest, now! I'll get the rest of the kitchen work done for you! You have done enough today. And... Ayya gets no cake. She doesn't deserve it. I also ground her to her room for one month!"

She heard her mother stomp through the kitchen and come to the doorway. "She is a child. That is way too long!"

"Don't you dare question me! You are in no condition to make any kind of decision like that with any sound mind. Go smoke some cigarettes and watch TV. Mind your own business!"

"She *is* my business! She's my *daughter!*"

Her father stood up, throwing the chair to the floor.

Ayya felt deadly calm and moved right in front of her mother in determined silence, forgetting for a moment how afraid she was of him.

Lanna turned away and walked through the kitchen and down the hall.

As Ayya faced her father, she didn't budge in either her expression or position. She heard Aaru growl, and it magnified her already strong anger even more. She knew what was coming.

Her father pulled off his belt and folded it in half, but held the bent end this time. "You will come home from school and go to your room. If I catch you out of that room for any reason, I will make you regret you are even alive. On the weekends, you will stay in your room. I don't want to see your face. You make me sick! If you aren't in school, you better be in that room."

He held the belt out, pointing toward the den, and Ayya couldn't help but focus on the buckle dangling there, swinging slightly, making that tinkling sound.

Ayya turned and walked into the next room as Aaru growled and lurched. She turned as her father closed the multi-paned glass French doors behind him. His face had the most inky-mist that she had ever seen around his head. She didn't think there was much of her real father there anymore.

— Don't let him hit your head, Ayya. Survive.

Something caught Ayya's attention. Charlie had jumped up on the windowsill outside and was trying to peck his way in frantically.

She smiled, despite what was about to happen, then turned her smile toward her father, never letting it wane.

Then she thought to herself and to that voice, *You are right; I have a lot of help and people that care. They just might not always be the normal kind.*

The echoes of Charlie's honking and pecking were all that she concentrated on.

9 Convict

Ayya

Ayya looked at the ceiling. She couldn't see it very well because it was so dark. Thinking about how much help she seemed to have had in the past, she judged by the quietness everyone was in bed.

That voice, there was something about it that made her feel trust. It was stern, but it seemed to care.

As much as she hurt, and as much as she felt scared for her mother, she never cried except to make her father stop when he thought she had reached that 'she's crying hysterically now' mark.

Unfortunately, her mother heard it because when she went back to her room, she heard her sobbing.

She looked at the clock and it said 1:11. Ayya figured it was okay to get up and sneak out to the bathroom and pee, as well as do other business. She opened the door quietly, grateful that her mother oiled the hinges a few days ago.

Ayya stepped into the doorway and looked across the hall to the closed door of her parents, then up the hall to see if there were any lights in the living areas she could see. All was dark the other way, too. She had to pee so badly, but she had to be careful.

This was the tricky part. The wood floor in the hall was beautiful, but it creaked in places. She was so glad in times like this that she and Trevor would play lava monster. If they stepped in a place going down the hall that made the floor creak, they died by lava. So now she knew exactly where those spots were, but there was little room for error.

Reaching out to hold the chair-rail molding, she stepped out on the outer edge of the wall, right up against the lower molding. Then she reached her left foot over and stepped down three quarters of the way to the other side. *Three more steps and I m there.*

Right foot down ahead of her left. Left foot ahead at the floor molding, and then the last step was the hardest. She leaped as high and far as she could jump and landed as quietly as she could, right in the middle.

No creak.

Ayya stepped into the bathroom with a sigh and hurried to get her pants down to pee. She slid as far forward as possible so it wouldn't make the water splash too loud in the toilet. She had made that mistake once, and she wouldn't do it again. *Ahh, it feels so good to pee!*

Ayya didn't mind peeing in the bucket she snarfed from the garage two nights ago and pouring it out the window, but she didn't enjoy pooping and dealing with all that.

While sitting there, she double checked to see if there was anything she might want to get while she was out of her room. Then it hit her that her magazine was probably still buried in the mail pile in the kitchen by the phone. She also wanted her pad of paper she got two weeks ago for a school project.

Ayya finished her business and got cleaned up by taking a sink bath. She put her pajamas back on and picked up a clean wash cloth just in case she needed one. She stuffed the wash cloth into her pajama bottoms and started the long, careful walk down the hall of lava.

As bad as the hall was, the kitchen was worse. So she would go around through the carpeted living room and reached into the kitchen from the other side, climb on the phone chair to the counter and get her stuff.

Yeah, good plan, she told herself.

She made it through the hall of lava and carefully walked on the left side of the living room so the muffled creaks wouldn't happen. She stopped halfway through and checked for den lights. Seeing it dark in there, she breathed a sigh of relief, then continued.

She rounded the corner to the left, stepped through the dining room and took one quick step into the kitchen, and climbed up on the chair. Thankfully, there was a built-in night light there and she could see pretty well, though it seemed bright to her.

She found her pad and pens, but she couldn't find her magazine. But there was another one that her mother liked and grabbed that one instead. She carefully put the two in the front of her pants and put her shirt over the top of it all.

Aaru thrummed a growl that filled her insides. *Oh, no, no, no, not now, please. Sorry, Aaru, not really yelling at you. I'm just thinking.*

Ayya quickly climbed down from the chair and into the dining room. Just inside, to the right, was an antique serving cart that her grandmother had given her parents long ago. It was at an angle in the room's corner, and it gave her the best hiding spot at night. She slipped behind it and squatted down in the corner space.

Things got silent. Then suddenly she couldn't remember if she closed her door or not. She felt ripping panic run through her. How could I be so stupid not to know that? *No wonder you get in so much trouble. Stupid boy! I mean...* Ayya sighed... *girl.* She didn't want to keep living like this, but she didn't want another beating either.

She heard a thrumming growl, but louder this time. The thrum from it seemed to vibrate her body. Ayya realized it was through her outer ears, not her head. She held her breath and told herself to disappear... just disappear.

Footsteps and creaks came through the kitchen, coming toward her. Then she watched the legs go past her with a dark mist that seemed to glow a little red, shifting in and out of them.

Nooo, Daddy, nooo. What is happening to you? She carefully placed her hand over her mouth because she didn't trust herself. He went into the den and shut the doors.

Ayya made herself calm down as she saw the light flip on, wafts of mist moving around the room. She couldn't see her father on the right side of the room because of the wall, but she saw enough dark mist that she almost peed all over again.

After about five minutes, she got up slowly and made her way back into her room. To her relief, she had shut the door behind her earlier. Grateful, she opened it and walked in her room quietly. Ayya carefully shut it again, making sure she turned the knob before she closed it.

She breathed a sigh of relief and put the things down on her desk and crawled into the bed. She looked at the clock and it was 2:22. It had been over an hour. This was day four of her grounding. It would be a long month, but she was enjoying the time away from the stress of her normal life. But she missed seeing the trees and Trev.

Her eyes opened wide, remembering what Trev had told her before he left that day about her present. She smiled. Ayya had something to look forward to tomorrow.

She talked to the voices.

"If anyone is out there listening. I think we are doing good and thank you for the help. But if you are listening, I'm not sure I know what to do about all this. Can you help me? I'm not that great of a good person, and I know I really don't deserve it, but I would like to be better and would be grateful for the help.

"There, I said it.

"I promise I will keep trying to do good. I can't seem to help but get in trouble all the time, and I just don't want to hurt Momma anymore. Please help my momma. She cries a lot these days. I think Ms. Angel Queen has died. If she isn't dead, please help her.

"Good night."

Ayya woke up hearing the family noises in the kitchen on the other side of the wall at her head. She laid there and listened for a while, glad she didn't have to follow a lot of rules right now.

She finally got up to go pee. Aaru growled, so she pulled her pajamas off and peed in her trusty old bucket and went that route.

After she cleaned up and dressed, she opened her window and held the pail outside and poured it out. She whispered to the bushes. "Sorry, I promise I wouldn't do it if I didn't have to."

Just under the window was the spigot for the hose. She hopped up and bent over the windowsill like a jackknife. She slowly turned the water on and let the water leak into the bucket. Once there was enough, she swished it around and poured it out. "That should help us both a little." It felt good to smell fresh air and feel the sunshine without a window between her and the outside.

She cleaned her two washcloths and put them on the windowsill to dry. So, she pulled herself out of the window, turned around, and looked at the bed to her left and put the bucket between the bed and the wall.

Ayya grabbed the clothes from under the bed and got into her jackknife window position again and washed them out. She remembered Trev, but she would have to get that hose out when her father wasn't home.

Once she was done, she pulled herself back in again and draped the washcloths on the sill and looked out over the backyard to see if she could see Charlie.

"You know, you could just ask for help with that and I can throw it in the laundry."

Startled, Ayya jerked her head up and hit it on the window as she turned around. Her mother was standing there, closing the door with a smile, holding a tray of food.

"I'm sorry, Momma, for being so much trouble. I don't mind doing it, it's kind of fun, and I just don't want to get you into trouble."

Lanna said nothing and sat her tray down on her desk.

Ayya picked it up and put it in her closet on the floor and shut the door.

Her mother frowned, but nodded. "Katie wanted to come visit you, but your dad told her you had homework."

Ayya couldn't help but smile. She loved her sister. "I miss her too."

"One more thing, Trev came by and asked to see you. He handed me a note to please tell you to remember he was there and that your birthday present was in your closet. I really like him. He's so much like you. And I love you to the moon and back. Whatever you two are conjuring up, have fun, but I don't want to know about it." Her mother laughed softly.

Ayya smiled. "Okay, Momma, can we play spite and malice, rummy, or gin soon?"

Her mother laughed. "I have created a monster! How can I turn down a chance to beat someone in Spite and Malice? We will do that when your father isn't home, if I have time."

"Thank you, Momma. It will be fun."

Then Ayya heard Aaru's growl just as she saw her father open the door. Panic ripped up her stomach and up into her face.

"No, you will not play with her. She is under restriction. Come on, Lanna, she doesn't deserve company."

Her father's eyes were red and bloodshot. He was drinking early today. She looked up at him and wondered if something had happened. "Are you okay, Daddy?"

Her father stared at her, then back at Lanna. "Come on, Lanna, we don't speak to people like her."

Lanna looked at him, and her face flushed. "Ayya, I need to go see your aunt for a few days. Your cousin is sick, and she needs some help. I will call and check on you."

She whirled around and glared at her father. "She is a child, not a convict. And I will speak to her when I am god-damned ready to speak to her."

Her father sprung to life in a rage, then lifted his hand and slapped her incredibly hard across the face. "Don't you *ever* talk to me like that, woman! Who the hell do you think you are?"

Then he looked at Ayya with such hate that she thought she would fall over from shaking before he walked out.

Her mother held her face, and Ayya could tell she just couldn't bring herself to look at her. But as she walked out, she said, "I love you, Ayya, and I will see you in a few days. I'm taking your sister with me."

"Good, she will be happy. I love you very much, Momma. I'm sorry," said Ayya as the tears surfaced.

When her mother left the room and shut the door quietly, Ayya sat down on her bed. The rage she felt for her father was the highest it had ever been. "You stupid, stupid, selfish person, Ayya. You should have never asked Momma to play cards."

Ayya laid on her side and cried herself into a long, but disturbing, nap.

10 Bye-bye

Ayya

She woke up with a start, covered in sweat. As she sat up, she tried to shake off the snake dreams. Ever since she had that encounter with the one at school, she had been having nightmares. Random people turned into snakes. The people with inky eyes, she knew, turned into snakes.

She used to love snakes, now she only tolerated them. But she definitely hated them in her dreams. Sometimes she would wake up not knowing which world was real anymore.

Ayya rubbed her face and turned toward her wooden-slat accordion-styled closet doors, and thought about the tray her mother brought in. There was a lot of food there, and not one, but two pieces of cheesecake. "Yum. Thank you, Momma," she said appreciatively.

Under her plate of two sandwiches and assorted sides of chips, there was the magazine she couldn't find the night before. It meant a lot to her because she had gotten the subscription from Ms. Josephine for being so good and helpful while her mother was sick.

It had short stories and a lot of pictures. Ayya thought about how smart and kind her mother was and said to her, wherever she was, "Thank you, Momma."

She used a knife and cut the sandwiches in quarters, ate one quarter and a few of her favorite chips... cheese puffs. Setting the magazine aside, she covered up the rest of the food with napkins loosely.

Ayya put the tray on a shelf in her closet because her father never went into it. Then she put the magazine with the other on her desk with her pad of paper and pens. Then she remembered Trev. She wiped her face and hands off, then listened to see where her father might be. She didn't hear him at all, so he was either drinking away in the den, half passed out, or gone. There was one thing about her hearing, it was extremely good.

She hopped up on the windowsill and jumped out. She was glad the windows on that side of her house were low and could get back in easily.

A couple of years ago, they used the excuse of a school project to get their parents to agree to create an underground messaging system. She and Trev had experimented with blowing paper messages through a hose to each other to see if they could get them across the yard. It had worked great, and they had a blast goofing off with that.

Then Trev's dad helped them dig a trench for a hose to reach from Trev's window to hers when her dad wasn't around. Her momma knew about it, of course, but they had kept it a secret from her father. But instead of a regularly linked garden hose, Trev's dad had helped them put in a much wider smooth walled tube so they could experiment with other means of getting messages and things through.

When they didn't figure out a way yet to do it with such a wide hose because they didn't have enough air in their lungs to create enough force to blow something through it, they capped each end off to keep moisture and creatures from getting in. They still had the regular hose right next to it.

As Ayya dug up the tube wrapped around the bush at the base from under the mulch, she remembered what Trev's dad had said... that when they were ready, they would figure out a way to use the large one, but to hide it in the meantime.

Trevor's dad was some sort of science researcher for the government. Unfortunately, he wasn't home often because of his work, but he and Trev talked a lot on the phone. They were really close, and she couldn't help but wonder what that might be like. She supposed it was like how close her mother and she were, but without the stress of her father, to go with it.

His dad said they had some left-over tubing from an experiment they were doing for a NASA project and said that it was special. Ayya figured he was just trying to make them feel good. Dads didn't do that kind of thing for kids to make them feel special, did they? She decided she would ask Trev about it the next time she saw him.

Ayya hoped she could cover the mulch up right when she finished, so her father wouldn't get suspicious and start digging it up. She eased the mulch so it wouldn't get mixed up with dirt while she listened closely for her father. Right now, she didn't think he was home. It was just too quiet. But it felt good, and she breathed easier.

She noticed something that concerned her. Someone had recently messed up the mulch. It was too loose and some of it seemed fresher; in fact, the entire line of that mulch looked the same. Whoever had messed with it made sure the entire row of bushes looked consistent. Had Trev come over when she wasn't around?

Ayya felt bad that she had not yet looked in the closet for her present. He knew all about her father and how weird he was, and had seen it too many times to be a chance. She was glad she had a friend that understood. He had said there was no way he could take it, and that he worried about her a lot.

She smiled as he felt the end of the tube and pulled it up. Ayya looked at it and realized it was a better tube than they had before. It seemed... more... well, just more fancy, smooth, and shiny, but it felt like some sort of metal woven cloth.

The cap was hard and screwed on. It had a light on it that blinked. She wasn't really sure what to do and didn't want to mess anything up, but she also knew what this was supposed to be, a fancy version of their message hose.

Ayya thought she better hide this for now and check their normal one and then go look at what Trev left for her in her closet in their hiding place.

They used the message hose a lot when they played secret agent. She and Trev had watched a spy movie with her mother once, and that was it—they were hooked on science gadgets and secret agent stuff.

The pair had told her mother once they were on a mission. She had played along while they solved the mystery of the missing cookies.

Ayya laughed as she slid the mulch back over the dirt. She realized it was almost dark, so it was just as well. She wanted to be careful about opening that thing.

But she opened the special cap for the regular hose, hidden by the household-coiled hose hanging there, as well as the mulch. The cap allowed air through, but it was watertight. How they did that, she had no clue. Trevor's dad, Mr. Sadler, had given them to Trevor for their regular message hose about a month ago, saying that they would be testers.

They put the message inside a special tiny canister that she and Trev made of a chapstick tube originally, and then they blew it through the hose. Mr. Sadler replaced it with one he made with special caps for each end that were magnetic.

When the message inside would get to the end of the hose, it would magnetically stick to the hose cap at the other end. They could send no more messages until they took it out because it blocked the airway. They had made three of them so each one of them would have one at all times.

Ayya almost forgot to write Trevor a note. She knew he was worried about her. Somehow, she felt it. Quickly, she climbed back in, and scribbled a note with the secret code that it was really her:

Dear Trev,

I can tell you are worried. Daddy's really bad. I almost got caught, but I hid. The mist filled the den. I don't know when I will be able to send another message, but I will as soon as I can.

Thank you for my present, even though I haven't got it yet. He's been home a lot and I don't want to take a chance that he will find it and throw it away.

Yep, it's me, Aston Martin DB5.

Ayya took out the special tube in her desk drawer, opened it, then rolled up the message tight. She slid it inside and replaced the cap, then climbed back out the window quickly.

She took the tube Trev had sent her out of the hose and replaced it with hers. After screwing on the hose cap, she took a deep breath and blew hard into it. After repeating it the standard eleven times, she couldn't blow into it anymore and knew it had gotten to the end.

Getting paranoid, she replaced the cap and put everything back into place, making sure the mulch was smooth and matched the rest of it as best she could.

Ayya brushed herself off and climbed back in through the window. She grabbed a washcloth and wet it under the spigot and washed herself off. Then she risked going to pee. She put the message container into her drawer. It would have to wait. Nothing came before a much-needed bathroom break.

Turns out her father wasn't home, so she ran to the kitchen, put her cheesecake into the refrigerator, grabbed two new pieces, put them into a container, and poured herself some soda and took it back to her room.

Just as she got the door shut, she heard her father yell from the other side of the house, "Ayya, where are you?"

Ayya almost choked on her drink. She rushed to the closet to hide the cheesecake and soda, wiped her mouth and yelled back, "I'm in my room, Daddy!"

Then she scrambled to her desk and opened the magazine that she had gotten last night and picked up a pen and started pretending to draw a face she saw in the corner near the binding part of the page. It was a hand drawn picture of a pirate.

A loud thump from something hitting her door made her jump and go into an immediate panic. The door opened and her father stood there. The surrounding air around him seemed grey. His eyes were bloodshot, but the black mist seemed to recede just before he struggled to say. "I'm...-sorry. I know you... know. No m-matt-er what, s-surv... vive."

Ayya was confused, but she listened closely, but didn't dare to move closer. She stood and backed up slowly, darting her eyes briefly to see her options. It surprised her she didn't hear Aaru. He was clearly struggling to speak, but there was something about what he said that was sincere.

"I only hate... you be-cause you are s-stron-nger, and you are not male. No, that's-s not right." Her father shook his head, shaking off something she couldn't see. Then she saw a tiny semblance of her old father in his eyes, and he pleaded, "Ayya, kill me."

"W-what, Daddy? No! I love you! I wouldn't know how, anyway. I didn't mean to even kill the duck. Daddy, whatever is happening to you, you have to fight it!"

Her father leaned against the wall just inside the doorway and dropped his head. Then all the grey air around him seemed to come together to form that black mist. Her daddy looked up at her. His eyes filled with the most hate she had ever seen in them. Whatever was doing this to him was back, and she pressed up against the windowsill.

Aaru growled and thrummed. It gave Ayya a newfound confidence, and she glared back at him. Then Aaru thrummed again and Ayya felt her skin tingle as it seemed to escape her body.

The eyes of her father seemed to startle, and for a brief moment went wide, but then reverted.

"Whatever you are, black mist, leave my real daddy alone!"

Well, she knew she had made a mistake then when he rushed toward her and slapped her so hard it knocked her sideways into the wall beside her desk. Aaru thrashed all around inside her, thrumming. She almost blacked out as she tried to struggle to her feet.

Ayya stood and wiped the blood away from her nose, and looked up at him. She was not sure how she got the courage or where it came from, but she looked straight into his eyes and said, "Every time you do something to me, you make me stronger."

Just as he raised his arm to hit her again, Ayya never blinked or wavered her stare, determination, or her stance. "Daddy, thank you for fighting so hard against that thing inside you."

He stopped, then backed up. The black mist dissipated into the grey air around him, but it didn't last long. She wanted to call out to her father, but she knew he was gone.

When her father slammed the door, she knew she was in for a hard few weeks, but she had affected him somehow. Feeling very defiant, she decided that next time she wanted to pee, she would go to the bathroom, whether or not he was home.

Ayya realized she had really never met her true father face to face. It was just that over time she just saw less and less of the man from a distance.

She turned toward the door squarely and put her hand over her heart and said softly, "Bye-bye, Daddy. I love you."

11 Me Too!

Ayya

Ayya wasn't sure why, but she was excited when she got up the morning after her father walked out of her room. She didn't understand what had settled inside her, but she was grateful. Though still scared of her father, an understanding of the night before seemed to sink into the crevices of her mind.

She got up and got ready and went to school, but she didn't see Trev. Ayya asked Ms. Harrison if she knew if he was okay or not.

Ms. Harrison said she got a message that he wouldn't be in today because they were working on a project with her!

That confused Ayya. All she could do was look up at her and say, "Me?"

Ms. Harrison smiled, leaned over, and whispered, "If you want to wait a few minutes, I will drive you over there so you don't have to wait to go home by bus. I think it might be important you go home."

Ayya smiled bigger than she thought she might have

ever smiled. She nodded vigorously, feeling like she would explode from excitement for many reasons. She whispered back to her, "Do you know where he lives?"

Ms. Harrison stood up straight, smiled, and winked at her with a nod.

Her teacher told everyone to settle down and get their things put up and get ready for the next class. She announced a substitute teacher was going to be taking over for the day, but that she might be back.

After things got settled, Ms. Harrison motioned for her to go outside the classroom. The kids started laughing, probably because they thought she was in trouble again.

Clapping her hands hard, she said sternly, "She did nothing wrong, class. In fact, she is going to get an award. Mind your own business and do what you were told."

An award? Ayya wondered what kind of award she was talking about. She decided that she honestly didn't care. She was going to get to spend some time with Ms. Harrison, even though she was just driving her to Trevor's house.

When her teacher came out of the classroom, with all her personal belongings, Ayya asked her if she wanted help to carry a few things.

"You are sweet, little lady, but I'm doing okay. Thank you for the offer."

"You are welcome, Ms. Harrison." They walked out to the parking lot and Ayya fell in just slightly behind her teacher, since she had no idea where she might have parked.

She looked out at the cars in the parking lot, wondering what car Ms. Harrison would drive. Ayya loved the cars she liked but didn't care about knowing details about a car she didn't. She loved her grandmother's car, but thinking about that made her feel sad, because an inky-eyed wolf in the field behind her grandma's house had killed her. Then she wondered if Ms. Harrison would drive a Volkswagen.

Ayya looked up at her and decided she would probably drive it. She was the type she could see her having fun pretty much everywhere. Once she came to school dressed in a Hawaiian ceremonial dress just because she wanted to teach them about different cultures and their celebrations.

Then she saw a car that made her so excited that she wanted to scream. Ayya pointed hard with excitement. "Ms. Harrison, look!"

Ms. Harrison didn't seem surprised at Ayya's outburst. "What is it, Ayya? What are you so excited about?"

"It's a DB5, Ms. Harrison! It's a... *colorful* DB5!"

"Why yes it is! Imagine that! A car like that here in this parking lot!"

"Does that mean that the famous spy agent from the movie is here? Are they test driving one for the next movie? I wonder if they are here to ask the science teacher for advice. He has an entire team that makes all his gadgets, you know!"

Ms. Harrison laughed and seemed to bounce with joy, almost losing her purse.

Ayya caught it and said, "I got it for you, Ms. Harrison."

"Thank you, Ayya. We are almost there, so go ahead, carry it for me."

"Yes, ma'am!" she replied, happily.

She was so glad they were walking in the general direction of that car. "Wait till I tell Momma about this! She will smile, and that is the best part ever!" She could barely contain herself.

To her, it looked better in real life than in the movies. "My uncle is a big car mechanic and, from what I hear, he is the best in the state. He says that a DB5 has three Weber carbror-rator—"

"Carburetors," her teacher corrected.

"Yes, ma'am, *and* revised camshaft profiles. I don't know what it all means, but isn't it neat? *And* it goes one hundred and forty-five miles an hour."

Ms. Harrison laughed. "You are a DB5 enthusiast, to be sure! It goes to show you, you don't have to know all the details to be a total fan!"

It still perplexed Ayya the more she thought about it. Then asked, "Wonder who would paint a DB5 with all kinds of color, trees and flowers? I *like* it!"

"Me too! As for who would do that, I would! Can you get my keys out of my purse and unlock and open the trunk for me, Ayya?"

Ayya wasn't sure she heard what she said right. "I'm sorry. What did you say, Ms. Harrison?"

"You heard me right," she said as she turned and smiled. "These are getting heavy. Hurry along and get my keys from the side pocket and unlock the trunk. Careful not to scratch the flower paint. I worked hard on that!"

Ayya squealed and ran to the trunk and stood there in amazement for just a second before pulling the keys out of the purse and carefully unlocking the trunk. Then she opened it and backed up, stunned.

Finally, Ms. Harrison unlocked the door for her and prompted her to get inside. "No feet on the seats. There are already some of those."

Ayya didn't get what she meant until she looked inside. The seats were an off-white leather with seamless footprints sewn in of different colors. "This is the bestest car ever, Ms. Harrison!"

"Best, Ayya," Ms. Harrison corrected. "Now, let's have an enjoyable ride."

"Yes, ma'am, best. This is the best car ever. I love these seats!"

"Me too!" she said, as she shut the door for her once she was in.

Ayya remembered little about the first part of the ride because of the excitement and shock. She took in all the details of the interior of the car in awe.

On top of the dashboard, she had a little painted rock with a big smiley face. Ms. Harrison's smile was just as big to match it. "This is the best day I ever had in my life, Ms. Harrison! Well, besides, when Momma came home from being sick. That was better, but this is different!"

"That is something that I understand. Paul wanted to come visit you today, but he is quite busy. But you will see him soon."

Ayya beamed at hearing Paul's name. "Really? I hope so! Can I ask a question?"

"Sure! Ask away," she said as she turned the blinker on and slowed down to stop at a light.

"How did you meet Paul?"

She smiled. "We've known each other since we were born."

"Oh, that is nice! So you actually liked each other for that long, huh," said Ayya mater-of-factly.

Ms. Harrison busted out laughing so loud that it startled Ayya. Electric panic ran up through her body, and out of reaction, she turned and leaned up against the door.

Her teacher glanced at her and immediately stopped. "It's okay Ayya, I was just laughing... loudly. You have done nothing wrong. I just like laughing is all."

Ayya calmed her breathing down, surprised at herself that she would have reacted like that with a laugh. "It's okay Ms. Harrison. I guess I just didn't expect you to laugh at what I said."

Ms. Harrison pulled into a parking lot of an ice cream parlor and said, "It doesn't take a very smart person to see that you are struggling with things at home. I would like you to try something, even if it is only with me. Would that be okay?"

"Yes, ma'am."

"Okay, let's have some fun with answering questions, and there is only one rule. You can't use your head or open your mouth to answer. Got it?"

"Yes, ma'am."

"Oops, you used your mouth. Try saying yes without opening your mouth or nodding."

Ayya felt a little stunned and wasn't sure what to do. She looked at her hands, then she lifted one and gave her a thumbs up, totally proud of herself.

"Good! Now, try another way without using either hand."

"Hmm."

"That is closer."

"What?"

"What you did was close to the way to say yes without using those other ways." When she gave her teacher a confused look, she continued. "I've been doing a lot of research on the unique designs of humans for many, *many* years. You are a responder and your aura invites questions, people, and events to come to you. You're designed to respond, then act if it feels right."

Now interested, Ayya turned toward her and put her knee up on the seat. She cocked her head, then said, "But what if I attract bad things, and bad luck?"

Ms. Harrison turned off the car and turned to face Ayya with a gentle smile. "Here's your first question, and I want you to respond with the same rules. Do you really feel you attract bad things and bad luck?"

Ayya felt a little cornered because she wasn't really sure what she was after.

Her teacher said, "I'm not asking to get anything out of you Ayya, I'm asking you so you can learn to be strong inside."

Did she just read my mind? How did she know that was what I was thinking?

Then Ms. Harrison smiled and asked her the question again, "Do you really feel you attract bad things and bad luck?"

She thought for a moment. Ayya cocked her head, making sure not to open her mouth, and sat on her hands.

Ayya let out a steady, "Mmm," in thought.

Ms. Harrison surprised Ayya by saying, "Let's break this down, Ayya. How would you say yes?" Then she closed her mouth and leaned toward Ayya slightly.

Ayya couldn't help but mimic her.

Then they both said, "Mmmm," in a normal tone, Ayya slightly behind her in her mimic. "Then..." Her teacher closed her mouth again and let out a "Hm" in a higher tone.

Ayya repeated, "Mmm-hmm." She finally got what Ms. Harrison was trying to help her understand. "But Ms. Harrison, my momma and daddy said I couldn't hum anymore. And you saw what happened when I was in the first grade at school."

Ms. Harrison held up a finger. "First, that isn't humming. Second, just as you have seen, there is more than mouth and hands to say 'yes.' In the same way, there is more than one way to hum and respond. Why do you think you like humming so much?"

"Because it makes me happy, I think. I don't know Ms. Harrison."

"Do a really long hum using one tone. Try to feel it,

then tell me what you discover."

Ayya did just that. It felt good. She felt it in her throat, head, chest, and down to her hips. Even her nose vibrated. It tickled. It felt right... and good. Oh, how she missed humming. She closed her eyes. Her one breath seemed to go for a long time. Then, when it was over, she opened her eyes.

"Well? What did you discover? Take your time."

She thought a minute, and she wasn't really sure of what the teacher wanted to hear. "I'm not sure what I'm looking for to tell you, Ms. Harrison. I'm sorry."

"It's quite okay! Let's do a fun lie detector test."

"I'm not lying, I promise!"

Ms. Harrison laughed and said, "Oh, I know! It's a different kind of lie detector. It's more of a... know if something is right for you or not kind of detector. Think about how you feel right now, being here and going about our day."

Ayya nodded, but Ms. Harrison let it go even though she smiled and had that look like she had caught it.

"Now do the long tone again, but pay attention to the area around your belly button."

Right now, she felt like it was the best day of her life. Then she closed her eyes and started the long hum. While she hummed, Ms. Harrison told her to think about her day and pay attention to the vibration of it.

Ayya thought she was going crazy to do this kind of thing, but she did it anyway, and paid attention to her stomach.

As she hummed that tone, she felt her nose tickle and almost giggled, but rubbed her nose instead. Then she went back to concentrating. She felt a vibration that seemed stronger there. The more she concentrated on it, the more she heard and felt what the vibration said.

She took another breath and resumed the hum. Then Ms Harrison said, "Don't stop, answer with the tone. Does that feel right inside?"

"Mmmmm-hmm," she toned.

"Remember how that feels. You can stop now."

Ayya opened her eyes slowly, then asked, "Why does that feel right, Ms. Harrison?"

"Because it is how you are built. It is your design. What is right for you as an inner authority may not be for others." Ms. Harrison thought a moment, then said, "Before you were born, I can tell you, you were… a unique design, though the same type of aura. An aura is the energy that is around you. When you were born, your design authority anchored in the sacral / belly area. That is your inner authority. Do you remember what that felt like when you were humming and things felt right?"

Ayya thought a second before almost nodding and said, "Mmm-hmm."

Ms. Harrison clapped and said, "Good, good! Now let's do the lie detector test. Pay attention to how that little vibration feels right now and say, 'My name is Ayya.'"

She paid attention to how that little buzzing felt, then said, "My name is Ayya." There was no change. It still felt like it did before. Ayya shook her head and said, "Ms. Harrison, I don't feel any different."

"Was your day feeling 'right'?"

"Yes, ma'am."

"Did it feel right when you said your name was Ayya?"

"Mmm-hmm."

Ms. Harrison smiled and then asked gently, "Then why would you feel any different?"

"Oh! That makes sense. But what use is it?"

"All in good time, Ayya. Now, remember how you feel in your body, then say 'My name is Ms. Harrison.'"

Ayya cocked her head like she had gone mad, giving her an apprehensive look.

"Your body already responded. How does your body feel right now? Pay attention," Ms. Harrison instructed.

She concentrated again and realized that she could hardly feel the buzzing and vibrations. Then she took a chance. "My name is Ms. Harrison."

The subtle vibration all but stopped and her body felt heavy in her belly area. She knew that feeling well and felt it most of the time. "This is really fun Ms. Harrison. I like *this* kind of school."

"Ayya, even if your mind can't make sense of things, your body knows what is best, no matter what your inner authority is. Yours just happens to be in the sacral, the belly area. So even if you don't understand something, listen to your vibration in response. If something doesn't feel right, don't do it or get away from it if you can. Okay?"

"How do you know this stuff?"

"Let's just say I've been doing research and dabbling in things like this for many, many varSas. And it will help you stay alert and wake up more."

She lost the rest of what she said after the new word, so she asked, "What is varSas?"

"I'm sorry, Ayya. It is another language, a word for years."

"I like that word."

"Me too! Now, would you like to be naughty and get some ice cream before we get lunch? They aren't quite ready for us yet at Trevor's house."

"You're weird, Ms. Harrison, but I like it!"

"Me too!"

12 The Test

As they pulled up to Trev's driveway, Ayya couldn't help but look two houses down to see if anyone was home. She didn't want to get into trouble.

"Trust me, Ayya, it's okay. I've spoken with your mother."

She felt a jolt of panic at those words. "Is she okay?"

"She is fine. Ayya, if something was wrong, I would tell you. I promise. Would it be okay to trust me? Listen to your insides."

Ayya closed her eyes and listened. She realized she didn't have to do that. Ayya could already tell. She opened her eyes and told Ms. Harrison, "Thank you for the truth detector."

"Don't thank me. Thank yourself. It's perfect for a generating aura. Your aura gives special things to others, and I'm glad I could help you see your *own* truth detector. Just like saying yes or no, there are many ways to do it. There isn't just one way."

"Thank you, ma'am. But if it is okay, I still won't hum

on the outside and make my family mad.”

“Nothing wrong with doing it when you are in the right situation or all by yourself.”

After they got some ice cream, they got back in the car and drove to Trevor’s house and talked more about her what-was-right-for-her detector.

Just as they pulled up to Trev’s house, Ms. Harrison turned on the blinker. As she pulled into the driveway, she asked, “Now, ready to go see Trevor?”

“Yes, ma’am, I’ve missed seeing him!”

Ms. Harrison opened the car door. “I’m sure you have, Ayya.”

Ayya got out of the car herself and pushed the heavy door closed. That had to be the best car she would ever see. She stepped back and looked at the whole thing, trying to get the image in her mind to save. “I need a poster of this car! This is better than the secret agent’s car on TV. Ms. Harrison, you are the best teacher ever!”

“Why, thank you, Ayya. And you are a wonderful friend.”

She was shocked. No adult had ever called her a friend. Ayya wasn’t sure if she heard that right, so she let it go. She heard a door open, and she turned around in time to see Trev running outside.

“Ayya!”

“Trev! What are you doing here?”

Trev stopped in his tracks and put his hands on his hips. Then they both laughed, ran up to each other and hugged and bounced, making it rough waters for the hug. But she didn’t care. She was just glad to see him.

“Thank you for my birthday present, even though I haven’t opened it yet because things have been a little—”

“I know already, but you *will* want to open it soon. I can’t wait to see what surprise dad has for us.”

"For me too?"

"Yes! He said on the phone it was, and I quote, 'An opportunity for you and Ayya.' He's not home yet, but should be soon. Dad said that he wouldn't tell me till he told you, too!"

Ayya didn't know what to say. This whole day seemed surreal to her. She looked back at Ms. Harrison, who was standing there smiling like the sun. She couldn't help but think she had something to do with this whole thing. There was this overwhelming feeling to go hug her.

Ayya ran over to her and she lifted her up and gave her a hug. She tucked her head into her teacher's neck and felt a tear roll down her cheek.

Ayya whispered, "Thank you for everything. You aren't going anywhere, are you?"

Ms. Harrison pulled her face back from the hug and looked straight at her. Her teacher smiled and her black freckles seemed to dance on her smooth chocolate skin. "I'm not going anywhere, Ayya. I might not always be your teacher, though I am again this year, but I'm always going to be around to support you, even if you can't see me."

Ayya hugged her again and let her loose. Ms. Harrison put her down, and she ran to Trev. Both of them walked into the house, through the entranceway, and into the large sunken living room.

Trev and Ayya sat down on the floor and started playing cards. He was the only one of her friends that liked playing strategy games with a deck. They were told Trev's dad would be here any time, so while the adults talked, Trev beat her two out of three hands.

"Oh well," said Ayya. "You played good!"

"Yeah, but if we had played spite and malice or gin, you would have won again. You got to let me win in another game every once in a while."

The two laughed and went into the kitchen to get some cookies and tea, and sat up on the seats at the counter. About half way through their snack, they heard a door open. Both of them looked at each other with full cheeks, then toward the door.

The anticipation had to be killing Trev because he hopped down and ran over to the entranceway. "Dad!" he ran to his father and jumped up, disappearing around the corner before he landed.

Ayya heard two sets of footprints on the floor. First, Trev's dad came into view as she took a drink of tea to wash down her cookie. Trev's dad had caught him and held him tight. But Trev's face looked a little leery as well, like there was someone there he didn't know.

Ayya hopped off the bar stool at the counter and walked over beside Ms. Harrison. "Hi, Mr. Sadler!"

"Well, hello Ayya. It's good to see you! Where is my hug? Or has Ms. Harrison taken them all?"

She smiled and ran up to him and gave him a side hug so she wouldn't mess up Trevor's grip on his dad. When she let go of him, she saw the man that had come home with Mr. Sadler.

A thrill ran up and through Ayya's body, and her breath caught before she squealed. "Mr. Paul!" Ayya ran and jumped and squeezed him so hard that he finally said, "Can I breathe while we hug, little phoenix?"

"Oh, I'm sorry. I will let you breathe." But Ayya never let go. She felt his warmth and love and they just held each other. "I've missed you Mr. Paul."

"I know, and it is good to see you too, my girl. It's been a while, hasn't it?"

"Mmm-hmm." Ayya felt Paul look toward Ms. Harrison. Her smile grew.

Finally, Paul put her down, and they all went to the

kitchen to get coffee, tea, and cookies. Ayya stood between Ms. Harrison and Paul. She didn't think there could be any better a day than what she was having right now.

After about thirty minutes, Mr. Sadler looked at Trevor and Ayya. "So, are you two ready for your surprises?"

Trev and Ayya both said a variant of, 'Oh yes, please!', in unison. Everyone laughed.

"Dad, we were waiting patiently," said Trevor, almost bouncing. "You always have good surprises."

"This one is a little different, son. This one is about your futures."

Ayya and Trev looked at each other, confused, then back to Mr. Sadler. She had never once thought about her future, really. Ayya was very interested, though.

"How would you all like to go to my research lab to do a special test?"

Shying away slightly, she leaned against Ms. Harrison. Ayya felt her pat her back several times. Then she bent down and whispered, "Remember today's detector test so that you know how to respond."

She nodded, then looked up to Paul, Mr. Sadler, then to Trev, and listened inside. Paul smiled proudly, and that made her feel really good. It felt... right. Then she thought about Mr. Sadler's question about the lab and the test. She felt excited, then realized the humming didn't change.

"Mmm-hmm, I'll go."

Trev's face lit up and he threw his hands into the air, "Yes!" Then his excitement morphed into his typical bouncing up and down.

With that, Mr. Sadler piled everyone into a van with dark tinted windows. She had never seen anything like that before. She and Trev sat next to each other and played rock, paper, scissors. The winner punched the other one in the arm.

Ayya was still a little nervous about going some place without her mother's direct approval, but Ms. Harrison had told her that her mother had agreed, and she trusted her freckle-faced teacher.

As Trev punched her in the arm again, she laughed while she thought about how she didn't seem like just a teacher to her. She seemed like more than that. From the first day she met her in that bathroom till now, she seemed more like a friend with something extra special about her.

"Pay attention, Ay," said Trev, "or I'm going to get to punch you again."

"Okay, one more," she said, still contemplative. She noticed the vibrations in her belly and her thoughts about Ms. Harrison felt right. Then she thought about which one to pick. At first, she thought rock, and the humming vibration went quiet. So then, she thought about scissors. Again, it was quiet.

Ayya looked at Trev and said, "Ready." She noticed that Ms. Harrison and Paul were both looking at her with smiles. "You can count off this time."

Trevor did so as they tapped their palms with their own fists each time he counted. *<tap>, <tap>,* and Ayya opened her hand flat to represent the paper.

Trevor had chosen a rock. "Aww, you win." Then he winced, readying himself for the punch.

Ayya just put her hand on his face and pushed it sideways a little. "Done."

Trev seemed surprised and looked at her weirdly.

"If I beat you to a pulp, I won't have anyone to play with later." Then she giggled.

They all laughed.

Mr. Sadler announced, "Hey, here we are!"

In front of them was a big tall gate with barbed wire at

the top slowly opening.

"Are we going to jail?" asked Ayya nervously.

Trev laughed a little. "No, silly, it's just where dad works. It's top security. He told me all about it a while back."

"That's right, Ayya," confirmed Mr. Sadler.

"Wow, I never knew this was what it was like." Ayya watched with interest as they went through another gate not long after the first one. "I bet we are safe in here!"

Everyone laughed. Paul was next to her at the window and patted his lap. Ayya gladly got on his lap and watched out the window. She could see much better. "This drive is long to get here, but it is beautiful!"

"We still have a way to go, little phoenix, but we are at one of their facilities. We will stay here for the next couple of nights."

"Oh, okay. Does Momma know?"

"She does. And when we get there, we can call her up and talk with her too, if you like."

"I would like that. I can't wait to tell her about all this and Ms. Harrison's DB5!" Ayya leaned back against Paul's chest and watched out the window as the buildings came and went. Paul wrapped his arms around her and locked his hands together. She felt safe and excited all at the same time.

Some buildings were tall, single floor buildings. Others had more floors with a lot of glass. She wondered what it would be like to stand on the top and look out at everything, and it surprised her it was out in the middle of nowhere. She looked over at Ms. Harrison in the front seat, looking ahead, and couldn't help but smile.

"Mr. Paul," she whispered. "Are you going to marry Ms. Harrison?"

All the adults chuckled.

Paul looked at her from above her head and to the side. "Well, she is wonderful, isn't she?"

"Yes, sir."

"Well, I might do that, but it really wouldn't be right."

Trev sat up straight and asked, "Why?"

"Well, because she is family. She is my sister."

Ayya looked at Ms. Harrison, then at him. "Well, you are kind of married in a different way. I guess I wouldn't marry my sister either, even though she is the best."

They all laughed and Paul said, "Now you are getting it."

As she looked out of the window, she felt Trev lay his head on her leg and she closed her eyes, exhausted from all the excitement. She mumbled, "But my dad is going to be furious. I broke my restrictions. I hope momma doesn't get in trouble."

Paul squeezed her gently and Ms. Harrison said, "Your mother won't get in trouble. We have already taken care of that part. You are here at the government's request and they will compensate him. Money very much motivates your father."

"Oh, okay. Thank you, even though I don't understand all of that. I need to learn those things, don't I?"

"In time, Ayya," said Paul. "Right now, just be a kid and have fun learning."

Ayya smiled and closed her eyes and felt herself drift off.

13 The Results

Aqum Interruption:
— We are transmitting an event with utmost secrecy —
Current Place: Research Facility
Relational Time: 3 Earth Days Later
— End of Transmission —

As Paul sat in the room with his brother, chatting while waiting for the children's results, he thought about how much more comfortable he felt in talking now that they kept using their Earth names just in case someone overheard something.

They had learned the hard way when they both worked at the fire station that it wasn't worth the trouble of trying to explain, and definitely wasn't worth the chance that they could mess this up for Ayya.

It was still hard to remember that Rtu was Dulce Harrison. The form he had chosen for Ayya's teacher seemed just like his brother, but a female. He couldn't help but grin at her and those freckles on her cheeks.

"I'm actually nervous, Paul," said Dulce. "I hope this goes as planned," she almost whispered. "But I'm pleased with how things are going so far."

"Waiting for these results is indeed difficult. I just hope we can get her away from her father, and I couldn't be happier that her mother wanted the same thing so bad that she would consent to this. I offered her help to get Lanna away too, but he has her so scared for Ayya that she feels like if she leaves, he will chase them down."

Paul sat down, feeling his muscles tense, but still calm. He scratched his head just over his ear and couldn't help but think about all the details he hadn't addressed... like her entire future. "Connor is risking a lot doing this. Ayya does not know that Trevor's father will play a part in her future."

"I'm glad you saw his potential and approached him." Dulce sat down in a chair across from him and continued. "He seemed *thrilled* to come visit us and spend time to update him. At least there were no rules about involving willing participants in the challenge when they believe in the cause; after all, it *is* a multiverse-wide challenge anyway."

"Yes, but honestly, he had me worried at first. He accepted all this way too quick for a human in this time period. But then again... he *is* a quantum scientist. But in this part of Earth history, that is a loose title and considered an insane conceptual science meant for the mentally eccentric."

Dulce got up and poured some tea for both of them. "So was Albert Einstein, who fairly recently died. But he was a theoretical physicist."

"Oh, tell me about him."

Dulce turned around and looked at him in shock, still holding the teapot. Rhom knew that look—he should have remembered him.

"I'm not sure why you are not integrating back into your visage-hood better than you are. Something is indeed off about that. For you to not remember a famous scientist, is more than weird."

"Yeah, it's getting a little aggravating and I'm a little more than concerned, but there is nothing I can do about it now."

As Dulce put the teapot down on the tray, she said with a thoughtful tone. "Do you think he will hold up his end of the bargain, Paul? I mean, about taking his family with him after this is over and living at the Phoenix Order facility?"

Paul nodded thoughtfully. "I actually do, oddly enough. Ayya and Trevor are close, and Trevor and Connor are close."

"The wife will be the one to hold him back if he goes back on his word. Do you think she will do the same thing? I'm not sure about her, environmental sciences or not, she isn't the nurturing type and can be a bit sarcastic. Her snarky humor is something I admire, though."

"Not everyone can be typical, my dear sister. I detect nothing really off about her. Maybe we are just not giving her a chance just because we don't know her. We are limited in these bodies, remember. She's just not as social as most. I hope she is okay with things, though."

Rhom leaned back in thought, then continued. "Her specializations in terrestrial ecosystems and biology would be very handy. Neither one of them is up on advanced technology, but Connor is very excited and willing to learn. And don't forget, Connor agreed to have a little *mojo* done, as you call it, to wipe the memories of them if they decide not to go."

"And because of the agreement, we can always follow through with that visage-like last resort. We have the balances for it and with what they are pulling, we would have balances for thousands of varSas to equal what that dark visage has done."

A knock came at the door, and a familiar voice said,

"It's me, Connor."

Paul got up from his seat and checked the peephole. He unlocked the door and let the scientist in. No one else was with him. As soon as he was in, Paul shut the door, locked it, and shook the man's hand.

"You know, waiting for those results is like waiting to have a baby, not that I know what that is really like," said Rhom.

Connor laughed. "I know what you mean! I can tell you it is *just like* having one, since my son is one of the ones being tested." He turned and reached his hand out to his sister to shake it. "Hello, Dulce."

Dulce laughed, then shook his hand and gestured to the chair beside her. "Have a seat! Tell us! We're dying to here!"

He sat down.

Paul sat back down in his chair. "Would you like anything to drink? We have some tea here all ready."

"Sure, I'll tell, if you pour," he said, laughing.

Paul could tell by his energy and expressions that he had mixed news, but part of it was good at least. It was good to have a relationship with someone that didn't treat him like a visage or high seer.

Then again, they didn't tell him of their visage status, either. He just thought they were some high-tech human aliens with quantum science tech on a mission for Captain Zreyas. He brought his thoughts to Zreyas, being in a leadership position he never wanted, despite the anxiousness to hear the news from Connor.

"So, Paul and Dulce..." He took a sip of tea, then put the cup down and folded his hands together and leaned forward. "They have undergone so many tests, as you know, and the kids are really sick of them at this point. Trevor told me he felt like a lab rat and he was putting his foot down on anymore."

Connor laughed. "I told him I respected that, but we had to take one more and I promised he and Ayya were done."

"Ayya was a lot more patient than I thought she would be," said Dulce. "So, how did they come out?"

"All their health scans came back okay but one. Ayya's lungs are like a person who has smoked for a decade. She has been around too much cigarette smoke way too long and it is showing. Then again, it might be the dark mist adding to it, too. There is no way of knowing without a lot of other types of testing. Anyway, the good thing is... she is young enough that she can totally clean that damage up in time. Other than that, they were really healthy... physically."

Paul got up and looked out the window. Then it hit him *how* Connor said what he said. He turned around and looked at him. "What do you mean by that?"

"That is what I was going to ask, Paul," said Dulce with curiosity on her freckled face.

"Now, don't panic. I don't think it is anything to be concerned about. It's just... different."

"There were also a lot of scans done on several energetic and frequency levels. We analyzed them separately *and* together."

Paul went back over to his seat and sat down, put his elbows on his knees, and leaned forward.

Oddly enough, Dulce did the same thing, waiting for the news.

Connor looked at them both and chuckled. "Trevor, when he was alone doing something he didn't like to do, gave results of lower frequencies and slowed body function in some cases, and in others, he had huge amount of stress chemicals. No surprise there, right?"

Everyone shook their heads, knowing that was normal stress.

"But when he was doing something he liked alone, he had above average frequency activity. He even showed patterns of frequencies we have never seen before. I measured him first. I was curious, of course. Then we did the same tests on Ayya."

Dulce rubbed her palms together. "And?" Then she reached for a cup of tea and took a sip.

Connor lifted his hands and slid them down his face once, and shook his head. "I've never seen anything like it." He took a deep breath and let it out. "When she was alone and doing something she *didn't* particularly like, her readings were as high and active as Trevor when he was doing something he was happy with. But when she was doing something she *liked*, it was all four to ten times higher, and one of those times, we didn't have the instruments to track it accurately."

Paul held up a hand and asked, "What was she doing in those times?"

"Good question. When she was at the four times range, she was trying something new, drawing."

Dulce grinned. "I'm not surprised for a few reasons. Go on, please."

Paul looked at her, curious, but said nothing. He just listened and waited. Knowing Ayya as a Viduri, as an energetic body as he put them together in that dying dimension, and then as a child on earth, that didn't surprise him.

"But when I told her to do what it was she liked to do most, she asked if she would get in trouble. I told her it didn't matter what it was, and that if she needed something, I would go get it. She just shook her head and said, 'I'm all I need.'"

Paul covered his mouth, trying to hide the grin. He knew what it would be, and so did Dulce, judging from the look on her face.

"She just sat down and laid on her back, expecting her to do something, but she just laid there and—"

"Hummed," both Paul and Dulce said in unison.

Connor looked shocked, but he laughed. "That's it! And the readings went off the charts, literally. We don't have the instruments in this type of lab to register the emissions she put out. But that isn't the weirdest part."

Now *that* really got Paul's attention. It grabbed Dulce's too, but neither one said a word.

"Trevor was on the other side of the test facility, through layers of all kinds of doors that isolated and/or blocked all kinds of energy frequencies. I mean, it *is* a research facility with a lot of layers put in place for safety and test accuracy."

"That makes sense," said Paul as he sat back.

"We were still monitoring Trevor for other things. When Ayya would hum and the readings went off the charts, she would pause. During those first hums, Trevor would turn and face her direction even though he couldn't see her. When she paused, Trevor would hum, as if answering, and then his readings would raise four to ten times his normal 'I'm thrilled with what I'm doing' frequency."

"When my assistant asked why he was humming, he just shrugged and said he suddenly felt like answering Ayya about what they were going to do next time they played."

Then Dulce got up and put the teapot away. "Wow! You couldn't even consider that to be coincidental."

Connor shook his head emphatically. "No way, come on, you need to see this. They were still doing it when I left to come talk to you. We can talk as we go." He got up and headed toward the door, clearly excited.

Paul and Dulce followed him. He looked at Dulce and made a V with his first and middle fingers, putting each one to his brow like he was tracing them. It was their signal to get the visage part of Rtu that couldn't come through the challenge. His visagely side would come and assess things.

Dulce nodded.

Walking down the hall now, Connor continued. "Every single time over the next hour, it was spot on. It gets weirder, too. They got to the point they seemed to communicate through this humming, because they were in perfect harmony with each other. Some tones were dissonant, but it was a perfect transitioning dissonance like what you would hear in a classical piece of music."

It shocked Paul in part, but not so much in other parts. He wasn't a visage right now, so he didn't have those extra sets of abilities to get the other levels of what was going on. But Rtu would do that part. He could tell by her glance that it shocked Dulce, too.

That was the wonderful and frustrating part about being incarnated in the challenge. You kept the memories and knowledge, but had to live within the awareness of an incarnate.

"When my assistant asked if he wanted to go home, he said no, that he was not leaving Ayya. Understand, the boy loves his games at home and could spend hours playing alone. He loves it. But when my assistant told him he had to go home, he had a fit of anger and said he was not leaving her in this place."

Astounded, Paul contemplated and felt the need to verify, but Dulce beat him to it.

"What? Trevor?"

Connor nodded. "Then my assistant called me in and I calmed him down. I just asked him if it would be okay to get some more readings while we finished up with Ayya, that he didn't have to leave. He agreed. I left the monitor on him and took him to the entrance of the facility, and you know how far that is."

"Yeah, quite a few miles," agreed Dulce.

"Well, when I got back to the monitors and equipment that measured all this, they were still doing it! And the readings were just as clear as if they were two rooms away."

"I'm not surprised at that part. The quantum has no limits and they are using their humming to communicate, and they aren't adult enough to be conditioned by limited thinking," said Paul.

"I never thought of that!"

"Have you ever thought about someone, then the phone rings and it is them?"

"Oh, yes, Paul, I have." Connor said, nodding in understanding.

Dulce nodded. "The two children have been best buddies at school since kindergarten. But, from what I understood from Ayya, they hardly ever got to play together because of her father."

"That is correct. That is why I tried to help them out with their garden hose experiment. Trevor was much happier when that hose was near. And even lately, Ayya hasn't been using it much because of being afraid of her father throwing it out if he discovered it. He's been home a lot more lately, from what Trevor told me. I just recently put in a large one in the hopes of this future experiment."

"Mmm, or because they communicated unconsciously," said Paul as he contemplated.

Connor's face paled as he opened the door to the

observation area full of monitors and equipment. Then his jaw hung a few moments in the silence with an expression of realization. "One time I came home from work and Trevor was at the hose. He was listening with his ear to it. Then he would hum a tune into the hose. It wasn't like a kid's tune, though. When he saw I was home, he hummed a few more seconds, then capped the pipe and came over to greet me and give me a hug."

"Oh my gosh," said Dulce. "They have been communicating all this time."

"That is probably why they don't get upset when they are apart. But the behavior from Trevor to leave her in this unfamiliar place, well, he would not have it. I have been thinking about it ever since the test started and it just dawned on me now. He used to act like that before he met Ayya. He couldn't keep still and he was antsy a lot, like he was looking for something."

Paul rested his elbow in his palm and rubbed his chin as he thought, "Interesting."

"Look at them." Connor pointed at a monitor to his right and walked over. There sat Ayya on the floor, doing slow rolls as she hummed. Though it sounded like a single tone to his ear, he thought he heard the fluctuations of communication, but wasn't sure. He looked over at Dulce, and she nodded slightly.

— It's me, bro. This is rather interesting. You know the Viduri even better than I do. But to me, this sounds like a toddler version of the Viduri Tantra Song. Like it is still in development.

Oh, what wonderful news! Thank the stars. Can you tell if it is bouncing back from Trevor or if he is reciprocating?

To keep things going with Connor, he routed his thoughts a moment to lean forward to watch and say, "Interesting, have you detected variations in the frequency?"

"No, but let me double check. They did not make our

instruments for this kind of thing."

I hope he doesn't find them because he needs to be in full commitment and off this planet before we can tell him everything.

— I will make sure he doesn't find them. Good thinking, brother. It would be too big of a temptation for a scientist to go off on an obsessive tangent of research if he did. Trust me, I know. You are my brother.

Connor shook his head, then said, "Unfortunately, our equipment isn't good enough to detect something like that here in this facility. But now look at Trevor." He pointed at another monitor.

Trevor was doing slow rolls in an empty day care room full of toys he hadn't even touched.

Dulce spoke next. "They are in total synchronization. Look! How fascinating!"

Paul had a realization like a lightning bolt. *By all the visages, Rtu—*

— No need to say it brother, I think you might be right on that.

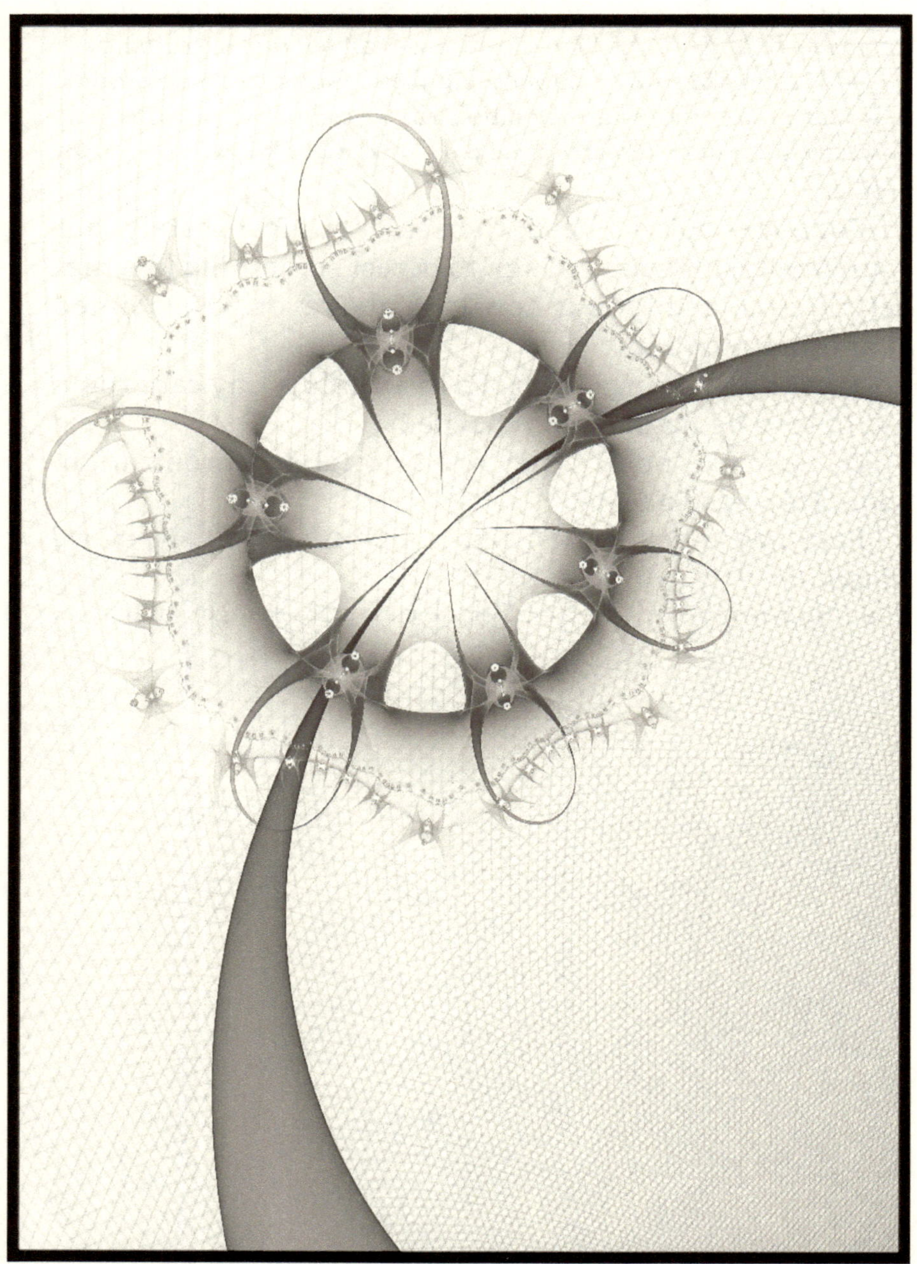

14 Lanna's Invitation

🁢🁢🁢 *Ayya* 🁢🁢🁢

Aqum Interruption:
— We are informing you with even emotional frequencies —
Relational Time: 3 Days Later… again
— End of Transmission —

She woke up groggy, and it took her a few moments to remember where she was supposed to be. They had traveled the whole day yesterday back to Trevor's house. But she didn't remember arriving. They must have moved her.

Ayya propped herself up on her elbows and wiped her face with her hands. Then she sat up in a sleeping bag on the floor in Trevor's living room. Trev was still sleeping next to her.

"Good morning, sleepyhead," said Ms. Harrison.

"You two slept in! It's almost nine, and your eyes have almost closed their dungeon doors forever from lack of light," said Mrs. Sadler.

Ayya giggled rubbing her eyes. "Good morning, Ms. Harrison and Mrs. Sadler."

"So polite, young lady. You can be a little less formal with me, Ayya. I'm just the resident, weirdo science geek waiting to experiment on you. Just call me Ms. Cerys if you *must* use a proper title."

Ayya laughed again harder. "Yes, ma'am. I'll try to remember that, Ms. Cerys. And by the way, if you don't mind me saying so, you're weird, but I like it."

"I'll take that as a compliment then. Good to see your dungeon doors opened. Your eyes are beautiful, can I borrow them? You can use mine."

She blushed and laughed at the same time. When Ayya stopped laughing and rubbed her belly from the cramps, she finally replied her thanks.

Giggling, Ms. Harrison asked, "Would you like to have some breakfast, Ayya? We have our meeting in an hour," as she worked on preparing food.

"Oh, yes, ma'am!" She reached over and shook Trev and said, "Trev, wake up! Your dungeon doors will shut forever, and there is food!"

Trevor moaned and turned over, mumbling, "Mom, not the dungeon door thing again. I told you dungeons don't have to have light, it's part of being a dungeon. Besides, sleep is better than food."

"Oh, no it's not!" Ayya got up and rushed over to the stools at the counter and climbed up. "Thank you, Ms. Harrison!"

"You are most welcome, Ayya. After the last few days, you deserve a fun breakfast."

After she said that, she reached over and set down a plate. A stack of huge pancakes were on it with eyes made of strawberries, hair made with bacon, and a big plop of butter for a nose.

Ayya felt her eyes go wide, and she squealed out a thank you and said, "This is better than Ms. Josephine's breakfast!"

"Shhh, don't tell her that. You might hurt her feelings." Then she set down a jug of raw maple syrup for her.

"I have to, Ms. Harrison. It's my duty. It will help her

improve. But I will tell her it is in the dessert breakfast category, not the regular."

Both of the ladies looked at each other and said, "Her duty?"

Ayya shoved pancakes into her mouth and after a couple long mouthwatering chews, let out muffled and blissful, "oh-daht-goo."

Ms. Harrison laughed. "Don't talk with your mouth full. You might lose all my hard work."

Ayya happily nodded and chewed. It was the best breakfast ever. She *loved* pancakes, bacon, and strawberries.

Trevor sleepily climbed up onto a stool next to her. When Ms. Harrison put his plate down in front of him, his eyes grew wide.

Ayya swallowed her bite. "See, breakfast is better than sleep."

"*This* breakfast is!" In an afterthought, Trev looked at his mom. "No offense, Mom," as he shoved one of the bacon hairs into his mouth.

"Hey, I killed the pig and made the bacon, I'll have you know!"

Both Ayya and Trev laughed holding their hands in an effort to keep the food in their mouths, then both muffled out their thanks.

After thirty minutes of blissful eating, listening to Ms. Cerys' corny jokes, Ayya couldn't finish all of her breakfast. She thought about how good it would be to have it later. "Umm, Ms. Harrison?"

"Yes, Ayya?"

She looked up to her just as Ms. Harrison put a large paper bag on the counter with a smiley face drawn on it.

Ayya looked at her again, curious, then she opened the back up slightly to look in and there was a whole other pancake breakfast in there with extra. She looked up at Ms. Harrison filled with gratefulness. Her eyes watered and her voice cracked. "Thank you, Ms. Harrison and Ms. Cerys."

The front door opened and Mr. Sadler and Paul walked in.

Ayya jumped off the stool and ran to Paul. He picked her up and gave her a big, long hug that seemed better than breakfast. She kissed his cheek and hugged him again.

"Hey, I see you have had one of Ms. Harrison's breakfasts!"

She pulled back and said, "How did you know?"

"Well, little phoenix, there are two reasons I know. One, the smell in the house. And two, my sticky cheek."

They all laughed as he put her down. "Let's wash up a bit, shall we?"

Paul got a cloth, wet it and washed her mouth and his cheek. Suddenly, Paul and Ms. Harrison stood a little straighter near her. She cocked her head and watched.

"What's wrong?" she asked.

Ms. Harrison looked at her. "Oh, it's okay Ayya, we are getting a special message." Then she looked over at Connor. "Zreyas will need us soon, so we need to have this meeting."

"Wait... Zreyas... I know that name," Ayya said thoughtfully, not quite able to place from where.

Paul looked surprised, then leaned down closer. "Where have you heard it from?"

Ayya thought a few moments and said softly, thinking out loud. "I know I've heard that name. It was—"

Aaru vibrated inside her. It wasn't an alarm kind of growl, just a communication. She thought about her grandmother and sadness came with it. Then it dawned on her…

"I remember, now!" she said excitedly.

Ayya pointed at Paul. "My toy that you gave me! My father threw it into the woods the day you gave it. I remember seeing him after Ms. Angel Queen showing up around Momma and a hurt bird in the yard. I know this sounds like I'm crazy, but I'm not making it up."

"Don't worry, Ayya, we believe you. Go on," encouraged Paul.

"Well, one time when I was at my grandmother's house on the day she… well, I visited my grandmother and my cousin and I went into the library to look at the books, but there was no light. So Jackie went to get a flashlight. While she was gone, lightning struck the library. I got up on a ladder at the window because the fire trapped me inside."

"I love this story!" Trev bounced on the balls of his feet. "Don't forget to tell them about the book, too."

Both Ms. Harrison and Paul both said, "What book?"

"Well, first I was up on that ladder looking outside while the building was burning and the flames were coming close. My uncle was outside telling me to get a book and break the glass so I could get out. It all scared me and I couldn't think. I am not sure if he showed up before or after the book. It's a little fuzzy. But there was a large old book, and I picked it up but it was so heavy I almost couldn't manage it."

"Then suddenly her toy showed up right on the bookshelf!" Trevor interrupted excitedly to help with the story.

Ayya nodded emphatically. "Yes, and he introduced himself and told me his name and calmed me down. I wrapped my leg around the ladder as my uncle instructed me to do for safety. But the book was still so heavy. Zreyas said he knew I could do it. He said some other things too, but I can't remember them."

"I like this part coming up the best! Tell them Ayya."

"Well, I remembered the spine of the book. The words were like a picture to me. I figured out what it said. It said, 'Heart of Odium.'"

Trevor started bouncing in excitement. "And Zreyas jumped over to where the book used to sit."

"And he knew my name, and that surprised me. He helped me get the window started by cutting the wood part with his axe, but he told me I had to break it."

"And she did it! Ayya broke the glass, flipped out of the window and her uncle caught her!"

Paul and Ms. Harrison looked at each other, shocked. They seemed a little pale, like something was wrong.

Before she could ask, Mr. Sadler told them it was time for the meeting.

They spent the next couple of hours reviewing the tests. Ayya had trouble with things that Trevor didn't, and vice versa.

"Ayya," said Mr. Sadler. "Your scores for mechanics and engineering were amazing!"

"Really?" she said, surprised. She wasn't used to being great at anything but climbing trees, football, and sneaking around the house between boards.

"You scored at the ninety-nine point six percentile in engineering and ninety-eight point eight in a mechanics division."

Ayya just looked at him, waiting for something she could understand, feeling a silent questioning tone go out.

Trevor turned to her and explained before anyone else could say anything. "That means that ninety-nine percent of everyone in the world that took this kind of test scored lower than you. Dad taught me about it a while back. You are a genius!"

"That pretty much sums it up, Ayya." Then Ms. Cerys went on. "Trevor scored really high on other things like social skills and languages. But children, you both scored extremely high on resonances, frequencies, and higher brain activity."

Mr. Sadler continued. "That is correct, and it is very exciting. But we don't need to get into those details. But we have an offer for you both, but you must choose together."

Paul chimed in with that accompanying look he got when he wanted to reassure her. "And you do *not* have to take the offer if you don't want to. Dulce, would you like to do the honors since you are their teacher?"

"But I can't take any offer without asking Momma first. And I miss her too. Can I go home to wait for her after this?"

"We thought you might want to do that. So we decided we would help you consult her. Here is another surprise adventure for you." Ms. Cerys stood and opened up a panel on the wall where a large screen sat.

Trev whistled in amazement. "Woah, I didn't know that was there!"

Mr. Sadler chuckled, then said, "I tied it to our facilities and Lanna was close to it, so we brought her in."

The screen came on and Ayya instantly recognized the room she had been in at the facility. There was one thing that immediately came to her that was different, though. Her mother was sitting there with a smile on her face.

"Momma! I've missed you!" Ayya got up and ran up to the screen. But it was so high up she couldn't get too close or she couldn't see her.

"You look good, sweetie!" her mother said.

Ayya looked a little suspicious, then said, "What game do you like to play with me? I'm sorry, I need to verify."

Everyone in the room laughed, even her mother.

"Spite and malice, of course!" said her mother.

"It's good to see you too, Momma! Is Katie okay?"

Her mother smiled and nodded. "She is! Katie is with your aunt today while I do this with you."

"Please, can you give her a hug for me, Momma?"

"Hi, Ms. Lanna, it's Trev!" he said excitedly. "You look good on our wall."

Everyone laughed.

Mr. Sadler interrupted the reunion. "So, shall we get on with our meeting so your mother can go back to help with your uncle?"

Everyone nodded, even her mother.

"Ayya," her mother said, "I want you to listen to them carefully. I think it might be really good for you. I already heard about your test results and I'm very proud of you. It will be an excellent opportunity and it will get you away from your father. I will support you either way you decide, though."

A little concerned. She thought about what her mother said. "Yes, ma'am. I understand. But what about you and Katie?"

"You just let me worry about that."

"Yes, ma'am. It sounds like you want me to do this no matter what I think, though."

"Honestly, I do. But it isn't because I want to get rid of you. In many ways, you are my sanity and rock when things aren't going well. But that is also why I want you to do this, because it will allow me to see where the problem really is. But, Ayya, listen to them with an open heart, and if you decide not to do it, it will be okay too. I get to have my hugs and play spite and malice with you more."

Ayya wanted to cry, and she didn't even know what it

was all about yet. She closed her eyes and looked down so no one could see her face, feeling the warm liquid escape through her eyelids, no matter how tight she thought she had them.

She felt Trev's arm go around her back. "I don't know what it is, but if you don't want to do this, I won't do it either. It just wouldn't be the same without you."

Nodding her head, she looked up, wiping the tears. She figured if her mother thought it was important, that it was worth doing for her.

Somehow, she knew this meant that she wouldn't be seeing her mother as often. She thought about Zreyas too and that they were needing Paul and Ms. Harrison's help, so something must be wrong somewhere because he was strong for a little toy.

"Would you listen to them for me?" asked her mother.

Then Ayya felt a low hum from Aaru. He was trying to tell her something, but it wasn't an alarm. Feeling stressed, she let out a long, sustained, single-toned hum. "Mmmmmm" It felt right in her body. "Okay, Momma, I'll listen for you."

Paul walked over and sat beside her. "My girl, don't listen for her. This is *your* life. Lanna, correct me any time if I say something that is not correct for you."

He waited till they saw her mother's nod and smile, then he continued.

"You are only eight, yes. You need guidance, yes. But you still need to live your own life using your talents to do what you want to do with it. You are in a rare situation that you now have the power to change your circumstances, and maybe you might even help the world starting in a few months if you choose to."

Ayya, hearing that whatever this thing she was supposed to decide on was a few months out, set her mind at ease. She had time and she could see her mother again soon. She felt the stress leave.

Paul smiled and looked at the two of them. "You and Trevor have talents that are powerful and could help many people. You are *both* important."

Then he looked at Ayya and said, "Did you know Zreyas came from many universes away to help rescue you when he found out that you were in danger?"

Ayya felt Aaru let out a hum of contentment. Something clicked, and she asked, "Is Zreyas Aaru's brother?"

Everyone in the room went silent for a long several seconds. Everyone seemed to her like she had said something wrong except Trevor.

He leaned over and said, "I think you said something that they didn't know you knew."

Ayya leaned in and touched Trev's head sideways. "I think you are right. I think they are going to drool any second now from their jaws hanging open."

She looked at Paul, who was close enough to hear their conversation, grinning from their comments.

"Mr. Paul, you really didn't think I knew about him?"

Paul and Ms. Harrison chuckled, then Paul said, "We knew you knew about him, but we didn't know you knew his name, much less make the association that they were brothers."

Ms. Harrison added, "It shows us you are growing in awareness, and that is good news, Ayya."

Her mother looked as if she was confused. Ayya look at her mother and felt guilt and sadness. "I'm sorry I'm so weird, Momma. I know it is more trouble for you."

Everyone in the room turned to look at her mother, who seemed like she was about ready to cry.

Paul looked at Ms. Harrison, who nodded back. Then

he looked at her mother. "Lanna, we have been friends for a long time. Do you trust me to give you some... really way-out-in-space sounding information about your daughter that might fill in some gaps for you? Ayya hasn't heard any of this either, though she might have figured out pieces we didn't expect."

Ayya's heart went out to her mother, feeling bad she was causing so many issues. Lanna looked like she was at her wit's end. That was one thing that really bothered Ayya, and that was to see her mother cry or be upset, especially if it had to do with her.

"I would like to understand more, but honestly, I'm not sure if I want to hear it at the same time," her mother said.

Paul nodded his head. "Understandable. It will be an enormous amount of background information. But I feel you are strong enough to handle it gracefully. It will take more than a few minutes. In fact, we can make a seminar about it all. You don't need to worry about the time it will take. We can arrange everything for you. Ayya needs to be updated on it, anyway. It's your decision, dear friend."

Ayya's mother wiped a tear from her cheek and nodded emphatically, trying to not cry. "Yes..." She sniffed and swallowed. "Yes, I want to understand."

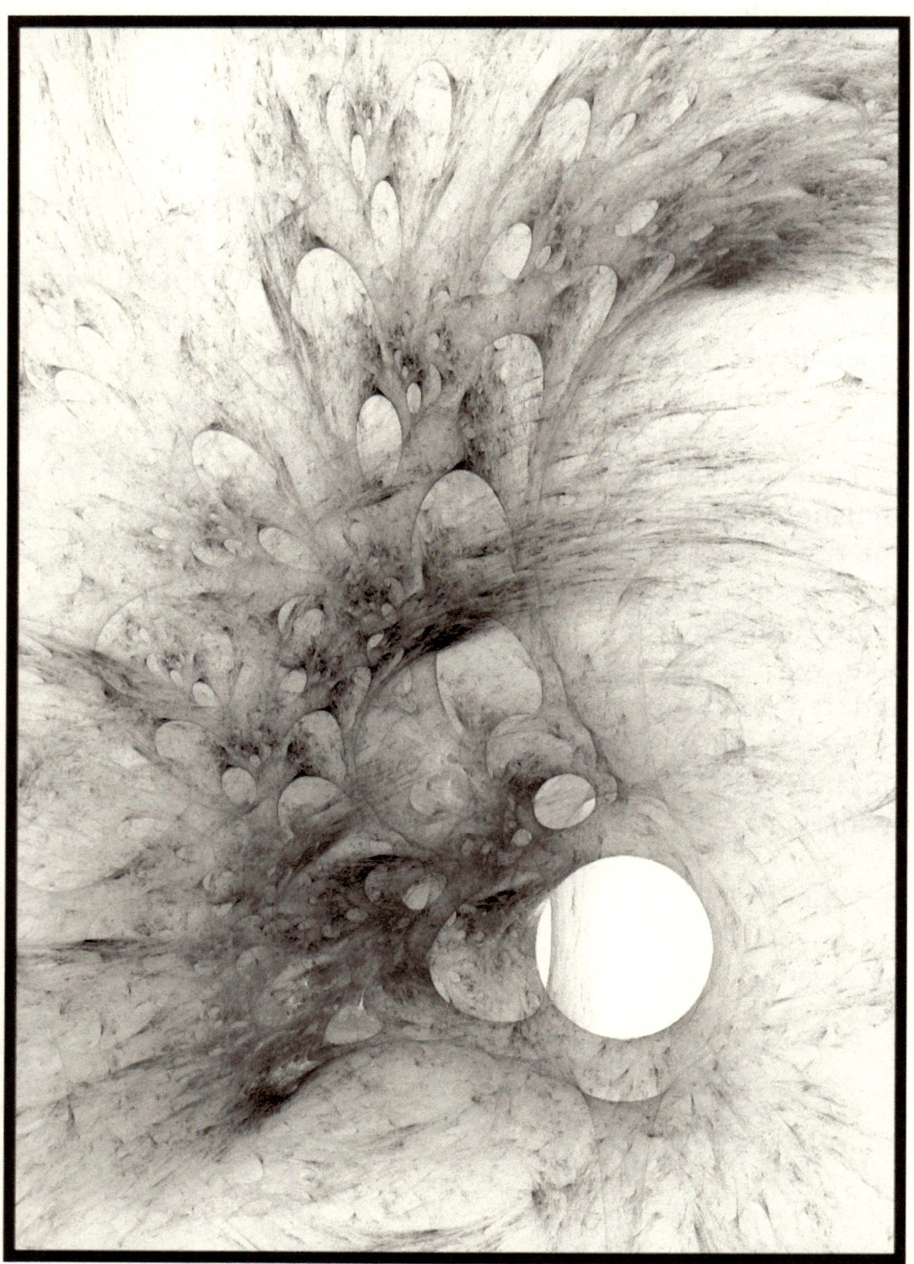

15 Waking Zreyas

ꙮꙮꙮ *Zreyas* ꙮꙮꙮ

"Captain, wake up, Captain. It's Tap and we need you to wake up."

Zreyas faintly heard Tap but nothing really registered. He did notice, however, he felt better than he did the day before. He could tell his body needed exercise, though, or his eyes would deteriorate and swell.

He shivered at the thought about that old warrior that lost his legs in a war, but continued to train new warriors. But the inactivity made his eyes swell and eventually burst. He wouldn't have believed the tales if he hadn't seen it happen. It brought up the total mystery that he was always trying to figure out surrounding the Janquar's eyes.

— Captain, I have extended your room a little and put up a treadmill for you to exercise. If you don't like it, you can adjust it. Maybe that will make you get up. Not only does the crew need you, Ayya, Lanna, and the twins need you for a very important talk. They are doing your idea. You can exercise and I can update you on what is going on.

Taps words slowly filtered in and it finally registered

what she was saying. He sat up quick and stood, alert. "Are they in trouble?"

"Not yet, Captain, but they will need you soon, I think. Freckles just told me they were doing a little 'proof mojo' to help them adjust to the news they were about to get."

Zreyas hopped off the bed and walked over to a wall, where he waved a hand over a sensor and a wall slid away to reveal a kitchen area. He poured water for himself, feeling a bit disoriented. As he drank his water, he walked over to a mirror wall panel nearby that covered from floor to ceiling.

He slightly turned his head to follow how far up that gold splotch had grown up to.

"It has grown, Captain. Are you ashamed of it?"

"Hmm, n-no. I just don't know what it is. Maybe the old man or Freckles will. I don't feel any different other than like I just went through torture and the relief you get after it is over."

A hologram of Tap wafted into his view to his left. He noticed it was to his size scale. He appreciated her sensitivity to wanting him to not think about how different he was size wise. Her hologram was blue and seemed like water.

"You went through something torturous; I know. It was hard to watch, Captain."

"Are you crying, Tap?"

"Yes Captain, Master Rhom said it is what incarnates do when they feel thrilled or really sad. He said it was good to show how one feels."

"I see. Maybe that is why the old man cries literal waterfalls. He must have a lot to cry about, with so much weight on his shoulders being a visage."

"Yes, captain, I imagine it is so because I know how I feel when I have to watch things you go through, and you are just one person."

Zreyas looked in the mirror, using his free hand to trace the huge splotch of gold that had grown in the center of his chest. It was like someone with gold fractal paint splattered a ball of it on his chest and ran their closed hand up the left shoulder, around the back of his neck, up the right side of his face over his right eye to the middle of his forehead. He liked the gold part, but the part on his chest was more transparent and could see the faint outline of his heart, yet it was as solid as ever.

"The more I go on this journey, the more weird things happen to my body."

"Captain, as you say..." Tap mimicked his voice exactly. "Ticking-hell, oh we-ell!"

Zreyas blinked and then laughed. "Ha!" He walked over and put his cup on the counter and made his way to the treadmill that was already running. When he hopped up, it adjusted to his size and he saw all sorts of stats and numbers. He didn't care about them, all he cared about was exercising. "So tell me about what is going on, Tap."

Tap's hologram turned to a pleasant, dusty green. She usually turned that color when she got down to business. Then she directed him to look at his vision interface.

All he needed to do was think about it and he realized he had already been looking through it, but just hadn't been paying attention to it. Around the edges were his health readings. He didn't want to see that stuff right now, so they disappeared. "Nice work on that, Tap."

"Thank you, Captain, but I didn't do it. You did. A few days ago when you started your... wave of... many things. I am still learning, but I think all of that weird processing you did was worth it. Our bond and potential have grown. And you feel less... murky, and more... clear and strong."

"Yeah, I don't know what the ticking-hell that was, but

I'm glad it is over for now. All I did was start grieving over Aaru. That was not what I call a fun time. That was more painful than the hall of waves in the challenge."

"Well, it looks like your heart cleared, literally. Speaking of challenge, Captain…" Tap created a screen in his vision interface, making it convenient to run and watch. A picture came up with a round corridor with three doors and a hallway leading into it. Silence and the cub were laying on each side of the center door between that and the outer doors.

"Another tri-fork. This is on the ship, but where?"

"That center door is your quarters, Captain. The other two doors are the quarters of Silence and the cub. They would not leave your door when you went in the last time for your… change time. What you are seeing now is the second dimension outside your own. Your quarters are now nested three times. Yours is one, your protectors there live in the second one, and the third…"

Tap backed the view out again, pulling them through another door.

He felt his eyes widen when he saw Aqum, the challenge node. "So Aqum is protected in a nested, separate dimension, within the ship?"

"It looks like that, Captain, and it is, yet it isn't. I hide these dimensions through me, but not *of* me, you included. You hide them within you, but they are not part of you."

Zreyas waved his hands around in front of his face. "I have too many questions and that is a sign I should just let that bit sink in. Let's have a lesson on that later."

"Noted, Captain. All you need to understand now is that they are very safe from the big D.O. as you call it… at least with his skills now. The reason Master Rhom and I did this was for the following reasons:

1. We wanted you to be safer.

2. We didn't want you to have to enter the chaos of the ship in a challenge emergency.

3. Silence and the cub seem to distract the crew a little for different reasons. And...

4. They deserve their own place. And since they would not leave your side, we wanted to keep them from blocking the corridor.

"It sounds logical. Well done, thankings to you. Now what is the status on the gate and us?"

"Captain, all is peaceful. We are hidden."

"Good, now give me the update on the old man and Freckles." Zreyas ran faster now that he was warmed up some. It felt good to run again.

Tap did something then that shocked him. She changed into a full-bodied person and started running with him as she talked. It made him feel... odd, like he used to feel when he did things with Aaru. It seemed like varSas ago.

"Captain, they went ahead with your plan."

"Uh..." Zreyas thought hard, trying to think of which plan she might be talking about.

"Captain, when you were going through this last change, I relayed a conversation Rhom had with you. I was your speaker. In your mind, you had an idea to get Ayya out of the fatal situation she was in. You said she would die if we didn't get her out of there. You were holding the tryst, and you said you talked to the stars."

Disturbed that he didn't remember any of that, he slowed down his run to look around and think. He squatted in his favorite thinking position, sitting on his heels.

"Captain, I know not remembering bothers you, but I took the liberty to record it, though most of it I couldn't record. Apparently, my incarnation skills didn't have the technology to do it, but I can show you what I have."

"Thankings to you Tap, but we will wait for that. So I made a plan based on the stars. Rhom is good with that kind of thing. We should ask him about it later, but for now, I came up with a plan to help Ayya get out of there and safe. Tell me about this plan."

"Captain, Rhom came to you for help because there was a situation where an entire block of time with all directly involved participants on the challenge had red auras that said those events and people couldn't be influenced."

"That's bad."

"That is what you said then, too, Captain. You said that it was time to take advantage of the 'spaces' in the rules again."

"*That* sounds like me. Go on."

"Yes, Captain, it does. You started spurting out a plan that Rhom could barely keep up with in all the details that involved informing Ayya and Lanna about the truth of everything. Aqum confirmed that there was no reason to forbid the direct contact and informing that it was inside the spaces of the rules. His reason was because of the Dark One—"

"Ticking-LFO mag-shit."

"Yes, Captain, agreed. His reason was because the ticking-LFO mag-shit was interfering directly too, but through others. When Master Rhom told you about all of her situation, you took it all in without questions."

"That doesn't sound like me. I always have questions."

"Agreed, Captain, but that gold thing on your chest was... growing at the time. Maybe you didn't need to ask them."

Zreyas grunted and thought about everything she was saying. "Then?"

"Rhom told you about her best friend Trevor, his father and mother being scientists, and—"

"What kinds of scientists?"

"Ha! That is what you asked before, Captain."

Zreyas couldn't help but grin at Tap's laugh.

"His father is a quantum scientist, though for earth it's primitive in our technology, and—"

"Heh, not in *my* mind. I bet you I'm more primitive than they are. Go on."

"—and his mother is one of the top scientists on Earth. She is a specialist in environmental sciences and microbiology. You advised to first involve her friend's father and mother directly. You wanted Rhom and Rtu to ask and see if they wouldn't join your team on the planet side base when it was established, since the ticking-LFO mag-shit was making things look grim."

Zreyas didn't mean for her to call the Dark One that name all the time, but he liked how it made him laugh inside, so he let it go. "That sounds like solid strategy."

"Yes, Captain, it is. But then we weren't really sure how Ayya was doing exactly, so you proposed a ruse to test both Trevor and Ayya for an experiment. And yes, Captain, you did. But that is when we ran into a discovery that was both amazing and troubling... and why Rhom and Rtu needed your help."

"Go on, list it for me and I'll ask questions if I need to."

"Yes, Captain.

"1. They ran the tests on both Ayya and Trevor separately.

"2. Trevor is at genius level in some areas like people skills, mathematics, and quantum concepts, etc.

"3. It seems Ayya is a genius of high capacity in engineering, mechanics, and sound. They never got to really test her on quantum capacity because that is where they figured she was already a genius."

"Why is that?"

Tap explained the whole situation to him about how she hummed and they communicated with each other, and how he wouldn't leave her in that research facility. Tap explained about the pipe experiment and how it all tied in.

"Then you told them to bring the whole family in. If they didn't like it or didn't do well, then the visages could wipe that part of their memories and let them live on earth normally. But then the whole connection situation revealed itself. Now they want to tell Lanna about it all, because Ayya knew your name and asked if you were Aaru's brother in front of Lanna. Being visages, there are certain decisions that they can't make, because it is not just through the challenge."

"Yeah, balances. Always the balances, even though the ticking-LFO mag-shitting-bandhula is doing what he wants to destroy them. In a way, we are off balance to offset the balance."

Zreyas shifted his weight on his heels. "What do they have in mind?"

"Captain, since you hatched this entire plan, they thought maybe it might be easier if you came and explained it in person for a few days. It's too much for just an hour or several hours. You can come back here at night to sleep and do work here if you like. They will sleep there like normal for being challenge participants."

"And if they don't want this?"

"Then they will wipe their minds and let them live out what life they likely have left and we will have lost the challenge, Captain."

Zreyas stood and immediately went to shower and put his armor on, weapons, tryst, and all. He wasn't taking anything for granted.

"Is the larger part of Freckles here on the ship?"

"Yes, Captain, Freckles is here, but he has most of himself on Earth right now, though I'm not sure why."

"Ask him to meet me at the challenge node living area so I can get details of when I should show up and exactly where."

"Yes, Captain."

16 Solution!

◪◪◪ *Paul (Rhom)* ◪◪◪

Paul stood and looked at Connor and Cerys. "Do you have room for another guest?"

Cerys immediately said, "It would be wonderful to have another here." Then she addressed Lanna. "We don't get to talk much, Lanna, but I feel like I know you well through Ayya. It would be nice to have you if you will come, as long as you don't mind dry and terrible humor. Your husband doesn't have to know."

Connor clapped his hands together once. "Then it is settled. I will send a driver over to come get you when you can pull away from your responsibilities there. Your husband will think you are still there, then you can go home afterwards."

Dulce Harrison held up a hand and said, "That won't be necessary, Connor." Ms. Harrison looked at Ayya and smiled meaningfully, though Ayya was a little confused.

Paul knew why, but waited to see what his brother was up to. Though as limited as he was in that body, he knew his brother. *Are you going to do what I think you are going to do?*

— Of course! We have the balances. Even though the rest of the participants aren't using balance, it will catch up to them, eventually. Plus, it will give both Ayya and Lanna an awakening on what Ayya's world is really like. Neither understand. Unfortunately, for everyone's sake, we need to tell them, and that means they have the weight of it too.

Yeah, I don't see her lasting here another year. Go ahead, you know human nature better than I do right now.

Then Dulce asked "Lanna, do you consent and trust to take a brief ride with me through the quantum to get here? It will give you an idea of what Ayya and yourself will be involved with. Ayya will understand some things she has seen that no one else would understand but you. It will be proof to help you feel more comfortable with all this."

Lanna took a deep breath and nodded. "I consent and I trust you all."

Paul looked over at Ayya and motioned her gently for a pickup hug.

Ayya got up and came to him, reaching up. It melted his heart when he looked into her face. He realized she was like his daughter in almost every way but the sperm it took to make her. He was the one that wanted the hug and it comforted him as much as it probably did for her.

He didn't relish the shock they were about to experience. This was all Zreyas' idea, and it made too much sense to not do it in such desperate times. He held her close, and she did him too.

Paul did not know that Lanna had watched it so closely until she said, "You know, Paul. I know this is horrible to say, but you should have been Ayya's father, because you are her daddy in every way. Thank you for that. She needs that."

Paul realized the crushing blow of mistrust Lanna was about to have come down on her when she found out the truth about him. His chest almost heaved. It almost felt like betrayal, but he really valued her friendship and realized he loved Lanna almost as much as he did Ayya.

"You might not feel that way once you hear all this. But I want you to know I love you both very much. I think I would have asked you to marry me had things been different."

Dulce patted Paul's shoulder, then turned to Lanna. "Do not let it alarm you, it's just a little like light and confetti." She smiled and watched the screen.

— Brother, Zreyas is up and running again. He will come there after I move Lanna from her location to where you are. Zreyas will land in the foyer so make sure no one is there. We don't want any unfortunate accidents.

Paul heard the voice of Rtu in his mind and sighed with relief at hearing the news. *Sounds good, dear brother. No one is there now, but there must be a reason you warned me about that,* he thought back as he nodded to Dulce.

Paul watched Ayya as he saw a bright light appearing behind Lanna. In a few seconds, the light formed into a similar shape that looked like Rtu, but with wings. *Flare for a grand statement?* he thought to Rtu.

— There is a reason. Watch Ayya.

He did as his brother instructed and Ayya's expression immediately went wide in just about every feature. She put her hand over her mouth and pointed with the other one. He barely heard her say, "Ms. Angel Queen?"

Paul held her close to reassure her.

She had tears in her eyes as they watched her mother disappear and appear on the other side of the room near the screen. Then the light version of Rtu settled on Ms. Harrison and slowly dissipated.

That might be too much too fast, Rtu. You just took Ayya's childhood view of her mother, even though that image has nothing to do with her mother.

— Have faith in her Rhom. This is my realm of things. Trust.

When Lanna landed, he watched her put her hand on

her chest and the most blissful expression he had ever seen on her face.

Ms. Harrison turned toward Ayya and smiled.

"All this time, you..."

Ms. Harrison nodded and motioned to take her in her arms. Paul let her go and transferred her to her teacher.

She held Ayya close, then pulled her away enough to talk with her. "Your mother is still Ms. Angel Queen. I just wanted to help her from getting killed. But she is still Ms. Angel Queen because she is worth saving, and an angel to you."

Then she looked at the still shocked Lanna and gently asked, "Do you remember the bird that you picked up when you lived near the fire station?"

It seemed to wake Lanna out of her disorientation and she answered, "Yes... yes, I do. We went to go see Paul and..." She stopped in shock a moment, realizing something, pointing to Dulce. "... and you... at the firehouse, and we came back to eat our cookies on the steps. All this time you were a fireman, a teacher, and a visage."

Ayya face lit up. "... and Ms. Josephine."

Dulce nodded to both of them. "A terrible visage called the Dark One, inflicted it with a poison, not native to Earth. They weren't really trying to kill you, Lanna, they were trying to kill... another."

"Who were they trying to..." Lanna's expression went wide in horror. "Oh, no..." Lanna looked at Ayya and then at Paul.

Paul nodded his head in confirmation, then said, "As we talked about before, this is Dulce Harrison, but she is not a normal human."

He sighed and started his confession. "And quite honestly, neither am I, though everything about our friendship and my love for you is genuine. We came here to help and protect her." Paul deliberately left Ayya's name out of it so it wouldn't upset and close her down internally.

Trevor ran over to the foyer and stood there tall with a protective air about him. "We know someone is trying to hurt Ayya. She told me all about the inky-eyed stuff going on. And I've seen part of it happening, too. You don't have to protect her from the information you are trying to keep from her."

"Trevor, there is a guest coming that will land there any time now. I ask you to come over here by Ayya and myself."

Everyone in the room other than Dulce and himself looked surprised.

To his credit, Trevor did as he was told and Ayya let her teacher know she wanted down. Then she stood beside Trevor in front of Paul and he let his hand rest on each child's shoulder.

Dulce continued. "Because Ayya didn't pick it up, you did. Had I not come to help, it would have killed you instead. While Ayya has always seen the Ms. Angel Queen in you, seeing me just brought attention to it. Hence why she has always called you that."

"Ayya, I am sorry I didn't believe you," she said to her daughter.

Ayya ran across the room to her mother's arms and hugged her tightly. "It's okay, Momma. I wouldn't have believed me either."

Lanna let Ayya go, then sat down on the floor cross-legged, rubbing her eyes and forehead. "I'm sorry, this is a lot and I need to sit down."

Ayya sat on her mother's lap, and Trevor went over to sit by Ayya.

Paul smiled. "We figured it would be, and it's quite okay, dear friend. There is one more piece of basic information we need to give you before we have that little seminar we plan to do together."

Paul sat on the floor too, crossed his legs, and leaned on his knees. "Ayya, about Zreyas..."

As soon as he said that, a light flashed in the foyer briefly and Zreyas shimmered into view, fully armed and arms crossed.

Once Paul's eyes adjusted from the light, he saw Zreyas' face and the changes that had occurred. The shock ran through him, but he tried to keep his composure and just looked at Dulce. He wanted to ask Zreyas about it right away, but he held off, knowing it was not the time.

Zreyas looked at Paul and took a couple of steps up and stopped.

"My toy, Zreyas! Ayya got up and ran, picked up Zreyas, and held him close. Then she kissed his face many times before hugging him again."

Zreyas looked at Paul with one of those expressions like, "Ticking-hell, I'm going to explode."

"Uh, Ayya," Lanna said, before he could say anything. "It's important that you put him down because he is not what you think he is."

Ayya quickly put him down, backed up and stood there, watching him apprehensively.

Zreyas looked up at her. "I'm giving the thankings to you for putting me down, but it was okay to give me the huggings for a short time."

"Can I do it one more time? I missed you!" as she stepped forward.

Before she could step again, Zreyas held up a hand and shook his head. "Once a day is enough for me." Then he sat down on the edge of the step and asked Ayya to sit next to him. Trevor got up and sat on the other side.

Zreyas looked at him and said, "Greetings to you, Trevor."

Trevor reached over and touched his horns out of pure curiosity.

Paul almost lost it and laughed, but he held his hand over his mouth with his eyes watering from holding it back.

Zreyas leaned away from Trevor a little with that look again and said with a slow, deliberate pressured containment, "Are you going to keep doing that?"

"Probably. They are so cool!"

"Trevor, leave him alone," said his father, also grinning now.

"Solution!" Zreyas pointed to the floor in front of him.

Trevor jumped at the loud word that came from the captain.

Zreyas pointed both index fingers in both hands in front of him now. "New game. You two, enjoy the floor in front of me, so I can see you! We need to give you information."

Then he Q-leaped from a sitting position back up to a standing position on the edge of the step.

Both kids said, "Woah!"

Ayya looked at Trev and said. "See Trev, I wasn't lying about him, just appearing in the library during that fire."

Paul snuck into the conversation to get things back on track. "Ayya, you understand Aaru and that he is within you."

Ayya turned toward him and nodded while she said, "Yes, sir."

"Lanna, we will explain that part soon. Don't worry, she is still your little girl, but she is not... like other humans either."

Lanna nodded apprehensively. "I have a feeling this will make a lot of sense when you are done with this, even though I might not like it."

He nodded to her. "Thank you for your patience."

Paul looked again to Ayya. "Little Phoenix, when you inquired earlier about if they were siblings—Zreyas is indeed Aaru's brother."

"And..." Zreyas paused only a moment before saying, "I am Captain Zreyas Rittak, of the quantum ship called The Potential, leader of the Sleeping Phoenix Order."

Trevor and Ayya looked at each other with wide eyes, then back to Zreyas.

Ayya, in awe and in disappointment, said, "So you were never my toy?"

Paul chimed in quick. "Yes, he was for a time, to help protect you from the inky-eyes, as you call them. That is why he showed up at the fire at your grandmother's library. And many other times."

"So that is why my daddy threw you away into the woods?"

"Yes!" confirmed Zreyas. "But as you can see, I came back to show you I was still around to help you."

"Thank you for helping my daughter, Captain Zreyas."

"Bah, it was fun. Well, not the doll part, but I'm giving her the likings, anyway!"

Paul chuckled. "Apparently you kept trying to take his armor and weapons off and carried him around by his neck."

"You kept slapping my hands, I remember!" said Ayya.

Lanna gasped and tried not to laugh. So did everyone else.

"Ha! It's okay to have the laughings. Humor is good for the stressing relief!"

Ms. Harrison, still laughing, said, "That it is, Captain!"

"Do you want to hear all the explanations why we have come to you with all this shocking news?"

Lanna, Ayya, and all of Trever and his family said, "Yes."

"Okay, we will tell you many things when the time comes. We will also show you many things. But after, you must agree to join us, or stay, after it is over. If you do not want to join this cause of the Sleeping Phoenix Order, then we will let you go on with life like before, but without memories of us in your life."

Zreyas pointed diagonally outward conversationally as he continued. "*That* is the only way you would have a chance to live through this. I'm not coating this with the sugarings. However, we *will* continue our efforts." Zreyas lifted his hands and put the final stamp on his stipulations. "Understood?"

They all nodded and confirmed.

Zreyas waved a hand in front of his stomach upward and took out a tablet that materialized. It grew larger as he put it on the floor beside him. Everyone in the room but Dulce and Paul gasped in amazement.

"If you agree, place your hand on this screen to get scanned and provide what will be your signature by doing so. Then you will be provided with a uniform to wear during these talks to monitor your body and overall health. In addition, it will protect you in case something happens with the inky-eyes."

One by one, all of them, without hesitation, went up and did as they were told. Paul thought it was probably more out of curiosity more than anything else, but it was better than nothing. It would get the ball rolling.

Paul looked at Zreyas admiringly. He stood there shining in his role as a captain, unaware he was even doing it.

He couldn't help but fix his curiosity about Zreyas' skin change, as he placed his hand on that tablet to show the others he was not so different from them as they might think, at least until they talked at the next gathering.

17 New Eyes

Before he could see anything from his teleport to the ship, he heard a familiar voice.

"My boy! Welcome home!"

When he could finally see and talk, he laughed. "You act like you haven't seen me in years, old man!"

"Well, it seems like it, little buddy. It's good to see you!" Rtu bumbled up happily and picked him up and gave him a big hug like a child would a rag doll.

Feeling testy with all the sudden huggings from Ayya and now Rtu, but humoring the two, he talked to himself. *Okay, Zrey, remember you love them. Don't punch them, you lo-ove them.* Then he said between the pulses of Rtu's squeezes, "But... you just... saw me five... min-nutes... ago."

"That was Paul and Dulce, not us!" Rhom paused, then said, "Uh, Rtu—"

"Oh, I love you, little buddy. I'm so glad you are okay

from your tough week. Hmm, Rhom?"

"I think he's had about as many loving embraces as he can take for one day. He looks red, but I'm not exactly sure if it is because you have squeezed him to death, or he's getting angry."

Rtu immediately held him out in front of him like a rag doll, legs dangling, and Zreyas realized he probably had a nasty-looking expression because he felt like he was about to explode. "Yes, I'm giving you the lovings."

As he dangled, Rtu started to hug him again in his excitement, but Zreyas held out a hand. "But I am informing you that if you give me any more of the embracings to the point of drowning, I don't claim responsibility for my actions."

Rhom held his hand over his mouth and bounced.

"Go ahead and laugh, old man." Zreyas' heart melted watching the old man he had grown to give the lovings to so much. He gave the lovings to Rtu too, but Rhom and he had a special bond of a different kind. "And yes, I will give you one of those embracings, but not so hard."

Rtu laughed and handed him over like he was one of Ayya's dolls. "Why do I end up in these doll toy positions all the time?" he said, disgruntled.

Rhom held him out in front of him with a grin. "It's the size, my boy. Incarnates like to love little things. Get used to it. Remember, it was your choice to stay that size."

"Yeah, yeah, okay. Do the huggings so we can get to work."

Rhom grinned and brought him to his shoulder and let Zreyas hug him if he wanted to, and he did. He wrapped his arms around his head, covering his eyes, making Rtu laugh. Rhom patted his back a couple of times.

"Okay, okay, don't make me explode."

"Funny you say that, little buddy. Tapping the backs of

babies is what many species do to help get the air out of their stomachs so they don't get gas. Sometimes they spit up."

"Oh, that's it, I can't Q-leap away cause you have too much hold of me, put me down."

As he put Zreyas down, Rhom gave Rtu a dirty look.

"Peace, brother, peace." Then he turned his attention to Zreyas. "I apologize, little buddy. Neither one of us looks at you in that way. We just love you and missed seeing you. We were a little concerned."

Just as Rhom put him down, his head felt light. He put his fingers on his forehead a moment, but the twins said nothing. "Thankings to you for the lovings. Sometimes it's hard to remember that the lovings is—"

Zreyas looked up at the twins and a flash of the day he first saw Rhom change into his true visage form with all his elements played before his eyes superimposed on his normal vision. He remembered how strong he looked in his simple form. It was more significant this time, though, maybe because he understood more.

These sudden visions were getting on his nerves. He just wanted to move on. His experience, this time, was like the first time, but with a blend of conscious presence of mind and extra dimensions.

⁊⁊⁊ ⁊⁊⁊

"Whoa! Rhom, you are so... so..." Frustrated at his lack of good vocabulary, he finished with a simple ending. "Well, you look good now!" Zreyas' jaw hung as he stared at the visage, manifesting himself before his eyes more solidly.

—I remember feeling that awe. I still do, he thought as he experienced it again.

Rhom's body was powerful, and he had multiple skin color tones that mixed with each other.

—*He seems more powerful this time than the last time I saw this.*

His left arm and shoulder, along with the right leg and hip, were a blue-tinted tanned skin. The opposite of his arms and legs were red. Both sides had flecks of purple mixed in with it, subduing the vibrancy into something pleasant to look at. His torso was a subdued dusty purple that blended gently into the other colors.

—*I have decided I give the lovings to the color purple... there is something about it. There are many colors of purple on him. They are living, just like the neutrinic-gleam.*

Zreyas wanted so badly to go over and touch Rhom's skin. It drew him in. He didn't seem painted; it appeared almost like its own dimension.

—*Yes, I see the dimensions now.*

Rhom was someone he didn't even know anymore. Zreyas had nothing to say. He wondered what would happen to him now.

 The leather pouch on Rhom's hip was simple worn leather with a thin strap that went diagonally across his chest.

Zreyas loved the simple necklace he wore. As shiny as Rhom was, Zreyas wasn't sure if he made it of shell or bone, but leather knots separated each segment.

—*I have always given the lovings to that necklace. I don't know why.*

He felt his present day chest warm as he looked at the necklace.

—*Those represent something, but they are the curled heart of a shell, not bone.*

Rhom's body had iridescent white tattoos all over it, but they stopped at the middle of his thighs and his elbows; none past those points. They moved and lived on his skin.

He wore a simple headband and wristbands, both made of leather that long-used and dirty, a contrast to the opulence of everything else about him. After Zreyas thought about it, he realized it was like the earth part of Rhom that grounded him.

—*Yes, that is exactly what it is.*

Once Rhom coalesced into a firmer fleshy form, the misty faces at each shoulder and the surrounding mist disappeared into his body. He stood there in all his glory.

Rhom slowly turned his face toward Zreyas, both in the vision and in the present. That was when Zreyas noticed the brilliant light-blue irises.

Rhom's eyes seemed to pierce through him in the past and present. "I'm still here, my boy! You are safe." And then he smiled that very Rhom-like smile that always shined in any form, past and present.

Zreyas looked at Rtu and saw dimensions in him he had never seen before. In many ways, he was stronger than Rhom. Though he never had a *true* incarnation, Rtu could relate to being an incarnate by his very earth nature. It was why his respect for him had grown so much that day he punched him down the runway.

He decided Rtu was the strongest in incarnate ways for now, the fiercest, yet he showed his lovings to things openly. Rtu had something important to teach him, and he would watch and listen to him. He was a warrior, and he had always underestimated Freckles.

They were both strong and powerful in their own ways, yet equally gentle. That perplexed Zreyas. He shrugged. "You two make my head hurt. Ha! Let's get to the bridge and talk strategy. We got a new home to claim!"

As Rtu turned to follow him, he clapped. "Yep, he's back, brother, he's back. Better than before, even if he is more grouchy than normal."

Zreyas couldn't argue with that. "I'm saying the aplop-o-gies to you, but I'm not saying the sorries. I'm informing you that my head seems to be swimming in different worlds right now. So, get in the boat and ride or start swimming!"

The twins laughed and followed him to the bridge, making jokes.

18 Heart Out Your Face

After meeting with the ship's crew, Zreyas discovered they had done a lot while incapacitated with processing his grief, and whatever else that was that happened to him. Being startled at how different he looked in the face, Zreyas knew he had to decide about how much he was going to tell them.

They all gave him their new salute, fist to their forehead, and then everyone went silent. Silence and the cub were there in the room with him too, one sitting on each side slightly behind him.

As hard as it was, he decided he was going to be honest with them all. There was no point in starting a relationship as a captain with dishonesty. He knew that there would be those times that he couldn't give out information, but it was part of the job at times—this... wasn't one of them.

"I want to tell you how pleased I am with all your progress in just a few days. I'm also giving you the thankings for your concerns to all of you. What started out as grieving for my brother ended up in some weird transformation I don't understand. I haven't had a chance really to speak with anyone about it, yet. You are my crew, but also advisers, and we are a team of choice... a new family."

Zreyas took in a deep breath and let it out, looking out at all of his advisers' faces. "This time... though it might not always be like this, right here and now is the first time I have spoken about it, other than to Tap. You deserve to know what transpired. You worked hard for me and the cause, so I am returning the respects to you as your leader."

"Captain," a familiar voice came from nearby to his right.

Cree stepped forward and saluted. It wasn't out of protocol, because he had not given orders for anything like that. The Janquar didn't do it either, not even to the emperor. They had started doing that fist to the forehead salute after his fight with the nagodara and saving the cub at the crevasse.

Zreyas nodded. "Yes, Cree?"

"Captain, can we see your full mark?" Cree pointed to the golden color coming from the back of his neck forward and across one side of his face to his forehead.

He thought it an odd request, but nodded. "I can do that." Zreyas took off his chest piece and outer helmet so they could get the full view. It felt more than a little odd, and he felt vulnerable. Though he was a little nervous, he decided that if he had come this far with it, he might as well follow through.

He took off his gloves and Cree held them for him, then he stood there.

His crew had a mixture of shock, gasps, and awe.

He was the most vulnerable he had ever felt in his life. Zreyas looked around for the old man and Freckles, especially the old man. It was times like this that he was the one he would look to for wisdom. He didn't see them anywhere. Had they left? *Tap? Where are the twins? Where are you?*

No answer.

Zreyas swallowed. He realized it was one thing to be vulnerable for leadership purposes, but it was another to go overboard and be a spectacle for them to gawk at.

Just as his indignation rose to near capacity, and he was about to reach for his armor, Cree spoke up. "Captain, your heart shines out of your face, just like when you fought the nagodara. All the light came into your chest, then it came out of your face."

All the crew mumbled and nodded in agreement.

The artisan he knew that was now named Tracker stepped forward. "Captain Zreyas, being one of your advisor's now, I would like to say..."

Tracker stepped to the front of the room and turned his body to the crowd so that everyone, including Zreyas, could see his face. "I have known the captain the longest of you all. Myself and the late tracker, who the captain named Everyone, got to know each other on a one-to-one basis because we were not captain and crew then.

Zreyas cocked his head slowly sideways, listening to Tracker. He felt his emotions swell for the original tracker that lost his life and almost lost control of his emotions. But he listened and paid every bit of attention to his new adviser as he could. He felt it was important.

"You see, we didn't know each other, and we were hunting him, yet he came to help us. He was going to teach us the ways to make water and survive, and yet knew we might give his hiding secrets away. The Captain knew we might try to kill him, and he told us what our nation was doing, that it was killing the multiverse.

"But he treated us like equals. He talked straight like a commander, yet he didn't command us. The Captain even knocked on our heads when we were thinking stupid things and taught us to laugh when there was nothing we could see to laugh at. But there was one thing the tracker, and I knew, and we talked about it…"

Using a head nod and hand gestures to emphasize his words, he said with conviction, "We could always see his heart on his face and through his eyes. He was true and, like my late brother said, his tracks are good."

Then he pointed to his chest. Zreyas' attention seemed blurred from the surreal vulnerability. Zreyas could tell his chest had a glow about it out of his lower peripheral vision. He wanted to interrupt him, but he stayed quiet. He owed him that.

"The Captain taught us about the quantum in different ways on that trip those two days. I think that Captain Zreyas has put his heart out there so much in the last few weeks that his heart has changed and it can't help but come out of his face."

Zreyas expected the people in the room to laugh, but they didn't. Tracker held his open palm to his chest, then put his fist to his forehead, but that didn't surprise him near as much as the entire room followed his gesture without a word.

"Captain Zreyas, I hope my heart always comes out of my face too." Then Tracker backed up into the crowd.

Zreyas took in a sharp breath, doing everything in his power not to lose it. He put his hand on his own chest, swallowed, then put the thumbed side of his fist to his forehead in salute to them and realized that they had yet changed their salute again. It was then; he saw the twins fade in at the entrance of the room where he himself had entered. They had been there all along.

He guessed they weren't going to let him lean on them through that one and assumed Tap did the same.

— They love you, Captain, and so do I.

That wasn't something he was going to respond to right now, with his emotions bouncing all over the place. He reached over and took his armor back and put it on.

Once he was all put back together, he asked, "Are you ready to go claim our new home?"

The entire room erupted. "Yes, Captain!"

"It's going to get crazy before we get there. Are you still sure you are ready?"

Again, the room erupted, but even louder this time. "Yes, Captain!" The entire room started thumping their palms to their chests in a steady rhythm three times in silence, then they paused for a beat, then all together they started a four-part rhythmic drumming of their chests and chanting.

Zreyas felt it throughout his body. He grinned and slightly bowed his head to show it. Then, as they all did their last beat, still in the Rhythmic style, they yelled, "Heart out your face!"

They all laughed and punched each other, then Zreyas said, "To your posts! We got a lot to do. Just in case, be ready for a fight, but I hope we don't have to do that. Dismissed!"

The entire room went into motion with various commands going out from different crew members that were now in authority positions, and Zreyas couldn't help but smile. They were doing so well.

As he turned to head to the command deck, just before jumping off the table, he was greeted by Silence and the cub coming into the room. The cub jumped up on the table and gave him a huge lick that felt like teeth on a saw. It was a good thing he had armor on. Then she rubbed her face up against him, purring.

"Mother, she is learning well, but she will not go away from your door or wherever you are. She will watch for you and is extremely diligent in doing so."

Zreyas chuckled and stroked her neck. "Giving you the thankings, little one, for your focused unwavering dedication. But I am asking you to listen to Silence, Tap, as well as Switch and Tracker. They will help you learn to be better at being... dedicated to me."

The cub stopped nuzzling and sat down in front of him, who was now just a centimeter or two taller than himself. She let out a muffled growling roar, then a series of guttural noises that were a cross between a purr and a normal large-feline roar. It was quite intimidating, even to him.

"Mother, she is telling you that you need to learn her way of speaking like I have. But she will never leave you unprotected, no matter who tells her to."

"Thankings to you, Silence, for translating and for guiding her. I'm assuming she understands me from her reply."

"You are welcome, Mother. You teach me, so I will teach her too. But she can't do the leap of the quantum, she doesn't want to. She is afraid because of where she came from."

"It's okay, I don't blame her and we are all different. She will discover what she is best at with time," he said as he looked into her eyes. "To help and protect me is sometimes done through doing things away from me, too."

The noises came again from the cub's throat and Zreyas mentally paid attention to feeling the frequencies and remembering the sounds.

Before he could ask Silence what she was saying, he translated.

"Mother, she said that you can be remedial at times, so she was not going to leave you unprotected."

Zreyas laughed and found he couldn't argue with that. Then her name came to him. "What do you think about the name Determination?"

A long string of guttural sounds and an edgy roar emerged from her.

Silence cocked his head, then translated. "It'll do."

"That is all she said out of all that noise-making?"

"Well, Mother, she also said she loved you and asked how she could learn to save you from yourself, just like I told you once before. Our goals are aligned with that, Mother."

Zreyas chuckled. "Good question. I'm not sure I can answer that, but we don't have time for that right now. I'm not sure we will ever know that."

"That is what I told her, Mother."

"Hey! It might seem impossible, but there is always hope. Anyway, I need to finish getting to the bridge and assess information I haven't yet seen. You two help with labor or communications while I do that, and you know how to speak with me if you two need anything, Silence."

"Yes, Mother. We are happy to do things to help and make ourselves stronger." Silence looked down at the cub with a little more predatory energy than normal. "Isn't that right?"

The cub let out a small roar that made Zreyas almost laugh.

Silence looked at him and came closer putting his forehead forward.

Zreyas leaned forward and met with Silence with his own brow. Then he looked at the cub, and he couldn't help himself and had to show some of the affections bubbling up inside. "Just like Silence, I'm giving you the big admirings. You are strong and I am giving you both the thankings for protecting me. And I think I have decided on a name for you, and it isn't determination."

The cub circled quick and sat down.

"She is excited, Mother, and says, 'it's about time. What is it—what is it?'"

Zreyas laughed. "I'm not great with names but I think this one will be perfect for you. I hereby name you, Resolute."

The cub got up and rubbed her head against him, and a loud purr resounded from her that seemed to reverberate.

"I've never seen her do that before, Mother. She says she loves the name and she plans to live up to it."

Zreyas grinned, petted her, then said, "Good. Now be 'resolute' in my instructions. You go help with the labor. Make yourself stronger. Go see Tracker since he is overseeing a large crew of labor and artisans. Work hard."

Resolute let out a roar that was tame as she opened and closed her mouth several times.

"Did she just mock me?"

"Perceptive, Mother. She did, but she also said she would work hard for you and listen and learn."

"Good! But do you really have to keep calling me Mother? You do realize I'm not female, right?"

"I know you are not female, Mother. But I call you that because I want to. It is what you are to me. It makes no difference your gender."

Zreyas' eyes fell to a crass wilt, thinking about how a seasoned warrior being called 'Mother' was just comical.

He turned to make his way to the bridge almost chuckling, feeling the lovings in his heart for those two, almost forgetting he needed to talk to Aqum. Zreyas turned around again walking past the two, who were staring at him inquisitively as he headed toward the challenge node.

19 The Bribe

The last thing that Trevor had told her to do was get her birthday present out. He had said he didn't want to tell her because he wanted her to have a surprise while she was stuck in her room.

When the hired car brought her into the driveway, her father came out of the door and stood there, a dark mist swirling in and out of his eyes.

Ayya's stomach knotted up for the first time in days just seeing her house. She had forgotten how much it did that when she was home, and reminded herself that humming was not an option again.

She did as she had been instructed—to wait till the driver opened the door for her. The car windows were dark tinted, and she knew her daddy couldn't see her. Ayya sat up and watched as the chauffeur, who said his name was Light Warr, got out. He had a dark suit on with black sunglasses. She knew he was a good person, but he *did* look intimidating and she would be scared if he were to approach her as a stranger.

His co-driver got out, who was Mr. Light's twin brother

using the same name, which she thought odd, looking more intimidating than his brother with his muscle-y build. She liked it; it reminded her of the secret agent movie she loved so much.

She couldn't help but wonder if the stuff in the movie was real. If it was like this, it was scarier than she thought it would be.

The co-driver, who she called Mr. Warr so she wouldn't get confused, winked at her just before *almost* closing the door. Ayya didn't know his name, but she really liked him. Instead of closing the door, he left it partially opened. It wasn't long till she understood why.

Mr. Light reached into his pocket and pulled out a thick envelope. Ayya's eyes went wide. He didn't give it to her father yet, though.

Mr. Warr pulled out a pad, almost like the one Captain Zreyas used that took hand prints. He held it out for him, gripping each side with both hands, keeping them out of the way of the surface.

Using the envelope in his hand to punctuate his words, Mr. Light said, "If you want to get payments for your daughter's service to the government, you had *better* make sure she stays safe until the end of the term of service."

Mr. Warr then added, "If *any* harm comes to her at any time, the government will issue a warrant for your arrest and prosecution in a... *special* government court of law. Trust me, we will know if you harm her or if she has any... accidents. If that happens, you will never see the light of day again. If you agree, put your hand on this screen as a signature."

Her father looked at the screen being held by him, who seemed to tower over daddy by a head and a half. He didn't seem to know what to do with it. Those kinds of things weren't normal, and it sure seemed to intimidate her father.

Then as if he understood her daddy was clueless, he advised, "Just put your open hand on the screen until it beeps."

"No hand on the screen, no payment, no daughter. We will take her to stay at another facility. The only reason she is staying here, is due to balances and a few other things you wouldn't understand."

"Balances?" Her father looked confused.

The driver gestured with the hand holding the envelope, waving it.

Ayya wished her father wouldn't do it. That would mean she didn't have to stay at home while her momma was away.

Her heart sank as her father opened his hand and pressed it to the screen. It beeped, and they instructed him to do the other hand, and he did so, clearly unsure of what it was all about.

After seeing the screens and bleepy monitors in the research facility as well as in Trevor's home, then with Captain Zreyas, she knew this was not normal for Earth. Her mother's TV had antennae and tinfoil on the ends to get reception. There was none of that anywhere at the facility or in Trevor's house. She had no idea what she had gotten herself into, but she both loved it and feared it.

After it was done, the driver held out the envelope. "Treat her well, or the deal is off and you know what happens."

As her father took the envelope, the driver took a step forward, still gripping the money. "Do you understand?"

Her father seemed to smolder the inky mist but nodded. "Understand, now give me what you owe me."

The driver let go, almost making her father stumble

backward, because he was pulling on it so hard.

Then he came over to her door and opened it. He, too, winked at her. "You are home safe and sound, Miss Ayya. We will see you again in another week or two, depending on your schedule."

She picked up the bag of stuff they had given her on the seat beside her and got out. They were treating her like a princess or something and she felt very awkward, but she played along as she had been instructed earlier. "Thank you, sir. I look forward to seeing you again next time."

As Ayya walked toward the door, she heard, "Thank you for your service, Miss Ayya."

When she turned around, both men bowed their heads briefly and waited at the car doors facing her, with her father between them.

He just stood there gawking.

Ayya was filled with gratitude and the drivers seemed familiar somehow, but she didn't know why. She wanted to go hug them and let out tears because she felt them and the gratitude filled her. It was almost like she was remembering something about who they were, but couldn't put her finger on it.

"I'm glad I can help, Mr. Light and Mr. Warr. Thank you for all you do." Then she looked at her father, knowing there wasn't much of anything left in him somehow in that mist and knew she would learn more in that next meeting as to why.

She was afraid to say what she was supposed to say next, but she did it anyway. She took in a deep breath as calmly as possible, looked at her father again, and said, "I know I'm still on restrictions. I'll get some food and go to my room. I know my place here, and I will use the bathroom to shower and do my business any time I feel like it. If you don't like it, take it up with them. It's part of the agreement you just signed."

Her father jerked toward her to grab Ayya, but Mr. Light and Mr. Warr were already all over him.

Ayya had to blink. Did they just do what Captain Zreyas had done in the burning library?

Mr. Light held him, and Mr. Warr pressed a palm against her father's chest.

Ayya's eyes spilled with tears as she watched in silence as her father's eyes went wide. After a few seconds, they let him go, and her father seemed to relax.

"Do we have an understanding?" asked Mr. Warr.

Her father nodded, rubbing his chest.

Mr. Light added, "You can still back out if you like," as he grabbed the corner of the envelope in her daddy's hand.

Please don't take it daddy, then we can be on our separate ways.

Her father jerked his hand away with the money. "We have an understanding, as you say."

Ayya couldn't take anymore and went into the house. As she walked in, her guts squirmed at how dark her home seemed. She wanted to cry at the stark difference coming back in here.

She rushed into the kitchen to get out of the den. She would have stopped there to catch her breath a bit but she was afraid her father would come in. There was no sense in pushing her luck.

When she turned the corner to go down the hall, she found a new door with an odd sheen to it half way down. It had a print of a solid red bird that looked familiar but couldn't quite place it in her mind at the moment.

Ayya opened it and her bedroom was on the right as normal, but there was something odd about her parent's door. It looked like it had been blocked off, but there was a shimmering look to it. Everything else in the hall looked normal.

She knew the food in her closet would be too old now to eat, so she had to do what she didn't want to do in the first place, go back to the kitchen and risk seeing her father.

Ayya dropped her bag of stuff on her bed and made her way back to fix herself some fresh sandwiches, cheese puffs. She was happy to find out she could add cheesecake to the tray, still there from her birthday, though it might be risky to even in the fridge being a week old.

She heard her father come in and close the door to the den, so she hurried out of the kitchen before he came through.

She went through the new door in the hall, using her forearm to close it behind her. Once in her room, she unloaded all she had on her desk, then shut her door. She took a few steps, then stopped and turned around to lock the door.

Ayya went to her desk and sat down sideways in the chair, and just sighed. She looked around her room. Everything felt comforting, yet alien. Her whole life felt like it was warping out of control. She missed her momma badly.

She turned to face her desk and smelled her cheesecake. She sighed because her mother had made it for her. It didn't smell as good as it should have, so she reluctantly put it aside and ate her cheese puffs instead as she thumbed through one of the magazines.

Halfway through her second cheese puff, she thought about what her mother had said to Paul, about him being more of a daddy to her than her real father. She cried silently and didn't know why. As her mouth salivated from the cry, she finished chewing as she thought about it.

Ayya figured it was because she felt alone, maybe. She

felt loved by some, and she felt like she was disliked by many because of how odd she was. But the one she wanted to love her most, besides her mother, hated her. Then she told herself that the person was dead or buried so deep that he could never come out of that inky mist.

She rested her forehead on the heels of her hands and cried, feeling sorry for her father. She reached out to him inside and realized that she didn't feel him anymore other than a speck far away. Then she sobbed as quietly as she could.

She looked up and croaked out, "I love you, no matter what, Daddy, but now I have to say bye-bye because I can't reach you anymore. There is a part of me that won't give up on you, but I know you are so far away now that the inky-eye in your body will hurt me. I just ask you don't hurt Momma or Katie."

Ayya stood, wiped her eyes, and picked up the rest of her food and put it in her closet. She picked up the old tray of food that was now six or seven days old and took it into the kitchen, seeing no sign of her father. She could tell he had gone somewhere. There was no mist on that side of the house. Even the den was free of it, other than a little smidgen here and there.

Breathing easily, she looked out into the backyard through the door and felt an uneasy peace. She would take that, though. Since it was almost dark, she decided to do something fun in her room. Ayya didn't know why, but she had this urge to draw.

Ayya walked to the bathroom and decided to take a hot shower first, since her father wasn't home. She never felt comfortable taking a shower while her father was home, even with the door locked unless her momma was there.

As she put her head under the shower, she closed her eyes and felt the warm water run down her body. She realized it had been so long since she felt this much peace and quiet. As the water streams hit her head, she started to pay attention to each one and how each felt when they came in contact with her head.

Before long, she found herself in a dream. Ayya was floating in space and she was talking to the stars. What was odd was that she knew she was dreaming, yet enjoying the experience anyway.

At first, she didn't understand anything the stars were saying, but their sounds were soothing to her. Then she realized it almost seemed like a memory because it was familiar to her. It wasn't long, and she began to see faint images, though blurry. The stars seemed to chatter about it, but she couldn't understand them.

For a brief few seconds, she saw a large navy-blue version of Zreyas near a smaller one of his species with no horns. She felt Aaru give a long-contented growl that seemed to bring her almost out of the dream, just before she left the vision, she turned to see a dark inky mist in the distance coming her way and the stars' saying a few words she almost understood, something about 'love well.'

Ayya found herself laying down in the tub of the shower facing up. Though it felt good, she stood and had the urge to get to her bedroom. She felt safer there for some reason, though she did appreciate the shower time and the wonderful little dream.

She lived with dark mist every day, so seeing it in the distance actually made her feel better. It wasn't up close to her in the dream.

Ayya couldn't help it, she hummed while she dressed and combed her hair.

20 Savage!

Ayya turned on the light sitting on her desk. For some reason, all the clutter was bothering her. Her father still wasn't home yet, so she cleaned her whole room, threw sheets and blankets in the wash, got new ones out and made her bed. Before she knew it, she had cleaned it all and even part of her closet.

She took out a notepad she had specifically to send Trevor messages. She sat down at her desk and wrote Trev a note.

Dear O-neg,

I'll get your present out tomorrow morning. I know if I open that now, I'll want to get myself in trouble. I always do.

Right now, Daddy is gone, and I want to draw. The night is peaceful, and I got to take

a long shower. I even had a little dream while
I did.

The drivers of the car were funny with
Daddy. He was scared of them, I think, but
it went well. But there was a new door in
the hall and Momma's bedroom door is
blocked off. It is a little weird to come home.
Did your mom and dad install these new
weird doors?

I miss you, but you can always hum to me.
Tell your mom and dad, I said thank you and
hello.

Signed, DB5

After sending the note off to Trevor through their
message hose, she took out her two magazines, pad, and
pencil.

As she thumbed through her magazine she realized,
after the exciting week, looking through her normal
magazine bored her. So she put her mother's magazine on
top and started turning the pages. She forced herself to
take her time to occupy herself and see how many words
she could recognize. It was all adult stuff, but she didn't
care. It would make her learn, and now that she knew she
wasn't stupid, she wanted to learn more.

She saw a picture of a book that had a girl flying in the
air that caught her attention. Under it was an ad for a
company named something she couldn't pronounce, but
there were no words under the book—only another

picture. She knew what it was though, because Ms. Harrison had taught them about it. They were still used today in some things, but mostly used in the past. It was a golden scale.

She was not really sure why it was interesting, but it was. It only had some kind of gold powder stuff on each side made up of slightly squished squares that made the squares look a little skewed. She sat back a little and found them fascinating.

Suddenly she thought about her favorite childhood toy, the camel saddle cap. Then giggled as she thought about her second favorite toy that she thought was a cute doll, but finding out he was a famous warrior captain from outer space. She really looked forward to seeing him again. Now that she knew who he was, he was a little scary in a fun way, but wished she could hug him again.

Ayya stood and went to the kitchen. Before going through, she peeked around to see if she could see the black mist in the den, but didn't see any.

Ayya ran through the kitchen and into the den. The cap was missing from the camel saddle. It had been there earlier. She started looking around.

Just beside the trash can by her father's desk, she saw the camel saddle cap. It had been smashed. Panic ripped through Ayya's guts as she heard the door keys in her father's hands outside.

She picked up the cap, and ran as fast as she could back to her room, shutting and locking each door behind her as quietly as she could. So much for a peaceful night, but she was grateful she had the time she did. She sat down at her desk and looked at the crumpled brass cap.

She tried to unfold the top part so she could see the picture, but it wasn't as easy as she thought it might have been. The top had been molded to make the picture. She could see the person that did it in her mind.

After all these years, it dawned on her where the person was that had made the cap. She... was from Egypt. One day she would go there, she vowed to herself. Ayya wanted to meet the woman. She would have to tell Trevor about this. So, she just pretended to talk to him and found herself humming.

Ayya caught herself, put the cap on her desk where she could see it, and went back to the magazine to look at the scale, comparing the shape of the scale to the one on the camel saddle, what little she could see of it.

After a time, the powder on the scales seemed to churn and vibrate, first on one end of the scale, then on the other.

She opened the drawer of her desk and pulled out some scissors she had had since kindergarten and cut the scale ad out, giving it plenty of room at the edges with the extra room at the top.

Pulling out thumb tacks from her drawer, she hung it up beside the desk on her wall. She put one on each corner.

She stepped back to look at it and then talked to it. "I didn't know scales did that. My teacher told me about them in a class and drew one up on the board. But I didn't see it do what *you* are doing."

Ayya watched it churn and move a few more seconds before saying, "You are good company." *It's a good thing no one is around*, she thought, because they would have thought she had gone mad again.

Sitting back down at her desk, she turned the page. Ayya felt Trevor's tones inside her. She thought back tones of communicating a hug. Then their tones mixed and she knew he was sending her a hug, too. Though they couldn't really say anything complicated, it was still nice to get a hug from her friend.

"Well, you got my note, I see," she said as she turned the page of her magazine. Again, something caught her eye on the left-hand-side page under where she cut out the scale ad, a black and white hand-drawn pirate face. It looked like it was drawn by a very black pencil.

"Art...something." Her reading was okay for an eight-year-old, she guessed, but that was a long word she had never seen before. And there was an address.

She spent the next hour looking words up in a dictionary and finally understood what the ad was saying. People were supposed to draw this pirate and send it to the address to see about getting accepted into this art program. She could do that. It would be a fun way to keep her mind occupied, at least.

She didn't want to forget the stuff Ms. Harrison taught her about doing what was right for her. So it was good to practice it on something that wasn't stressful. Ayya let out a tone and checked how it felt to her and it felt right to do.

Ayya felt satisfied and pulled out her scissors again. She cut the article out and pinned it on the wall to the left of the scale picture right in front of her at face level.

She wasn't a great drawer. She knew that by her momma's responses to pictures she had drawn in the past—'Oh... that's nice dear.'

Despite that, she was excited to at least have a focus. She put the magazines in her desk drawer and put her drawing pad and pencil in front of her.

Deciding to get a soda that she had seen in the refrigerator earlier, she ran to get it. As she opened the refrigerator door, she felt like someone was staring at her.

Ayya looked left through the dining room to the glass doors of the den, and there stood her father, looking straight at her, facing her straight on. There was no movement, almost like he was an inky-eyed statue. Chills ran through her, but she knew there was no danger because Aaru was quiet.

She knew he had been drinking. She could always tell. The inky-eyes and mist were always really bad when he did. So, she knew what he had done with the money he was given... at least in part. She might only be eight, but she wasn't stupid.

Ayya decided to not push her luck and hurried to get a glass, ice, and took the bottle with her back to her room. She would just put it in her closet with the rest of her sandwiches and cheese puffs she had stashed. She really didn't love to eat that much, but she didn't like starving either, and Ayya had no idea when her father would be out of the house again.

She couldn't help but wonder as she got back to her room and poured her drink if her mother saw the mist and inky-eyes now. She had always been afraid to ask because her mother always defended him.

After putting the bottle of soda in her closet, she sat down and picked up her pencil. "Okay, Ayya, remember it doesn't matter that you don't draw well, but let's have fun drawing." She glanced at the scales from the ad and watched it for a few moments. They were balanced. Then she stared at the picture of the pirate. How the strokes seem to go.

When she was satisfied where she would start drawing, she spent a couple of hours trying to draw the pirate. When she was done, she tore it from the pad and pinned it up to the right of the scales because there was no room under the pirate on the left side.

She decided to get a few of the cheese puffs and eat them while she stood back to look at it, comparing it with the one from the magazine.

Ayya cocked her head at her drawing. It wasn't that

great, but she felt proud. Just as she decided to sit down on the bed while she looked at it, she noticed the scales moving. She blinked, taking a step forward in amazement. The scales were now tipped toward the magazine pirate on the left.

She crammed the last cheese puff in her mouth and swore she remembered the scales were balanced before. Ayya took down the drawing she made, realizing it wasn't good at all and the face looked like a messed-up bunch of... well, a melted mess.

When she looked back up, the scales were balanced again.

"What the..."

Scrunching her face up, she pinned the picture back up making sure to use the same holes as before with the thumb tacks so she didn't have so many to repair.

Sure enough, the scales tipped in favor of the magazine pirate.

"You know, that is just *savage*! I know that one is better, but you don't have to smear it on my face!"

Ayya sat down at her desk hard and looked up at the scales. "If I hadn't seen so many weird things, I would ask who or what you were. But I have decided I don't care. You are like my father... you will just make me stronger, even if you judge... my terrible drawing!" She sighed, narrowing her eyes at the scales.

The scale seemed to move a little and clink back in the same position.

"Pfft, this is just wrong. I'm sitting here listening to a picture of a scale in a magazine and having a conversation with you. And worse, I'm listening to you compare my picture to some art company's pirate!" She threw her hand down at the scales and turned to the blank page in front of her.

As she started drawing on a fresh piece of paper, she continued ranting. "I'll have you know they said I was a stupid genius! Well, they didn't say stupid, but I am in some areas, I admit."

Then things got quiet as she drew. Things went a little better this time, and before she knew it, it was bedtime, but kept going.

"No one is going to care. It's late anyway, and I don't have school tomorrow. I will get this, Grumpy-Scales."

She worked on it till it was done. Ayya held it out in front of her and smiled. She got up and took down the other one. The scales balanced as she laid it aside. Then she took a breath and pinned the new one up.

Ayya stood back and watched the scales rapidly tip toward the magazine and clinked.

Frustrated, Ayya fell back on her bed and looked up at the ceiling. "Graah!"

Realizing she was tired, she sat up and pointed at the scales as she spoke. "You are judgmental, just saying."

As she took her shoes off and got ready for bed, she went over and took down her picture and picked up the first one she did and compared them. The first one actually looked better than the second one, except for one area in the beard.

"Well, I got a lot of days to spend in this room, and I will get this. Then I will send it off to the address just for fun. I don't know who you are, but you are rude, but at least you are honest."

With that said, she got in bed and quickly fell asleep.

21 Quirky Weird

Waking up refreshed, Ayya used the bathroom and checked to see if her father was around. After seeing he was nowhere in the main part of the house, she decided to quickly make herself breakfast. She had no idea if he was in his bedroom, but she wasn't going to check. His car was in the drive, so he was likely sleeping in.

She got a pan out as she realized how much she missed Ms. Josephine's company. But she didn't come around anymore since her mother was no longer sick. Ayya was glad she wasn't, but she missed Ms. Josephine's cooking and the talks she had with her. Then again, she wasn't really Ms. J. She sighed.

Ayya cooked enough eggs and bacon for two and made a plate for her *and* her father. She toasted some English muffins and put butter on them. She set one plate on the kitchen table and put the other on a tray to go with her. Getting the urge to hurry, she quickly washed the pan, dried her hands off, put her cooking stool away, and picked up the tray.

She looked back at the breakfast on the table that she

arranged in a smiley face. Proud of herself, she left.

As she ate her breakfast in her bedroom, she looked at the drawings. Today was her father's skeet shooting day. When he left for that, she would open Trevor's present.

After finishing her breakfast, she congratulated herself on how good it was, then attempted a third drawing. As usual, the scales tipped in favor of the pirate in the magazine. But she noticed the tip wasn't quite as violently quick to flip.

"Well, it's getting better," she told herself proudly.

Ayya heard her father's car door and knew he had left. Before going into the kitchen to clean up the dishes, she said, "There is hope. I will get this drawing right!"

When she entered the kitchen, she came to a halt as her mouth hung. The food she had fixed for her father was scattered everywhere. It looked like it had been slung from the plate. Egg yolk from the sunny-side-up eggs was all over the wall.

Now she *knew* her daddy was gone—whatever was left, she didn't know. That was the one thing her daddy loved about what she did, and that was to cook him breakfast... especially eggs. Maybe she should have done the soft-boiled eggs instead.

Ayya cleaned up her own dishes and then looked at the mess. She picked up the plate and silverware and washed those, but she decided to leave the mess. She would help her mother clean it up after she got back. There was no way she could reach most of it, for one reason, and the other reason was that she wanted her mother to see what he had done when he got back.

She would eat the pancake brown-bag package that Ms. Harrison gave her for supper. She wouldn't have to come back out here after her father came home. But she fixed a peanut butter and jelly sandwich for her lunch and grabbed the last soda bottle and went back to her room. *Sorry, momma. You aren't here to drink your soda and someone has to do it for you... It's my duty.*

Ayya put the wrapped sandwich on top of the pancake package, then went to the back corner of her closet on the other side of the built-in shelves. She pulled out the panel on the wall she and Trev made for their secret agent games.

She reached in to get her present and realized it was heavy, so she grunted to pull it out. The hole was only a foot square, and the package was an odd shape and kept shifting. It took her a few minutes to get it out, but she did, then replaced the panel.

It was wrapped up sloppily in birthday wrapping. Yep, that was Trev's style of wrapping. She giggled, then quickly jotted a note out for him to let him know she was about to open up the present.

Ayya threw open her window and bent over, grabbed the hose, and unscrewed the cap. There was a message in it from Trev from last night. Trevor didn't do mornings well, so she knew it wasn't from this morning.

She took the capsule out of the cap and inserted hers, replaced the cap, then delivered it. Ayya pulled herself inside the window again and shut it. She unscrewed the top of the capsule and pulled Trevor's message out.

Dear DB5,

I'm glad you are going to open up the present tomorrow. Make sure you do. I saw your dad today, and he doesn't look good. You might need it. I even saw all the mist and inky-eyes really clear. And you know I don't normally see it that well, unless in certain lighting.

I think you will like your present. I know I do. Remember that tunnel we started to build in secret? I kept working on it when Dad and Mom weren't around. Dad will kill me when he finds out.

I also have news. Dad told me to tell you that your mom called. She will be home next week. Your uncle died, so she will stay till they settle all the arrangements. Ayya, I'm sorry about your uncle. I know you didn't know that one very well, but still.

I'm going to go to work with my dad tomorrow to learn new quantum stuff. I'll teach you when I get back, if you want.

Signed, O-neg

P.S. – Burn this one. It has top secret stuff in it.

Ayya didn't have to be told to burn this one, but she was glad Trevor was so good about reminding her that she was a secret agent. She ran through the house, not worried about her father being home, to the one place she knew there was a lighter, her father's den.

She opened the glass paned French doors. One step in

and she stopped cold. The stench almost made her throw up right there. The room seemed dark, even though her father wasn't home.

"Whoever you are, you are not allowed to be here. Get out!" She heard nothing from Aaru, so she felt brave. To her surprise, the mist dissipated.

Ayya decided it wasn't safe to come back here anymore. Something in her gut told her it was the last time. Instead of grabbing a lighter from her dad's desk, she opened the cabinet under the bookshelves and reached in to pull out her grandfather's old lighter and a can of lighter fluid.

She closed everything and made sure she left no evidence that she was in here. *A secret agent has to be careful,* she told herself.

After burning the note from Trev in a bucket just outside her window, she put her grandfather's lighter away in her closet in the secret panel. Satisfied, she went back to her bed and sat down. Throwing her right knee up on the bed to face the present, she smiled.

Wanting to draw this gift out as much as possible, since it would be the only birthday present she would get this year, thanks to her father. She decided she had a good gift already, just by her mother doing her best to do all she did for the party... *and* the cheesecake.

Ayya was even grateful for the beginning of what her father did for the party. At least he *seemed* a little normal then.

She carefully unwrapped the paper and a cloth bag with a drawn picture of a DB5. She laughed at the terrible magic marker picture and decided she loved it. It was almost secret-code-bad. But she could relate, remembering the pirate pictures she drew.

Ayya didn't care what was in it. She picked up the bag

and hugged it. "Thank you, Trev. You are the best friend ever. I lo-ove you-uu!" Her words morphed into a soft toned hum, at least until Aaru let out a warning growl.

She knew then her father must be home, or arriving. Ayya stopped and listened to make sure that she didn't hear him coming. As she put the bag down, she felt something loose in it.

After not hearing anything in the house, she opened and loosened the drawstring of the bag and reached in. She felt something fuzzy. She jerked her hand back instinctively, letting out a little giggle.

"What have you done Trev, you weirdo?" There was a note inside. She grabbed it and put it beside her on the bed. She opened the bag wide. It was a tennis ball. She picked it up and realized this was what made the bag heavy. "What did you fill this with, Trevor? Holy crap!"

Ayya knew that the note would shed some fun light on what it was all about, but she was enjoying the mystery of it all. She set the ball aside on her bed and pulled two more out, each as heavy as the first. There was nothing else in the bag except a square piece of card paper that had Trevor's best print on it:

I.O.U.

O-neg owes DB5 another present that is started but isn't finished yet, but will be soon.

Signed, O-neg

Ayya loved Trevor's creativity. She hugged the card and decided that the hope of seeing what he created was enough, even if she never got it. She loved everything about Trevor, even his quirky weird thinking.

She quickly opened the note. She ran her hand over the paper to smooth it out, feeling very appreciative of the fun. There were parts of it where the ink had smeared and seemed rubbed thin, but that was Trev.

Happy Birthday Ayya, (Yes I'm using your real name because this isn't secret agent stuff)

This might not seem like much of a present, but it is your next step to being a proper secret agent! We are a team and my job is to help you be better than the one in the movie! Well, you are better at pretty much everything than I am, but I can still try.

I got one thing on my side that you don't! DAD! He doesn't know about this part of the present, and he thinks I finished the other present and gave that one to you. He also doesn't know he helped me through my stealthy questions on pretend projects. I'm glad he didn't ask me outright what I was doing, cause then I would have had to tell him.

Giving you the secret agent missions and

being the front guy gets a little boring sometimes, even though I like it and it was what I wanted to do.

So, I am initiating a new plan to make sure you have a special hideout when the bad guys discover or blow your other one up. By the way, I decided I like doing this kind of masterminding.

Here are the instructions for the special tennis balls:

Ayya giggled. She loved this! "This is the best present ever!"

She decided she would wait until it got dark to start these instructions because she needed to leave the house and go to the live oak woods. Plus, it would be more secret agent-like. She would send Trevor a note to let him know.

Those woods were her most precious sanctuary that Paul had given her. Buying the land so she would always have a place to go still overwhelmed her when she thought about it.

None of the bullies in the neighborhood on the other side of the woods didn't come there anymore after Paul intervened on her behalf when things were about to get nasty. She didn't know exactly what he did with their parents, but Ayya had not seen them since, and that had been a year ago at least.

She shrugged and put the note in the bag and then put it all in her closet.

She spent the rest of the day drawing and eating.

She tried reading a book that was given to her by her mother to help her learn to read better during the summer last year. Ayya really wanted to read it because it was about a lion and a witch in a closet. But every time she read, she felt sick to her stomach and had to read the lines too many times over to get any meaning out of it. So, the reading attempt didn't last too long after about fifteen minutes. "I tried, Momma."

It was odd, though. She didn't mind re-reading the lines on Trevor's notes, even though she had to re-read the same thing. But she figured it was because they weren't that long and she could hear him almost saying it as she read it. Either way, she still felt sick to her stomach.

That entire problem was why she was surprised she scored so high in engineering and mechanics on those tests at the research center. It was probably because there were more images than words.

Ayya pinned the first of three drawings she had made over the course of the afternoon, then turned away immediately so she wouldn't see the scale tip, at least for a few seconds, while she went into her closet to get the pancake bag.

She reached into the bag and pulled out one of the large pancakes, rolled it up and bit the end as she turned around toward the wall. As she chewed, she tried to say, "At least it isn't taking me as long to draw them."

The Scale tipped toward the magazine pirate as expected, but at least it seemed to have to think first. As she ate the pancake in her hand, she looked at the drawings and compared the two. She was beginning to see the problem in some areas.

Ayya stuffed the rest of the pancake into her mouth. She took another out and laid it on top of the bag, then got up and took the drawing down and replaced it with the second one she did.

Before she could even get the second pin in the scaled tipped hard with a clink.

Her eyes grew wide, and through a full mouth, she complained. "Savage! You were obviously never a mother like mine!"

She spat out the pancake ball in her hand. "That is cold-hearted. At least let me put the pins in!" Then she put the pancake back in her mouth, grumbling in muted insults while she took the second one down and put the third one up, half expecting the same thing to happen.

Ayya finished putting the pins in the wall and backed up to the bed to pick up the second pancake. She watched the scales as she rolled up the pancake with slow growing excitement that the scales hadn't tipped yet.

Nothing happened for an entire bite and swallow worth of pancake as her eyebrows lifted slowly in excitement.

Then the scales violently tipped with an obnoxious clink.

Ayya's eyebrows and shoulders drooped. She scowled, dejected, then sighed. "You made your point. I stink at drawing."

Frustration filling her, she picked up her pencil and, with a grip that made her knuckles white, she wrote on the next blank page; *I QUIT DRAWING!*

She ripped it out of the pad and pinned it up on top of the drawing she just put up and stormed off to go pee.

While she was peeing, she heard a repeating faint, 'Tink... tink... tink...' She hurried and went back into the hall. It was coming from her room.

Ayya slowly walked in, looking around. She didn't see anything out of the ordinary. She turned to the right to look into the closet, but as soon as she turned, she knew the sound wasn't coming from there.

Turning toward her desk, the wall caught her attention. The scale on the ad was repeatedly tipping with that 'tink' sound. When she was close enough, she noticed what she had written had slightly changed.

Instead of the '*I QUIT DRAWING!*' that she had written before. They faded some letters out.

Ayya read the strong letters out-loud.

"*I QUIT DRAWING!*"

The scale tipped like a metronome in the silence.
"Trev will *never* believe this one."

22 Agent DB5

෴෴෴ *Ayya* ෴෴෴

Ayya knew it was childish to keep pretending to be a secret agent during what Trevor called the age of dark mist, but she couldn't help it. She loved it. After all, she *was* a kid. She loved pretending to be someone special that could save the world from bad guys, without having to do the hard stuff to *actually* do it.

She put a few things in her little backpack. Most of it was already in there because a secret agent never knew what they would run into: flashlight, drawing pad, pencil, jack-knife, garden hand shovel, water bottle, sandwich, and string for building traps.

Ayya had written a note to Trev earlier, and she picked that up off her desk and sent it off on the way out of the window. She quietly climbed out and carefully slid it shut. Then she pulled her flashlight out and used the lanyard to throw it over her shoulder, across her chest. She wouldn't use it yet, though.

There was no moon tonight, so she might need it later. But for now, she didn't. She was going into *her* territory and sanctuary. She knew the way, and she knew those woods better than her own house, and that was saying something in her way of thinking.

She looked down at her feet in the light coming from her bedroom window and grinned. They were her old red high-top tennis shoes with white toes that were for tree-climbing, and they were well-worn and felt like gloves on her feet. They were her secret agent shoes.

Ayya turned and walked quietly against the fence of her half-acre backyard into the woody part. Just before she climbed the fence, she looked back to make sure no one was behind her that might be one of the inky-eyed mutants—after all; it *was* the age of the dark mist.

Climbing up the fence next to the tree, she stood on the top of it to get her climbing mind and balance primed. Once Ayya mentally got her tree legs ready, she ran down the top of the fence to the back corner at top speed—well, top speed as much as possible for having a backpack full of stuff. She decided to go for the lower branch for safety.

As she stepped on the corner of the fence, feeling her muscles burn from not doing this for what seemed like an eternity. She grinned as she launched off the corner of the fence into the air. She pulled her legs up as high as she could to clear the smaller bushy branches before extending them out to land on her targeted branch. Holding her arms out for balance, she giggled quietly after landing, exhilarated by her jump.

Then she stopped to do the ritual she had started after she found out Paul had bought the land for her. Ayya had sworn that every time she entered the forest, she would stop and pay a secret agent tribute to him. She made it up with all her imagination, but it still felt sacred to her.

"Thank you, Paul, for the secret agent land. This is agent DB5. I honor you, Top Agent of the good stuff. In this age of the dark mist, I hope the live oak forest provides a safe place for those that fight the inky-eyed mutants and bullies that want to cause harm to me or my friends. May these woods be too pure for them to enter, so that everyone inside this sanctuary will have protection... except if they want to come over to the good stuff side."

Ayya let out a relaxed long exhale and lifted her arms into the air, watching the stars, not even thinking about where she was. She was so comfortable she really didn't think she was standing up in a tree, but she was mindful of the weight and bulk she was carrying.

Trevor and she had decided on a meeting place. If they weren't meeting, they had made a rule—if they were going to spend any time in the sacred wood headquarters that they would always go to the same place first, just in case there were messages there. She loved going there.

Dropping her arms, Ayya started her tree-tapping run. Just because this was her territory and safe space, didn't mean that she didn't have to be careful, so she took her time.

It would take about twenty minutes to tap and climb her way up to her favorite spot. It was the tallest of the live oaks. Now that she was going to be part of the Order of the Sleeping Phoenix, she could watch for the ships from there. That thought thrilled her as she climbed and jumped as if she had been born in the trees.

She imagined sitting up in her spot watching the sky and waving to Captain Zreyas on his ship. She wondered if it would look like a falling star or if she would actually see it. Then another random thought came, and she wondered if things could be born from a wish.

Ayya decided it didn't matter, it was fun to wish and hope. Right now, she loved her little spot in the woods, and it was a whole world for her. No one had been able to climb there yet, except Trevor. She had shown him the secret of climbing up in two places.

Jumping up at one of the tricky spots, she thought about how one of the bullies that had given her a hard time had tried to get up there but he had gotten himself into serious trouble, and had needed help from her to keep him from falling.

Ayya felt like she was in heaven being out in the woods again, hearing her footsteps, leaves rustling as she stepped and jumped, night time noises, and her breathing.

Once she reached her favorite spot, she sat down and looked up at the stars. It wasn't long before she heard Trev's clicking noise he used when he mocked a dolphin call. He was letting her know he was there. She answered the call with her own, a dove call, to let him know she was there. She didn't expect him to come, but she was glad he did.

After all, she had no idea what to do with her present. She could follow the instructions, but it would be so much cooler to do it with him. She loved when their insides connected. But she had to admit to herself, sometimes she was a lazy agent, not wanting to read too much.

23 Breathe

"Captain, the talks are over and they have made their decisions. They are ready for you. And they said you could land in the same place."

Zreyas looked up from the chart information he was looking at, with all the records about what species they were looking at, swim-sailing around gate forty. "There isn't much in the records about them, Tap. I would rather be peaceful with them than have to fight. We will need to go through this gate again and it would be nice to have them on our side, rather than an obstacle. I can't even find out what language they use."

He stood and made sure he had everything he was going to take with him, including the capsule that Rtu gave him to wipe their minds. "Have they been fitted with the uniforms so that we can make sure they are not serving the big D.O.?"

"Yes, Captain. They rather like them, especially Ayya and Trevor from what Freckles told me."

"Good, well, they have had to digest a lot of new information, let's hope things go well. Ticking hell, I hope I didn't make a mistake in strategy." Zreyas turned around and looked at Tap's hologram. "Thankings to you for everything that you have been doing to relay and help in this."

"Captain, there is no need to thank me. I already know how you feel. I'm wishing you the fortune of the potential in what is to come."

Zreyas nodded and went out the door of his quarters and said hello to Silence and Resolute. He gave each one a few strokes. "I promise as soon as we get you more trained, you will be able to come along with me at times. Sending to you the thankings Silence for all you are doing to help."

"It is good to see you again, Mother. I look forward to spending some time with you. But we are fine and happy here."

The cub gave a playful growling purr as she licked Zreyas.

"Ow, that tongue is dangerous," Zreyas said as he scratched her ears causing her to purr loudly.

"Time to go." He headed into the challenge node and said hello to Aqum.

— We are speaking with friendly greetings — Hello Captain Zreyas.

Thank you for not doing the A-word thing. Until I find out about that, I don't want anyone to know, and I don't want to hear it—it's distracting. There has to be a reason you redacted that. I don't need any extra load on me right now.

— We are showing giving of glad tidings to do so for you, Captain Zreyas A-word.

Zreyas chuckled yet still felt a little irritated. *Look I know you know who I am. You do not need to use my title every time you address me. If you want to show respect of a title out in the open, use Captain Zreyas. Otherwise use Zreyas.* "Take me through."

— We are saying in understanding tones — We will comply for you, Captain Zreyas. Transmitting in three... two... one.

As Zreyas landed in the same foyer, he saw everyone sitting around eating, but facing him. He felt like he was at the center of some arena.

Cerys walked toward him with a plate of food. She held it out for him. "Would you like some breakfast?"

Zreyas had no idea what customs were in accepting food on earth or what the proper etiquette was. Not that he cared, but he didn't want to start the whole meeting off with offending anyone. He looked at Paul and Dulce, and both slightly nodded to encourage him.

He reached for the plate and took it. "Sending the thankings to you." He looked at everyone in the room watching him and awkwardly sat. He looked at the plate consisting of eggs, bacon, and round cut bread of some kind with some sort of thick sauce on it. It smelled good.

Dulce spoke up first. "Captain, I know you know what eggs and bacon are, but the rest of what you see is called biscuits and gravy, a loved dish by this part of their country. It's wonderful!"

Paul added, "Indeed! It's probably my favorite food I think, though nutritionally it isn't the best food we could eat."

Trevor spoke up. "But it is so-o good!"

"*If* it's made right. If not, then... bleh," added Cerys.

Zreyas lifted an eyebrow and looked at her. "Is this made right?"

A long second of silence elapsed before the whole room started laughing.

"Ha! Guessing so." He picked up the fork that was on the plate and tried some of the stuff that was apparently made right. He noticed the room got quiet, so he looked up and chewed slower wondering what they were wanting now.

He swallowed and said, "What is wrong?"

Cerys shifted her weight and asked, "How do you like it?"

No one had ever asked him that question before, and he wasn't ever in a position to be particular about food enough to turn it away if he didn't like it, either. There were more important things. He looked down at the plate, took another bite, then chewed it up paying attention to the flavor.

Zreyas looked at the plate and said, "It must be fixed right."

Everyone laughed and Paul said, "Good answer, my b—" Paul cleared his throat and said again, "Good answer, Captain!"

Zreyas grinned, finished his breakfast and then stood up. "Good meal. Now, what is it you would like to tell me."

Paul spoke first. "Captain, everyone has had time to let everything settle over the last day since you left. The Sadlers have even had a chance to talk among themselves as a family, as well as Ayya and Lanna."

"And all together too!" added Trevor excitedly sitting beside a nodding Ayya.

"Captain Zreyas." Connor stood and walked forward till he was in front of him a few meters back. "If it would be okay, I would like to say a few things."

Zreyas crossed his arms, then he flipped a palm up and extended it conversationally. "This is your home, Connor. I am the new..." He couldn't think of the word he wanted. He realized he was a little nervous for some reason. He looked at Paul and Dulce. "What is that word that is for not-quite-friends?"

Paul smiled and said, "Acquaintance?"

"Yes, that one." He looked back to Connor and said, "This is *your* home and *I* am the new acquain-ance. There is no need to ask for permission. You are not under my command."

Zreyas looked straight into the man's eyes and said, "Thankings to you for listening for so many days to the situation. You didn't have to do that." Then he looked at all of them, including the small ones. "All of you."

Connor cleared his throat, clear to Zreyas that he was nervous too.

"Breathe," said Cerys. "I hear it helps you live. All the rest is easy."

The quantum scientist laughed and nodded his head. "You have a point."

Connor looked at his wife and she came forward, too. Then Trevor walked up between them. He looked back at Zreyas and said, "I want them to make their own decision. Though this is a family, I have learned through this whole thing that each person has a life they need to live. We are just doing it all together in our own way, helping each other out."

Cerys looked at Connor then to Zreyas. "Connor and I decided that Trevor needs to also make his own decision in this whole situation."

They both got down on their knees, holding each other's hands. Connor spoke up first. "Captain Zreyas, I'm not sure what you expected, but I would like to pledge my career and life to the cause you are fighting for. None of Earth knows what is going on, but I would like to be the first to say I would like to help. I'm not sure how much I can help with as primitive as we are compared to the rest of the... multiverse, but surely you need researchers and someone that is used to leading others in the same area."

Zreyas looked at him as he ran his fingers and thumb down his face on each cheek and looked down in thought. "Is there anything else you would like? What is your... trade requirement? And what is your personal interest in all this?"

Everyone in the room looked at Connor.

Connor took a deep breath and let it go. "Honestly, Captain Zreyas, I never thought that far ahead. Research is a love I have, and a passion. I am married to it more than even Cerys. She is the same way and it has always been an understanding between us. The love is there but it is also with what we love doing. I don't need anything in return except for my family to be taken care of with mutual respect, with all their needs generously met if at all possible."

"I was reading about family-oriented species while I was away so I could understand Earth and humans better. I didn't grow up in a species that cared for their families like that, as you probably understand by now. They are large, cruel, and self-serving."

"I know two of them that aren't, Mr. Captain Zreyas," said Ayya quietly with tears in her eyes. "I'm sorry I took your brother away to help me. I know you might miss him a lot." She wiped her face, then leaned against her mother, who held her tighter in her lap.

Zreyas almost lost all composure right there and then. His chest cracked so rapidly that it shocked him. He closed his eyes a moment till he got himself together inside enough to open them again and could speak. He smiled and said with a cracked voice, "Well... I didn't expect that." He paused a few moments.

"I'm sending to you the lovings to you and my brother." He took a breath and shook his hands out. "Now, back to the research I was doing. I know that family is important, even if it isn't blood family. It will be the only thing that will get us through this war. Though it is not officially declared, it is a very serious one."

Everyone's expressions showed they were very aware and serious right now, and he could tell they understood that this wasn't a simple adventure.

"What I'm trying to say is that your whole lives will change and so will your family dynamics. I want to say this again... your *life will* change. You might not even be in the same place for long periods. It will be a long time before you get a home like what you are used to, if ever. Now that you understand what we are all up against, once you commit, there is no going back."

Zreyas wasn't sure they understood the entire gravity of it all, but he knew that once they saw some of the hideous things they would see, it would typically be too much for many. "You will see some ticking-hideous, gruesome, mag-shit. Those of you that commit to this, will be hunted. There is no taking the easy road. Now is the time to refuse and live your lives without any memory of this."

Ayya stood and sat down by Zreyas without a word. He looked to her and nodded. Her face seemed like it was an aged human at the end of her life, not eight varSas. He knew she had seen some nasty mag-shit already. Zreyas wasn't sure he wanted to know what she had seen, though.

"I... can't imagine the full image of any of it, truth be told," said Connor. "But I can't imagine saying no to help save so many, especially my family and my friends I've grown to love in a short period. If this is an indication of the kind of family you speak of, I can handle that."

He looked at his wife and then turned back to Zreyas, lifted his chin, and spoke with assurance. "I one-hundred percent pledge my service to The Sleeping Phoenix Order for the love of my family, friends, and science. And if for some horrific reason my family doesn't make it, then I do it for those that are still here. That menace can't be allowed to exist anymore."

Cerys stood again stepped forward. "Unless you want to hear the same ten-minute speech with mom jokes, as Trevor calls them, mixed in," she grinned at her husband, "I will say I second that and make the same commitment. I pledge my service to The Sleeping Phoenix Order as long as naps are allowed.

"Also, we are rich as far as Earth standards are concerned. I can give financially to help too if needed, at least if there is a way to exchange currencies for the one you need."

Zreyas grinned. "I see you are trying to learn the humors too. Ha!" Then his face grew serious. "I accept your pledges and service, thankings to you."

Through tears, Ayya said in a cracked voice, "Thank you, Mr. And Mrs. Sadler. I'm sorry you need to do this."

Zreyas looked at Ayya. Her face sitting down was still higher than his head level, but he could still look into her eyes. She seemed so grown up suddenly that it broke his heart. He knew her heart was breaking. It just dawned on him the brevity of how she must feel, thinking all this happening because of her.

He hesitated, but he lifted his arm slowly and he touched her cheek with his hand and held it there.

Ayya looked at him with silent tears streaming down her face. The look in her eyes was grief-filled with apology. "I promise, Mr. Zreyas... I won't touch you, but I just want you to know that I want to give you a hug even though I know it won't help. You lost everything because of me."

"No, Ayya. I lost everything I had because a ticking piece of mag-shit will do anything for power and hate. You didn't take Aaru away, he gave himself to you. And I lost my old life, but gained a new one, and a new body... and a family. I am sending the thankings to you for being here. If it wasn't for you, I would not have met Visages Rhom, Rtu, and Tulyata. Then I met all of you—plus more on my ship. We can't always pick the circumstances by which we receive the good things in life. But we must always focus on the good things, not the surrounding storms, or we will forget the most important things and lose our way."

Zreyas reached up and pulled Ayya to him to do an awkward embrace. It wasn't so bad when he initiated it. She held him tight and felt her doing the cries.

He didn't know what to do, so he looked at Paul and Dulce. Their eyes had tears but their faces smiled, which was confusing to him.

When he paid attention to Ayya again, he felt her yan and it wasn't sad anymore; it was with the gratitudes and joys.

He looked over at Paul, wondering if he was doing the right thing with this hugging of a child... well, of anyone. Paul and Dulce nodded once with smiles on their face that seemed to beam. He wasn't exactly sure why, but he figured it was a good sign.

Ayya let him go and wiped her face with her shirt.

Then Trevor stepped forward. "Captain Zreyas?"

Zreyas turned to face him. The boy had an expression on his face that was determined.

"I'm just a kid, but—"

"So was Aaru in our varSas, but look what he did. It makes no difference how young or old you are, whether you are big or little. You have as much potential as anyone else, if not more. Now, go on."

"Yes, Sir, you are right." Trevor straightened his back and pulled his chin up with determination. "I want to help too, and I want to be on your crew and learn to fight, not on planetside. I want to fight for my friend and those that this inky-eyed piece of whatever it is you said he was, want to hurt. I don't want Ayya to get killed. She is... I don't know how to say it."

"Your future mate," said Zreyas.

Everyone looked at him, shocked, except for Trevor and Ayya.

"Yes, sir. And I understand her more than anyone. Ayya will need me to remember her, and I want to. I know that sounds weird, but I can tell something is coming. I understand why Aaru gave himself to her to keep her alive. I don't understand as much as all of you yet, but as dad always says, 'I'll grow into it.'" Trevor straightened proudly. "I'll grow up fast for Ayya and the multiverse."

Zreyas knew they wouldn't know the significance, but he wanted to show how he felt about it, so he inclined his head without taking his focus off his eyes. "Welcome to The Sleeping Phoenix Order, young man."

Trevor grinned proudly. "But, Captain Zreyas, I really need to pee. Can I go now?"

The entire room laughed.

"Ha! At least you have on easier armor to take off than I do! Go, go, go! I'll go back and do the same thing real quick." Then he winked at him.

Trevor scurried down the hall with everyone in the room chuckling.

24   Body Slam

Paul got up and walked over to Lanna and sat down beside her. He rubbed her back with his hand and said, "You are not alone, dear friend," he said softly.

Lanna looked up and fixed her gaze on Zreyas, her face red-blotched from silently crying. All sorts of realizations came to him as he watched her lean on Paul.

In three days, Lanna found that her mate was a demented commander of the Janquar in a past life that was awakening. She had been sleeping with a man that was being taken over by the Dark One, and that her daughter should have died at child birth but now her body was filled with a Viduri Tantra that had been attacked and almost killed by the very one, or ones, she had been living with all this time. And she had another child made with this man.

Zreyas didn't know what it was like to have a mate but he did know what it was like to be so invested in someone, like he was with Aaru, that he could imagine that it would crush him too. He couldn't help but feel for her. Her whole life must have felt like a bad dream or a manipulated ruse. She probably felt like she was left with nothing.

He walked toward Lanna. Zreyas felt himself being led to her with his chest. He wanted to cry for her but that wouldn't help. Standing there a moment he gave the best smile he could, and she thankfully seemed to understand in a way what he was trying to do by the look in her eyes.

Zreyas sat down in front of her cross legged. "Yours and Ayya's situation is difficult. I cannot even begin to understand this for you. And I'm not a good one to know what to say like the old man here and Freckles over there," he said with a half grin using his thumb to point behind him.

Lanna couldn't help herself and half chuckled once, trying to wipe her eyes.

"Look, I'm not good at this mushy-moo stuff, I'm just learning it myself. But I do have the feelings of it." He paused a moment to try and find his words.

Lanna looked at him and smiled through the tears, but he could tell she had no words right now.

"What I do best is not what you need right now, but I will say to you..." He made sure to look into her eyes without wavering with focus. "No matter what you decide, I will do my best to protect you as much as I would Ayya. I'm saying the... em-pla-thies to you about who you thought you mated with. I know it must be a shock. The man you mated was a good man in the beginning... It's just... if we don't clear the past it always comes back till we clear it. It happens to me with my anger or when I don't... face the... chest-cracking stuff. Bah! I don't know this mushy-moo stuff."

Zreyas stood and let out a sigh, not really knowing what else to say, wiping his hands on his pants to clear the sweat from them.

Lanna looked at Zreyas and despite her overwhelming situation, she smiled and said, "You are a good man, Captain Zreyas. Thank you for all you have done and... intend to do."

൐൐൐ *Cerys* ൐൐൐

Cerys was listening to the conversation with interest but she was getting anxious and wasn't really sure why. She supposed it was because she was away from the lab for so many days. She knew she needed the break from it. Though she loved what she did, the politics of it all was way over the top lately.

The corruption was out of hand in the government and military leaders. Everything was being bought out and manipulated to make money and take power by large companies, not for the betterment of the environment and mankind. It saddened her that the deep pockets and power were winning, and it was really getting to her.

She had eight-hundred eighty-two days of vacation mounted up and this was the perfect time, and cause, to take some of it. Looks like she would be taking a permanent leave now. Maybe her science work would actually be used for good things for a change.

The nervous energy was getting to her, so she stood and put her cup on the counter. "I apologize, I will return. Trevor must be goofing off doing something and getting side tracked. Plus, all this talk about peeing has made my bladder jealous. I'll round him up after I take my own bio-break."

Everyone nodded as she rounded the corner to walk down the hall to her bedroom ensuite. Through the laundry door on her left as she passed, she noticed the front door of the dryer open with towels hanging out of it. There was something dark spread on the floor.

Curious, she walked in slowly trying to identify what it might be. Had she been away at work and come home, she wouldn't be surprised what she saw laying around the house with her son and husband having full reign without her supervision. But she had been home for a week and this wasn't here this morning.

She bent over and picked up a few pieces of it between her fingers, crushing it and rolling it around. "Huh, some sort of charcoal-like matter. Well, little guy, let's see what you are made of."

On the opposite side of the washer and dryer she set it down on the wall-to-wall counter. She pressed a button on the right and a door slid back and a mini lab raised. She opened the drawer and pulled out a knife and a box of slides. "I might not be at the lab but science is never done. What has my kid gotten into this time. My bet is on Trevor using grill charcoal again for chalk for the sidewalk."

No, he's been way too busy with all of us. This was getting weird. She put the sample under her microscope and put another sample into a test tube with a solvent in it to see how quick it would break down.

She heard Trevor run down the hall as she realized it was some sort of charred flesh. "It's about time you got back in there, young man."

She dialed her microscope in and found herself stumped for the first time in a long time. Some of it seemed status quo, other parts something she had never seen before, which was also normal. The combination of the two, made things rather strange. She found it exhilarating, because she had never seen anything quite like it.

Cerys decided to look at it later after everyone left in an hour or so. She left everything as it was, and turned around to put the knife in the wash tub by the dryer. But after almost tripping on the clothes and debris on the floor, she bent down to put all the clothes and towels on the floor into the washer first.

She cocked her head as she looked into the dryer to get the rest out, noticing the back of the insides were gone and a hole in the wall behind it. "What the..."

Cerys stood, feeling the anger rise a little at her mischievous boy going a bit too far this time. As soon as their guests left, he was really going to get it. That stunt ranked up there with when he decided to *renovate* his room a couple years ago, knocking the wall between two studs to merge his play room and bedroom.

Trevor had said he couldn't be bothered to walk one and a half meters to the next doorway, saying it was more efficient with the wall gone. She found out about it because he had called her up at work asking her to order a saw to take the rest of the wall out.

Cerys told herself she should be used to this kind of thing by now, between him and Connor. They drove her crazy but she loved them both. Her son couldn't be a normal little boy, no-oo. He was so much like Connor. She never knew what she would walk into and find with those two.

Right now, though, she had to pee, and it couldn't wait anymore, even for science. As she turned the corner to go down the hall, she saw part of her ensuite floor through her open bedroom door further down the wide hall. There was a dark red liquid on the floor. She didn't need a microscope to know what that was.

A little foot slid through the liquid into view. Stunned, she froze a split second. "Trevor?"

שׁשׁשׁ *Zreyas* שׁשׁשׁ

(A few minutes earlier, just as Cerys left the room)

Zreyas turned to return to where he had been sitting before

"And Captain..."

When he looked at her, Lanna continued. "I've watched him for many years now. Just as you empathize with me, I do you, too. Knowing that is your father, what he has done... and doing. I have thought about it many times for Ayya's sake. You can both probably understand each other in that. But just like I told Ayya, just because your father has done those things, doesn't mean you have to take on responsibility, guilt, and shame of it. Don't wonder if you will become like that, because you won't."

Then she said something that made chills run through him because her face was stone cold and resolute. "The man I loved, is dead already. It was confirmed when Ayya told me what she saw while I was gone recently. I've also watched it happen over time, taking a piece of myself every day with him. It took Ayya telling me that yesterday to realize what had been happening. It cost Ayya her childhood."

Lanna stood and started pacing slowly in thought at the same time Trevor ran into the room and sat down by Ayya.

No one said a word, not even the young ones. After thinking about it a moment, he really shouldn't view them as young ones. They are far more grown up in ways than *he* was probably.

She finally turned and said to him, "Did you have plans for me if I said yes?"

"No."

"That's it? So you were going to have me stand around being poor Ayya's mother?"

"Again, no. Our order is built on trust, choice, and taking responsibility to do our part. Some of our crew had no skills at all, but they are now discovering what they want to do. Also, sometimes things have to be bent in that temporarily but so far it has always worked out for all of us.

"So no, I'm not demanding, planning, and taking charge of your life. That is for *you* to do. But once you choose, then you will answer to me and your superiors like any other organization. If you don't have skills that you want, then we will train you in what you would like to do if we can."

Lanna dropped her hands to her sides. "I'm going to stay."

"Momma, n-no!"

"It's not me he has a problem with. If I leave, he will go nuts and that might make things worse."

"Then I will stay with you, Momma." Just before she could object, she said, "You said it was my choice. I can stay as long as I can, at least." She turned and faced Trevor, and they both closed their eyes.

Trevor started humming, which was odd, even with what little he knew of him.

Ayya shuttered and started a toned song that had brief blank gaps in it. After a good minute, she started all over again; but this time, Trevor started toning the gaps, so complete and accurate he wouldn't have known they were there had he not heard the first version.

On the third time, the tones seemed like they were speaking with each other.

Everyone held their breath, and jaws dropped. Most had their hands on their chests. Zreyas felt it, but it didn't shock him. He knew Trevor was her mate. Ayya had made up for what she had lost in her body through him, and she would sing her song—just not as traditionally done in the past.

Ayya and Trevor just changed the game, and not even the Dark One knew what was going on. Rtu had put this house in a dimension to secure their talks and Aqum assured him it couldn't be breeched.

As he listened, he asked Tap, *Are you recording this?*

— Yes, Captain, every bit of it.

Good because I want to listen to this song sequence again so I can learn her language and see the progression. Do not tell anyone. If Ayya wants to tell, then that is okay, but I'm not going to take that choice away. She will be protected more if she doesn't at this time.

— Yes, Captain. I agree with you.

Part of Rtu is still there, right?

— Only a small part of him, Captain.

Can you tell if Paul and Dulce are understanding what is going on?

— Their readings say they don't, Captain. It is as if the frequencies beyond hearing capacity are being filtered out around them. Maybe Ayya or Trevor are doing this.

Have you noticed that Ayya seems to be older and more aware when Trevor is around? It's like he completes who she was. Have you done any closer looks at this yet? If not, do so now, we don't know when they will be together again like this.

— I have noticed that, Captain. I will start analysis now. Very wise of you, Captain.

Zreyas grunted more in his mind than externally and let himself get caught up in the tones Ayya was singing.

Something hit him and he said it a little more urgently than he meant for it to sound like. *Tap! Ask Aqum if there was a change in the Rsi Torana, now.*

— Yes, Captain. Right away. It wasn't long at all and she was back with an answer. — I can't see it at all since it is not within my quantum space, but Aqum said, and I quote, "It changed as it should have and should not have.

What the ticking hell does that mean? Wait... oh no... no, no, no.

A blood-curdling scream from Cerys rang through the house.

"Ayya! Stop! Don't finish the song!

Zreyas Q-leaped forward between the two kids facing Trevor, drawing his weapons. "You are giving away a key and a way for the Dark One to summon—"

A long knife burst out of the front of Trevor's chest with such force that the boy jolted forward.

Cerys stood there, still holding the knife in the kid's chest with an expression of pure wild rage.

He hadn't noticed her come in the room because he had been so focused. It surprised Zreyas she would kill him, and his shock surprised him too. As hardened to war as he was, it bothered him.

She made contact with his stunned glare, and he knew something terrible had happened. He had to trust that look she had on her face. This was a protective mother.

Zreyas Q-leaped up on the boy's shoulder and swiped his axe across his neck hard. Zreyas jumped down and followed the rolling head.

He used his axe to crack the skull wide open to make sure he was dead with no lingering mental functions to draw on.

Ayya gasped and seemed to... wake up. When she saw the body of her best friend, head smashed on the floor, she screamed hysterically.

Paul ran to her, scooped her up in his arms and tried his best to calm her. Her body shuddered in shock.

Black mist slithered out of the corpse and snaked around like it was looking for a way out.

Rtu's light-form appeared right next to it and he reached out toward it. He contained it in an invisible bubble, infused it with blinding high frequencies and light until it ceased to exist. Then he disappeared.

Connor, looking wild with horror and grief, ran over to the body.

He could only assume Connor thought Zreyas and Cerys had just killed his son. It wouldn't matter why they did it to Connor right now.

He watched Connor come for him as he sheathed his weapons and he consciously converted his inner armor to one hundred percent physical protection, rather than a mix. He knew what was coming, but he refused to hurt him.

In a fury, he picked Zreyas up and body-slammed him hard between him and against the wall. The rage of the scientist was powerful and Zreyas felt his teeth slam together as his head took the brunt of the force.

Paul yelled out to him to stop.

Then Connor went over and grabbed his wife and threw her against the wall.

Even as Zreyas fell to the floor and landed, he let out a pulse of war aura to disorient him, at least enough that he would stop. It did more than that though.

Connor fell to the floor and threw up.

"You can't kill your wife for killing a challenge form that the Dark One sent to pose as your son!"

Connor threw up more of his breakfast and barely said, "Wha-at? Cerys?"

"Stop talking and finish throwing up so we *can* talk, and make sure your wife is okay." Zreyas straightened himself, now concerned for her but he had to find Trevor.

"Cerys, I know you are disoriented right now but where is Trevor?"

She was still trying to breathe and weakly pointed toward the hall. "All... the sciences I... know... and I can't... help my... son." Tears spilled down her face. She curled up and cried, pushing Connor away weakly.

"She wouldn't have screamed her ticking-head off for nothing, Connor!" Still angry at all that was going on, he walked toward the hall pulling his weapons. "Connor, you should *never* act without making sure of things during these times. You are lucky I understand why you did what you did and converted my protections. That sickness I gave you is your best friend, otherwise, you might have done something you would have regretted the rest of your life."

He wasn't as irritated with Connor as much as he was the situation, but he didn't care. "Come on Paul, she came from down that hallway. Lanna and Dulce, watch Ayya. Connor, help your wife, and don't leave this room!"

Paul handed Ayya to Lanna and rushed to catch up with Zreyas.

He and Paul rushed past the Sadlers on the floor and ran down the hall checking each room as they went.

Zreyas said in a low voice, "I don't want anyone but us to find whatever it is that prompted Cerys' response. It must be bad."

"Good call, my boy. We need to find a bathroom in here. That was why she left. This house is huge. You take the left side and I'll take the right."

Zreyas nodded and went into the first room. It had two machines in it. One had a clear window in the side with what looked like clothing in it. He Q-leaped on top and saw what looked like a trap door in the other one. He opened it and nothing was in there but a center post with fins. "Ticking-hell. What is this technology?"

Just as he jumped down, he heard Paul urgently call his name. As he reached the hall, he pulled out the tryst. One beam led to Ayya back the way he came from, and the other beam led in the opposite direction through a wall.

Zreyas ran down the hall and found the closest door. As he entered, he saw a nice bed to the right and another doorway on the left side where he saw Paul stooped over something on the floor. He ran in as he put the tryst back in his vest pocket and entered the tiled room.

There on the floor, laying sideways, was Trevor, unconscious, or dead, he wasn't sure which. It surprised him that his S.P.O. suit was not anywhere to be seen. That ticking mag-shit impostor waited till the boy had his pants down, literally.

Zreyas shook his head feeling like he would throw up any time. He had seen a lot of death and unconscious states, and he could usually tell if they were dead or not. But he really liked Trevor. There was something pheno about that kid, and he was too invested in the boy already. Zreyas froze and gawked.

"Zrey, go get Dulce, she has medical training from being a paramedic in this world."

"On it." He Q-leaped faster than he ever had before through the room and down the hall. He reached the room where the five were and Dulce was tending to Cerys, who seemed stunned and hurting.

"Dulce, we found Trevor. Cerys had been coming to get us for help. He's still alive, come quick!"

She stood up and immediately kicked her shoes off and ran.

Connor looked shocked, and then remorse seemed to rip through his expression with the realization of what he had just done. He looked at his wife and started caressing her cheek. "I'm so sorry, Cerys; please forgive me. I'm so sorry..."

His voice and comments faded as Zreyas ran down the hall again with Dulce in tow. When they reached the doorway, he pointed. "In there!"

Zreyas stayed out of the way while Dulce and Paul worked on him. He knew one thing, the boy was still alive or they wouldn't have stayed bent over him that long.

Tap, I know Rtu probably knows this already but we have been compromised. Asking for advice on how to get them out of here, and keep you, and the challenge node, safe.

— Yes, Captain. I'm on it. Rtu is here and aware. He's thinking. Freckles says to look out the window. That is why he can't change the dimension.

Zreyas Q-leaped to the window and he saw all types of men in black uniforms with weird things in their hands that he could only assume where some variant of the shotguns he had run up against outside of Ayya's house when she was little. They were targeting the house and going in and out of it. They just weren't seeing them because they were in a different dimension. He *really* needed to research those kinds of things.

Tap, when this settles down put an entry on my list in the number one position to research weapons made on earth.

— Done, Captain.

Hmm I have an idea. Zreyas ran down the hall back to where Connor was. Thankfully Cerys was aware and they were hugging each other.

"Connor, Cerys... I know this is a difficult time, but your son is still alive, and I need your help right now. We are in trouble. Dulce is the best paramedic on the planet, so we need to let her work. But I have a plan, but also a problem, because I lack the full understanding of your technology here.

They both turned toward him, expressions serious. Both nodded.

Cerys shuttered in shock. "Thank god, he's still alive! I didn't think he would last this long with as much blood as he lost." She struggled to get up.

Zreyas put a hand on her shoulder, holding her back, glad of his Janquar strength. "You can't go in there, a mother's protection instinct shows no strategy."

Putting a hand on her chest she nodded, still showing signs of still being stunned from the body slam, her head bleeding a little. "*Anything*, what do you need? If there is something so evil to stab my little boy like that, the best thing I can do is help you get us out of this mess, whatever it is."

Zreyas updated them on what he saw, then told him they might want to look for themselves since he was so unsure of technology on Earth.

Connor helped Cerys to her feet and they went with him to the two-machine room. They all looked out the front windows. Sure enough, Zreyas could tell by the grave expressions on their faces they knew things weren't good.

Connor spoke as he looked out the window, face grim and even tone. "What is your idea?"

25

Dad, Don t Kill Me

As Zreyas watched Ayya walk into the room and climb up to the window, he asked, "I don't know who you know in that research place, your warriors, or whatever you have here, but can you order a strike team with more... technology to take them down?"

Ayya touched the glass and said with horrified wonder, "Look at all those inky-eyes out there!"

Zreyas turned back to Connor and Cerys. "Will anyone help you? You seem to be in a high position to do the things you have done already."

Connor thought a moment while Cerys looked out to where Ayya was looking.

He continued, thinking out loud. "What I don't understand is how they got so many here. They have to be in breach of the challenge rules." *Tap, ask Aqum if the other side is breaking the rules of the challenge beyond the spaces.*

A few moments went by and Tap returned the message — He won't answer, he is in calculation mode. He said 'please wait, we are under a calculation stress sequence, not in the spaces.'

"I'm speaking with my ship and getting reports." He paused a moment. "I assume that means that the whole challenge system itself is under attack somehow," he said to both Tap and those listening so he wouldn't have to repeat anything.

"We need a distraction here so we are not being targeted and can go back to the ship."

"Wait," said Cerys. "The General owes me a big favor that he can't refuse, or it would mean his career. I know something he is trying to keep covered up. I just need to make a phone call. Plus, when he finds out our house is under attack, and they might lose two of their best scientists... well that might provide a little motivation. They don't need to know they will lose us anyway."

She walked over to the phone and picked up the receiver, then shook her head. "No connection."

"Wait, hold on. Tap might be able to help." *Tap, can you ask Rtu to put a little communication-mojo in, and connect the lines. We are way out of balance on this challenge, it's ticking broken.*

— Yes, Captain. I don't mind saying I'm getting a little concerned.

Me too, Tap.

— Captain, he said for everyone to move into the bedroom by the bathroom where Trevor is and use the phone there. He didn't have to do anything other than make the dimension a little smaller where the phone is. It's exposed now. He said make it quick and as soon as the call is made, step back away and he will enlarge the dimension again.

"Okay everyone, Tap said we all need to go back to the other side of the house in that bedroom. You can use the phone there." As they all walked back quickly, Zreyas continued, "As soon as you use the phone, hurry back away from that corner of the room."

"Now I know more than ever I want to help. This Dark One is a damn tyrant of the worst kind," said Connor.

Zreyas turned to look at Cerys gravely. "Don't be tempted to run to your son. Run to that phone and make that call or we are all dead. Once we get a distraction, we can attempt an escape. I promise you I will do all I can so you can have time with your son."

A moaning sound came from the bathroom and Zreyas turned to look as Cerys ran to the phone and did something that made a tick-a tick-a tick-a sound.

He hoped that tick-a sound was a good sign, but Zreyas made no move to go in there.

Paul and Dulce were talking and coordinating. They asked Trevor questions about his feet, toes, and where he was. He thought they were ticking going mad, not understanding why they did that.

Connor darted toward them and he heard Trevor say, "Dad?"

Zreyas breathed a lot easier and Ayya's face lit up and looked at her mother. Lanna hugged her with a big smile.

"We need to help, Momma," Ayya said softly. "I know what those inky-eyes are like and, well..."

Her mother put a finger on her daughter's lips and said, "Shh, I promise you, we will help. Let me think on it a bit, okay?"

Ayya nodded, and Zreyas paid more attention to what Cerys was saying and moved closer.

"Yes, General. I wouldn't ask but if we don't get help soon, none of us will ever live to finish that research you wanted. And I swear to you if something doesn't come within half an hour, I will use my last breath to—"

She paused a few second then said, "Yes, that should do it. Just call to evacua—pause— I know you know your job." Then she hung up the phone hard making it ring a little then stepped back more into the room.

"Tap, she is done."

— He already knows, Captain, and he has made the adjustment in the dimension.

"Stand by, Tap," he said out loud. Though he would rather just use his mind communication than out loud, it would be too hard to try and explain why there were huge gaps in conversation. *Think, Zrey, think.* Even with a distraction, if they went running out of there, they would eventually catch them.

Then he had an idea. "Paul and Dulce, are your tokens available to use?"

Both of them looked at each other then they shook their heads.

"Ticking-hell, we need a way out of here without being seen. But we will take what we can get. Cerys, what does your General say he can do?"

Just then, he heard a distant fa-fa fa-fa fa-fa. There were some ticking strange sounds on earth with technology.

Cerys' head cocked to listen as she spoke. "Captain Zreyas, those are helicopters, we aren't far from the airbase. He wasted no time. Thank gosh, the general came through."

The closer the sound got, he realized there was another sound with it. Then the air started to vibrate.

"Oh no... That bastard is going to—" Cerys ran out of the room and Zreyas wasted no time following her.

Cerys ran into the room he had been in earlier with the two weird machines that held clothing in them. He Q-leaped up to the window sill and looked. Hundreds of inky-eyes swarmed around the house. Neighbors were fleeing the neighborhood in the chaos, but they didn't bother them; they only had eyes for the house and what was in it.

Something caught Zreyas' eye up in the sky. Several air machines with things that turned in a circle over the top of them was coming closer. "What *are* those things?"

"Armed Helicopters and there are heavily armed planes behind it, higher up," said Cerys as she pointed. "That son of a bitch," she whispered.

"Wait, isn't that a good thing?" he asked with incredulity.

"Yes and no... He will get rid of our problem, but he is going to also get rid of *his* problem."

"What is his problem?"

"Me... I know things about him that will ruin him, he is going to create a casualty of war that will be very convenient for him. The good thing is, they are not in a hurry. They are calculating how to do this with the situation, otherwise we would be gone already. He values his reputation more than our work."

"Ticking-hell, will he go for them first or us?"

"Them... I think."

A weak voice came from the tiled room. "Captain Zreyas?"

Zreyas turned, ran down the hall and walked to the bathroom opening.

Dulce looked toward Zreyas. "I will save you the question. He will be okay if we get him help soon, but he is very weak. Don't talk long."

It was then he realized how much blood was on the floor around him. Paul had blocked his vision of it before. No wonder Cerys went to such an extreme to kill the impostor. There was no doubt she thought him dead. Then he heard Trevor's weak voice again, pulling him out of his assessment.

"Captain Zreyas..." he grunted out painfully, sweat beading down his face from the pain. "We can get out of here."

Connor looked at his son. "How? We don't have another way out other than the back door and it is swarmed with those things. Actually, they are in the house but we are in another dimension."

"Dad, you are going to… kill me."

"Let me do that later, right now it is more important that we live so I can kill you later," his dad said with a grin.

Zreyas could tell it was an attempt to make his son feel more at ease, and apparently it worked.

"In the basement… can you help me get down there?"

Without any communication between the two, Paul immediately moved around Trevor slightly, picked him up slowly, and all the while Dulce kept the bandages and pressure in place.

They all hurried down the stairs as fast as they could. Connor brought up the rear, after Lanna and Ayya, and shut the door. Then the scientist slid another door closed just on the inside of the regular basement door, and it was metal.

"Are you prepared for war or something?" asked Zreyas. He wondered if this was the kind of thing all Earth families did. Putting up unnecessary defenses who weren't true warriors in a true fight.

Connor shrugged. "I guess so. In my line of work, one can never be too careful. Someone is always wanting to destroy what you have worked hard to achieve, steal it from you, or make you look bad over it. In any case…" Connor latched the lock on the door and slid yet another one across that was recessed into the wall.

"And I thought Janquar were paranoid. At least it will buy us some time in this case," said Zreyas.

"That would have been my idea, Captain Zreyas," said Cerys. "Don't judge him too harshly, I'm the one that had those… squirrelly connections, like the General and his secret."

"Over there behind the shelf. Slide it to the right," Trevor said weakly. "It will slide easy, it's on hidden tracks."

Connor looked at Zreyas and shrugged, then they watched the shelves move easily over as Lanna and Ayya pushed them along the wall.

"I used the extra metal left over for the doors for this small door. Dad please don't be mad, for a year I been working on a tunnel so I could help Ayya leave her house in case her dad got too... mean. It's not done, but it does go out into Ayya's live oak forest, well Mr. Paul's really."

Paul smiled and looked at him. "No, you had it right the first time, it is her inheritance and a gift to her. Well done!"

"I agree, son, it was very smart of you. I would have helped you had you just asked."

Trevor grunted and looked pale. "I... just wanted to do something on my own, but I guess I should have. I'm sorry dad. I'm not exactly sure where it is. Things are kind of... fuzzy, but there are too many large roots to not be in her forest. Maybe Ayya remem...bers."

"Good work Trevor," said Zreyas. "You have already served to help us and didn't even know it till now. "Sending the thankings to you. You might have just saved the multi-verse."

With that, Trevor passed out and head flopped to the side.

He assessed inside the tunnel, then turned back to Connor. "We need to find something to put Trevor on so we can slide and pull him down the tunnel, because I don't think any of us, but me, could stand in that tunnel."

"I have just the thing." Connor ran over to a shelf and pulled down a long sled sitting on hooks mounted to the wall. It had a rope on the front.

"Perfect, said Dulce. Just put it down here and we will get him settled. Do you have a sheet that we can wrap him up in to keep pressure around him since we won't be able to do it while going through there?"

"Yes, I have one in the dryer upstairs," volunteered Cerys. "I'm not sure we have anything clean down here like that."

After several looked around in the basement, Lanna said that she only found some foam wrap for packaging and a few dirty car covers.

Paul laid Trevor down on it and stood to help look for a solution.

Zreyas hopped up to a high small window on the side of the house. He couldn't see much, but what he could see, were those... things... that were moving between the front and back of the house like mindless pacing tigers.

"Paul, get that dirty cover for me, and Lanna, get those packing foam sheets." Then Dulce followed up with an explanation that sounded like perfect strategy. "We can wrap him in the foam and then use the thin car cover to wrap that around the foam. He stays clean, keeps the pressure on to help with the bleeding, and he will also be cushioned a little from the bumps he is going to feel."

Zreyas would have to remember what Dulce did in case he would ever have this kind of problem in the future. All his life he had been one of the ones out there pacing trying to take advantage of any opportunity to kill that he could. Now he knew what it was like to be on the other side of those invasions.

"We are ready, Captain Zreyas," said Connor.

Zreyas grunted. "Good. I will scout ahead. I can see clearly in the dark." He was growing way past impatient now because of the situation, but there was so much he didn't understand.

He realized that was really the source of his frustration. Not understanding how things worked on Earth and its technology. He found it hard to strategize and felt incredibly helpless. He was used to being on the offense, with a lot of information ahead of time, not the tactical defensive retreat side.

Deciding to use this as training exercise in his mind, he felt the stress and responsibility ease a bit by just re-framing it. A sense of adventure started to creep in. He refused to let himself think of anything else right now.

Connor told them he was going to go in last so he could hide the tunnel properly. He mumbled things about how well-done Trevor had done with the tech for that whole door system.

As Zreyas went into the tunnel, Dulce said they would have to duck-walk through, or crawl, but that it was plenty big for Trevor's sled in width.

Zreyas walked back and grabbed Trevor's sled rope and pulled. "Bah, easy. Let's go." He put the rope over his head and let the rope wear on him like a diagonal sash. Though he was small, he never lost his strength. "I will be your work animal for you. I will send a request for trade later, ha!"

Everyone half chuckled, and he realized his attempt at humor was almost a failure. Then he added, almost in a barking order, "Cheer yourself up, we are fortunate. Trevor saved us all, and I didn't have to do it. You don't have to carry Trevor, we are all alive, not enthralled, and instead of bomb in your face, you have bad humor in your face... from me!"

Everyone laughed harder then, except Trevor.

Ayya had a concern in her voice when she spoke. "Trev is sleeping, so I will tell you what he can't. There are lights in here for at least a short way. I've never been in this part before but Trev told me about it. The switch is hidden behind a panel that looks like dirt, but I don't know where that panel is. We never got a chance for him to fully show me my secret agent birthday present. I mainly saw the end ahead."

"Very helpful, Ayya. Thank you," said Paul. "In you go, right after Trevor. You can help push if Zreyas needs it and still be near Trev. Dulce you go in next so you can administer to Trevor more easily if he needs it. Lanna, do you want to go next?"

"Sure."

Ayya ducked her head a "Trev also said that when he started this tunnel, he could stand up in it."

Connor laughed. "He has been going through quite the growth spurt. I've bought two different sized shoes for him this year. How did he get all this dirt moved is what I would like to know. Did he start from the other end, Ayya?"

"I don't know, sir."

Zreyas looked around as he walked and he began to see supports. "He did start from the other end. This is where the supports started, which means he ran out... look."

"That is where all the timber went for the renovation, look Cerys, the same stain too."

"Well, that little shit. I owe that company an apology. Now that I think about it, that was when he used his money to buy a sled and a wagon on sale. But after a day I don't think I ever saw them again."

"He has been working on this a year or more," said Connor, amazed. He's a building genius. Imagine what he could do when he has years under his belt."

"Mr. Sadler, I am sorry to say, he isn't a genius. I mean, he's my best friend and all but, he is good at it by now. He told me about the idea and that night I had a dream."

Zreyas listened to her carefully as she spoke. There was something about what she was saying that seemed important. *Tap, record this whole thing. Something about this is important, but I don't know why. My neck is prickling.*

— Yes, Captain. Also, this is the perfect time to show you something. Bring up your vision interface and think about scanning the environment around you. You can turn on and off different types of vision layers. For example, structural, electrical, etc.

Zreyas did so, and the wonder of what he saw made him stop for a moment.

26 Temperature Reading

All around him, it was as if he was seeing a technical blueprint hologram of everything. He also noticed scientific data on the boarders he didn't understand. But there were some things he definitely got.

Zreyas could see that the top of the tunnel was almost exactly five meters below the surface, and how long the tunnel was ahead. It even gave a visual color of stress points in the supports and how over, or under, stressed they were.

"Is everything okay, Captain?" asked Cerys.

"Yes, I'm just getting readings on the area. It seems Ayya and Trevor are ticking-good at planning structures, dream or not."

Lanna chimed in, sounding rather proud of her daughter. "Well, Ayya *did* score genius level in engineering and mechanics."

Connor followed up with a confirming, "Yes, she did, Captain!"

Zreyas was surprised. He had not heard that bit yet. "Oh, did she. Hmm. Go on, Ayya, I would like to hear more."

He started pulling Trevor again with more speed now that he knew what was ahead. His dark vision was valuable but it didn't tell him things like this. This new ability was amazing. *Tap, giving you the thankings for this new ability.*

— Don't thank me, Captain. It was yours already, you just didn't know it. I discovered it only a few minutes ago. I guess we have grown enough together to see it.

Interesting... "Go ahead Ayya, I won't bite. This is good news."

"Yes, sir. There was this underground city somewhere. Then I saw another city that had white brick and a crystal. But there were a lot of the same things in how it was built in the walls, even though it was different materials."

Zreyas stopped and whirled around. "Did it have a crystal triangle in the middle of it with pedestals?"

"Yes, sir, how did you know?" she said with a shocked look on her face.

"It's a real place," he replied.

"Interesting, little phoenix," said Paul. "This is important, tell us everything you can remember."

"It's fuzzier now than it was, though. That dream was a long time ago. I told Trevor about it the next time we played together in the live oak woods. We sat in my favorite tree and drew little parts of it. He said we should build something. I thought we would be building a fort or something for fun, because we wanted to be secret spy agents, like the one in the movies, but..." She hesitated painfully, then said, "Because of Daddy, we really didn't ever get the chance."

A long silence filled with only the sled sliding on the ground somehow made it sound more silent. Then Ayya asked, "Can we please get my present from Trev from my closet, and my drawing stuff?"

As Zreyas looked toward the end of the tunnel he saw a widened part that might be a rough room. "Hopefully soon, but not now, Ayya." He turned around watching the adults struggling with the crawling. "Let's stop for a rest."

Grunts of relief sounded from all of them. They all turned, sat, and rubbed their knees except for Ayya because she had been walking a little stooped over. She just sat down at Trevor's head and stroked his hair a few times before leaning back.

"I'll be back, I'm going to scout ahead. Just whisper, just in case someone gets close. We are only about five meters underground." Zreyas pulled the rope over his head and dropped it. He carefully started to not only look for what was ahead but for any live bodies that might be in the area. All he saw were energy signatures of insects and an animal here and there. He was surprised to see so many insects. They were everywhere!

Ticking-hell, too much information. He consciously turned off the insects and other small distracting things. Zreyas decided he liked his delusions that there were not that many insects around him. They were much larger to him now than they used to be, and the thought of those things swarming him was scary-real.

Another thing he noticed right off was that the dirt here had a lot of clay content. It looked like the walls were wet down and rubbed to make them smoother.

Zreyas saw the dark scars of heat in the walls too. He touched the wall where it was dark and rubbed his fingers together. It was recent, and the walls felt more like fired clay than raw clay. Did something burn the walls?

Curiosity got the better of him in the whole artisan aspect of it all. He also noticed marks where Trevor must have dragged something over it to smooth it. As he looked closer down the walls, he realized they weren't just marks. All the way down the tunnel was an entire sculpted story.

As he walked, his eyes lit up as he recognized a small section of it. It was the Viduri people, sitting around that ritual place. They were happy and there was an old one with a beard speaking to them. That had to be Rhom in his incarnation. Stunned and frozen in awe, "This... is pheno-mi-tastic," is all he could manage to say under his breath.

Tap can you get a whole picture of this tunnel so I can look at it at the ship?

— Yes, Captain.

Are there any energy signatures other than Trevor that have been here?

— That is a Freckles question. Without me being closer I can't analyze that properly with our current level of growth.

Oh, okay. While he waited, Zreyas started to jog quietly. He wanted to see what that room was all about ahead and he was almost there. The further he got the more things looked burnt and he realized he was getting warmer, too. *What the ticking-hell.*

Zreyas looked at the interface in his vision and didn't see anything about temperature. He figured something like that had to be there somewhere. But he wasn't going to stop to look through all the details. So, he consciously thought about bringing the temperature readings to his attention.

A number on the right-hand side of his vision flashed, and when he focused on it, it brought up the world in colors. Blueprint lines became colors according to the temperature. When he looked back, the further away colors were green and blue. The closer they got toward where his friends were it changed to a light greenish-yellow. He was standing in the range of a yellow with an orange color.

Then he looked ahead and there he saw the colors of deep yellow-orange with a lump of red that seemed to have a motion of breathing.

Uh, Tap? Forget the previous task I gave you. I got the answer right here... whatever it is. I'm not sure what is about to happen.

Then he heard that whispering female voice he had heard back in the hall of statues in the challenge. But this time he heard it both in his mind and with his ears.

"— Come forward, Zreyas of the Atra. Do not worry, you and your friends are safe and protected. Though danger comes soon, we have time. You know my voice from the Hall of Statues. That should be verification enough to give trust."

Zreyas ran ahead and skidded to a stop as he tried to comprehend what he laid his eyes on. The temperature color was blinding red so he turned all that off.

Ahead of him, in the sunken floor of the room was a large creature of flames. It looked like a bird of some sort curled up asleep. He had never seen anything like it before. He realized just how big the room was because that bird was huge. *Ticking-hell, Tap. Is Rtu seeing this?*

— Yes, Captain. This is unexpected. Even Aqum is glad to find out who that was in the challenge.

I wonder... wa-ait... I know who this is. "Are you the fire missing from Rhom, the visage of fire, water, and aether?"

"— That I am." The bird opened her eyes and raised its head and looked at him. "— You did well, though I am sorry you had to go through that pain. I will now ask you what you once asked your brother. 'Was it worth it?'"

Shocked at the question, he cocked his head in thought. After a few seconds, he nodded. "Yes. Though it provided a way for the Dark One to attack once, it was worth the pain because of what I learned from it all and in finding a safe portal room, and... something else."

The bird stood and stretched, spread its wings slightly, and shook itself, flames lapping out in all directions without damaging things around it.

At least now he knew why the walls seemed like they had been burnt. He couldn't help but wonder how deep that clay had been fired in those walls, floors, and ceilings.

— About five meters, the fiery bird said in his mind, obviously reading his thoughts.

"Were you the one that gave Ayya the dreams?"

"— No, not really. They were my dreams, but Ayya is attuned to me by design, even before I came into existence. She is why I am here. Quite the sacrifice Rhom made. It has been, and still is, extremely difficult for him to adjust to. I regret to say that he will never be the same as he once was."

Zreyas noticed a golden glow that didn't seem to fit the rest of the fire. It must be Tulyata's power.

"— You are observant."

"Do you always read people's minds?"

"— Yes."

"Would you stop? Ticking-hell, everyone has a right to their own thoughts."

"— No."

"No, what?"

"— No, I will not stop reading your mind. Privacy is an illusion. Every thought you have goes into the multiversal quantum space. It is part of who I am, too. I'm here to help. I have better things to do than use thoughts for something unproductive. But, I admit they are good for conversations like this."

Zreyas grunted with a little humor in it, and couldn't help but grin. "I don't know why, but I am giving you the likings. If you are attuned to Ayya and made from Rhom, you are okay. So, what do we do? Why are you here in this place? What is your name? I should remember from the vision Aqum showed us about your birth but I don't. What is your mission?"

The fiery bird chuckled and it sounded like a closed-mouthed whispered version that seemed to echo in his mind.

"— As inquisitive as ever, I see. I would be disappointed if you weren't, little one."

"Little one!" he blurted out, forgetting for a moment he was little. But still he took offense to it, though he didn't know why. He liked his size now. "You regularly insult those you just meet?"

The large fiery bird cocked her head and chuckled. "— Do you often forget you might not be insulted when someone says that name for you? Did you not call the one you now call Silence by that name of endearment? … and the cub you named Resolute? The endearment name doesn't make you less… or weak as you call it."

"Oh… Ha! Okay, okay. I get your point. I'm sending you the aplop-o-gies. So why are you here? Though you could be useful in baking thousands of bread loaves in here because it… is… ticking-*hot!* I can't help but ask, what happens to you if you get in water? Does it boil? Ha!"

The head of the bird seemed to suddenly be centimeters from his face and body. Zreyas' head slid back on his shoulders suddenly aware he might have just gone a little overboard and not everyone was like Rhom and Rtu.

"— To answer your last question, I will peel your skin off in layers with steam."

Zreyas' war aura suddenly flared in reaction but he held his temper. "That… is… rude! Rhom and Rtu been teaching me some etiquette." He pointed his finger at her face as he talked, trying his best to keep his rage down. "And this… is ticking-*ru-ude!* If you are a visage from him you taint his line! I was just doing the jokings with you." Then he mumbled to himself, "I think that is how you say it." Then he looked straight into her eyes. "Tulyata used to try and push me around too like a little play thing, and

I didn't let her get away with it either. I *used* to be rude. Yes, very rude."

The fiery bird started laughing a little, then she started laughing a lot as she backed her face up. Then she roared in laughter.

"Oops," he said deflating. "What did I do this time?" Zreyas watched the huge bird laugh so hard little flames darted around, eventually dissipating.

After a few minutes he scowled sourly. He eventually just got up and walked back to his friends, leaving the laughing bird alone. "What the ticking-hell is happening to that ticking-match-stick?"

When he reached his friends, the first thing he did was address Paul. "Your ticking spawn-of-a-match-stick is up there ahead," he said, thumb pointing behind him. His dented pride seemed to darken his mood even more. "I will say she is *rude*. You spawned that thing from you? She wouldn't answer any questions and... well, let's go see the baking-oven fire. You will see what I mean."

Everyone just looked at each other, incredulous, clearly not understanding a thing he was saying.

Zreyas growled. "Come on, I'll show you. Let's go." Zreyas grabbed the rope and started pulling Trevor ahead and everyone started moving forward in silence. "Paul, you might want to go back and get Rhom the visage and tie a knot in that beak."

He heard Paul and Dulce chuckle. Then Paul said, "I have no idea what you are talking about but I can't wait to see this."

"Bah, you will in a few minutes, ticking-rude!"

"Someone's ego is bent out of shape," Dulce remarked with a chuckle.

"If it is who I think it is, then it is likely you asked the questions in the wrong way."

Zreyas thought about it a moment and the logic just didn't make sense to him. "A question is a question. What do you mean I likely asked wrong?" He wasn't in the mood for any more mysteries. He felt antsy and grouchy, but he couldn't figure out if it was because of the situation, and being uncomfortable with it, or if some of his old life was surfacing. Either way he didn't like it.

Just in case, he consciously tuned his sight. As he adjusted the rope on his shoulder, he scanned around them for any signatures of life.

Then he heard faint muffled sounds of, '*tink... tink, ting-tink, ting-tink,*' and he could tell the others heard it from the looks on their faces and heads turning.

"Did any of you notice when you looked at what Ayya calls the inky-eyes if their skin looked normal or black?"

Paul responded first. "I never thought to look at that. We were in a bit of a hurry."

Everyone nodded in agreement with short apologies.

The sounds continued as Zreyas thought about it. Tap, these readings I'm seeing, can you make it see something that seems to be living but dead like those bodies we saw on Tarq after the ship's defenses killed them? I mean they were already like that but—"

— I understand what you mean, Captain. Give me a moment, I have records of the energy signatures they had. I'll let you know when I get it done, Captain.

You might want to hurry; I think we might be in big trouble. Then he coached himself. *Wait for the waves to calm Zrey, wait for the waves. Your guts are way too antsy, so calm down before making any decisions.*

27 Nice Try

Zreyas

After Zreyas considered the situation, he started walking faster. "Let's pick up the pace, just in case."

He heard confirmations of some form of, "Yes, Captain."

"Is everyone okay back there? Need help with anything?"

Dulce spoke up. "Several of us have knees bleeding from all the crawling. How far is it till we can stand?"

Zreyas looked forward and concentrated on distance from himself to the fireball ahead. "Hmm, it looks like about one-hundred meters or so."

Groans came from all of them except from Ayya and the unconscious Trevor.

Tap, is there any kind of modern tool that could assist with this kind of thing to help with pushing weight? I don't know new technology. The only thing I can think of is a flat cart with wheels.

— Captain, that solution sounds perfect. I know what you are thinking, but remember, you *can* change more than the tool itself with the balance of energy.

Can I use my weapons to make the tools or weapons like I would build something out of clay? Or do they come already fixed?

— You have to answer that, Captain. But I can tell you, everything you are, and all the tools you have are made from the energy of your potential and choices.

Zreyas thought a moment, not quite sure of what she was talking about at first. He pulled his bow and looked at it, forgetting he had his technical view still going until he saw the energy signature.

It was more condensed energy more than anything else he had seen in his view. Even the fireball bird ahead didn't have that same density. After thinking about it, it made sense because his weapons were made from neutrinos and potential. He had no clue how that worked but he decided to at least try something.

"Hold on, rest a bit. I'm getting some readings."

Sighs of relief came from behind him and they all sat down on their asses and checked their knees. They were bloody to be sure and he suddenly felt quite bad. He had no idea they were having that problem.

"Next time, tell me before it gets to the point of something like this. I don't want you to suffer if you don't have to carry out an order or what you *think* is an order."

They all nodded.

Zreyas pulled his dagger and looked at its signature. "Anyone have a metal instrument or tool of some sort, like a knife? If you do, hold it up so I can see it."

Tink... tink, tin-ng-tink, tink-tink.

He could tell people were scrambling to try and search pockets.

Paul finally called out that he had a pocketknife, unfolded it, and held it up. Zreyas was fascinated that there was such a thing like that, though he shouldn't be surprised given what he had seen in his ship. He really did need to get up with the modern technology.

Zreyas looked at the energy signature of the knife verses his dagger, and though he had no way of understanding the reasons for the differences, since his own weapons weren't the same, he now had a little more understanding just seeing their energy structures.

"Here... catch this, Paul. Put it back in the back on the ground, then stand away from it and get ready to catch my axe." He tossed the dagger, hilt first.

Paul caught it, paused to look at it and feel it, and then did what he had asked him to do as he pulled his axe out, repeating the process with each weapon.

They ended up with his three weapons laying on the ground spaced out, just like he wanted them to.

Tink... tink, ting-tink, tink-tink.

Zreyas nodded in thanks and then he concentrated and started with the dagger in the back. He accessed the quantum by sending out the signal of what he wanted and then visualized the wave patterns coming back to the dagger. It immediately morphed into a defined flat cart with metal wheels as big as he could make it and still have some potential left. He left the loop of the rope for it still not defined for now.

Then he did the same thing with the axe next. That cart was a little larger and longer. Lastly, he did the same with the bow. That cart could hold two people. Then he finished his construction, attaching them via the ropes, connecting them into one long train, including the sled. Then with the excess energy he put it in the potential to decrease the weight of what was on it.

Tink tink, ting-tink.

Everyone had backed up when he transformed them, then said, "It won't bite, get on. If you are in a position to help in some way, good. If you are not, then, good. Let's go."

Tink, ting-tink, ting-tink.

What is that noise? he asked himself. Zreyas put the rope back over his shoulders and started testing his strength again. It had been a while since he had assessed it.

He looked back and when everyone was on, he leaned in and filled his war chamber, trying not to make it too invasive. Trevor wasn't well and he didn't want to make him worse.

To his surprise, the sled slid forward fairly easily. Once he got his momentum going he started running. It was awkward but it was doable.

"Well done, Captain!" Paul said with amazement. "We will help keep the carts from grinding on the sides of these beautiful walls!"

Ting-tink, ting-tink.

He heard 'woah's and giggles coming from behind. That made things a little less tense in his gut. It made him grin.

— Captain, I have that adjustment done for you to see the not-living-living. Turn it on whenever you are ready.

Zreyas almost forgot he had asked for that. Tap had put in a new button for him to choose with a thought. He did so, but nothing really looked that different until he looked up and back.

There were hundreds of what he assumed to be the enthralled Janquar above them in the form of humans. They were making digging and pick-mining motions.

"Ticking-hell." He poured on the speed to get to the fireball bird that was up ahead. He noticed everyone had gotten quiet. There were no more fun sounds.

He didn't know what he was going to do, but everyone behind him was important to the survival of the multiverse. That ticking LFO was somehow cheating the system because there was no way that many of his minions could have gotten through with the balance system of the challenge node, even with... the spaces between the rules.

As Zreyas ran into the large room with all his people in tow, everyone got off and stood. He willed his weapons to turn back to their original state and picked them up quickly, putting them in place.

The fiery bird was ahead of him laying down, more like a wolf would than a bird. It looked like it was... asleep? Surely that thing knew what was going on and it's sleeping?

Tink, ting-tink, ting-tink.

Incredulous, Zreyas said, "Hey, wake up, we are back! "This place is under attack!"

The fiery bird snored softly. Zreyas just looked at Paul. "Did you create this? Is this where your fire went?"

Paul chuckled. "No, but Rhom's fire was used to create this new visage to bring in the new age."

Zreyas looked at the bird then back up to Paul, stunned. "I thought the sleeping phoenix was figurative, not literal!"

Paul was outright laughing by this time and said, "Well, it's both."

Then they all heard faint sounds of aircraft coming closer. The tinking sounds stopped.

"Uh, oh," said Cerys. "That would be the General's... help." She looked at her husband. "I'm afraid our help is here dear. I am not sure our house will survive this... aid of his."

"I was just getting that house all decked out with nice stuff too." Connor sighed. "But we won't be needing it very long anyway."

Zreyas walked up to the head of the phoenix hesitantly as he heard the aircraft sounds grow louder. "Hello-oo! We have an air attack coming like right now!"

When the phoenix didn't move, he started scoping the place for exits, mumbling his typical obscenities. More out of the situation than the useless fireball laying there asleep.

Tink, ting-tink, ting-tink.

As he turned around to look at the group, everyone was standing there doing the same thing, but alarm ripped up through him as he saw Ayya laying on the ground by Trevor.

"What the ticking-hell happened to Ayya?"

Everyone turned to look at her.

"Ayya!" Lanna ran a few steps over to her in a panic.

Dulce and Paul went to her too. After a few minutes, Dulce looked to him with a stunned look on her face and said, "Captain, she's... asleep."

Zreyas reached out with a palm up. "Are they ticking communicating or something?"

Paul, still examining Ayya, turned with a serious look. "I'm not sure."

The entire place boomed and the ground shook. Everyone that wasn't already on the ground ended up there. Even those already on the ground were knocked prone.

Zreyas looked around incredulous as he rose up from the floor with a Q-leap. He scanned to see if there were any openings using his new... whatever kind of sight it was. There was a start of a tunnel but it only went a few meters in. He assumed it was going toward Ayya's house.

He pointed toward the construction. "Connor, is that the direction to Ayya's house?"

Connor finished standing as he looked where he was pointing just as another large boom hit, almost knocking him over again. He looked as he went to the wall to stabilize himself. "Yes, Captain. Yes it is, Captain. But..."

"But what?"

"I don't know what this material is that these walls are made of. There is no way Trevor could have dug through this, not with his tools."

"This fireball of a bird did something with heat. The ground has high clay content, but..." Zreyas Q-leaped over to the wall where Connor was. He ran his hand down the smooth glass-like sides, then knocked on it with his knuckles and it seemed to make no sound.

Zreyas flipped out his axe and threw it at the wall. It bounced off unnaturally. He then put his face almost touching the wall. Laid the free hand on it, pressing his palm against it firmly. He opened his mouth and let out an open mouthed mild but forceful roar. His hand didn't feel it and the sound dissipated like it was snuffed out. "What the ticking-hell?"

Connor watched him curiously and then did the same thing as Zreyas, but instead of a roar, he did a forceful 'aaah' sound. Then he looked at him. "Well, without my instruments, there is no way to check if that material is affected at all by sound. That is... impossible, isn't it?"

Connor turned back toward the others. "Cerys, this is more your field of expertise, not mine. Come look at this, my dear. I think you will find this fascinating."

She stood and walked toward them. "I've only got so much knowledge in Earth sciences, not anything that this pot pie oven might have made. I have a feeling this might be way out of my realm judging by the sample I found in the laundry room."

Zreyas chuckled sardonically. "Trust me, I understand *that* ticking-feeling. But it would be like being stuck in the mag-shit if there was nothing to learn about."

"What is the mag-shit? Is that a real thing or a figurative expletive," asked Cerys with a tone that reminded Zreyas of Tulyata when she didn't quite believe something.

Just as he was about to reply with a bit of aggravation, Dulce turned toward her. "Oh, it's real all right."

Zreyas shivered as he said, "I can't imagine a worse type of death."

"Is it like pools of quicksand or something?"

Tink, ting-tink, ting-tink.

"No, it's worse than that. That would be kind compared to mag-shit problems. You can study it later, right now I need to find out what we are dealing with here since the ticking-sleeping bird won't talk to us.

— Little buddy, Rtu here. I have some bad news for you. The explosions have obliterated the house and rendered the dimension I had for your protection useless bec—

"What?!" Zreyas looked to Dulce, her eyes looking distant.

— They have breeched the tunnel between Samsara's protection and mine. They are on their way to you. The only way out is using the other entrance. And—

"What other entrance?" Zreyas began scanning the walls to see nothing but solid walls just like where he was standing. Just as he looked at the sleeping Ayya, his eyes darted toward Samsara, who was sleeping too.

Zreyas turned on his new vision to see what he could find structurally that would look like an exit. He saw nothing anywhere. Where Samsara lay sleeping, he couldn't see anything past her. The signature of her body seemed to be integrated with all the walls.

It dawned on him that they were literally within Samsara, in a way. He was beginning to understand energy signatures and what she had to be doing might really be taking quite a bit from her, visage or not. It looked to him like she was literally making herself smaller in order to protect them.

"Rhom! I mean Paul! Wake up your fireball! She is hurting herself to protect us maybe, and the only exit is behind her.

— Little buddy, I can't help you anymore from here. The only advice I can give is when you get out of there, run to Ayya's room. It's protected and they won't be able to get to you, though that also means we can't teleport you out. So it is best you find a way out and not let them see you, or all is lost. They will camp and wait till you all die. They have no time constraint due to numbers… we do.

"I understand." Zreyas looked at Dulce and spoke. "Thank you, Rtu for all you have done for us. If things go bad here, at least the multiverse still has part of you."

She looked at him with a tear in her eye and nodded quietly, her eyes saying everything.

His heart filled with the gratitudes, then he looked at the dark tunnel and the anger replaced the gratefuls at the thoughts of them getting to those he had come to give the lovings to.

As he slowly started walking toward the tunnel entrance, he calculated. After a few steps, he said with grave focus, "Paul and Dulce, do what you can to wake Ayya. Maybe if we wake her up, so will Samsara."

Desperately trying to come up with a plan so he wouldn't have to tell them what was really going on, he stopped his walk and sat down on his heels facing the tunnel as he started to hear the noises echoing up toward them of grunts and war roars, though they didn't sound like normal Janquar roars. They sounded more... demented.

He thought about the hall of waves again, but this time the statue of himself had no glowing red eyes. Things weren't always what they seemed in the hall of waves, yet they were, *after* he had gotten the hind-sight.

This time he recognized all the statues in the hall on the left. He also recognized the deserter on the right. Thankfully he didn't recognize any of the others on the right. That made him sigh in relief.

As soon as he did, an idea came to him. Sometimes things had to be worked out backwards from what the mind knew at the time. But he didn't know how that was going to help him right now. He didn't have time to get hindsight because he started hearing clinking of weapons along with the echoes of running feet.

"Captain! They are coming down the tunnel!" Cerys screamed. "This seems like one of your mag-shitting deaths to me!"

Zreyas stood in the tunnel entrance. He made sure his emotions were as even as they could be as he focused on the tunnel, yet still seeing the hall of waves. As Cerys' statue came up and slid to the left, he gave a command.

"Cerys, wake up your son, and tell him to communicate with Ayya to wake her up. Tell him what is going on so he can relay it."

She immediately ran over to Trevor and started to shake his shoulder.

Dulce interjected gently. "Be careful. You don't want to hurt him further. Trust in your heart to wake him."

Zreyas focused down the dark hall, adjusting his vision. "If that works, tell him to tell Ayya to let Aaru help her. I'm going to need her help. She will have to grow up fast today if we are going to survive."

He pulled his two long swords off his back and crossed them in front of himself, sizing up the swords in comparison to the tunnel opening, glad the tunnel wasn't any bigger. It was the only reason why they hadn't reached them yet. He willed them to turn into a crossed barrier. They widened and melded together, but when he tried to attach them to each side of the tunnel, they wouldn't connect.

It didn't surprise him. He would need permission to do that. Samsara was a visage, and he doubted that would even be feasible without a lot of balance costs. He might not understand it all, the balance thing, but he was beginning to get a feel for it from his quantum mirrored experience where he saw the energy of the scales and how they worked.

He felt the panic in all of them that were awake, so he figured he needed to tell them the bad news just to keep them focused. It was better they have the details so they could strategize, at least it was for him.

"Our only exit is behind Samsara," he announced. "She is using herself to protect us. We are literally inside her. Now they are coming inside her too."

Zreyas reverted his swords and returned them onto his back. "And no ticking-way I'm letting that happen for long. She might be rude, but I am sending her the lovings for what she is doing for us. Move *everyone* close to Samsara. I don't think the burning visage will hurt us... I'll try and talk to her."

He moved over to the wall at the tunnel entrance and put his palm against it. Zreyas let out a deep breath and tried to calm himself enough to understand the energy signature.

He realized there was no way he could understand a visage, but if he could at least send a frequency out that would communicate to retreat herself back enough to close the tunnel off, it would at least keep them *outside* of her. Something told him that if they got too far in, they would kill the visage and all would be lost. It might not be accurate but it was his gut feeling so he had to listen to it.

Taking in a deep breath, he concentrated on putting his thoughts and mind to the energy signatures he could see that belonged to the visage. He tried to visualize the frequencies that matched what he wanted to try and say to her.

Samsara, I don't do the pretendings of understanding the visagely-wooza you do. But we are in trouble and I am thinking you are in the danger soon. I am asking for yourself as much as for us that you close up your protection from the tunnel and make a barrier so they can't hurt you or those inside.

He felt no change in the walls of energy running down the tunnel. *I do not ask for myself, I ask for you and the others. You, Ayya, Trevor, and the visages must get out of here safely or all is lost. This world would mean nothing to me without them, yes, but the multiverse can't do without them and you.*

Zreyas looked quickly down the tunnel as he heard a distinct clang on the floor of a weapon. He gave up on trying to contact Samsara, because he realized he just wasted precious time. He didn't even know this new visage. For all he knew, she wasn't a very good one.

Pulling his bow and standing at the doorway of the tunnel, he gave one more order. "Do your best to get around that useless fireball that might just be our death instead of an ally!"

Then Zreyas thought about the arrow he wanted and drew a flaming arrow, nocked it and pulled back taking aim.

28 Head-Room

▣▣▣ *Ayya* ▣▣▣

— Ayy-yaa… came a far-off voice.

It sounded familiar to Ayya but she couldn't seem to place it.

— Ayy-yaa… wake up Ayya.

Trevor's signature tones seemed to vibrate through her, almost like they were her world. She was content and she found herself inside the space in her head that she always shared with him. She assumed it was her head, but she wasn't sure.

— Ayya… The inky-eyes are coming, you need to wake up so the firebird will wake up.

She tried to wake herself up but she was just too content where she was. It was nice to feel satisfied and at peace, even if Trevor *was* yammering at her. The love she felt around her was too much to resist. She even felt it breathe.

A sustained thrummed roaring tone shook her whole existence. She grew frustrated that something was messing around with the satisfying peace she had been experiencing.

— Ayya… The inky-eyes are almost here! Wake up or we will all die!

Another resounding thrum ripped through her. Between what Trevor had said and what she now realized was Aaru's warning thrum, that got her attention.

— Ayya, please help me and listen. It's hard for me to stay awake. I think I might be dying because of my injuries.

That *really* got her attention this time. She couldn't imagine a world without Trevor. Thinking about that made her remember what had been going on when she suddenly felt drowsy. She remembered a gentle voice soothing her and asking for help, that when the time was right, she would need to—

Fear ripped through Ayya as she thought about her mother, Trevor, Paul, her parents, and Captain Zreyas. She knew they were now in trouble. The first thing she did was send her tones to Trevor to help him somehow. She didn't know what she was doing but it felt right.

She tried to make herself wake up but it was like something was keeping her from doing it. So, she used their communication tones to tell Trevor she was stuck. They had those little short toned patterns for general things like 'I'm in trouble', 'hello', 'I love you', 'let's meet', 'hideout', etc. Then she asked *'what?' 'going?'*

She noticed the language between them had grown beyond those simple words in the past year, but it was still short simple words. she had to revert to the short simple communications. She gave him the basic status that she was having a hard time waking up.

— Thank you Ayya. I feel so much better now. Mom is gasping at what she says is a miracle. Mom is smart but she still has a lot of growing up to do. Anyway, we are in big trouble.

It was too advanced for her to understand right now. It seemed garbled.

Ayya replied back. *'DB5 code'* and left off the tone for 'name'.

Trevor filled Ayya in on what was going on using their simple code tones. She was grateful because the frustration subsided. He communicated in short small words, and from what she gathered he said... — 'inside'... 'sleep'... 'no' 'little phoenix'.

A pause came, then the tones filtered in to say, — 'inky-eyes'... 'go'... 'head-room'... 'let's meet'.

Head-room... head-room... she thought to herself. Ayya couldn't quite remember where that was. Then it dawned on her it was somewhere north, or was it west? Then she realized she seemed to be all over the place. And not quite all in her body because she could see her legs. No, that wasn't right, that was normal for being in a body, just not while she was asleep. *Am I still asleep?*

Shock gripped her as Aaru's thrumming alarm ripped through her. It was so intense that she felt like cowering in a corner.

— 'Head-room'... 'Ayya, hurry!'... 'secret meeting.'

Three thrumming roars resounded from Aaru. Whatever was going on, it was bad. That thought seemed to jolt her mind a little more, and some clarity trickled in.

Ayya found herself inside an oval room. The walls seemed to be organic in nature. It seemed familiar. There was a crystal in the center of the room that looked like it was a pine-cone shape. It was at the top of a triangle that seemed to go through the organic, but a see-through floor.

She felt presences here and it all seemed familiar. After she thought about it for a moment, it was more refined since the last time she had been here.

She remembered something. Ayya had been sorting out this room so she could organize her thoughts and talk to Aaru and Trevor better, but she didn't remember how she was doing that.

Almost startling her, a figure made of rainbow-colored mist wafted down from high up on the wall to her right. It approached her with gently pulsating colors and it grew arms and legs, almost as if it were trying to make its form relateable to her.

Not sure what to do, Ayya looked to see if she could see any evidence of inky-eyes, but she didn't see anything like that. They didn't feel like one either. She had gotten to know how they felt too, but this mist didn't feel like it. In fact, it felt very bubbly and excited, but she couldn't help but be suspicious after not recognizing Trevor being an inky-eye.

The guilt washed over her at the thought of that. And to her surprise as it did, the colors of the mist in front of her went tinted with an overall dirty orange. "Hello. Who are you and why are you in my head-room? How did you get in here?"

— Ayya, it's okay, came Trevor's communication. — The inky-eye was an exact replica of me. You couldn't have known. Even mom didn't know until she saw me on the floor, and you know how moms are.

There was a pause and the misty entity in front of her seemed to recover to their original rainbow colors.

The entity threw up a hand and waved. "Hello, Your Highness! I'm Gulloo, and I've always been part of you! I'm very happy you can see me now! I'm one of your elders, the alchemist."

Ayya had no idea what it was talking about.

A thrum resounded again from Aaru.

The mist entity, apparently named Gulloo, immediately started pouring something she couldn't see into something else she couldn't see.

That confused Ayya. "Hello Gulloo, I can't talk now I have to try and figure out what is going on. Aaru does that when there is danger."

"I've noticed the war-horn-blowing-protective-psycho has a habit of doing that. Because of the effects he creates inside you, he keeps me working over-time."

— Ayya, I have a message for you.

"Okay, Trevor. I'm listening."

— Captain Zreyas said we didn't have much time left. He's the only one that has any fighting weapons and they are gaining ground in the tunnel, even though he is burning them with those arrows he's shooting.

There was a pause and Ayya idly watched Gulloo mix invisible things in the air. Every once in a while, Gulloo would hold up a three-dimensional chemical looking symbol. She learned to recognize those kinds of things hanging around Trevor and Mr. Sadler for so long.

— Ayya, he said that you need to speak with Samsara. She is the phoenix visage protecting us right now but the inky-eyes are starting to get inside her and you need to tell her to retreat enough of her to block the tunnel. It will buy us time to figure out how to get out of here and get her to get out of the way of the entrance I made for you for your birthday present.

"But I don't know how to talk to her! How am I supposed to do it?"

— Captain Zreyas said you are connected in some way. He said that it might be like how he has to communicate with Tap, who is part of him, too, but in a different way.

"I'm not sure who Tap is."

— I think that is his ship. Paul said to just reach out to what you feel is surrounding us all and you will know how, just like you do when you are in your tree spot. Ms. Harrison said to trust yourself and relax, but try and hurry, because this is worse than the big snake.

Gulloo, stood with a bounce. As he talked, he became very animated with his body language. She almost giggled at him. Was it a him or a her? She didn't know why but she felt like Gulloo was a him. This seemed almost like a memory. Still, she felt like she was grinning as she watched him talk with his body. "You can be happy in your tree spot. And when you are happy and satisfied, you see lots of things that are real, just like the old man in the sky that you knew before that one time."

Ayya had no idea what he meant but right now she suddenly felt the urge to sit down where she was and be in her tree spot. She pretended she was sitting there, and she felt herself sigh and relax. The more she did, she noticed the less colorful and transparent Gulloo got.

— That's it Ayya. I will be here if you need me. I'll also tell them you are trying to do it now.

She nodded and imagined closing her eyes, even though she knew they were already closed because they couldn't wake her body up. It made her wonder how she could be asleep and still be so awake here and talking to people in her head-room and not be dreaming. *Trev, do you have a head-room? If you do, we can meet there sometime.*

— Yeah I do. I think everyone does. But we just tend to meet in yours I think. I never thought about meeting in mine. It's such a mess. I need to set up a room for us to chat just like you have. I like how you have made up rooms for different things so thinking won't get so cluttered. Mine has piles in it. But before I met you, everything was just all over the floor.

She turned the awareness of herself around to see behind her and sure enough Trevor was standing in the glass room, respecting her space, in the open doorway smiling.

If the piles work for you, that is better than everything scattered on the floor. As she closed her inner eyes again, she said one more thing. *Just change things because they are right for you, not because I do it another way. You don't ask me to change, I don't want you to change for me either. You of all people should know what it is like to see and meet another just like yourself, even though that was different.*

— That was scary Ayya. Every time I close my eyes, I still see him. You are so much better at living with scary stuff than I am.

As she concentrated on feeling out around herself for Samsara, she still kept paying attention to Trevor. He was scared, really scared, just like she was, but she would rather them all die than leave him feeling like he was being deserted while scared to death.

I don't feel brave, Trevor. I still feel scared, almost all the time. I've just had more time in the scary than you have, is all. Maybe I can help you learn to push it to the flame like I do. When we get done helping Captain Zreyas, we can sit and talk about it if you want. We can even do it in your head-room so we can both see where it is on the floor and find it all.

Ayya could tell that Trev was now sitting down getting calm and quiet. Behind her she felt the crystal in the center of the room start to glow as she felt her inner hum resonate through her body. She was glad Ms. Harrison taught her how to do that, though she wasn't sure she meant in this way, but she felt satisfied and content, so it must be the right thing for her according to Ms. Harrison.

Then a tone came from Trevor as he left her mind-room, and she knew all was right and good with him for now. He had let her know he liked that idea and he would leave her to do what she needed to do.

29 Explosive Steel

ⴲⴲⴲ *Zreyas* ⴲⴲⴲ

As he pulled his arrow back, Zreyas was alarmed how fast those ex-Janquar could move on their knees. He tried to think how he could make more of an explosion, but until he could, he would use fire. They were bound to be flammable with that coal-like flesh.

The first arrow hit, and sure enough the... *thing* started to burn, but it was unaffected in movement. It horrified him that they were so far gone that they didn't have fear, or try to put the fire out. He talked to himself while he pulled back again trying for the one behind the first. *Think, Zrey, think. They are like charcoal, they burn, and they are unaffected by—*

Zreyas hit the advancing ex-Janquar and thought about how he needed a word for them since they were no longer Janquar. "Paul! See if anything here is flammable. If you do find something, throw it into a pile in front of me."

Then he had an idea. He didn't know if it would work though. "Anyone tell me what is the heaviest and hardest metal material that is also flammable."

Silence filled the room other than some footsteps he could hear.

Dulce responded first. "Plutonium is easily flammable but it is also radioactive and that would render much damage to nature and people. All metals are flammable but it takes extreme heat to make it happen most of the time. Some only need air. But—"

"Nevermind, I have an idea. Paul, Cerys, and Dulce, come close, I want to make sure I have this right."

All three ran to him as Zreyas created an arrow that had a steel ball on the end, aimed at their knees and hands, compensating for the weight. The neutrinos in the arrow seemed to understand what he wanted and Zreyas felt it... *adjust* for him. When he let it loose, it wreaked havoc on their limbs.

He rained arrows through there as fast as he could, and even took off one of their heads by shattering it. Zreyas let the arrows go as fast as he could in the hopes a pile would start accumulating—his idea was working.

As he loosed more arrows while the ones behind tried to move the debris away, he explained what he was thinking. He remembered what was in the belly of Tap and it was the only element he knew of that wouldn't take much to create an explosion.

Paul nodded and seemed distant a few seconds before he said, "This will work if you use a tiny amount but condense it on the surface of the ball."

"Yes," added Cerys. "The heat will accelerate the process."

Dulce rubbed her cheek and nodded. "Contain it until the impact to be safe, the impact will finish things."

Connor suddenly stood at Trevor's side. "It is also radioactive, but it vaporizes fast. As little as you will have to use, it is a much better alternative than plutonium."

Zreyas had almost forgotten about him. He had been so quiet by his son's side, that he almost made himself invisible in a way.

"Thank you for your council. Back away, just in case. And I hope you give me the forgivings if I blow us all up, but we are all dead anyway if we can't get Samsara to wake up."

As Zreyas started concentrating on the same metal ball arrow with the modification of the spot of E-87, he mentally told the neutrinos to contain it till it hit.

Out of nowhere, a name came to him for the ex-Janquar. He had no idea why that came to him while he was focusing so hard. He reasoned it must be because he had been doing so much naming of the crew recently.

Zreyas raised his bow and concentrated hard to make sure this arrow was prepared right. The ex-Janquar had started pushing the debris forward quickly and they were only meters away from the wall of debris coming into the room.

As he took a breath and aimed, he noticed the walls shimmering slightly. It almost broke his concentration.

"I... hereby," he said, as he listened to the line on his bow get tight.

"Name you..."

He made sure his aim was spot on where there were still a few flames from the flaming body in the debris.

"A new species called... *The Charred*, you ticking... life-sucking... monsters!"

The opening of the wall contracted rapidly.

He adjusted his aim quickly, reminding him of how he had to jump through the fracture closing on him in the dying dimension that seemed so long ago.

His focus was so intense that it felt like the arrow was moving in slow motion as it left.

Good timing Samsara. Sending the thankings and appreciates to you.

— You are welcome, but we are not out of the woods yet. You are going to have to help each other, and you will need Trevor and Ayya to get out of here. This explosion was what I was waiting for, but it will not kill all of them. Ayya will know the spot you need to go to.

I understand.

As the arrow went through the hole in the golden translucent barrier, Samsara slammed the opening shut. On impact the entire tunnel erupted in an explosion that shook the entire room. Though the integrity of Samsara held, Zreyas could tell the earth around her was blown apart and now cracked in several places.

"Everyone, go to the back of the room where Samsara is now!" Zreyas struggled to pick himself up off the floor, sheathed his bow and watched everyone scramble to move.

The fire on the other side of the tunnel wall was intense, at least until the ground collapsed on top of it, snuffing it out. Then he thought he heard a tree crack. The confirmation came when he heard the loud series of branches cracking as they hit the ground. A vibrating thump as the trunk hit the ground made everything seem surreal.

Then he heard Ayya let out a wrenching tormented scream that seemed to rip through him. That woke her, and Trevor convulsed.

"No-oo!" she screamed as she reached out toward the tree, before going into a screaming inconsolable cry.

No matter how hard she tried, Lanna couldn't get her to calm down. Ayya was shaking all over.

Paul rushed over to Ayya and looked at Lanna as if he was asking for permission to try.

Lanna nodded as tears streamed down her face.

As Zreyas reached them, the look on Lanna's face was of utter loss as to what to do.

Zreyas just stood there while Paul did his magic just by being himself. The love for both of them was palpable. Dulce walked over to stand beside Zreyas with an empathetic expression on her face.

While Paul picked Ayya up and held her, whispering to her, he heard Samsara.

— To answer your question burning in your mind, Ayya is very attuned to those trees in the woods there, and she had asked for protection for the trees and those that enter the woods long ago.

Aah, I understand, at least a little. If it's anything like how I feel about all of us, I really understand.

— It is.

Zreyas waited for himself to calm down and emotions even out, along with Ayya.

She was still hysterical, but with less of an edge after a few minutes.

His ears still rang from her scream. Of all the people he had murdered in his life, no one had ever screamed like that. He felt like his insides were shuddering from the trauma, like residual vibrations.

Zreyas also noticed that Samsara had not yet left. His guess was that she was waiting for Ayya to calm down enough so the little genius could help get them out.

He was growing concerned for Samsara though. He knew two visages well, and they weren't invulnerable. She had to be suffering.

Paul was growing sterner with her in order to shake her out of it without physically shaking her. Even though he was a pseudo-incarnate, he still had that same look he got when he was an incarnated Viduri. It was helping but she was still hysterical. Then Paul turned his head toward Zreyas as if to question if he would help.

Zreyas nodded to him and motioned for him to lower them down.

Paul sat on his heels and made sure Ayya was facing him, but she was in her own panicked world.

Zreyas had no confidence in himself as to what he should say to her. All he knew was how he would deal with Aaru. But that was a very different culture.

He knew one thing, though, and that was that this little human girl was one of the handful of keys in the multiverse's survival. Things were serious. It was out of any of their control that this child would have to grow up fast. And he was not about to let a crying-fit like this doom the multiverse.

30 That Knowing Look

Zreyas

Zreyas knew it was time now for drastic measures and he used his aura to push out his words, but said calmly with authority, "Ayya, do you want to kill your mother?"

She drew in a sharp breath and looked at him with horror etched in her face.

"Why are you choosing to put in danger everyone you love? I understand that the loss of one of the trees is difficult. But unless you want to kill everyone in the room and in the multiverse, you need to get your ticking-shit together. You can mourn the trees later."

Ayya sniffed in shock.

"You are not a stupid little girl, and you are accustomed to dealing with a lot of pressure. Getting attention should not be your main goal now. Like it or not, you are one of the keys to the multiverse's survival. Do you want to doom us all so you can get the attentions?"

Ayya had a lot of expressions morph across her face that seemed to be a mix of anger, grief, and determination. Then she said, "Nuh-uh, no, sir."

Dulce bent over to look at her. "Remember your inside detector. Do you want to help us get out of this mess?"

"Mmm-hmm."

Paul smiled, then added, "All right then, we need your help. You are smart and you know the design of this place. Though Trevor built it, it was your design."

Ayya lifted her head from Paul's shoulder as if in realization. She looked at him, cocked her head, and smiled. "I know you. You were the old man in the sky."

"Yes, little Phoenix, I was. It was in another life before, and you were there."

She looked at her mother and said, "I love you, Momma. I'm sorry I put you in danger."

Before Lanna had a chance to say anything through her own tears, she continued. "I'm ready to help." She wiped her eyes. Then she wiggled away from Paul to stand.

Paul stood and smiled as he reached over to hold Lanna's hand, who was now staring at him. But he didn't look at her, though Zreyas could tell it was just his way of keeping himself from getting more emotional.

Ayya stood up straight as if she was finding her resolve. She looked down at him and saluted like he assumed they would do on earth. "Captain Zreyas, I'm ready to help. Agent DB5 reporting. What do you need me to do?"

Zreyas smiled and almost chuckled at how cute she was. She reminded him of Aaru when he did things like that just out of the tunnel. "Now *that* is the Ayya I have grown to give the lovings to." He decided to play in her world a little.

"DB5, you know the design of this place, and Trevor is not in a position to help. You, secret agent of the Sleeping Phoenix Order, are our last hope to get out of here.

Because Trevor cannot give you your mission, I will. Lead us out of here, or at least tell us what to do."

Ayya nodded sharply and then turned around toward Samsara.

As soon as she did, Samsara started slowly dissipating as if she was melting into the walls of the room, receding from the walls on the end that the visage had been.

It seemed to surprise Ayya but she quickly regained her composure. She looked around getting her bearings.

Finally, she pointed toward the dead-end short tunnel. "There is a mechanism built into both sides of that eight and one-half foot tunnel."

Zreyas saw nothing that would indicate that there was something built in the wall. Fascinated, he said, "Good, go on, DB5. I'm listening."

"Yes, sir. You can't see them, but they are behind each wall, but at the end there, it's not a wall. It's an emergency entrance or exit. Once it is used, it has to be rebuilt and disguised because we didn't have the materials, but at least it works."

"I'm proud of you, DB5. I'm guessing there is something tricky about it. Explain."

Ayya explained to him that both sides had weights and mechanisms that were anchored into the tree above them. From the outside, she had to use weighted balls in three different places to activate it. In theory, she had to run in before the area collapsed behind her.

"I know it will work. But if we try to tamper with it, dig it up randomly, it will trigger a collapse, and the entire secret hideout and tunnel all the way to Trevor's house will cave in. In theory, but I know it will work."

Connor's jaw was hanging to match the concentration and awe mixed in his expressions. Finally, he spoke up. "I have no doubt it could work. Where are the mechanisms and can you guide us to safely get us out?"

Zreyas listened while he checked the other tunnel. Samsara was melting through the walls in that direction but also leaving at the same time. "We are running out of time."

Ayya quickly said, "Yes, sir. It won't take long." Then she walked over to the short tunnel and stood at the center of the area and looked at the wall to the left. "Captain Zreyas, you have a pick, right?"

"I have an axe with a pick in the back, yes." He took it off his belt and willed it to fit Ayya's size. Just as he did, she looked at it.

"Captain Zreyas, can you make the pointy part longer? There is a weight in there and I need something to keep it from falling down."

He did as she asked and made it a bar with a point with a handle at ninety degrees.

She used it to make a circle, then said, "It needs to go in at least one and a half feet but no further than two."

Zreyas nodded. "I'll make a mallet to hammer that in from my dagger. Connor, can you give me a little help? I'm a bit too small to help in this without using the quantum." Then he looked over at Paul and winked.

He knew he could help because, though he was little, he had the strength of a Janquar, but something inside him told him they needed to be the ones to do it. They couldn't rely on him all the time, and he wasn't designed to do everything. It wasn't feasible or efficient—nor did he want to be the one doing everything.

Zreyas loved being active, but he had to train himself to be a leader more than ever now. He had done the part they couldn't do in that room. It was time for them to step up to gain that feeling of being part of a team and empower themselves.

Connor and Ayya worked together to get the bar in at the right depth. Zreyas had made it the perfect length, so all they saw was the handle against the wall, lengthwise.

Then Ayya turned to the other wall and stared at it. Everyone was quiet. The only noises were the tings of some of the Charred trying to pick-axe their way through the room. Zreyas assumed that when Samsara fully left the area, they would get through.

Ayya pointed upward and explained what needed to be done next. She took them through the process step by step, Zreyas making tool adjustments along the way for her.

"That works," said Connor, and he proceeded to do the same as with the other side. After it was done, he nodded to Ayya. "Now what, little genius? I mean, DB5."

Ayya smiled and explained that both side ropes in the wall had to be cut at the same time.

"Connor, I don't know Earth technology, but is there something I can make from my weapons that will do both at the same time? We could carefully dig in there till we see it."

"Captain Zreyas, you can invent what you need. There are cutters that cut at one end. You could always make a two ended cutter with one trigger in the middle."

Ayya looked at the floor in front of them and asked if he could make a magic marker out of it so she could draw. Connor explained what one was to him and Zreyas finally got the idea.

"The only problem is that it will be large," he said as he took the mallet hammer from Connor.

"I don't mind, Captain Zreyas. It's still a marker."

He made the marker for Ayya and she picked it up from the floor. She drew out something large. Though the floor was hard clay-dirt, it didn't draw very well, but it was enough that he could see what she was doing.

As he started to get the idea of the design, he said, "Oh I see now. That is smart, Agent DB5." When she turned around to look at him, he smiled and winked at her. "Thank you, you can put the marker on the floor now."

He concentrated on what he wanted and since it was more unfamiliar it took more time. There were several attempts that didn't work, but he finally fully understood it, and made one they could use. The cutters on each end also had spikes for working through the wall first.

Cerys stood. "I need to work off some of my panic for Trevor. Let me dig through the wall. I'm trained to work with and around things with a careful eye. Lanna, would you like to help me?"

"Yes... I believe I would. I feel useless," replied Lanna.

Zreyas could see and feel Lanna in an odd way. He casually crossed his arms and watched her, cocking his head. It alarmed him when he realized she almost felt like how Janquar had felt like when they had been injured so badly they were suicidal because all purpose had left them.

She suddenly felt alien to him. He could not imagine what the female human was feeling. Though her daughter was alive and well, she lost the child she thought she had. Her mate was now one of the Charred, and so, he was dead. And her other child was conceived after the charring process started and he wasn't sure how she felt about that. Either way, she had the look of someone who had nothing left and lost all purpose in life... and that gave him concern.

Cerys woke him from his thoughts. "Captain Zreyas, we are done."

"Well done. Paul and Connor, your turn. Line everything up and then coordinate the cut. The two levers there in the center will need to be used to cut at the same time according to agent DB5."

He started to say to Lanna that she should be proud of her daughter but he stopped that thought abruptly because she was really struggling with Ayya not literally her daughter, even though she had her daughter's body that would have been dead due to a defect. This situation needed to be addressed somehow soon or he bet that she would commit suicide in some way with doing something drastic.

"That's right, Captain," said Ayya.

"Would you supervise what they are doing so they make sure they are doing things correctly? You have a sophisticated system here."

Connor looked at the walls with awe still on his face. "That she has. I'm impressed they both came up with a way to compensate for not having materials."

"I also see a lot of missing things from the house here in these walls too!" accused Cerys. "Look, there is one of the weights of my grandmother's grandfather clock." She looked like she was about to explode, then she just busted out laughing, shaking her head. "I can't be mad at them. This is too ironic that they would use those weights in a mechanism like this. My grandmother would have loved it."

Ayya grinned a little sheepishly, then looked at Trevor, who wasn't looking well at all.

Tap, can you ask Freckles if Trevor is going to make it? Because if that boy dies, we will have a mess on our hands, more than the Dark One. I know Dulce is on it, but she's pseudo-incarnate and limited in sight.

— Captain, Rtu said that it depends on…

There was a pause that was awkwardly long. He tried to distract himself with watching them carefully line things up. He sat on his heels and thought while he assessed the room. Samsara was still there but slowly retreating, like a timer. She was about six meters from the corners of the wall that the tunnel was in.

Trevor and Dulce were in the middle of the room and she was still furiously concentrating on him. "Dulce, do you need me to do anything to help?"

Dulce looked up toward him briefly, face grave. She looked toward Ayya and the others before softly saying, "We need to get out of here and to a hospital, he's lost a lot of blood. Honestly, I am surprised he has lasted this long."

Zreyas nodded and walked closer to the tunnel, now blocked by the golden visage's barrier. *Samsara, how is the boy doing? Is there anything we can do to help his condition with what we have? I'm not hearing back from Tap and Rtu, which concerns me too. But I can't think about that right now—first things first.*

More silence. He knew Samsara was there and okay, but she wasn't speak—

— quantu— —ocked.

Someone didn't want them communicating. He took that to mean that someone was using some sort of interference.

Just as he turned, the two men cut the ropes.

There were several muffled *thunks* and *clinks*. Everyone froze and looked up to the ceiling, even Ayya.

Ayya went up to her mother and hugged her. "We did it, Momma! You are a secret agent now!"

The seriousness on Lanna's face almost didn't break, but it did. She smiled weakly. "Thank you for being so smart and brave." Just for a moment, Lanna lost that look and feeling of being suicidal.

When it returned, Ayya looked up at her mother and she showed slight sadness in her face. "Momma? Are you okay? Did I upset you?"

Lanna half smiled and said, "Not at all, Ayya. How could I be mad at you for being so smart and saving us all?" She leaned down to look at Ayya. "You are an amazing agent, DB5. Thank you." Then she gave her a big smile and grinned.

Ayya's face lit up like the stars.

Zreyas reluctantly stepped forward not really wanting to interrupt, but the captain in him was sure it needed to be done. "Agent DB5 isn't done yet with her mission. Trevor isn't doing well, and we need to get out of here. I'm proud of you Ayya, but now is the time for the next step... getting us out so we can help Trevor. Dulce, let's get Trevor close to where Ayya thinks is best to get him out quick."

Ayya pulled away from her mother and nodded with determination. She went over and pointed to a spot near the exit in the wall. "This spot is the third place we need to cut. When we cut this one, the wall at the end there will crumble and we need to get out quick. We will only have about ten to fifteen seconds before the whole room will collapse. But it will start cracking apart before then.

"We will need help to pull out the poles the captain created with his weapons to get them back. But, remember the place will already be collapsing, so you will need to hurry."

Paul walked up to one of the inserted poles and positioned his body on the room's side, grabbing the handle. "I got one of them."

Connor moved to the other and wrapped his hand around the handle. "I'm beginning to see the inside guts of this thing, and from what Ayya—uh... DB5 has told us, we will all need to cram in this one area to be ready."

Zreyas went over to where Trevor was and put his hands on the sled ready to push, then nodded to Dulce. "Ready to push when you are."

"Thank you, Captain," Dulce said, never changing her expression away from her serious grim face.

It was so unlike her that it made him realize things were not good. Once she nodded, Zreyas pushed the sled while Dulce pulled and steered. Cerys joined her son and got in position to help pull Trevor through beside Dulce.

Lanna stood beside Ayya.

Once they were all in that area, Ayya gave one last instruction. "Don't lean on the end wall here because it will kind of... do a crumple explosion, so you might want to turn your backs to it."

She took a deep breath and used her fingers to stroke her bangs away from her eyes, clearly a little stressed to Zreyas. But he smiled at her and nodded, trying to let her know she was doing good.

Then she looked up at her mother. "Momma, can you please cut the rope with the cutter? It's important, so we need you to do it."

Lanna snapped out of the mag-shitting-hell she was in for a moment and said to her daughter, "It would be an honor, agent DB5."

31 Namdlo

ᓄᓄᓄ *Zreyas* ᓄᓄᓄ

Ayya nodded as she looked into her mother's eyes. "I love you, Momma."

"I love you too, sweetie."

Then, with some effort, Lanna used the two ended cutter and snapped the handle closed with some effort. Two *thunks* sounded on both sides.

Zreyas willed his weapon to revert back to its natural state, and caught it as it slipped out of Lanna's hand and put it in its place. He smiled up at her and nodded. "Well done, Lanna."

The sound of ropes running through something echoed for a few seconds before a loud crunching pop, and Zreyas felt debris hitting his back.

Ayya then said, "*Now!* Hurry!"

Zreyas and Dulce started pushing Trevor as fast as they could through the debris, pushing it aside. Once they were through, Zreyas used his strength to start smoothing some of the debris down so the others could get through easier. Once Everyone but Connor and Paul were through, Zreyas looked at Ayya and nodded to prompt her.

Ayya took a deep breath while she looked around the top of the opening. "Mr. Sadler and Mr. Paul, you need to do this at the same time and run hard. Three... two... one... *Now!*"

Paul and Connor pulled the poles out, and there were two stereo muffled *thunks*. Then a series of expected cracks and crumbles started to resound around them.

Paul pushed Connor through first just as the whole room started collapsing in on itself. Connor dropped the weapon as he fell forward. The modified weapon slid and then bounced and tumbled forward. Zreyas willed it to turn back just before it hit Ayya and caught it.

He reached forward to help Connor through the opening. Just past Connor, he could see Paul trying to help him push him through just as the roof started coming down above him.

Panic ripped through Zreyas as the debris started falling down. "Paul! Dive forward now!"

Paul looked at him with a knowing look that made Zreyas feel uncomfortable even as he dove forward.

"Don't you ticking die on me, old man!" he yelled, just as he grabbed his wrist, barely able to hold on, as small as he was now, but he did. He felt the jolts of Paul getting hit by all the debris. Then his body jerked him forward as Paul was covered up.

The last thing he saw of Paul, other than the forearm he was holding, was his face. He had a slight empathetic smile.

"No-o!" Zreyas pulled hard as he scrambled to the side to let Connor get up and out.

Connor turned around and grabbed Paul's forearm, and pulled hard.

Even with both of them trying to pull Paul out of the debris, Paul wouldn't budge. But Paul's fist was still tight, so he kept pulling.

Lanna must have realized what was going on because she screamed. "Paul!"

Zreyas could hear Ayya gasp along with the others.

No matter how hard he and Connor tried, they couldn't budge Paul. The only thing they could see or reach after all this time was his forearm and fist.

Then Zreyas felt Paul relax and his hand opened. The challenge token in his palm. Everyone was already panicking and he didn't want to add to it. Unfortunately, he, as a leader, had to lead in situations like this, but this was to over the top for him to accept.

"No ticking way, old man!" Zreyas started slapping his wrists while he held the token in Paul's hand to keep it from slipping out, something that he was taught by the old artisans and healers varSas ago.

No reaction... nothing.

He saw a portion of the other hand sticking out of the rubble and ordered Connor to pull his arm out enough to follow along.

... nothing.

"Dulce!" he yelled "What can we do?"

With dead calm in her voice on a creepy level, Dulce uttered, "You are doing fine. I have nothing to offer in western or physical medicine."

In a panic, Zreyas tried the last thing he remembered being taught for someone that had the heart stop or stall.

"Connor, squeeze the last finger hard, and I mean hard! I don't know what it is called here." He showed Connor what he was doing and he followed his lead as he used his thumb to keep the token in the palm.

"Come on, old man! It is not your time yet!" he yelled, as he felt the tears run down his face just before they sealed.

He barely had enough presence of mind to give one more order. Ayya, lead everyone out of here... wherever we are.

"I can't, Captain," Ayya said as she sniffled. Then her breathing told him her chest heaved. "We have to wait for the tree to fall. It should happen any time. There will be cracking."

Zreyas squeezed Paul's smallest finger as hard as he could feeling a little cracking under his desperate Janquar strength. "Come on Rhom, think home! We got a lot to do!"

He felt a gentle hand on his back.

Just then, he heard a loud crack that seemed to come from everywhere. The gentle hand jerked away, obviously as startled as he was. He couldn't see anything, but he heard well, and more cracks came. A tree was about to die, right along with Paul.

A sniffle came and he heard Ayya's voice. "Get ready for the crash, the tree will fall on the room and the tunnel. We need to be on the opposite end, Captain Zreyas. Please, come."

The little one was being so brave for them all. Zreyas' chest heaved and it cracked right along with the tree. He heard rain begin to fall. He held Paul's hand to his face and he felt the fear and anger rise within him at the loss of Rhom.

He knew he had Rtu, but all he could think about was losing his friend and chosen father. The multiverse didn't know him, but it would soon know immeasurable losses multiverse wide. Spirits would begin to lose their fire to survive, frequencies would drop radically giving the Dark One more of an edge, and worlds would dry up, meaning no one had very long to live.

We are all lost without you, old man. Why did you do that? Can someone die from grief? It's just too much right now.

Connor sniffed softly. With evident shock and numbness in his voice he said, "He... he saved my life. Why did he do that knowing he was such a critical visage?"

As the rain fell, it seemed to encompass his soul along with the cracking of the tree, its haunting echoes gaining momentum.

Zreyas went from sitting on his heels to dropping to his knees while he held tight to Paul's hand. He didn't care who was watching—he didn't care about anything right now. His grief was all-consuming. He laid his head on the old man's hand and went into a numb state of oblivion.

How he could deal with so many deaths in his past, and yet recently be so devastated with it, made him angry. *Where will my lovings that I have for you go now—now that you are not here, old man?*

Another gentle hand touched his back. He jerked away from it. He heard sobs and wails all around him in the background as visions of the past came to him.

As they did he found himself mumbling *Namdlo dna Selkerf... namdlo... namdlo... namdlo.*

Stark visions came to him as the cracking wood continued around him. He briefly wondered why he hadn't heard Tap or Rtu in his mind, but he supposed that he wouldn't want to talk right now anyway.

He watched Rhom in his Vidurian incarnation in the dying dimension looking at him with those profound eyes during a conversation they had been having.

> "Yeah, okay I don't know this thanking of
> me is, but I don't know why I protected

your ticking-ass, either. My plan was to kill you after I found Aaru."

"I know, but you didn't. There is some good in you Zreyas Rittak. With a little time, you would be an outstanding leader. My instincts tell me you just gave up leading one type of group to lead another type of people."

"I don't *want* to lead. I was only where I was in the command line because I fought well. And the only reason I wanted to challenge the commander was so he would leave Aaru alone."

"Nevertheless, you mark my word, you will lead people. Let's go, we need to save ourselves so Ayya, Aaru, and you have a chance to live out your purpose... whatever that might entail."

He heard an angry wail escape his own shattered chest. Then another vision assailed him after Rhom had turned into his true form of a visage.

Rhom slowly turned his face toward Zreyas. That was when Zreyas noticed the brilliant light-blue irises. Rhom's eyes seemed to pierce through him.

"I'm still here, my boy! You are safe." And then he smiled that very Rhom-like smile that always shined in any form.

Zreyas tried to open his eyes but they were sealed firmly. When he morphed into the form he used at the crevasse, his eyes didn't seal. He had hoped that the eye sealing was done with, but it was due to his form.

Loud cracking sounded and he tried wiping his face. When he reached back down for Paul's hand he couldn't find it. Just then, he felt himself being picked up and turned quickly.

Dulce was running with him and he smelled fresh air. He could hear her sniffing. "Captain, we can't let you die. We need yo—"

A loud cracking boom resounded everywhere and the shock of it threw Dulce and himself to the ground. Just as he got up and his eyes unsealed, he saw a huge live oak root system flipping up into the air, sand and dirt flying up toward them.

They all shielded their faces with their arms. Just before the tree crashed down over where they had apparently been, the tree hit the ground. When it bounced, he saw a black stone statue with red glowing eyes at the edge of the forest.

Zreyas immediately narrowed his eyes, but just as he pulled his bow, it disappeared under the massive trunk of the bouncing live oak tree falling to the ground, slamming down on top of it. Pieces of the statue shattered out to the side just before it was completely covered up.

"Ticking-hell. How many of those statues are there?" Zreyas turned to follow the others. "Ayya, did you ever notice a black statue at the edge of your woods?"

"No, sir," she replied, sniffing and wiping away her tears.

"Take us to your most sacred place in these woods—your favorite spot where you asked for protection for the woods that Paul spoke of."

"Yes, sir. But it would mean we will have to climb."

"We will worry about that when we get there."

"Yes, sir." Ayya started running deeper into the forest.

Pure adrenaline, Zreyas supposed, kept everyone following her closely, even with Trevor. Connor and Cerys had picked up the sled at some point. Cerys held the rope over her shoulder and Connor, at the back, holding the sled itself.

Lanna was running just behind Ayya, moving her head around, almost like she was in awe. At the times he could see her face, incredulity and wonder morphed her features. He could only assume she had never really been there or knew about the secret life of Ayya. He wasn't sure which or if it was a combination of all of them.

As much as he wanted to stop running and scream out from the loss of Rhom, he was angry now about the statue. He supposed it was a form sent through for the challenge, and that meant the Dark One had somehow severely compromised the challenge rules, because he had hundreds of Janquar there *and* that statue with its radius of influence.

Dulce ran beside Trevor, periodically looking down at the boy's still form, jostling.

He stalled his run only a second when he realized that Paul must have known it was there somehow. The look on his face had been haunted with a clear knowing.

Tap, can you hear me?

No reply came. He turned on his vision interface and it worked just fine. He saw something blinking at the upper right edge. As he ran, he concentrated on it, and it enlarged. It was a message from Tap.

> Captain, things might seem very bad soon, and all will be lost. *Namdlo*. I have detected a concentration of the Dark One's energy near your location.

Namdlo. Aqum is under attack and we are trying to help him. We can't communicate normally because of that attack. We are not sure of its extent yet.

Aqum said that the challenge board of directors were also being attacked in some way, which is why we are experiencing exponential activity from the enemy's team.

Suggestions in the order it is received:

- Guard your thoughts.

- Rtu suggests to see if the time is 1:11.

- Leave without leaving (yes, you read that right) at the spot of the little phoenix.

Tap had been using Rhom's sacred name that he had given him to get his attention. That is why he had that odd knowing look before.

Zreyas knew about the attack but he had no idea it was that bad. He vowed to start checking this new interface a lot more often.

A prompt appeared, and it asked if he wanted to make messages from Tap show a blinking symbol automatically. He mentally said yes, and the prompt disappeared.

Then another prompt asked if he wanted to send a confirmation that the message was read to the sender. He thought '*yes, I got it, but a little too late*', then everything disappeared.

After it was done, he thought about how he had no idea what that really meant, and wondered if he had just played into one of the Dark One's tricks.

As they continued to run, he heard Ayya say as if it was in the back of his mind, "Almost there." He couldn't help but wonder about a few things in that message.

First, he pulled his thoughts out of the quantum, then he started thinking. He thought about how wise it was for Tap to use the name for the old man, and how it had worked because she was an extension of himself.

Second, his heart felt like it dropped down in his chest when he realized it had been sent before they got out of that room and he hadn't seen it.

Thirdly, he realized that he couldn't check about 1:11 because he couldn't access the quantum because of the ticking-LFO. He didn't know what Rtu was thinking. Was there something he didn't yet know?

"We're here, Captain," informed Ayya as she pointed straight up at the canopy so far up that the details of the leaves were a blur of color with light shining through.

Lanna gasped. "That is where you been climbing up to?" Appalled and in awe, she asked, "Is that where you saved the boy?"

"No, ma'am, it was over there." She pointed to a tree almost as tall but about four trees away.

All Lanna could muster was to shake her head and hold her chest.

Zreyas looked up and assessed the tree and its surroundings, not seeing how they were going to get up there as he rubbed his cheeks with his fingers and thumb. "Ayya..."

"Yes, sir?" Despite the circumstances, Ayya seemed bubbly in her tone.

He realized that this was her sacred place and why Paul bought the land, now. "Let me see, how do you get up there."

She looked at her mother and Lanna finally nodded, still in shock.

"It'll be okay, Momma, I been doing this since I was five."

"I can attest to that," confirmed Connor. "I been chasing her and Trevor here for a while now. "She gets up there differently than Trevor though. He's not as good a climber, so she made him a secret way. It takes longer but it worked for him."

Lanna looked at Connor as if his head turned into a mag-bug, and Zreyas couldn't help but chuckle.

"Go ahead Ayya," Connor encouraged.

"We don't have a lot of time." Zreyas grinned and nodded to her. "Show us one of your biggest talents."

"Yes, sir! I don't have my good shoes on but I can still do it."

"Those *are* your good shoes, Ayya," corrected Lanna.

"Not for tree-climbing." Ayya grinned and turned to face toward the tree that she said she had saved the boy from.

"I think I need to sit down," said Lanna as she lowered herself to ground.

Cerys walked over to her and sat down between she and Trevor, who seemed to be doing a little better. He would bet that with the balances as they were that Rtu made sure the boy wouldn't die.

Then Cerys smiled looking at Lanna. "Doing this is first nature for her, not second, according to Connor. In all the years she has been coming here, from what he said, she has only fallen once and that was because of a bully, *before* Paul bought the land for her."

As Lanna looked toward her daughter, following her as she broke into a run, he watched the tears stream down her face at the mention of Paul, watching Ayya.

"What... is she doing?" she said under her breath. "There are no low branches there on that tree."

"Watch her fly Lanna, I haven't seen her do this as much as Connor, but I'm glad you finally get to see this. That engineering mind of hers works constantly while she does what she loves to do. I would trust her safety doing this over riding a school bus."

That seemed to make Lanna breathe a little smoother.

Ayya passed the large tree trunk and hurled herself into the air to a smaller tree just behind it to the right. She grabbed the trunk with her curled wrists and feet like a monkey, landing right on the tree as if she had walked up vertically. She immediately launched herself upward, arms high and outstretched.

Lanna gasped as she caught the branch and then immediately, in one fluid motion, swung herself upward. She righted herself on the branch into a standing position, focusing on the huge tree ahead.

She broke into another run along that branch as if she was running on a floor. Zreyas was amazed because she wasn't using the quantum. He couldn't imagine how Lanna felt. When she got toward the end, she intentionally planted both feet on the forked part of the branch squatting. It bent stiffly under her weight. Then used it to spring herself up, launching herself upward toward the live oak tree.

Lanna yelped in horror as they all watched her sail through the air, lining her hands and feet up with two knots and a branch.

Zreyas thought any time the woman would faint, and Ayya was just getting started. As he watched her, he knew he could learn from her.

He wished Paul was here to see this, because he knew Rhom would have enjoyed watching his little phoenix. Then again, Rhom probably had seen it all many times, knowing him.

Zreyas took in a deep breath to ward off water in his eyes, and decided to watch her on an energetic level. He had seen her energy before in the tunnel, but he wanted to see her move and manipulate her intention while doing something she loved. So, he turned his new-found vision toward watching just that, and all he could do was gasp.

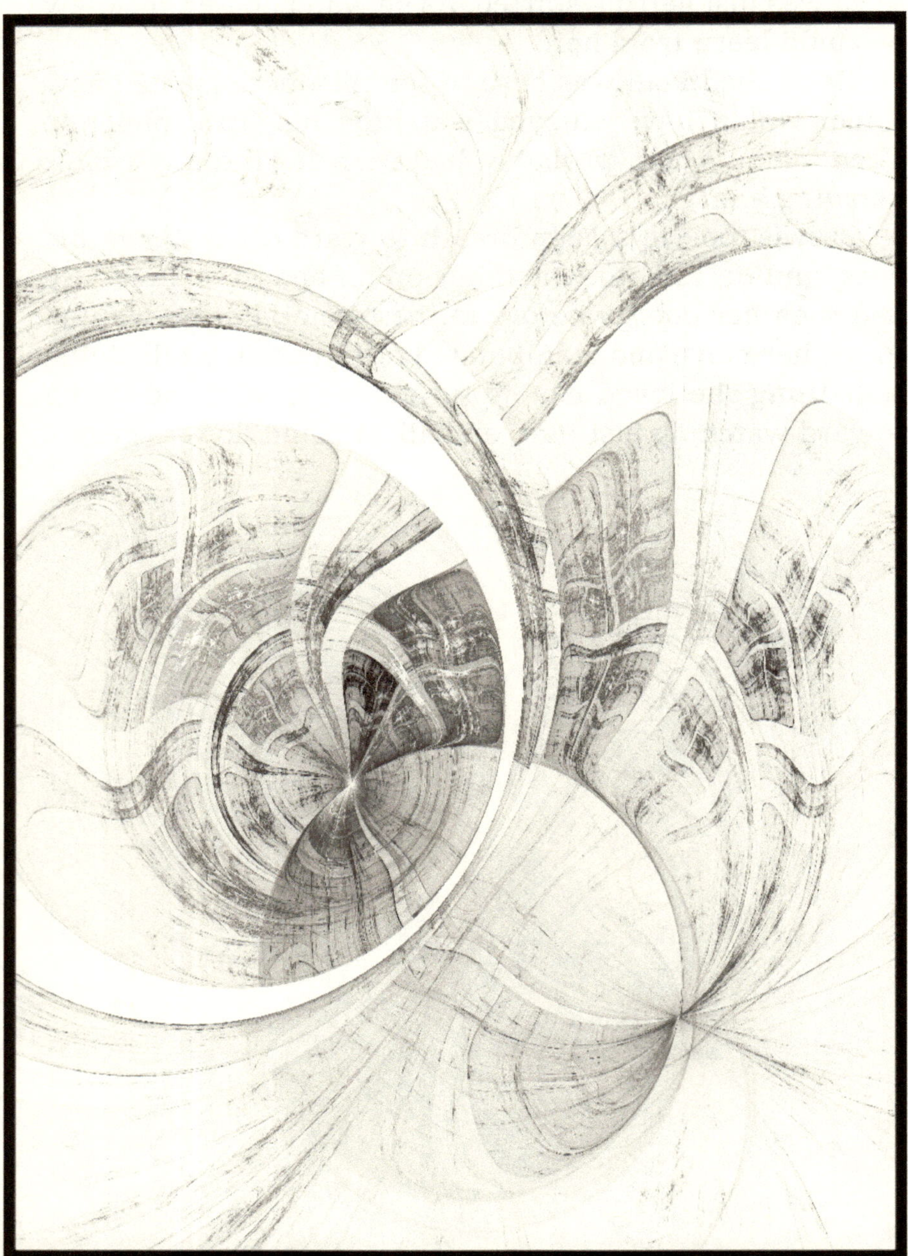

32 Inner-Authority Separation

ཀྲུ Tap ཀྲུ

Tap's hologram turned a dirty yellow watching Ayya. "Freckles, even if they all get up there. How will we get them out? With that barrier that the Dark One put up blocking all communications and teleportation to, and from, the challenge in that area."

Then they both saw a golden light come in from the corridor toward Zreyas' complex. She felt something in her body of a ship then it went away.

Rtu got up and ran down the hall. She didn't have to, but decided to follow Rtu with her hologram. He turned left into Silence and Resolute's sleeping and guard post. They weren't there. They must have been helping the crew. He opened the door to the next area where the challenge node and viewing room were, but nothing was there.

Rtu sighed and turned to walk back to the command bridge.

He wiped his eyes and sniffed. His face was red and blotchy from the tears that found their way to the surface. "It's so hard to—" He rubbed his face, took a deep breath, and let it out.

He dropped his hands to his sides and looked at her. "I need to get a hold of myself for the sake of everyone. I apologize, Tap. Rhom, our scientist and sagely adviser isn't here, and neither is Zreyas, our tactical strategist. If we don't get them out soon, we will all be grieving hard for the last days, weeks, or varSas we might have left."

Listening to Rtu was an honor, but Tap thought she might be feeling a little panic for her captain. She really would rather work on a solution, but she didn't know how to without the connection to her heart and captain.

While Rtu spoke, she would gather data about the surrounding area as much as possible. The big D.O. might have a bubble around the house and surrounding area, but it couldn't be infinite.

Tap put in several commands on as many threads of calculation as she could, to max out all of her computing power toward detection of life forms, scanning of dark frequencies, and the signatures of dimensions as she could. She could travel there using the quantum drive; but even if she did, it wouldn't put them there in time to help—besides, her captain hadn't told her to move, and Rtu hadn't either.

She discovered the multi-threaded calculations made her feel good and it seemed to comfort her in the absence of her captain. His lack of communication made her feel lost and the newer emotion of anxiety, and she didn't like that.

Tap decided that she would interrupt him. "Freckles, we need to do something. You know the balances, what do you suggest? I can attempt to communicate with Aqum again, if you wish."

"You are right..." Rtu ran his hands down his face, obviously very distraught.

Rtu wasn't used to being without leadership and neither was she. But she could detect his energy signatures and, right now, he was a mess. His visage energy was searching for something. She figured he was most likely looking for Rhom, which was understandable.

Tap decided to make her hologram the color of empathy... but it surprised her that she had no answer in her data banks for the color of empathy. Then it dawned on her to use her heart, not her data. It didn't take her long to figure out that empathy was the frequency of what she was empathizing with. She cocked her hologram head at Rtu as she detected his emotions and they fluctuated between the highest to the lower frequencies.

"The last time I checked we had the balances to do just about everything we wanted to," he finally said.

"That is a good thing, Freckles. Why do you lament so then for the others when they are still alive?"

"Because the balances are almost even now, and I don't understand why. Something is eluding me, beyond my control. I don't want to doom us all out of ignorance of the balances, tipping the scales too far."

"So that is what you are using your energy to do, feel out the balances?"

Rtu nodded. "Among other things, but yeah. I can't even find Rhom—dead or alive. If I look for my mother, I can still feel her, but not Rhom. If he is around, he's so different that I don't recognize him."

"I would like to remind you, Freckles, that he is within the bubble of that blocked area. It's so completely blocked

I can't even feel my captain and I know he is alive or I would be dead too."

"You have a point, Tap. Thank you. Du-ude! I need to pull myself together. All I'm doing is thinking what I *can't* do or feel. I need to focus on what we -can- do. I'm a visage for crying out loud, and even if I wasn't, that is good tactical advice as my little buddy would say! If I were watching him, what would he be doing?"

"Thinking Tactically, with a capital T."

"Yes! I'm just used to feeling and reacting out of instinct, because in a way, I'm part of all creation with my elements."

"Now you are thinking..." <pause> "du-u-ude."

Laughter just blurted out of him. Whatever it was she had done, it seemed to break his wall of stress.

ꙅꙅꙅ Rtu ꙅꙅꙅ

It just sounded a little weird because, being Tap, it was a little robotic to say 'dude', yet he could feel the curiosity in learning from her, but with apprehension and a *ting* of fear. She was so much like Zreyas in some ways, and he could tell she was in an ocean of confusion and anxiety.

He slapped his forehead at a realization. "Wait, you *are* Zreyas... at least part of him. What are some of your thoughts on what we could do, rather than what we can't do? He is your heart, as you once said."

Tap was silent a moment before responding. "But... my heart is my captain. He is my core and my leader. I just think and am his potential. Without him, I'm—"

"*But...* he's *not* here, nor can you contact him. He would want you to go on and do what he couldn't by proxy.

You don't have to do anything right now, just think out-loud. He gave me second command, along with my brother, until you can contact him again, I'm in command, correct?"

Tap's hologram disappeared. All of the lights on the consoles throughout the ship were blinking or fading in and out. It was as if she was malfunctioning or caught in a loop.

"Great... Now *she's* gone, too". He plopped down in a chair to think. It was the position he loved so well while he thought, created life, and ate.

"Tulyata, Rhom, and Zreyas are my personal world and now they are all gone. No offense to you, Tap, if you are listening, but I've just met you and just getting to know you. I helped create you but it's not the same... yet."

Something dawned on him like a load of bricks falling on his head, except for the pain part. He was glad of that part. "Tap... I know what you are going through. Would you like to hear what I have to say? Maybe it will help you."

After a few seconds, all the blinking stopped and Tap's hologram came into view in a weird red color that fluctuated slightly. With a static ridden voice Tap responded. "Yes, Master Rtu, I would."

Rtu blinked at how she had just addressed him. He took a deep breath, let his hand drop to the arm of his chair as he exhaled. "Tap, as you probably know, Rhom and I used to be one—"

"I didn't know that, Master Rtu."

Rtu nodded. "Try simulating me and Rhom as if it were you and Zreyas."

"Activating test simulation with real experience detail."

He looked at her at that comment, then continued. "Well, then we had to separate for balances to become who you know us to be today, sort of how you and Zreyas are right now. Right after we split, Rhom had to incarnate as a Viduri for twenty-four hundred plus.

"That part you know, but needed to state it to put it in perspective. It's kind of like how you and Zreyas are now in separation. You can't communicate or speak with each other. It's like losing half of yourself."

Different colors rippled through Tap's hologram. He might still be in distress but he was still a visage and helped make her, and he could tell she was developing empathy outside herself.

"But Rhom told me once in a very heartfelt and tough scolding I needed to hear about how we can't use each other to function in life. I will never forget it because I could feel his pain in the separation too. He told me:

> "Rtu, you can't use me either. We are separate visages now — different individuals from the same source, just like all the Janquar, Humans, Viduri, and so on. It is no different with us. In a way, we are incarnated with a different role and set of rules. Truth be told, I'm quite lost myself, but we must find our own way and live according to our own design."

"So you see, we need to live independently, but walk down life's roads together as much as we can. You might be part of Zreyas, just like I am part of Rhom, but we are still individuals and I think that is one of the hardest things an incarnate... or visage, has to learn in life. We are okay and are powerful potential by ourselves. Tap, you are more than just Zreyas."

Rtu sat back in the silence. After silence assailed the room for more time, he propped his chin on his hand and figured he needed to start thinking tactically alone. Living life as a pseudo-incarnate was difficult—He couldn't just wave a hand or a thought and make things better or worse. He began mounting up a list of things he had to work with.

    - He had a ship.

    - They were at gate forty and could move the crew through and out of the immediate range of the Dark One.

    - They knew the coordinates, sitting in Tap's data banks, to the new challenge node.—"

"Freckles..."

As he thought about his list, her hologram a dusty yellow, indicated she was unsure or worried. He looked at her.

"I want to help as an independent incarnation, but I don't want to live separate from my heart, unless I have to. My captain is my inner authority. I have calculated that I have an inner authority and voice but its purpose is to help my heart. My function is to calculate, translate, and watch to help my heart and captain. But if I have to function independently, my inner voice says it wants to help you, Master Freckles, so that you can make your decisions."

Rtu's eyes welled up with tears as he felt a warmth toward Tap, getting to know her softer side. "You are amazing Tap. You learn so fast, a lot faster than I do. Thank you for helping me. You have skills I was not born with. I'm built to create and watch those creations, though I am learning tactics slowly. Honestly, knowing my little buddy like I do, I think he would be proud of you."

Tap's color turned a beautiful greenish-blue, then transitioned to a slow oscillating purple-blue. It made him smile.

"So what do you think, shall we call in Tracker, Switch, Right, and Cree and go over some tactics? They don't understand what is going on right now but they are good and smart Janquar that Captain Zreyas loves and trusts."

"Master Rtu, I think that is a great idea." Tap immediately put out the announcement "Advisers Tracker, Switch, and Cree, Master Rtu asks that you report to the command bridge as soon as possible for an urgent meeting."

Rtu smiled at how Tap just could flip a switch and work through all she had in such a short time. She found a way to live independently but still honor her purpose and inner voice. He would be taking that lesson she had given him and using it as an inspiration.

It wasn't long and all three were running into the command room feeling the floors of the ship boom with their steps. Not surprising, considering their size and weight.

"Tap, I think you—"

"I'm already on it, Master Rtu. You should notice a difference already. Nothing but high-quality sturdiness for my captain and his crew."

Their steps became almost silent in comparison to the booming steps before.

"Thank you, Tap."

Rtu got up and said, "Well we have a council room, so let's use it. We've got a lot to talk about and we have a lot to decide in a hurry."

After an hour of discussion, going over data, trying to contact Captain Zreyas, along with the other part of himself in Dulce's body, with no success, he made his decision. After a vote, it was unanimous.

The plan was to contact the Screh in the hopes that they could go through gate forty without confrontation, and get to the planet so they could find the challenge node.

They decided to go that route in the hopes that the Dark One didn't know about that access point yet. The ship and crew would get to the node and help the group on Earth get out of their situation, and hope they would be okay and survive for that long. Sitting where they were would be certain death unless they didn't have all the facts to work with.

Without all of himself in one body, he couldn't do anything but light visage work. He was quickly losing awareness of himself and that was something he didn't like. He had been through that once before when he and Rhom separated. But if he didn't get himself back from Earth, he would cease to exist and only the incarnate form would live and lose all sense of self... basically brain dead.

As far as the Screh, he would be the spokesman, and take the risk. If they couldn't get through and help the group off Earth, all was lost anyway. They had decided they didn't want to kill the Screh or fight with them. He hoped he could explain what was going on with what little visage power he had with him.

The entire crew was ready for whatever might come. The bridge crew and Zreyas' advisory staff were there with him and Tap, except for Chief Engineer Right. He was preparing his crew and the engine room for the trip.

Rtu took a deep breath and gave the command to have Tap try and discover a frequency and language they could communicate with, whether it be through technology or through some sort of mind frequency. Rhom knew the species, as he did, but Rhom knew their language and history that was there before they were born. Without the other part of him, he couldn't tap into that. He was all but a normal incarnate in that way.

The only thing he could do is maintain his creations as they were, everything else, well... everything was limited and he was beginning to forget a lot. It alarmed him.

Before thinking about it too much he focused on speaking with Tap. "Found anything interesting or hopeful yet with communication?"

"I'm working on it, Master Rtu. I'm trying to—wait—I have a communication channel that is successful. I almost missed it. It is encrypted on both normal and quantum levels, Master Rtu. Before I could say anything, they sent a communication. I'll replay it."

> "This is the Grandmother Sheejee, grandmother of the Tragin Tribe. We have been expecting your communication, but we wanted to make sure you were worthy of our help so we buried and encrypted all our comms three times. Only those with your talents could have broken into our tribal communication. But the question is, are you worthy to speak with us."

Everyone exchanged glances in shock.

"Opening communications with Grandmother Sheejee, Master Rtu. On Screen."

33 The Screh Dimension

ოოო *Rtu* ოოო

Rtu told Tap to only include him in her view of the ship just before the screen came to life. There was a scarlet colored Screh with its fur slowly drifting around in weightless space. Her large round lidless eyes had depth and honesty about them, but also an undeniable fierceness.

Rtu bowed slightly to show respect. "Grandmother Sheejee, it is truly an honor to meet you. I have only heard about you and your tribes, but I'm afraid it is more handed down information. I am one of the two visages of the elements. But, I imagine you know this already."

She cocked her large head to look at him closer. Rtu looked into her eyes without blinking to show he was honest and sincere, but most importantly, open... truly open to see.

He knew that these tribes were ancient and fierce, but valued family and integrity over anything else. No one messed with them unless they had a death wish. Even if Zreyas, Rhom, and the rest of himself were there, they would be hard pressed to win, even with their defense system.

Finally, the grandmother spoke. "You are the one that overused his visagehood in transforming himself, then sacrificed your own power to become a warrior that fought the Heart of Odium, then helped imprison it, referred today as the Dark One."

Rtu winced as everyone in the room turned and stared at him, jaws hung. Even Tap's hologram did so.

Rtukaiah, you can do this. This is for them, not for yourself. He took a deep breath and said, "You left the parts out where I made big mistakes. In my self-pity, I accidentally created the Janquar because of my dark mood from the separation of my brother.

"I acted and did what I did for the purposes of delaying what is going on now in the hope that we could find a way to keep the Heart of Odium from wiping out my brother and all of existence."

Sheejee leaned forward, feeling like she was boring into his eyes and soul, so much so, he was paralyzed. But he expected this. This was one of the talents the Screh had, to bore into someone's soul and past events to find out truth.

The only way he could do anything for all he loved was to let her. He had been over it so many times in his mind, but he couldn't think of anything else but this to find a way to help them.

"So, the great prime visage Tulyata was killed the true-death way, yet you think she still lives. You blame yourself, and hide yourself. You don't seem like that great warrior now. How far you have fallen."

That was about all he was going to take without saying something that would clear this ugly matter up so they could move on to more important matters. "Grandmother

Sheejee, I have not fallen. I just hate violence and hurting. I've lived with the empathy of the Heart of Odium's containment all these varSas as well as all other creatures. But that is not a weakness, though I *have* made my mistakes. Trust me, I will fight again if I must to save anyone from this... thing."

He leaned forward, letting his warrior nature show to her. "No disrespect to you, but I know you honor honesty and stand for truth. Would you like to hear what I have to say, or do you want to play judge to spend time to entertain yourself?"

The Screh leader slowly smiled. "Now *that*... is what I remember of you. I will now listen to you, great warrior of the ages. You don't remember me, do you? Your transitions took a lot of memories, this I know."

Rtu squinted his eyes as he looked at her in thought. For the life of him, he couldn't remember even seeing a Screh before, much less know the grandmother personally.

Then she spoke up. "To be fair, I have changed more than you have. I wasn't quite so formidable as I am now."

He scratched and rubbed his chest as he tried to remember her. "I apologize, I do not. Maybe I will soon. We are short on time. Why were you expecting us? Forgive my suspicious nature right now but we are up against quite the deceiver with very low frequency yan. We are all masters of deception, though most of the time we don't know we are doing it. That is not the deception I'm speaking about.

"The one called Aqum is the extension of the one that said that Zreyas o—"

— This is an Aqum interruption — we say with urgent inflections — we are back only briefly to tell you that our council has been compromised and influ—

Rtu held up a finger. "I apologize, one minute Grandmother Sheejee. You might be interested to hear this as well because it is part of what we need to discuss. Go ahead, Aqum."

The ancient leader leaned forward.

"Go ahead."

A hologram appeared to represent Aqum.

Tap's hologram suddenly turned orange with static waves running through it. Just before she spoke, Rtu distinctly heard fighting in the background and someone he didn't know in the distance saying, 'get the blue and cyan one.'

Tap's hologram turned a sick color green. "Master Rtu, Aqum just hacked me! I'm trying to rectify it but he has disabled my attempts."

Everyone in the room jerked, then froze. He supposed it was because they had no idea what Tap was talking about, being that they were Janquar and just learning technology.

— Aqum is saying with exclamations and urgency — we are not hacking you for bad intentions. We tell you in secrecy that we did this so the Dark One couldn't track Aqum. We are in danger too, and ask to come aboard. We have released all control back to you, and ask you to verify.

"You could have just asked, Aqum," a little anger welling up in Rtu.

— Request from us to you that you accept apologies. — Saying with pleading tones — We were literally a few seconds from being compromised permanently. It was not easy to move our body. We request with pleading emotions that we stay aboard now that our body and node is safe because we wish to help.

"Oh, no, Aqum," said Rtu. "Is there anything we can do to help?

— Aqum says with touched feelings — We are safe and still helping the multiverse survive — with emotions of gratitude — you already have, and we ask that we can stay aboard till we find a new home and we will help you as much as we can.

How did Aqum know that? He was gone from the talks and had no way of knowing. Rtu felt like he was losing his mind way too fast to be healthy for what they had to do. Maybe he just didn't have his head on straight from the separation from himself for so long with the capacity he gave his last form.

"Master Rtu, he did release full power back to me. Thank you, Aqum. I understand why you did what you did."

There were now *three* Screh watching. Rtu figured she had something of an advisory team listening in as well. He would not reveal his for now because Janquar were a touchy subject.

Rtu turned toward Zreyas' advisers. "I could make a decision, but I would like to keep the captain's way of working alive and ask his team of choice what they think and advise."

They spent the next few minutes getting input and exchanging ideas. Ultimately it was a unanimous decision to let Aqum stay and work with them in safety. After all, Aqum had been helping all along from the beginning.

After that, Tap gave Aqum full control of their avatar hologram with limited access, just like any other crew member, but let them still have full control to use their access link to their own systems and encrypted connections in the same room as the challenge node. Tap explained that it was a nested dimension one layer deeper than it was before.

A deliberate clearing of a throat resounded in the room. Before Rtu could turn around and properly apologize to the Grandmother Sheejee, Aqum beat him.

— Aqum is saying with high apologetic tones and sincerity — We hope to not take up any more of your time with organization issues. We want you to know, it is important, even to you. We request that you listen to the Master Rtu and his reasons why we have been a little rude on our behalf.

That seemed to satisfy the grandmother because her features relaxed. "We know something is wrong, but we don't know the details. Why are you contacting us and what is it you want?"

Rtu was silent for a few seconds to gather his thoughts. "Grandmother Sheejee, we—"

"Just Sheejee is fine; after all, we used to be friends."

He had no idea what she was talking about but let it go. "Sheejee... we don't want anything from you. We just want to pass through this gate my brother and I created for passage through the new energetic channels to get us to safety.

"We hope to create a base of operations to try and save several of our critical team, along with the other part of myself, from a very critical situation on Earth. It's important that we do, because without them involved in the effort to defeat the Dark One with the damage it is doing, the multiverse is lost. The frequencies are *way* out of balance."

"I see... that explains a lot." She looked as if she was communicating with the two advisers, one a brilliant purple, and the other a dull, but beautiful, orange.

He couldn't understand them and began to wonder if he was losing power. It could also be his lack of experience with the Screh. He didn't create them and they were around long before he was born to succeed his predecessor.

She turned back to Rtu and seemed to sit just by the motion she was making with her body, though it was hard to tell with the solid black background behind her. "Tell us what you know, and perhaps we can help. Or, feel free to move through the gate without doing so."

Rtu looked back to all the others.

They all nodded.

Then he faced the Leader of the Screh. "We will tell you all you want to hear, but keep in mind we are under time constraints."

"You are not. When you created the communication, you entered a dimension that is timeless for two days, two hours, and twenty-two minutes in Vidurian time, so relax."

"Would you be offended if we said we wanted to verify that? There is too much at stake."

"I would be disappointed if you didn't, dear friend."

Her advisers nodded, their fur gently wafting about.

Rtu turned and faced Tap, who was now green and slowly turning a shade of blue. Her avatar nodded. "Master Rtu, from all my readings, everything points to no progress in time. Aqum, would you like to confirm or deny this as well?"

Rtu smiled knowing Tap was trying to show Aqum they were accepted as a part of the team.

— Aqum says with readings, reason, and acceptance — Creation doesn't progress in this location — We are agreeing with the Tap entity.

"Thank you Sheejee for the time to verify. Tap, can you have Engineer Right bring some refreshments prepared by the kitchens and let him know we need him to stay. He is one of the captain's advisers. Update him on the way, quietly."

Tap seemed to almost glow in a purple color, clearly happy about what she was doing and how things were going. "Yes, Master Rtu, I'm in a... joy to do this." She split into two holograms and one raced off in a blurr.

Rtu chuckled, feeling relief to laugh again. He wasn't used to being serious all the time, or having to lead.

Pointing to the larger purple Screh to her right, Sheejee introduced her advisers. "This is my daughter, Sheeja, my heir to lead our family when I am gone. And this is my other daughter, Katja, my military trainer, aid, and third in command."

"It is an honor to meet you both, Sheeja and Katja."

"And before you ask, yes there is a naming convention in our culture."

Rtu took a deep breath and continued. "I would like to introduce Captain Zreyas' advisers, but I ask you to wait to hear what we have to say before any reactions. Please trust me, they are quite amazing."

"You have my word." Then her daughters gave a single nod.

Just then, Engineer Right entered with a tray, put it down on a table that Tap created, then sat down by the other two Janquar.

"Tap, expand the view to include all of us."

When she did, all three of the Screh's heads jerked backward a slight bit, their fur straightening a moment from the movement. But to their credit, they still kept their composure and their hair went back to the slow lofty movement of no gravity. However, Sheejee immediately said with an edge, "You best explain... *them* first."

Rtu still had enough power left in him to know that the three Janquar behind him were confused by the comment. They began moving their chairs next to him in reaction to his hand gesture instructions to form a semi-circle.

He turned to the Screh, and took a deep breath. "Captain Zreyas had a strategic vision..."

34 Alliance

Rtu

The grandmother sat back and fluctuated in a ripple while she thought about all they had told her.

When Rtu looked at the three Screh, he couldn't help but fall in love with them. They were beautiful, graceful, and strong.

"You speak the truth, this I know. That out of the way, we will be helping you." The powerful leader leaned forward; the expression on her face transformed into that of an angry warrior.

It was clear to Rtu why these tribes were still thriving, yet feared. He felt sheer terror rise up in his gut getting caught up in her gaze. and it wasn't even for him specifically. Familiarity of something came back to him from the past, and it occurred to him that their tribes were the patrolling defense of the multiverse.

"We cannot let this Dark One succeed. Katja will coordinate getting the messengers dispatched to the other tribes we know the general locations of. We don't know where all our tribes are since we are nomadic. However, they will know of some that we don't and in turn do the same."

"We thank you for not only allowing us through, but also helping. Now that you know what our plan is, is there anything we can do to help you?"

The grandmother looked at them gravely. "That plan of yours is flawed."

"That is true, but it was all we could come up with that seemed feasible to be so far away." The stress that Rtu was feeling was beginning to get to him. He sat back and exhaled. It was one thing to fight for a cause when your actions didn't involve so many people, but yet another when it did... or did it? His past wasn't helping him right now and it frustrated him.

"It is not because your thinking was flawed, dear friend. The problem is because you don't know what is through that gate. We are space and quantum beings, but we don't use the same type of quantum skills you or your Captain Zreyas are accustomed to."

Sliding forward in his seat, now both fascinated and curious. "I'm excited to hear what you have discovered if you are willing to share."

Sheejee nodded. "First, I need to send Katja off to get the messengers dispatched so that we can connect our communications for this war. This is significant. We are smaller family tribes, but in times like this, if two or more tribes are of the same cause, we can invoke the Tookna-Connection. We didn't even use it during the last fight against the Heart of Odium. This should tell you how important this war is to the Screh."

"It is critical we waste no time then." He felt like his guts were scrambled, and wanted to get out of the body he was in and become his natural self. But that was not possible. Those on the ship needed him there.

Katja nodded to her mother, then turned to Rtu and the crew. "In order to waste no time with multiple communications, we would like to ask the consent to send a qunta-message with the recording of this meeting with our dispatched messengers."

Engineer Right spoke, curiosity tinting his tone. "If we can't get several universes away with the highest technology quantum ship ever known, how will you?"

The grandmother grinned. "I like this one, even if it is a Janquar."

Tracker stood and executed the Order of the Sleeping Phoenix salute. Then continued with obvious effort not to blow up. "I understand your limited optimism for the Janquar. We understand why you don't have it—we have *lived* the life of their treatment of others. But, I remind you, that none of us are more or less than you. Captain Zreyas taught us that. It would not be healthy to see us as otherwise because it jeopardizes the team of choice we are creating."

Tracker took a step forward, and with an edge to his voice said, "You want truth? You have just put Master Rtu through the torture of your scrutiny for hours, just like the Janquar Nation would, and you *knew* him before. You *know* he is a visage, yet you still did it. We have given you the honor and respect you deserve. Enough is enough. You are welcome to bore into my mind and life if you want to see the truth and what choices and sacrifices all of our crew have made. In fact, I won't vote to continue with this team of scrutiny if you don't."

Rtu raised an eyebrow as he crossed his arms and turned to see the reaction of the Screh, a very proud species with notorious history.

All three Screh squinted their eyes in a focus. Then Sheejee whispered venomously. "I accept your invitation to relive your life. Sit, or you might hurt something. I will get every truth out of you that your body can hold. Your arrogance will be the cause of your suffering."

"So be it," said Tracker as he straightened his back and held the salute of the new order.

Rtu was filled with empathy for Tracker. He didn't fear for his life, but there were worse things to suffer than his own death... especially for Tracker. He knew he would relive everything just as if he was living it for the first time all over again, except with the anticipation of what was coming. That anticipation is like a torture device that could break him in ways that the first experience would never have the chance to.

Then something happened that surprised Rtu and the pissed off Screh. Cree, Switch, and Engineer Right all stood up and stood around their brother, putting a hand on him in silence. They had learned enough from Zreyas and the visages to know that touching involved consent and unity.

Cree spoke first. "Me too, and I will both support and lean on my brother."

Switch added, "Me too, my brothers will not stand alone."

Engineer Right stood behind Tracker and laid both hands on each shoulder of the two and said nothing. It was clear he was all in.

The three Screh looked both angered and... was that a hint of respect? Then the truth-relive commenced.

"It is finished."

All of the advisers steadied each other and worked their way back to their chairs, sitting proudly together.

Rtu smiled with tears in his eyes. He swallowed, then with a cracking voice said, "The captain will know about what you did. Though he already is, I'm sure he will be just as proud to know you as I am right now."

All of the advisers held their head high with heavy swallows moving through their throats, but they never said a word.

Then Sheejee cleared her throat and bowed her head. "We thank you for enduring that. We have discovered something incredibly valuable. These... blue, as Captain Zreyas called them, are descendants of... No matter, the past doesn't help us now. But I will say to the captain's advisors, thank you for all you have done for the multiverse, even if you don't know what it is."

Rtu didn't make an announcement. He knew that the information would filter through the crew fast enough. "Tap, in case I don't make it through this, please make sure the captain knows what happened here today."

"I will Master Rtu. Captain Zreyas will be very proud of his advisors... and you."

"We have special scouts that have a gift. I don't have a word that you would understand in your language. But it is a large-area-scanning of no-seeing sight, and it is interesting what they found in this... channel, as you call it. It has a life of its own connected to creation."

"We call that a sampling aura," added Rtu. "But it sounds like this gift is much larger in range. Rhom and I noticed it when we put the gate in."

"You would be correct in how large it is. And this Gate's discovery, and the one on the other side, is what drew us to it. It was the first place we have ever found in our history that enhanced our tribal family in many ways at once. We digest better. Since we don't often eat, it is incredibly valuable."

"Interesting, can you tell me more?" asked Rtu.

"The energy of that gate when we go inside its channel, allows our family members to enjoy the digestion alone and we are able to finally rest, yet still allows for other benefits that our tribe enjoys. Since we have been here, our tribe has grown stronger because our individual members have bolstered in strength and vitality."

Cree observed out-loud with apprehension in his voice. "Though it might affect us differently, that doesn't *sound* like a bad thing. What is the part to be wary of?"

Sheejee opened her mouth as if she was going to start explaining, but then she closed it. Rtu felt humor radiate from her insides. Even with most of himself on Earth right now, closed off, he could still sense like a visage.

Then she resumed. "Let's just say our scouts report the further in we go, during the times the other side is open, it really strengthens our... community interactions. But remember, just like this gate attracted us, the other gate or gates you install in the future will attract others."

Rtu considered that. "Good point, Grandmother. That could be good and bad."

"We have also found our tribal interactions have altered some. Because we are connected, the things that our scouts have experienced we have too, remotely. We now bargain with each other and have opened up to talking to outsiders... like you."

Rtu propped his elbow up on his fist and rested his right cheek in his hand. "Fascinating." Somehow, he knew that was a precursor. "So... what is it you want? That was a segue into something else."

"You are still as perceptive as ever. I want to strike a bargain with you. We are drawn to, and thrive, in the gates you put in. It enhanced the energy of these places. Honestly, we are committed and... addicted to these two gates. Katja has been to the other side working with her scouts."

Rtu scrunched his brow in confusion wondering where this was going because he didn't know the Screh that well.

He stood and went over to lean on the captain's station to indicate that time was growing short, despite still being in their timeless communication.

"Listen, this will benefit you more than it will us, but we still consider this a fair bargain because of what we get out of it." Sheejee paused a moment as if she was hearing something.

Katja spoke to her mother, though they couldn't hear anything on their end.

No one on the bridge said a word, they all just watched.

Finally, Sheejee turned and addressed them. "An apology is in order. We were making life altering plans for our tribe and that takes a lot more time now that we bargain more. But we don't want to bargain so much with each other anymore, we would rather turn it into something that will benefit both us and outsiders."

Sheejee paused and Sheeja, her heir, put a hand on her shoulder. The grandmother nodded.

Sheeja faced them and spoke. "This is difficult for our mother, yet she saw the wisdom of breaking old ways. We want to help, but we also want to make our home here and not be nomadic anymore and create a capital for our Race. When our numbers strengthen, then we will break a tribe off and let them go to wander and protect."

"We are listening, but forgive us, we need to prepare for a departure at the same time. Right, we need you to get your engineering crew ready to depart. You can still listen in on what is going on here, but remember it is council business."

"Yes, Master Rtu, right away!" Right gave his salute and jogged out of the room.

"This is what we will do. I will list them in short for you and then we can talk more about each one to save time. Sound good to you?"

Rtu nodded. "Perfect!"

Sheejee straightened her back. "I will start with what we will do. We will divide our tribe into two families, but will operate as an overall tribe of two teams—half will go to the opposite gate, grandmothered by my daughter Katja and whoever she chooses as her second."

Rtu flipped his hand over conversationally. "That would be gate thirty-seven, and ironically enough, we nicknamed it the gate of family because it not only had the energy of family and community but it is the galaxy that we are going to be putting our base of operations in... our chosen family."

"Interesting, indeed... anyway, the gate forty side will be grandmothered by my heir Sheeja. I will still oversee them all. It will allow me to be more strategic in this time of war and interact with the other tribes while our family, as a whole, becomes stronger while they work, doing what they will be doing for the effort."

Everyone in the group nodded their heads in agreement. It was strategic and a great way to manage things. Then he couldn't help but coax her on. "That sounds very strategic... and?"

"Those that go to the family gate will bargain for us, because they are more open to outsiders and feeling more friendly. We will bargain for you too if you so need our services any time, without the need for further bargaining. Both gate tribes will defend your new home. Those on the gate forty side will also do the work to obtain, execute, and deliver, the things needed for the bargains.

"Both sub-families of the gates will exchange members as needed to make sure our line is strong. In times of war, we will cease to mate and use our males to fight."

"That sounds like a good bargain for all of us." Feeling the pressure of getting things started, he added, "We have less than one day and three hours till this communication dimension expires. We need to get going while we still have time on our side. Is that possible to do while still in your communication dimension?"

"I'm not done," Sheejee said with a firm tone.

Rtu exhaled and nodded in resignation.

"Whether you agree to the full bargain or not, we will allow you through, and in addition, all the previously mentioned if you will allow us to stay in your gates in peace."

Rtu's eyebrow rose feeling suspicion and curiosity rising inside. This was all so serious and it was beginning to get to him. He wanted to crack a joke, but refrained.

After a short pause, she continued. "In exchange, we would like to stay more educated about what is going on so we can protect our own and the Order.

"To do that, I would like to have three of our own work with you and have the ability to report back. Two would be in the galaxy in your base of operations, and one would be on your crew. We have several that have grown mature enough to thrive in atmosphere.

"I will warn you though, their size will change in atmosphere. They are free to live and choose as your people would. That enables them to understand what it is like in your culture, but also free of charge."

"Are you sur—"

"In addition," she interrupted, "I would like to remind you that we are bound and committed to truth. So, when I say, that it will all be done with secrecy so that your base and family are safe, then you know I am speaking our truth and integrity. We only ask that once every eleven varSas those three will be allowed to go back to the gates to mate and feed if they wish, bad timing or not."

Rtu looked to each side of him to the others.

Tracker spoke up. "What of your numbers? This could get out of hand and prevent travel in the future. How large will you allow your tribe to get before you create a new tribe?"

"Wise question, Tracker Janquar."

"Just Tracker is fine. I don't want to be associated or mistaken for the other Janquar."

"Again... wise. Once our numbers replenish from the last few centuries, to about one half again more than we have now, then we will start gathering qualified starters to live and wait outside this gate in preparation until they have at least eleven—a grandmother and ten others; two different aged males, and the rest females."

"This gate is called the Deliverance gate," informed Switch. "It is an appropriate name for us all it seems. I suggest that Master Rtu negotiate for this bargain because it seems fair and good for both groups."

Over the course of the next few minutes more questions were asked and answered, but ultimately, Rtu agreed to the bargain and had Tap help make it official in the records for both parties.

Rtu gave the order to approach the gate but hold just before going through, taking advantage of the timeless period they had left. "Who will be going with us? We need to get them on the ship. Have them come out. Tap can make a room for them all and carry the second tribe through."

"I will do that right away, Master Rtu. I can expand it to the size we need based on who you send, Grandmother Sheejee."

"There is only need for three spots. The others can move through physically on their own." She paused a moment. "On second thought, we have not chosen them all yet, but if you are willing to take those that have been chosen, then it would save their strength for the mating that will happen soon because we don't know when that other side will open again."

Tap flickered between several colors. "The no-atmosphere room on the ship has been created with a teleporter so they don't have to be subjected to atmosphere, Master Rtu."

Sheejee inclined her head. "Thank you, Tap of The Potential."

Katja then spoke. "I will be your crew member after we get settled on the other side."

The other two Screh both jerked their heads around to look at Katja in shock, fur radically moving.

"My sister Starnju will be acting grandmother of my family tribe in my stead while I'm out of communication range. She is as strong as I am. I am more of a wanderer and I will serve my family better doing what I am born to do. In addition, I would like to train under this Captain

Zreyas I have heard so much about. I have spoken, and so it shall be."

Sheeja nodded in agreement to Katja. "I hope you know how valuable a crew member you now have."

"As you have a valuable family here, she will also be learning from our amazing captain and crew, new Grandmother Sheeja," returned Rtu.

He and new *Great* Grandmother Sheejee instinctively recited together, "Good bargain," followed by a mutual nod.

Without a word, they watched the flow of Screh racing toward them. It was breathtaking to see all the swimming vibrant colored long bodies and flowing hair swarm toward them peacefully. Two of them had the extra set of arms that denoted males. One of the males looked like a child version. The rest were various colored females.

There were a lot more of them than Rtu expected. It was okay because the gates and channels were huge. "Please have your people nod yes if they are going to the gate, and no if they will be working for us. Tap, those that are going to the gate to live, let them in the new room. Those that are going to be working with us, we need a pledge, according to the rules Captain Zreyas instated. We will sort their jobs out later when we have time."

"Yes, Master Rtu, doing that now."

One by one, the Screh that came to the ship either nodded that they were for the gate or shook their head. In the end he knew why there were only two that were working for them out there.

Rtu looked up to the screen waiting for Katja's attention. Apparently, they had been saying their goodbyes, twirling their bodies in flowing spirals upward in messaging motions. Rtu could only put one hand on his chest and breathe at the beautiful sight.

When they stopped, Katja looked straight at Rtu and bowed. "My people will nod as their pledge since they have no way to communicate to you where they are in a way you would understand being in no atmosphere. Is this agreeable to you?"

Rtu nodded. "It is."

"I, Katja, and my two comrades, pledge our lives to serve in the Order of the Sleeping Phoenix under Captain Zreyas who stands for teams and families of choice."

The two waiting outside the ship nodded curtly.

"I also pledge that everything that happens will be relayed to the Great Grandmother Sheejee of our tribes in encrypted secrecy in the mode of your choice to educate and inform our home tribe."

Again, the two outside nodded.

"And one last pledge that I make for myself, the others can choose to do the same or not. I pledge that the members of the crew of The Potential are accepted as my new family, now and for life, though I will forever love and hold my foundational family close to my heart. I do this because anything worth doing is only worth doing if I fully commit my truth, loyalty, love, and protection for both my families."

The other two outside the ship looked at each other, turned toward the gate where the new Great Grandmother most likely was, and bowed. Then they turned toward the ship and nodded.

Rtu, trying to honor the new leaders, looked up to the newly arisen *Great* Grandmother Sheejee with tears stinging and filling his eyes. He bowed his head slightly. "We will not take your sacrifice for granted, Great Grandmother Sheejee of the Tragin tribes. Tiny particles of mist floated from her eyes into the no-gravity room as she nodded.

Then Rtu looked to the new leader. "I accept your sacred pledges, Grandmother Katja."

Katja watched her mother leave the room, then said, "You can always talk with my mother directly. Just let me know and we will create the communication space if we don't have something already created."

"All of you are granted access to the ship. Tap will teleport you, Katja. She will also set up communications between that room and us."

Katja nodded and left the room on the screen.

As they watched her race toward the ship, Sheeja spoke. "Thank you, Great Warrior and Visage, for helping our people and allowing us to live out our evolving design as a species. It is difficult for Mother, but to her credit and wisdom, she is the one that brought up the new plan after observing us living here with our changes.

"My mother is the strongest of *all* the Screh because of that. I'm glad she has your friendship. Don't forget her. She has needs too. Whether you remember her or not, you are her friend and she has missed you."

Rtu smiled warmly with empathy and a few more tears. "You three have just changed the course of history for you and other species. Sheejee's heir is as wise as the now great grandmother. I know you will guide your people well."

Sheeja smiled gently with a familiar strength Rtu couldn't put his finger on, then tipped her head.

The entire room bowed slightly in their Order's salute without prompt.

35

The Boat & River

Rtu

"All of the Screh are on the ship, Master Rtu, but they are not used to being in a ship with walls around them so I made the walls clear so it would seem like they were out in space."

"That is one of the reasons why I love you, Tap, you are thoughtful about working with others' needs without going overboard," complimented Rtu.

"I also have a screen up so you can watch and speak to them if you like, Master Rtu."

"Very good." Rtu looked around the room a bit nervous about having to fly Tap. Typically, Rhom did that kind of thing. "Everyone ready? It might get bumpy with me driving."

Everyone seemed a little nervous by the way they stiffened and held on to chairs, but they nodded.

"Tap, open the comms to the ship. I would like to make an announcement."

"Right away, Master Rtu."

A higher mid-tone sounded briefly, followed by a lower mid-tone sound, then Tap's purple hologram nodded as a silent prompt for him.

"This is Master Rtu. We are about to enter the gate of deliverance to our new base home. Though we still need to wait for the weather for the other gate to open, this is the first time in history anyone has ever used a gate like this. I want you to know I'm very proud of all of us in adapting to the changes we have had to make. We now have an alliance with the Screh and they are now part of the Order of the Sleeping Phoenix family."

Cheers erupted on the command bridge and through the corridors.

"Though we are up against a lot, our family is growing. The Great Grandmother of the Tragin tribe will contact the other remote tribes to gain more support for our cause to help the multiverse survive, and they may have a way to assist us in extraction of the captain and his team."

The cheers that erupted from that were deafening. He noticed that the Screh in the ship grimaced at the shock of the vibration of the sound.

He turned to Sheeja. "Are they okay?"

"We are relaying what is being said through our existing communication dimension. It is the way we communicate with or without atmosphere. They are fine. We appreciate your concern for the tribe."

"One last thing. We are all equal in this new adventure. We just have different roles. This role I am in is temporary until we can get the captain back. It will probably be a bumpy ride, but I'm doing my best. This is your first genuine test of working together. I know you will all do fine..." Rtu sighed, and had to release some of the tension now that the talks were over. "Du-ude, Master Freckles sitting down... and out."

Everyone buckled into their seats. Though a few were empty, they had made arrangements to compensate to get things done.

"I don't mind saying I'm sure wishing the captain was here giving me a squeaky ear, but we will make do. Take us to the gate and approach it straight on."

Silence and Resolute walked into the room and both sat on each side of Rtu.

"Master Rtu. Mother is not here, but we will give you the same support as we would him. We are all an extension of him. I will sing my song for us all. Resolute would like to roar your song with me to help?"

Sheejee came back into view, standing beside Sheeja. "Good luck to us all." After a brief pause while she seemed to watch the ship, infatuated, she continued. "I'll keep the timeless communication open until you go through the gate. We have discovered that inside the, what you call, the channel, time is suspended unless you are moving."

"That is correct. Your scouts are exceptional. It is how my brother designed the gates to compensate for the fluctuations of the weather of the channels since it might be the equivalent of many varSas before they appear again."

Soft bluish-white light began extending toward them until the entire ring of the gate had a connection around the ship.

"Tap, let the gate do the work. Don't fight it."

"Yes, Master Rtu. This is what you might call a little scary for me to let something else have control of our potential."

"It's not controlling your potential. Tap, trust me. It's carrying you *with* your potential to help you get through to the next place you want to go, which is potential as well."

Then Tracker said, "Like a boat carrying us up a river with less effort, but we chose to take the journey?"

Rtu nodded downward as he said, "Exactly! Tap, we tested this with another ship, remember? Though admittedly, I was in my full visage-hood then. It seems more invigorating now that I am more limited. Let's enjoy the ride! I'm all for having fun."

Tap's hologram turned a shade of brownish yellow-orange. "Yes, fun. I will note that this is… fun."

— Aqum is saying with empathetic tones — yes, this is… fun, Tap. This is living, yes?

Tap's hologram went from her normal figure to a sign that had three dots.

As Silence started the tones of his inner song, Rtu chuckled at the thought of everyone being in such a new situation no matter what the species, including Tap and Aqum.

Resolute started a deep resonating purr joined in with Silence in syncopated long beats. It was totally captivating to him and the others in the room swayed to the rhythms and tones. All the Janquar crew started adding grunts to it, giving it grounding.

Then Rtu took in a sharp breath as he felt the gate secure the ship. "Everyone sit back or lie down. Here… we-e… go-o!"

A waterfall-like roar ripped through the ship and reality seemed like it was about to lift them off. Then it halted. All screens went black.

Everyone went silent.

After a minute, Tap lit up and came into view. "Master Rtu. I would like to report that we have successfully entered the gate and are traveling through the energetic channel of deliverance."

Cheers erupted throughout the ship loud enough they all heard on the command deck. Tap had apparently opened the channels so everyone could hear her announcement. He was glad because he was more of a responder than an initiator. He didn't know what he would do if they lost Zreyas and Rhom. He could deal with losing the bigger part of himself, but he wasn't sure he could handle losing the team down there. Then again, if they lost them, it was all over anyway.

— Saying with informing tones — We will approach the dock of suspension in approximately thirty-three minutes, if time were rolling.

"Thank you Aqum for your information, and for working with Tap."

— Aqum says in welcoming inflections — you're welcome.

"Tap get everyone ready and on standby for what we need to get done after we exit the next gate. If it is as quick as it was to launch through the gate to get here, it should be relatively fast. And we need to get those coordinates ready for the challenge node. We need to head straight there so we can try to rescue the captain and team."

"Yes, Master Rtu. It is a good time to plan."

— Aqum says with alarming tones — now that we have more information to your plans, we have some bad news.

Rtu felt the panic rip through him and the exhaustion of yet another thing wrong. He wiped his face with his hand and let his hand drop. "Please tell me this bad news."

— Aqum says with an apologetic tone - When Captain Zreyas found out about claiming the node, he didn't know if they would compromise the node or another party.

"Smart thinking... and?"

— Our words are deflated — In an attempt to be safe, he locked the node from any operation except for himself until he unlocked it.

The entire room groaned.

As Rtu thought about it, as upset as he felt, he realized it was a very smart move on the captain's part because they didn't know who was involved, in nature or part of this war.

"As inconvenient as it is right now, what the captain did was actually very strategic. He had our safety in mind, and we still have Aqum, even if we don't have the node functional due to compromised communications."

— Aqum is informing you with an optimistic tone — we are working on a solution to reactivating the node with better security — we are also informing you that due to the changes in balance, there may or may not be new rules that may or may not benefit your cause.

Switch palmed his forehead and sighed. "I may or may not want to pound your hologram's head for that information."

"Ha!" Tracker punched Switch in the arm. "That was worth 'Ha'-ing about. Something good is about to happen. My tracking skills smell it."

Rtu chuckled. It was good to see a glimpse of the old artisan back again. He might be called Tracker now, but he would always be the artisan inside that he got to know by watching Zreyas with him.

"Well, I need to go help prepare for when we get through the gate, then I will be back, unless you need me to do something, Master Rtu."

"I don't need anything now, Tracker. In fact, all of you should. The only thing I need right now is peace and quiet to think. Thank you."

All of them nodded, saluted, and left the room quietly, except for Switch, punching Tracker back and both laughing once more before they disappeared out of sight.

He missed those days of being carefree. That was why he didn't want Zreyas to be pushed into leadership by giving him this ship. A part of a person died to make room for the part that would grow out of necessity to do what they needed to do. It was all good, too—just different. After he thought about it, no matter what a person chose to do in life... a part of that person had to give way to what new part would emerge.

Right now, like it or not, he was doing the same thing. He liked what Tracker had said. 'Something good is about to happen' and that would be his new mantra for the rest of his life... however long it would be. "Something good is about to happen... something great is about to happen. Something... pheno-mi-tastic is about to happen."

Rtu started laughing at how bubbly it made him feel to put that out there. It was the hope they all needed, not just him.

He pressed the comms button and talked to the crew and its Screh passengers. "I want to tell you something Tracker just said... 'Something great is about to happen.' I would like to add—no matter what happens, even if something bad happens... there is *always* something great coming around the corner... just look for it... expect it."

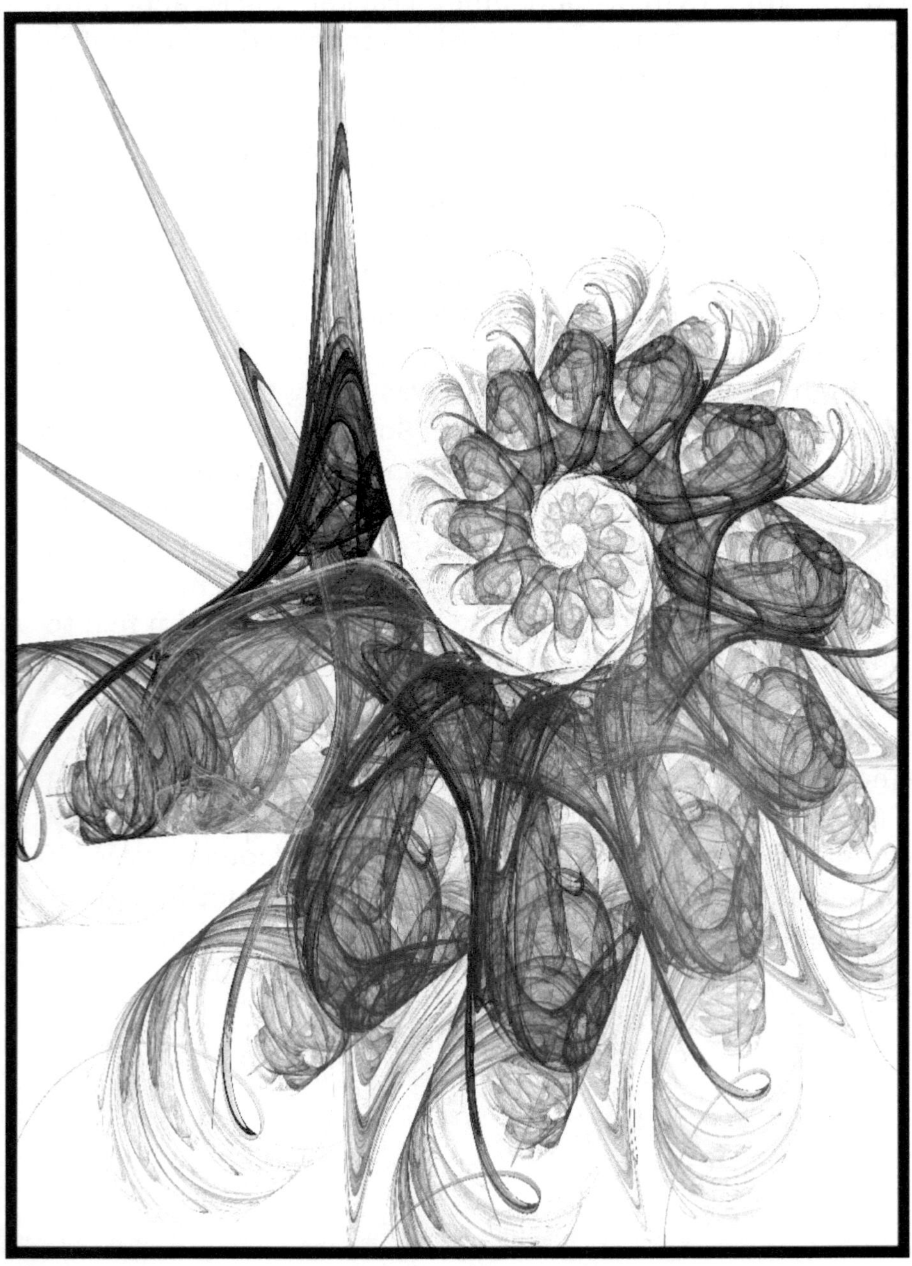

36   Rok, Paper, Shatter

Rtu

Once Rtu cleared all the docking procedures, he had Tap open the doors for the Screh that had been riding with them. Through the windows of the command deck, it was like letting out an array of colorful, elongated, flowing confetti. It brought Rtu a little relief and solace to watch them for a few minutes.

They didn't go far though, because the weather for the other half of the channel hadn't come in yet. There was no telling when it would, but he felt its energy. There seemed to be a pressure to go in, despite it not being there. For a moment, it tempted him to just do a quantum jump through.

He chuckled at himself, remembering that time didn't progress while they were stationary. It was a perfect opportunity to plan and look over data they had attained from when they discovered the channels.

"Tap, did you and Rhom build a holographic map of the planet we are headed to, and where the node is on that planet yet?"

"Only a partial one, Master Rtu. We were generating it when the weather changed in the channel. Would you like me to show you what we could generate?"

"Yes, I would."

As she pulled up the 3D hologram, Rtu barely noticed it, even though he fixed his gaze on it. He couldn't get his mind off his brother. It was like Rhom was calling out to him, but he had no idea where he was. The larger half of himself was calling out to him, too.

Being a challenge form for so long had made him grow used to being in a body and its limitations. When he signed up to teach as Dulce, he had no idea he would be down there for so many Earth years between Dulce and Ms. Josephine. When he went down as a paramedic at the firehouse, he didn't put as much of himself into that form.

That dimensional communication block was slowly detaching the other part of himself, and he was sure that was the Dark One's intention. It was like that thing knew what Zreyas had planned before they did it, every step of the way.

He grieved for himself and the others. He didn't want to end up being the captain of that ship when it wasn't made for him. He now understood, at least in part, what it was like for Zreyas to have something like this thrown into his lap with almost no real choice but to pick it up and run with it for the sake of others. An expounded respect grew within him for his little buddy.

He decided he was doing it for Zreyas and all the work he had put into building what he had established—it was mind-boggling. Rtu reminded himself that something great was about to happen. Then he smiled and looked at the hologram of the partial planet.

"There seems to be wavy weather in that system, Master Rtu. It's almost like the solar system is still developing, yet already established too. Master Rhom and I were talking about this in his lab."

"Everything about this whole new fracturing and the Dark One mess is wavy. I have decided they are unrelated... but the Dark One sure is using the fracturing to his advantage. I mean, it *did* release him."

Tap was silent a moment, then finally said, "Master Rtu, Aqum and I agree."

"So, let's look at this beautiful 3D model you have here."

Only one quarter of the planet's surface had been rendered, mostly the interior, rather than the outside. After taking some time to look at it, he understood why.

— Saying with apologetic intonation as we interrupt thoughts and collaboration — We can explain some of this if you would like. — In order to save us, we had to take liberties we didn't think we would have to take. If we had not, a raging catastrophe would have ensued.

Rtu nodded. "It's okay Aqum. I can relate to that as a visage with all my own past. When I was a full visage before half of myself ended up trapped on Earth, I knew your heart and motivations. I trust you. Though you could fool me now if you wanted to, I still trust you. Please explain to us what is going on."

— This is an official Aqum interruption –
— We are *struggling* to inform you with shocked and sad emotional frequencies —
Relational Time: Sometime earlier in areas where time was moving.
— on screen and transmitting —

֍֍֍ *Emperor Rok Phaar* ֍֍֍

He gasped for breath as the angry Dark One's enthrallment inside him seemed to dry up what was left of his lungs. "No!" Rok Phaar grabbed his chest hard. His last arm broke off and fell to the floor, shattering. "I will... not... become a demon... for you!" The scream inside his head made him lose consciousness for a few seconds.

— Get up, weakling! It will make you ss-strong for me! the voice said. — I will negotiate another foolproof win with the ss-stupid demons. While I do that, get up and prepare to go through and I won't tell you again!

"Yes, my King," he said as he thought about how he was just a fragment of the emperor he once was. He looked up to his commander standing against the wall beside the portal to the demon realm. The commander looked at him with empty eyes.

Was there no hope in all this? Was there something else he could do to stop this... *thing* inside him? He knew he would not be here much longer, but he didn't want to give up. Just to make sure he wasn't missing an opportunity; he ran through what had happened in his mind in the hopes he could come up with something before his king could kill him.

Rok knew he had made a mistake after he told the challenge node that they had been cheating in an effort to stop what his king wanted to do. He paid dearly for that being on the receiving end of his king's wrath. The council shut down that access portal inside the node room—that part was good, at least. The node told them they had to find another one—and if they cheated again, they would shut down the node completely and declare it an automatic forfeit.

He didn't even understand why his King would do all this. It started as a hunt, or so he thought. But then he discovered he was hunting the wrong person, and Bleyyas or Aasu tried to warn him of something. Were those their names? Rok couldn't remember what they tried to warn him about, either.

But sure enough, they did cheat again, and they struck a bargain with the demon king. They gained access to the demon realm because the nagodara were under contract for that bargain—if they failed to kill Za-rus... or was it Zirus... Anyway, if they didn't kill him, and the winged one, the demons would lose access to come to the physical world.

Oh, that's right, it *is* a hunt, but for different reasons— the King's reasons. The King gained access to the demon Earth world using one portal.

Once inside, there was something about having to create portals for them for six standard Vidurian varSas, but couldn't go through themselves, but the price was sacrifices, to be used for demon conversions so they could go through. The demons tried to take advantage of those portals, but there was an invisible force that wouldn't let the demons go through.

He briefly wondered why the Viduri varSa was the standard time used.

Then they started using portals from the demon realm to invade both the council of challenges and earth. He still couldn't remember how the king had found out who, and where, the council was.

Rok realized that the demon realm wasn't of myths and childhood legends. It was a place where even the good and strong people festered after it drew them in.

They became what most would consider evil over time because they lost free will to the festering low addiction.

They obsessed about going back to what they used to be with greed, and hating those that were.

Without knowing it, they ended up consuming what they wanted out of their fear of losing it. Eventually, what they thought their life was all about faded. Then they forgot their original best highlights in their life—or worse, demented and warped recollections, not remotely close to what really happened.

He had watched it happen to his people. Some were full mindless demons now, and they were calling for him to lead them. The communication network never deteriorated, even if they did.

Rok realized, for the first time, he wanted to apologize to the one that used to be one of them. Why, oh why, didn't he listen to him? For the life of him, he couldn't remember his name anymore, but didn't he almost have it just a few minutes ago? He had done some extraordinary things that he couldn't help but to respect, though he couldn't remember what they were.

He looked at the node. They had listened to him before. Maybe they would again. His King wasn't paying attention to him right now. He struggled to get up, using the wall near the dead-looking challenge node.

As he struggled to move toward the node, Rok wished it would light up. They no longer used lighting because the dark king didn't like it, and he longed for simple lights. He didn't want to consume it—all he wanted was to look at it before he died.

The way he led his people all those years had been wrong. He hadn't realized it at the time, but he had been leading his people down the path to the festering realm. All his people that were already gone were still calling for him... he had led them there and now they couldn't see a way out.

Somehow, as he got to the node, by some miracle, a single tear formed. As the festered king's screech ripped through him, he felt time slow as he fell face first into the node. As he fell, he knew he would shatter his head because his arms were missing. He felt more vulnerable than worn and aged paper.

The last two things he uttered as the scream ripped through him were, "Tell them... I regret I didn't listen. I didn't see till too late."

As he fell, his charred brittle face shattered and things went dark. He felt relief as the freedom of release lifted him out of his devastated body with one last thought. *I tried to help.*

— End of... transmission —

ᴨᴨᴨ *Rtu* ᴨᴨᴨ

Rtu's heart went out to the old leader, despite all he had done to so many. He turned to face Aqum. "Very sad, yet fitting. I feel sorry for the fella. But I'm sure the big LFO will use that commander next, no doubt. But, Aqum, I don't see why this would make you think you had done something desperate."

— Aqum says with urgent request to let us finish.

"I apologize Aqum, go ahead. This is obviously important, and until that weather comes through, we don't have any place to go."

Tap turned her hologram to look toward Aqum and Rtu. "Master Rtu, what they did probably saved my captain and the rest of the group on Earth."

— We are saying with agreement — Yes — But Aqum is saying it made things wobbly in the balance, though we realize we are trying to keep a balance in a time where there is no balance. — We feel it is better safe rather than sorry.

If Rtu could sweat, he would probably be sweating by now hearing this news. He sat down again and scrubbed his face with his hands. "Let's hear it. I'm sitting down."

37 Golden Dot

ᗰᗰᗰ *Zreyas* ᗰᗰᗰ

Watching Ayya reach the top of the tree, he was dumbstruck and in jaw-dropping awe at how she got up there with such grace without using the quantum. Well, if she *did* use the quantum, it wasn't the same way he did, or even Rhom.

She waved to them and sat down. He heard a faint voice come from up high. "Now it's your turn!"

Everyone looked at each other with incredulous expressions, even Dulce.

"Give me a few minutes to think of a solution." Then he squatted down, sitting on one heel, and propped his elbow on his knee on the foot-planted leg. He thought about how Rhom had moved them through the quan— *<gasp> The tryst!*

Zreyas' eyes grew wide with the realization. He stood and pulled out the tryst. The beautiful rhomboid shaped neutrinic-gleam tryst glowed starkly compared to other things on Earth. He couldn't help but smile at it. It was special to him.

The tryst still sported the triangle. The top dot on the triangle was already filled with a glowing cyan light, and a beam traveled into the air toward Ayya.

"Whew, it still works. I wondered if I broke it in some of my... adventures in the past."

Dulce stood from checking on Trevor. "Well, we know where Ayya is. Why did you... oooh!"

Connor waited a second or two, then couldn't help himself. "What?"

Dulce gestured to quiet him and whispered, "Watch. Rhom tied that tryst to three people: Zreyas, Ayya, and Rhom."

Zreyas nodded and looked back down at the tryst. His bottom left dot was lit up and a faint cyan beam reached out to his own chest. He knew he could see the third dot, but something in his mind wouldn't let him fix his gaze on it yet, ticking-hoping it would light up when he did. It was Rhom's dot.

He realized that Dulce had walked up to him with interest. Zreyas looked up to her face with a look that tried to communicate that they were in this together. Their exchange was a mix of anticipation and a grief they didn't dare submit to right now.

Taking a deep breath, he looked down at the third dot on the lower right and focused on it. *Namdlo.*

The dot activated in the same cyan color. Just as the beam should have reached out toward its target, it instead briefly flared a gold-fiery color. It sank into the tryst's third dot before going completely void of color or light.

Zreyas' chest felt like it went past the chest-cracking on to a shattering and beyond to oblivion. He clenched his jaw as he took in a sharp breath. Until now, it really never truly set in. He thought since he no longer felt Rhom's hand back there that he might have gotten out.

His thoughts went to Dulce. He apprehensively turned his face upward. *Selkerf, do you still feel him? With everything else going on, I hope this isn't accurate. I might be in the denials, though.*

Dulce was dead quiet. Then he remembered the Dark One had cut off all communications from where they were, then he whispered it again to her so only her ears would hear.

She had a look of indecision. She sighed with tears forming. Shaking her head and raising her shoulders, she finally replied. "I don't know, I'm cut off. But I think I will swim in that sea of denial with you for now."

Zreyas nodded with a weak smile. "The gold puzzles me, but let's keep the hope that he is still around somewhere and we just can't make the tryst work because of being cut off."

They both nodded to each other.

"Dulce... I know I know this, but I can't help but ask... if his challenge form dies..."

Dulce gravely shook her head.

Nodding, his anger flared—their multiverse was going to be snuffed out because of that... thing. If they were going to get snuffed out, he would cause as much damage as he could on the way out.

He vowed he would also give these people hope till the end. He thought back to the dying dimension and how it felt the same... being hunted, feeling helpless, but Rhom giving him that little glimmer of hope and light that kept him interested and drawn to him enough that he didn't want to kill him. Then he had even defended him.

Zreyas didn't know how long they had, but as he looked at everyone around him, seeing the lost hope forming in their expressions. Then raising his gaze up to Ayya in the tree, the only one who seemed to be in bliss. He decided though he couldn't ever be Rhom, he would be *their* Rhom for now in *their* dying dimension. Zreyas wouldn't lose hope and he would give them exactly what they needed, something interesting to hang on to... something to give them hope. He didn't know if what he had in mind would work, but all he could do was make the best attempt possible with no turning back.

Looking at the tryst, though he knew it was now useless, he reached out with his heart. *This is for you, Namdlo. I'm giving you the thankings and the gratefuls for all you have done for us, past, present, and future. I'm sending...*

Zreyas swallowed hard. *I'm...*

His chest heaved sharply as his chest cracked and crumbled. *I'm sending the most pheno-mi-tastic lovings to you I know how to send for all time and space. I'm with you, old man... always.*

Taking a deep anger-laced breath, he looked up at Dulce, who had a distant look on her face, though still looking at him. He Q-leaped to her shoulder to startle her enough to wake her. In her ear, he told her, "Let's get them out of here and give them hope, at least for a time."

Dulce nodded quickly a couple times, as if she was gathering her wits. "They might cut me off from myself out there, but I understand what you are going to do here. I'm afraid all the stuff that I can help you do this is in the other part of me. But I will help in other ways."

"That is all I could ever ask for. No matter what, giving you the thanking for giving me the teachings, the fun, and the lovings. I will never forget it, even in my death."

"I love you too, little buddy." Then, as if the old Rtu had possessed Dulce, she added loudly so everyone could hear, except for maybe Ayya, "Du-ude! Let's do this!"

Zreyas stood tall in his anger but put on an expression of hope and bright ideas. The fury simmered inside him and he fixed his focus on calculations. He thought back to all the lessons the old man taught him in that dying dimension that always seemed to come back to be a teacher or a guide. He turned to look around, using his adjusted sight for frequency, and it didn't look good. More of those things were out on a search party and somehow able to get into the forest despite the protection. He supposed it was because of the block.

Then he slapped his forehead, looked up at Dulce. "We are not in an area that is blocked, we are in a dimension that we didn't make. *That* is why we couldn't communicate—the same reason we change dimensions to hide from them."

Dulce blinked a few times as if in realization. "That makes sense. That is a good and bad thing. It means that the thing is now a full visage if they can create entire dimensions on a creation level unless they are doing it in another way. Who knows at this point? Right now, I'm limited."

"Everyone gather here. Do not lose hope. I got a trick up my sleeve that Rhom showed me back in the dying dimension. But I need your full heart's consent. The plan is that we all hold hands and I will attempt to move us through quantum space up to where Ayya is now like my Q-leaps."

Everyone told him they were happy to consent.

Zreyas pointed up. "I will go up there and get a more accurate layout of how those branches are arranged first so that when we jump, everyone is standing on something. If we stay here, we are all dead—they are coming into the forest. I'll be right back."

He Q-leaped up to the top of the tree in one jump. It was a long Q-leap, and it was further than he had ever leaped before. That was a tall ticking-amazing tree. It didn't seem to startle Ayya. He told her what they were going to do and asked her to move to a spot he pointed to on the branch and be ready to help anyone that landed unsteadily.

She nodded curtly. "Yes, sir, Captain Zreyas. I can't see them, but they are coming, aren't they?"

"Yes, they are. They have created a dimensional bubble down there that they are likely planning to... pop once they arrive, or at least near. I don't have time to explain any more.

"Can you ask Trevor if it is okay that I take him through the quantum, and to imagine he is healing? We need him able to run or he will die. It will also be easier to move them through the quantum."

Ayya nodded emphatically and closed her eyes. Her face looked like she was having a conversation in expression but without moving her mouth.

Zreyas cocked his head and couldn't imagine how they communicated, but he sure had the appreciates for it.

Finally, she opened her eyes. "He said he understood quantum now a lot more than he used to, and thinks he can follow your instruction. Just give him a marker on start, a marker just before landing. What does that mean, Captain Zreyas?"

"It's like saying the word 'go' to start a race."

"Oh, okay. DB5 ready, sir!"

"Time to get them. Trevor should land right in front of you. And I hope he will be standing and healed, or at least good enough to stand."

Zreyas Q-leaped back, preparing himself for doing something he had never done before. He just had to keep hope that he had learned enough from Rhom and Rtu to not kill them all. But either way, they would be dead if they stayed. There were way too many to hold off.

He informed the group of what was about to happen and got everyone's consent.

Connor was especially excited. "I can't think of a better way to research the quantum than go through it. Though I know we use it every day, and we don't realize when we are doing it, but I'm excited to see—"

"Okay, dear." Cerys chuckled. "Try to calm down so you can let the captain do what he needs to do."

Connor and Cerys lifted their son to a supported standing position, his head resting on Cerys.

Zreyas noticed that his wound started bleeding again profusely, but didn't say a word. He closed his eyes and had one hand on Dulce's leg and the other on Lanna's.

As he thought about where they were all going to land, just as if he was going to take just himself on a leap, he noticed the fluctuations and instability of each person. Though they had given consent, he now understood why Rhom said it was difficult to do in the best of conditions.

"Everyone, think of us all as one family and focus your energy on that. It will help me calm your fluctuations."

He told himself not to forget the marker for Trevor and decided to use the only frequency marker he knew to give him.

It was the frequency that was etched into his whole being by who he thought had been Tulyata in quantum space.

He realized he wasn't very proficient at that kind of thing. He hoped the intention would be enough. Zreyas concentrated again and fixed his mind's eye on where they were all going to end up.

— Yes — 1 1 1 1. All are one.

Zreyas took that as instruction from Tulyata and looked at each one of them in his mind and saw them as extensions of himself. Once he got that feeling down, he saw their bodies' reaction to his efforts.

Just like he had done in the dying dimension, he created the high frequency door, and instead of giving it to Rhom; he focused it in front of all of them. He felt the torus of energy begin to move around them.

The intensity grew, and he felt and heard all of his friends gasp, but they held on. It finally reached the point that the motion of the torus paused and began the reverse motion.

Zreyas directed the high creation and healing energy to the center of the torus in front of them all. Then he sang his song internally, hearing it in its pure form. It was grounding, yet it vibrated to the highest parts of himself. Then he gave the marker for Trevor. 1—1- -1—1

Trevor felt like he nodded energetically through the roar and song. He broke into iridescent particles, yet keeping his shape, and moved toward the center.

While he wanted to watch Trevor more closely, he had to concentrate on the Q-leap for them all. The rest was up to Trevor. Everyone seemed to be drawn in to the center, and when they did, he concentrated on their signatures and committed them to memory. He focused on their placement and destination, and he knew they were already there in the tree.

As they traveled through the quantum, he felt and heard...

— 1 1 1 1 — Focus. All the same.

Zreyas felt like he was losing who he was because of the fluctuations, then he remembered he was supposed to give a marker for Trevor before the end of the jump, and felt Ayya's presence.

Zreyas struggled to give the marker. 1—1——— 1—1.

All the particles converged. Zreyas realized Ayya had been humming to Trevor to help him.

He also felt Dulce's intentions had aided him. As they materialized, the realization of a newfound respect for Rhom and what he had done crashed into his mind with new scientific understanding.

Dulce gasped and almost toppled over, but Cerys grabbed her quickly to steady her.

ﻦﻦﻦ *Rtu* ﻦﻦﻦ

(Many universes away)

Rtu leaned over to look at the 3D model of the new planet they were going to be setting the base up on. He realized the node was inside the planet.

He gasped and slapped his hand to this chest with a thump at the sudden re-joining of himself on Earth. Then he said, "They made it out of the dark one's bubble dimension."

Tap's hologram fluctuated between cyan and purple. "Master Rtu! I feel my heart again!"

ﻦﻦﻦ *Zreyas* ﻦﻦﻦ

The awe he felt at what Rhom had done back in the dying dimension, hiding an entire house, and those in it, suspended in the quantum, left him feeling shock and his mind reeled. He took in the new knowledge he had just learned through experience as much as possible so it wouldn't fade.

— Captain, I know you are busy, but I wanted to let you know we have our connection back.

— Mother, I am here with you again. I knew you would find a way! Resolute says you are in trouble for not taking her.

Giving the thankings to you for checking with me. I'm glad we are all connected again, he said to them both.

Dulce's gentle voice brought him back. "Are you okay, Captain?"

Blinking a few times, he realized he was bending over with his hands propped on his knees. He nodded and sighed. Zreyas realized he had been holding his breath.

Dulce smiled with brightness in her eyes. "I will also tell you... I'm feeling like myself again."

Thoughts about Trevor assailed his mind, and he jerked his face over to where he should have been to find he was standing there on his own, awake, and smiling.

"That was an amazing healing ball you made, Captain Zreyas! I didn't have to work hard at all or heal myself. I just had to walk into it. And Ayya guided me on how to move inside the quantum to get in it. Thank you!"

Cerys jerked her face toward her son, realizing he was standing on his own and seemed perfectly fine. She started hugging and kissing him.

"Mom..." Trevor rolled his eyes when she didn't stop. "Mo-om... It's okay, Mom."

Connor had tears in his eyes, but laughed.

Zreyas started to thank Ayya and Dulce for their help, but a distraction caught his attention, and he couldn't ignore it. Where they had *just* been, it looked like it was sick. He didn't know how to explain it.

Then he heard Dulce's voice of appalled whisper. "That isn't a normal dimension they created."

"What do you mean?" As he waited for Dulce's response, he scanned the area closer. To him, it looked like a distorted version of the forest, but it had a greenish-rust tint.

She pointed toward where they had all come from. "Look to your right slightly, and up toward where the Sadler's house is."

"Sick," said Ayya in horror. "It's all sick."

Dulce looked ill. "Look at the place where they are touching. It's a portal. It's acting like a little bubble blower with a bubble stuck to it on both sides. They can't come here, but they still found a way to breech here through pushing dimensional walls. That portal is from another realm we are not familiar with. Sorry, I can't help it. I'm a teacher here and the habit of analogies is strong."

Zreyas looked at the details of what was happening, his brain taking in all the statistics to keep his mind going and not let his emotions get in the way. "This anal-thing is good for me. I had no education like that."

Amid the pure horror, all the adults and children alike looked at each other, shocked by what Zreyas had just said. He couldn't quite figure out why. "Uh, oh, what did I say?"

"The word you are looking for is, analogy," Dulce quickly corrected. "Anal is the opening part of the ass."

"Oh! Well... that looks like the anal of the ticking-LFO." Zreyas cocked his head. "So-o, appropriate. Giving the thankings to you for the corrections."

Everyone, including Ayya and Trevor, were holding their hands over their mouths trying to hold down the laughing to a minimum, even amongst the nasty situation. But in the end, they lost it, laughing hard out loud. Zreyas appreciated the mood lifting. They all needed it.

The color of the atmosphere and the tint of the dimension told Zreyas exactly where it was a portal to. He had seen one like that when the nagodara had given up on trying to kill him on Tarq because he was under the water. He wasn't about to say it, though.

When he looked back again at Ayya, the hopelessness and loss on her face looked as if she could lead the multiverse into eternal grief.

Zreyas wasn't about to let her undo all their hard work over another childhood fit. "Check yourself, Ayya."

She was an extremely advanced being, but she had not yet developed in maturity because she hadn't developed in most ways. That could mean disaster. He had been through that with Aaru, and he was mild compared to her.

Then he fully turned to warn her with as stern a voice as he could muster. "You will attract *exactly* what you don't want if you keep looking at the loss, and they are... very... close. This is *exactly* what they are hoping you will do. They *know* how precious this place is to you."

"I think he is right, sweetie," added Lanna. "We can plant more trees, and the forest will replenish itself naturally."

"I don't *want* the new trees! I want *these* to be okay, I know them!" Ayya started crying.

Trevor stepped up as if he would comfort her when a voice called out.

"Where are you, big girl?" There was a pause. "Ay-ya!"

Ayya sniffed in quickly and whispered, "Daddy?"

Trevor scrunched his face up slightly. "Ayya, I don't thi—"

"Daddy! Is that the *real* you?"

Lanna froze too, as if she had just heard a ghost.

"I can't see you, Ayya. Where are you? I went into your room to find you, but you weren't there!"

Everyone looked down toward the voice as they carefully stood on the large branches or plywood. Sure enough, there was the man, but there was no inky mist.

His skin looked normal for a human, and quite healthy. But he had seen Ayya's father earlier that day and he had been a mess.

Zreyas shook his head. "I might be assuming way too much. But I think that *has* to be an earth form or something from the challenge."

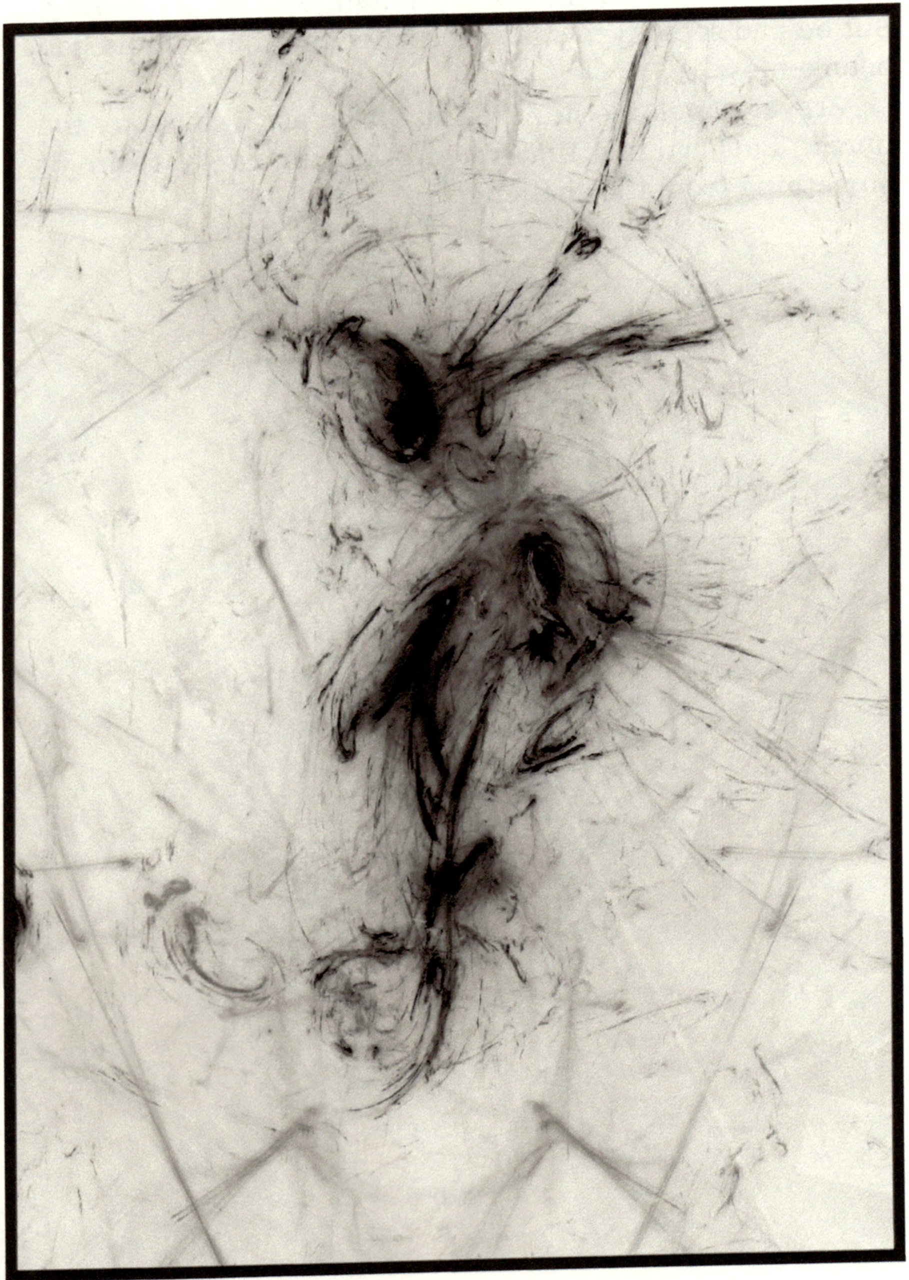

38 Mind Struggle

ᴨᴨᴨ *Zreyas* ᴨᴨᴨ

Ayya started to run back toward the trunk of the tree to get down.

Dulce spoke up with a tone that seemed to pierce the soul gently, but it made *everyone* stop, not just her. "Ayya? If you leave us, your memory of all of us, all events, will be gone. That would include your mother if she stays."

"Honestly, if Ayya goes, I will too. I cannot leave my child." She turned toward Ayya. "Please think about this, sweetie. After all you have seen and learned, can you really say that is your father and if it is the best thing to do for all of us?"

Ayya looked down at her feet and closed her eyes. From Zreyas' perspective, he could tell she was searching inside. "It's not, no." She paused a moment, then blurted out with anguish, "But I want my daddy. I know that is the real one! I can feel him."

As Ayya turned to run, Trevor called to her, making her stall. "Ayya! Please, don't leave... I know you want your real dad back, but leaving now, you know this isn't right."

Ayya balled up her fists and screamed with a slight growl, "Easy for you to say! You have a father that cares!"

Zreyas cocked his head and squinted at what he had just heard and felt. Her voice had an ever so slight tinge of a pushing growl. He could swear it sounded and felt like Aaru's signature in the war communication aura that they had been part of at the Janquar Nation.

Oh no, no, no, Aaru. You are influencing her and going down a dangerous path, he thought to his brother. Zreyas remembered how Silence had told him that Aaru didn't leave the life when he should have and that he had a new purpose now because he altered his.

He didn't know what this altered purpose was, but he knew what came from her was Aaru the warrior. *Namdlo, where are you? Selkerf, what are we going to do?*

Dulce spoke up. "It's time to go. Everyone that consents to be taken back to the ship, hold hands." She held her hands out and Connor took one and Trevor took his father's.

Ayya's eyes filled as Zreyas touched Dulce's calf and Cerys took Trevor's hand. Ayya was clearly struggling with the choice.

"Ayya! Where are you? Where's my big girl?"

Zreyas wanted to pound that imposter's head. They knew all too well how she was struggling. To his relief, she reached out for Cerys' hand and her mother grabbed her other.

Everyone sighed in relief in unison.

Dulce spoke up, sounding like a teacher. "Okay, listen to the instructions. Zreyas and I are in challenge form. Though he is as himself, they still consider him to be in challenge form because of how he got here. I will have to go back through the challenge but the second I'm there,

Rtu will be here to take you back, so it will seem like magic that suddenly I become Rtu.

"Zreyas won't go back until all of you are safe, just in case something goes wrong. Anyone have any questions?"

Everyone exchanged glances as they shook their heads.

"Okay, make sure you keep contact with each other. I'll be ba—"

As Dulce opened her hand, the token that appeared crumbled, dust falling down through her fingers.

Alarmed, Zreyas opened his hand and thought about going home. The token appeared. He sighed with relief, then it crumbled too.

The two exchanged glances.

"Look!" Connor let go of her hand and pointed down in the direction where the room was that they had been in.

Everyone, including himself, turned to see what Connor was talking about.

Approximately fifty of the Charred were running toward the tree, and five of them had large tools he had never seen before.

Zreyas squinted trying to see more detail. "What are those ticking-things they are carrying?"

"Chainsaws," said Connor. "They use gasoline as fuel and cut trees down with ease. You know, I'm getting *really* tired of being on the run from these things. I don't know about you lot. I understand what Ayya has gone through a little more now."

"Mag-shitting-bandhulas!" At first, he wondered how they got that close without him sensing them, but then he remembered—those things had been in the isolated dimension they weren't in anymore.

His guts churned as he realized that they probably *knew* they would get out of there and into this tree. Perfect strategy to get them cornered and be stealthy in surrounding them.

He took a few seconds to look around for the auras of the challenge to see what they could influence. He had almost forgotten about that feature Aqum granted them. It was in the spaces between the rules back when he had been at Ayya's home, when she had lived near the firehouse.

Once he concentrated on that, the world turned red around them, meaning those parts of the event they would not alter or influence. All the Charred coming toward them had red auras.

Then he noticed that there was one near the tree already that had a two-layered aura. He had never seen that aura before. "Dulce, look at the challenge aura on that one. What do you make of that? It's not like the rest of the red auras for the Charred."

Dulce turned toward where Zreyas was pointing. She had a startled look, and that told him all he needed to know. She focused and rubbed her freckled cheeks. "I've never seen a challenge aura like that before. And there is another one that is red coming closer, but from a different direction than the rest of the Charred. That one didn't have an inner lining in its aura."

Zreyas looked at it closer, then back to the Charred approaching. "Hey, wait a minute. There are two layers of the aura. We just never noticed it before. Each node has colors for the challenge. Ours is Blue and Cyan and the Janquar challenge node is Red with orange markings. But those coming through the portal have a sickening aura that matches that portal's color, not their challenge node's."

"So, they *are* cheating." Dulce's face was a picture of anger. It was the first time he had ever seen Rtu like that in any form.

"We just didn't notice the differences till now. Look at that other one... it has a red aura, but its inner strip of colors is purple and yellow."

"So... ours isn't purple and yellow—it's blue and cyan. So that must not be—"

"But you were under the ticking-LFO's influence at the time... you couldn't see the node, much less hear the voices. Remember?"

"Oh yeah, you are right! So, does that mean that challenge node you claimed was purple and yellow?"

"Right! It was! But what I don't understand is that they locked it for no use by anyone but me. So that has to be an override, some sort of official that we can't influence—or... someone has compromised the node. There is only one other thing it could—"

Dulce and Zreyas exchanged glances.

"I am inundated with information and visions from all that lost time separated from myself. Something has happened with Aqum, the challenge council, and Aqum's form has... changed and our node is... dead."

"Dead?! What the ticking—" He wanted to contact Tap, but right now he didn't dare. He didn't know enough, and it was too big a risk.

"Ayya, where are you?" came her father's voice again. "I know you are out here. I've been cured and myself again. What has happened? Come home!"

Zreyas watched Ayya out of the corner of his eye as he started spouting off questions, hoping Dulce's connection could get them answers. "How are you and I supposed to get back, then? And how are we supposed to get the rest of us to the ship? Can Rtu at least get them out of here?"

Dulce opened her mouth to speak, but it was like Zreyas' throat was spewing out questions of tactics and he had no valve to turn it off.

"And isn't Ayya's father under a contract enforced by the challenge council and visages? And how did he get into her room? Isn't that under the protection of the barriers put in place by the council and vis—"

"I'm trying, Captain!" she curtly said, exasperated. She took a deep breath. "I'm trying to find out the answers. I'm sure we all have the same ones."

"Oh, I don't know... The captain spouted off some that I didn't think about asking," said Cerys.

Trevor started giggling, but when he looked at Ayya for his friend's normal comradery, he didn't get it. She was frowning and seemed to seethe with anger, and it startled Trev.

Something wasn't right with her, and confirmation came when Trevor worked his way around his father on the opposite side. His expression looked like immense grief and... fear.

Zreyas could tell the boy was doing his best not to lose control of his emotions. Part of their connection had broken. It made his own chest hurt in empathy.

As he looked at Trevor, the boy looked back at him. He winked and gave a slight nod of understanding and said, "I understand, and I will help you get through that break. Everything will be okay. You and I got things we can do together. Something tells me I'm going to need your help—and you and your dad have a lot of quantum science stuff to have fun with." He gave a soft grin.

Trevor wiped his right eye, nodded, and did his best to smile as he leaned against his dad.

Connor held him close with his arm.

"I don't have all the information in yet, but I have some good news. We have made a permanent alliance with the Screh." And before Zreyas could ask how that could help them now, Dulce held up a teacher's finger, making him almost chuckle. "They advised us to get down out of the tree and run to Ayya's room."

"What!?" everyone said all at once.

Dulce held up a hand. "The room will protect us for a short time because it is too high of a frequency for them to get through. Though Rtu can't help totally with that, he can aid you, Captain, in taking us through the quantum as close as you can take us through. Our problem is these challenge bodies. Without my aid as well as..."

"What are you talking about, Freckles?"

Trevor put a hand over his mouth and giggled.

"Nothing, it doesn't matter now, anyway. We need to—"

Several loud machines started up. They were so loud that it made everyone jump. Then they revved up several times. Then they sounded like they were grinding something.

Zreyas scratched his cheek. "Well, looks like the Charred that carried the lame-jaws are cutting down the trees."

"Chainsaws, Captain Zreyas," corrected Trevor, giggling. "They use chained metal teeth to rotate around a length of metal really fast to cut, just like a plain primitive toothed saw, but about twenty-five times faster."

"Chainsaws... giving the thankings to you for the correction." As Zreyas looked down and watched them, he couldn't get over how Trevor wasn't nervous, or didn't seem to be. He had to admit to himself he was nervous, but it was time to get past it and assess the jump he would have to do with all of them... again.

Though it would take them a bit to get through that immense tree trunk, they have cheated many times and there was no telling if they would again. He estimated a few hours to get through that thing enough to make the tree fall as big as it was. If those saws cut twenty times faster, he estimated they would have about ten to twenty minutes, depending on how they did it.

They were cutting on the opposite side they were on so they would land outside of the protected woods, opposite from where Ayya's room was.

Zreyas looked in the portal's direction. "Trevor, since you are more cooperative right now, where is Ayya's room?"

Trevor walked up beside him and pointed toward a house the explosions had slightly hit. "The house that has the two toned red and white brick that looks so cool. The second window from the right is Ayya's Room, and it is unlocked usually since it is summer."

"Well, it will be a huge jump, but I think we can do it," he announced as he looked sideways at Dulce. "At least it will be a quicker trip to get home for Ayya and Lanna."

He turned toward the others with a grave face as he heard the chainsaws ripping through the tree and Ayya crying.

"After we get there, climb in the window," he ordered. "If it is locked, break the window, but do not go through the other part of the house. I got a bad feeling about doing that."

"Good thinking." Dulce held her hands out. "Time to hold hands for those that give consent."

As everyone did so, Zreyas wanted to get the rest of what he had to say off his chest. "They have snagged us into a strategic trap from the start. Because of balances, I doubt Rtu can pull both Dulce and I to the ship.

"My plan is to shut down that portal somehow. I can't get back since our node is dead, and everything is a loss if you all don't get out. Rtu can Captain the crew."

Connor stepped forward with a body language that was the most aggressive as Zreyas had ever seen him do. "I'm going with you. I want my wife and son safe. And I'm going with you to help. If it will ensure that they stay protected, then I'm going to do all I can for that cause alone, much less for all the other reasons.

"Plus, if there is anything left in the east part of our house that isn't destroyed, there might be a device there that might just help you destroy that thing, Captain."

"What are you... *oh!* Yes, dear, you are right! That just might do it!" added Cerys with excitement. "Looks like that crazy experiment of yours just might save us all."

Trevor's face lit up, and he nodded emphatically. "I would like to go too!"

Cerys thumped his head. "Don't even think about it squirm-worm."

Trevor sheepishly looked at his mom with a half grin. "Aww. Well, you can't blame a kid for trying to help save the multiverse."

"You already have, Trevor." Zreyas turned around and looked at him seriously. "Don't underestimate your contribution, young one, just because you are small. You helped us discover the impostor that almost took Ayya's key to the Viduri for one. Then you made that tunnel system to help us escape from Cerys' boss of obliteration."

He almost turned around to get ready, then had a question he wanted to ask, but wanted to see his face when he answered. "And I have a feeling you know something we don't, because you are not nervous at all. Is there something you would like to tell us, or would you rather keep it to yourself?"

All the chainsaws were running loudly all at once now so Trevor had to almost yell. "Thank you, sir—I mean, Captain. I don't know the details, but I promise it is good. I just can't tell you why... I just know it feels... bright and right."

Zreyas cocked his head, assessing both what he saw, and what he felt from Trevor. Truth is what he felt, and he was not hiding anything that he could detect. "Good enough. I trust you. Now..."

He made sure his face and voice were stern and used his aura to push the message home, making sure to fix his gaze on Ayya several times. "Everyone get ready and make sure you consciously consent to travel or you might end up staying in the quantum, land back here in a fleshy mess, and possibly kill others because you drag them back. So either commit, or don't. Don't jeopardize others by making a half-mag-shit-ass decision."

Everyone nodded in the sound assault of the chainsaws, then got as close as they could despite navigating the branches and partial floor that the children had put up there. Even Ayya enthusiastically took her mother's hand at the end of the line.

Zreyas exchanged glances with Lanna as if they agreed she would hold on to her daughter's hand tight. No one had confidence in Ayya at this point, with her father nearby somewhere calling out to her.

Once everyone was settled, Zreyas started the process of the quantum leap. Before he started, though, he wondered if he should attempt to put them back a few seconds just to make sure. But he wasn't confident enough with just the jump with so many for such a long distance, so he let it go.

He took a deep breath and focused on the yard right in front of that window, just as the first crack of the tree trunk sounded. Somehow, they had cheated... again.

39 Eyelid Sounds

ༀༀༀ *Zreyas* ༀༀༀ

As they jumped, Zreyas observed the signatures of the group members to make sure things didn't seem off. However, he didn't have much experience with manipulating a group of people through the quantum and was not really sure if he would even recognize something wasn't right other than himself. But there was one thing he *could* tell—he was getting help from someone.

It was like particles of protective guidance kept them all in an area so parts of themselves didn't get lost or scattered. It helped him to gain the general idea of how Rhom might have done this with all of them in the dying dimension. He loved learning stuff like this. It seemed natural to him.

As quick as it started, it was over, and he found himself face to face with the brick wall underneath Ayya's bedroom window, feeling the ground under his feet, and a bush at his back.

As he turned sideways to look naground the bush to check that everyone was okay, he heard another crack from the tree echoing through the woods, even as far off as it was.

From what he could tell, everyone made the jump with no problems.

Then movement caught his eye. Ayya's father was climbing the fence to get into the backyard coming toward them. Something wasn't right, though. He looked... good. He wanted to believe the real man was inside that body somewhere and no longer under the influence of the Dark One.

A tickle in his mind wouldn't allow him to be fooled because of wishful thinking. Something about him, though, just didn't feel like his former father. Had Ayya been right? *Okay, now you are getting crazy in your thinking... Focus, Zrey.*

Zreyas realized he was still not allowing himself to grieve and face that Rhom, his *chosen* father, was dead. Now, he wanted to believe this man was now cured, for Ayya's sake. "Ayya, go into your room and lead the rest in... now. If your father is safe to be around, he will be able to go inside that room."

Lanna grabbed her daughter's arm and opened the window.

"Ayya, come give me a hug. I've missed my big girl," her father said as he walked toward them with open arms.

Connor reached over and got a metal scrub, from what Zreyas had recently learned was called a charcoal grill. He held it leisurely on his shoulder, but ready.

Zreyas wanted to pull his weapons out of habit, but he could do that in the quantum if he needed to leap to kill. He was getting better at things like that since the day he took the archer's eyes out on Tarq to save Silence.

"Daddy?"

Another groaning single crack of that huge tree sounded, giving way to gravity and the lack of trunk to hold it up. But Zreyas could tell it was putting up a fight.

"I'm here. Come give me a hug. I've missed you. You've grown up so fast. I'm so sorry I let them get to me. Please, forgive me." He stopped a few feet away from them and held out his arms.

When no one moved to approach him, he let them flop down.

Out of the corner of his eye, Zreyas could see Ayya's struggle as her mother crawled into the window. Before Ayya might do something rash, he looked at his vision interface and turned on the frequency filter and studied her father. He blinked a few times at what he saw.

It was like the normal frequencies of a human were fighting the biggest battle of their life inside that body.

"Daddy!" Ayya ripped away from her mother and ran toward him before anyone could do anything about it.

Zreyas was glad that he still had his filter on because he witnessed the power of high frequencies as he picked her up and held her.

"I love you, Ayya. I'm so sorry I treated you so badly." Tears spilled from his eyes as he closed them and held her tight.

"I love you, too, Daddy. And I forgive you. Are you okay? The inky-eyes hurt a lot."

He chuckled at what Zreyas assumed was the love of a human father. It was weird to him, and he just couldn't imagine the commander holding him like that.

"I'm doing amazing, now, big girl."

The tree groaned and cracked again, longer this time.

Zreyas couldn't believe what was happening energetically. The higher frequencies were taking over and pushing the lower frequencies down into small areas throughout his body to the point they all became very stable, and just part of his body with no struggle.

Then he saw hundreds of the Charred running toward them in the background, climbing over the fence until they just knocked it down.

Zreyas drew his weapons and gave the command. "Everyone in Ayya's room, now! The Charred are coming, and it is the only way we can protect ourselves. Go, go, go! And you! ... Protect your daughter or I will come to kill you; but this time, I *will* succeed!"

He looked at Zreyas a moment with a knowing nod, and almost as if for verification, he said, "I've always admired your ability to strategize and act through fear productively. I was never good at it." Just as the man ran with Ayya in his arms, his back arched and he grunted.

Two loud cracks occurred together from the old tree. Zreyas looked up, but it still stood. But he could see an overall shake, settling and breaking down under the forces working against it.

Ayya pulled her head back to look at her father's face. "Daddy? What is wrong?"

He put Ayya down and said in a strained voice. "I'm okay, Ayya, I just got the wind knocked out of me. Run to your mother, and I'll be along soon. I need to make sure you are safe like a real father should." It was obvious he tried to stay calm, but it came out edgy. "Please, do as you're told... *now!*"

Ayya jumped slightly.

Zreyas knew what had happened—he had seen many men get hit from behind in war so many times. He didn't need sight because the memory of the sound an axe made when it was driven into the back had etched into his memory. Flashes of the past went through his mind, making him sweat and jerk.

Reluctantly Ayya nodded, turned, and ran toward Lanna the same time a gunshot went off from Zreyas' right.

Everyone either crouched or dropped to the ground. Zreyas either instinctively changed his sight that showed thermal wave pattern signatures from velocity, or Tap did it for him. He wasn't sure which. He saw two signature trails. One was much larger and more distorted, and the other was narrower. One ended right at the old commander's back, and the other went through his body and on past.

Whoa! Was all he could think when he saw the source of the shot.

In the distance, the commander of the Tsottan line of the Janquar Nation stood there as he lowered his gun. It looked longer and sleeker than the shotgun he had seen before. The Tsottan line had always been the Rittak line's competitor. Inky mist slid in and out of his eyes.

Beside him stood his second, both looking smug and proud. He wondered if they had seen him yet, but he didn't think so because he had been standing behind a bush from their view.

He pulled his bow and willed a camouflaged, neutrinic-gleam arrow to be used and nocked it, taking aim at the second in command without hesitation as he heard the tree give way with a resounding final crack and groan. He knew the second in command was the most dangerous from his history with the Nation. Without him, the commander of that line wouldn't be worth a pile of mag-shit.

He had an idea—As the tree slowly began its fall, he mentally asked the neutrinos if they would use the quantum for their flight and told them to sound a tone for his ears if they consented unanimously. Sure enough, it came. If he could take out those two, it would really hurt the efforts of the Nation and their new visage.

Several things happened in quick succession after he heard the tones. His old commander and father dropped to his knees, still holding himself up with a grunt.

Ayya had apparently turned her head back when she heard the gunshot. As he dropped, she screamed and ran toward her father.

Zreyas pictured where his arrow was to land and let it go just as Commander Tsottan stepped forward and his second stepped to the side, behind the commander. His mind screaming, *Nn-o! They knew this would happen!*

When the arrow appeared again in the middle of Commander Tsottan's neck, it exploded, and the rest of his body stood a moment before toppling over. When his body fell, his second was standing there behind him with a grin on his viscera-splattered face.

Then another familiar sound came, the deployment of a capture net with the signature sound of a distinct warbled whishing. Then the falling tree sounded, coming from his left. As he turned to look, the net was closing around Ayya and her dying father.

Zreyas pulled his axe and dropped his bow to waste no time in Q-leaping to them to cut the net open. It all seemed surreal as he landed at the net, both in it being pulled away so fast he couldn't react to keep up.

As the net holding them left the ground, he realized the Charred had tethered to the top of the massive falling tree, acting as a long-reaching trebuchet in the act of slinging its load toward a target as Ayya screamed, "Da-addy!"

Then it all stopped.

Everything went quiet.

The silence assailed his ears. He never really realized just how many sounds there were around until now.

It wasn't just the nature sounds or what was going on around him; it was his internal sounds in his body, too. Zreyas realized even his eye blinks made sounds, because it was quiet enough for him to hear them now. Then he realized his eyes were the only thing that wasn't frozen.

The only face he could see near him was Trevor's because he was facing the tree. The boy was looking at him. Trevor's eyes had wonder and excitement in them and he could swear he tried to shrug with his eyes—No panic.

— This is an official Grand Council interruption —
— The council has stopped time for the duration of this message —

Zreyas couldn't think clearly right now, but he knew that the voice didn't sound like Aqum at all. They sounded like an aged female with a weariness.

— We will report as abbreviated as possible. However, it will still prove long, because of the reasons for our intervention.

As he looked around to see if there was an entity to watch, he noticed that the tree Ayya loved so much was now in mid-fall, only one-quarter of the way down. That meant Ayya and her father would be thrown a long way when time started again.

Zreyas started calculating his next Q-leap as he listened. But there didn't seem to be an entity representing the speaker, anywhere nearby.

— We report the following event with gravity:

> - The Grand Challenge Council has been attacked, and they killed or incapacitated many of our members.

There was a pause that lasted long enough that made Zreyas feel an uncomfortable feeling rise within him.

> - Blatant cheating by the new visage, Ijin, has compromised the multiverse-wide challenge. In addition, this same said visage is responsible for the council attack and all damage to the council.

Who the ticking-hell is this visage of Ijin? The entire scene seemed surreal to him. He remembered Tulyata saying that time had been stopped when the beginning of the challenge started, and wondered if it was like. He had been in a visage realm, and they were different because they were timeless and still are. But something told him *this* time-stop was different. *Tap? Can you hear me now that time has stopped?*

No answer.

> - The council attempted to imprison Ijin to a dimensional prison for the multiverse's survival and allow us to gain a balance of the challenge design again and cancel it. However, the visage has retreated to a forbidden realm so deep that we cannot reach the new visage.

After Zreyas thought about it for a second, he assumed it was where that nagodara came from. He realized something small was flashing in his Tap-interface and he focused on it. He didn't know what that interface was called, but he liked calling it that.

> - If the council had not stopped time, there would have only been one survivor... the source. The council couldn't allow any more cheating or invasion of demented forms when all other sides were playing within balances to keep the alchemical equilibrium of the multiverse healthy.

The message blinking was a note from Tap. She knew about the time-stop ahead of time because Aqum was there on the ship. *Well, at least Aqum is okay.* Then it went on to say seconds before the freeze she couldn't speak directly to him and wanted to let him know that everyone on the ship was doing okay and to listen carefully to the announcement, and she would record it just in case he needed to hear it again.

— As a result of the total obliteration of the spirit of the challenge into something unhealthy for us all, the following will occur:

> - First. Because there is still one leader in the physical multiverse that follows the visage Ijin, the challenge will continue, but with some harsh adjustments in an attempt for the multiverse to gain some equilibrium. The council is the protector of the natural balance of frequencies, nothing else.

What was the point of the challenge now? This Ijin, who he assumed was in league with, or was, the ticking-LFO didn't seem to focus on Ayya or Aaru anymore than anyone else, really. If they cheated so badly, why didn't they do an automatic forfeit? Maybe it was because the one that cheated is no longer in the physical world and those left didn't do the cheating? He had way too many questions.

Ticking-hell, the Dark One made more effort to kill me and... oh no. Was this visage successful? Where are you, old man?

Nope, he couldn't think about that right now.

These... 'adjustments' didn't sound like they would be good for *anyone,* in his mind at least. Then again, adapting to change was not his best attribute, even though Rhom and Rtu had said he was to initiate it by design. Maybe they didn't declare it a forfeit because they had control of the council, or at least part of it.

There was one thing for certain though—not being able to move was driving him crazy. He focused on assessing the area, noting everything around him as well as a possible path to Connor's house as he listened.

- Second. Should the visage Ijin come back to the physical world, we will immediately trigger a permanent imprisonment in a dead dimension past potential space and exiled into null oblivion.

- Third. Since Ayya's father was involved in the cheating, causing much damage to life and multiverse balance, we will sentence him to a sealed dimension within the challenge realm, assuming he lives long enough to heal. He will be comfortable and have freedom within that realm only, because of his recent change of yan.

The council recognizes this was a remarkable feat. As a result, instead of being put to death, he will have the chance to put that recent change in motion. He will have a caretaker that will work with him.

As long as he is cooperative, his sentence will be as long as any of the following conditions have occurred:

1. For as long as any of his lineage is alive,

2. The visage Ijin is imprisoned,

3. Or the visage Ijin has died, the permanent visage death.

However, he will have the opportunity to show the change was not fake, or by any other unnatural means, to protect his lineage by helping to assure they survive and given equipment to do what is approved by the council. We are putting him under the command of Captain Zreyas Rittak of the Sleeping Phoenix Order indirectly. If said Captain Zreyas refuses his service, then the prisoner will be isolated.

Me?! What the ticking-hell! So, the frequencies fighting was real, and he really did change! Had the commander grown aware enough to do that? Or did someone, or something, help him? He gave into the Dark One so easily originally. Then again, he wasn't aware of the ticking-LFO at that time either. Before his possession, he had lived with a very low frequency yan. He lived to grandstand and was so attuned to the emperor that... *wait... had the emperor died?*

This whole thing was getting too ticking-weird, and backwards at the same time. *No one* changed that fast, unless maybe they died and came back from death.

A memory came back to him of something that had happened to a highly decorated commander of another line in the Janquar Nation. That Commander had died in a war. However, a few days later, he had opened his eyes while his body laid on a pile of corpses to be ground up for building.

He remembered when the commander had asked where the helpers went, and when no one said anything because they all thought him mad from his injuries, he immediately asked to have his horns cut off at the scalp and become an artisan.

It brought all kinds of shame to their line and the emperor dissolved it. The other lines killed most of them. Those that survived were integrated into other lines. Zreyas couldn't help but wonder if the old leader was dead or if he was one of the blue on his ship.

- Next, we will send Ayya, Lanna, and her other daughter with a caretaker to another place with different visages to live out their lives in peace until we consider Ayya an adult on Earth. We will implement the highest-quality frequency gene scrambler around each of them so their identities can't be detected by frequency or gene scans.

Zreyas sighed with relief that it would give them time to... wait. With no race of time to finish the challenge, how was all this going to end?—or *would* it end? None of this made sense to him. So how was there still a challenge left and what was it for if she was now protected and the Dark One banned from the physical plane of the multiverse?

This will give Ayya time to mature according to the human standards; however, after two Viduri varSas, the equivalent of twenty-two Earth years, all protections in place for Ayya will cease.

When time starts again momentarily, those mentioned parties will no longer be here, but all current events will.

And there it was... the catch. Was this even the original council, or someone that had taken over the council?

- The Janquar Nation Challenge node status: deactivated and destroyed.

Reason: penalty for the extreme rule breech and attack on the council.

In addition, we will compensate for the lack of nodes. The Council will restore the node that was destroyed by the attackers with the colors blue and cyan, currently possessed by Zreyas of the Sleeping Phoenix order.

 We will also create a new node to replace the one destroyed because of the Janquar penalty. However, it's placement is in another location somewhere within the Phoenix Ray Galaxy, bringing the original number of challenge nodes back to four—two claimed nodes, two unclaimed.

Zreyas looked at Ayya and tried his best to comfort her with a smile. At least he tried to, since they could still only move their eyes. He wasn't sure if it went across or not, but he hoped those amazing internal senses were still intact.

40 A Runner s Run

ඞඞඞ Zreyas ඞඞඞ

— At the end of the two varSas, if the Ijin team of the challenge has not found a challenge node, they will be granted the coordinates of the fourth node automatically if someone has not yet claimed it. They can then choose if they would like it where it is or choose to place it where their old one was. If all nodes are claimed by, or an ally of, the Order of the Sleeping Phoenix, the challenge is over and the leaders of the Janquar Nation will be contained in a dimensional prison.

Well, that ticking sucks mag-shit. So now we have to not only protect Ayya but also claim all four nodes in two varSas? **That seemed one-sided to Zreyas. Something wasn't right.**

— We would also like to note a disclaimer — the Grand Council of Challenge reserves, and uses, the right to withhold information in order to keep balances. However, *all* rules are stated openly and anyone can examine them at each node or at a Grand Council station in the capital galaxies multiverse-wide. You can also find them at the Order of History's station.

That is the place Rhom told me to go when I was ready. He didn't know when he would go there to do what he needed to do for Rhom and Rtu, but no doubt they probably had word of at least most of it already with all this going on.

This had to be about to end, so he figured he better start concentrating on his plan and to find out where Connor was so he could also make sure he was going. He knew Dulce would take care of Cerys and Trevor... somehow.

— The Grand Council interruption will end in five... four... three... two... one...

— End of transmission —

Zreyas almost fell on his face when time started again. As the net in front of him whipped away from where they stood, he was glad to see that it was empty.

Once he gained his balance again, he immediately scanned for Connor, who was already running toward his destroyed house, but looking for him.

Zreyas nodded. "Let's go! Dulce, you got the helm for Cerys and Trevor."

"Got it covered, little buddy!"

Right before he turned to focus on his run, he noticed Trevor was standing in the window with tears streaming down his cheeks quietly.

He turned his head back toward Trevor as much as he could while he poured on the speed to catch up with Connor, and yelled, "It will be okay, Trevor; you will see her again. We will do our best to make sure of it!"

Zreyas turned on his Q-leap-alternating run and kept pace with Connor, who ended up being quite a fast runner. "Connor, you run ticking *fast.*"

"That is what I do for exercise... running. I love it!" Connor had an expression of focused bliss, with no sign of being winded, even as fast as they were running.

"Maybe if you have time when we are out of this mess, you can train me to run like that."

"Any time!"

Zreyas had to do more Q-leaping than running. He was glad someone showed him some challenge. That was something he just now realized he missed from the Janquar Nation—the challenge in fighting physically that came from everywhere. That was his exercise. But he saw the strategy of being fast and small more than ever now.

He looked back and there were hundreds of Charred running from where the live oak forest was. His heart sank for both the forest, Ayya, and her mother. The Charred sped toward them and were gaining ground.

"Well, Connor, you love quantum science. I hope you can learn to Q-leap or run faster because they are gaining on us." Zreyas took a quick look back, and it was getting crowded. All the Charred were running toward them, not to mention the nasty anal-gy portal that was wide open with more Charred coming through.

"We have got to get that portal closed." Getting winded now, Zreyas was awestruck that a scrawny scientist could do that much running and not sound winded. He could barely tell the man had been running. "What do you have in your genius mind, Connor?"

"I have been thinking about that ever since we started running. I do a lot of thinking when I run."

"I'm like that too. How about you go as fast as you can and I'll Q-leap on your shoulder? We still have quite a bit to go with all that debris in front of us."

"So how do I do it?"

Zreyas Q-leaped onto his shoulder. It still startled him, though, and he almost fell. "Just run like you do, and head toward where you think your device is that you need."

"That's probably best. But we will trade in the future."

Tap, any ideas on how I can get back? I'm assuming Dulce can get back.

— Captain, Aqum's node is now operational, but Aqum says the rules say that you can't use it yet because it went down while you were there, and all passes to Earth were reset. That was the price for the reactivating of the node.

So, Dulce and the other two are sitting ducks... seal or no seal around them. Knowing them, they just might find a way to break it.

ꙩꙩꙩ *Trevor* ꙩꙩꙩ

Ms. Harrison watched through the window as she shut it. "They are headed toward the house and your father is running like a fiend, Trevor."

"Then Connor is in heaven. Dulce, that man loves to run." Cerys chuckled.

Trevor sat on Ayya's bed full of grief. He felt so lost. It was like someone ripped part of him away. Ayya might be somewhere, but she was not connecting with him anymore. It was like parts of him were reaching out to touch the other parts of her, but couldn't find their way.

Tears spilled down his face again when he heard his mother say, "Son, remember she isn't dead. She's just somewhere else, protected. It's what you want, right? For her to be safe?"

He nodded and looked at the window, watching the Charred try to get into the room. After a few minutes of many of the Charred being what he would call 'fried nasty,' he thought about Ayya. After a few minutes, they gave up and chased who he assumed would be the captain and dad.

Then he thought about her birthday present, and his dark mood lifted a little in the distraction. "Oh, I think I might have something that will help us, but I don't understand it."

Ms. Harrison sat down on Ayya's desk chair after turning it around. "What is it? And what was Ayya doing here?" She pointed at the wall with the scale and drawings.

He looked up at her pirate drawings and knew there would be no way she would believe that story. "Ms. Harrison, the story behind that one is so out there I doubt you would believe it, even being part of the visage, Rtu."

She flashed that freckle-faced smile that seemed to always melt him inside and feel better. "Try me. I might surprise you."

Trevor took a deep breath and told her the story Ayya told him—about how the scales tipped to show which one was better as she tried to draw the contest picture.

Then he told her about how Ayya was going to quit drawing and what the scales did in response. "Ayya said the scales were very strong about her not quitting with the clinks."

Ms. Harrison's eyes welled up with tears and she whispered, "Mother."

Cerys walked over and touched Ms. Harrison's shoulder. "Are you okay, Dulce?"

That seemed to wake his teacher up. "Oh, I apologize. Yes, I'm more than fine. Those scales tipping like magic tells me that my mother, the prime visage of balance, is still alive in some form somewhere. Zreyas told us she was alive, but we weren't sure."

Trevor felt hope surge through him. "You didn't believe the captain?"

"Oh, it wasn't that we didn't believe him. We knew what he was saying was valid from his perspective, but no visage has ever died that type of death and lived in any form... wherever it is in the quantum. She was supposed to be dead permanently. Tulyata was never someone you should underestimate, and it seems she has proven that yet again."

Trevor thought about Ayya's birthday present. He got up and bolted into Ayya's closet and opened the little secret compartment in the wall they had made years ago.

There it was, the bag that had her birthday present in it.

His mother called out to him. "What are you doing in her closet, young man?"

"I'm not sure, but I think this might save Ms. Harrison and the captain at least. Remember how during the talks when the captain talked about how the challenge node used tokens?"

"Yes," the two ladies said.

As he worked the bag loose and out of the opening, he explained. "Well, before all those talks happened, I was preparing these tennis balls to be heavy. They are, well were, the weights needed to open up the secret hideout we were in from the outside. They were to be placed in three different places to work the weights."

"You are a genius, Trevor." Ms. Harrison smiled.

"Well, this is Ayya's genius, not mine."

"Yes, but you were the genius at finding ways to execute her plans. Don't sell yourself cheaper than your value, Trevor."

"Here, here!" his mother confirmed.

A surge of a warm feeling made him take in a sharp, deep breath, almost like it pushed its way past the anguish of missing the connection with Ayya.

"Thanks!" He felt rather good after those compliments. Ayya always seemed to get all the attention when doing good or bad things. "Well, before any of those talks happened, I was the only one that knew about these balls." He handed one to each of them as well as one of his own.

Trevor reached into his pocket and pulled out a jack-knife and opened it. He walked over to Ayya's desk and pushed the point into the seam he had previously glued.

When it opened, the shotgun shot flowed out. Then he reached his fingers in, prying the ball open more. He pulled out a round poker-like chip token with purple and yellow colors, symbols etched into them. Then he held it up for Ms. Harrison to see.

Ms. Harrison's eyes widened and he assumed she knew what it was. She reached for it and took it from him, examining it. "This is a challenge token for the node Captain Zreyas claimed. But I don't think I can use it because the captain has to open up access."

"Can't you try to use it to make sure? How did you get this, Trevor?" asked his mother.

"You are such a mom, Mom. Can you try it Ms. Harrison?"

His mother and Ms. Harrison chuckled as his teacher closed her hand around it, then closed her eyes. Then she shook her head as her face seemed to melt into a sadness for a moment.

"So, all we need to do is get the other one to Captain Zreyas, Ms. Harrison?"

"Unfortunately, you might be right." She opened her hand, and right before his eyes, it sunk into her palm, disappearing.

"Wow!" he and his mom said together.

"Now, back to my question—where did you get that, young man?"

As Trevor took the ball from his mom, he explained. "It was weird, Mom, I don't really know, but I do."

He pushed the point into the ball like he did the first one, shotgun shot spilling out on the glass covered desk listening to the little tick sounds the shot made when they fell and landed on the glass cover of the desk, then the wood floor. There was something satisfying to him about that.

He giggled.

Getting distracted, he looked at the pictures of both him and Ayya that she had put between the glass and the wooden desk.

"Trevor Dan Sadler!"

"Oh, sorry, Mom. I just miss Ayya. I feel... dead." He took a deep breath and continued. "Anyway, Ms. Harrison, I put the plans Ayya and I made in a box on my workbench down in the basement that Dad and I made for my size. There were lots of pages.

"When I went back to get the plans for the entrance mechanism, the part about the weights was on top of the pile. It wouldn't be weird, but I put it at the bottom since it was the hardest part. Anyway, there was another drawing that we *didn't* do attached to that plan. I was going to use steel ball bearings from the old... well, it doesn't matter..."

Trevor nervously cleared his throat. —*achem*— as he looked up at his mom, who had that look on her face that said 'you might be in big trouble, buddy.' Then he quickly continued.

"The drawing showed a sphere with the words 'something heavy inside' with an arrow inside the half-cut sphere. Then there were these tokens taped on the paper with arrows pointing inside, too.

"... and that's it. I got the idea of using the shotgun shot when I was watching Ayya make shells for her father before she got into trouble. It's one of those jobs she did for him."

"Let me guess..." his mom putting her hand on her hip, "you stole the shotgun shot."

Trevor couldn't help it. He smiled proudly. "Yes, Mom, I did. I figured the bag of shot was payment for Ayya's indentured servitude!"

"I'll servitude *you*!"

Ms. Harrison smiled and held up a hand. "I'm not sure he really had much of a choice as connected he is to Ayya and this whole situation. While I don't condone stealing, look at how he became so obsessed about digging that tunnel, despite his weakness from the polio aftermath. He was driven by something inside. It strengthened him, too."

She gestured to his left side. "Cerys, you know how hard I can be on the children, but something tells me why he did it was more than just wanting something for himself in a normal theft this time. And I don't think Ayya had anything to do with it. Even in their communication, she never found out about the tunnel still being worked on."

Ms. Harrison mentioning his polio was something he hadn't thought about in a couple of years. He looked at his left hand, arm, and leg again, turning them. He just didn't think about it anymore. The more he thought about it, the prouder he felt doing all that with his physical disability.

"You are right, Dulce. Thank you. I noticed a few months ago how his muscles were filled in and how much more fluid his movement was."

His mom turned toward him and rubbed his head. "I'm sorry, Trevor, go on. We might not have much time and I think you are right. This is important."

Trevor finished opening the second ball and pulled out a much larger one that looked like three tokens stuck together, making a triangle that he had a hard time getting out.

"This one is the odd one of the three, Ms. Harrison. Look at this." He held it up in front of them all.

Ms. Harrison took that one and held it between her hands for a moment. "This one is for you and your parents, maybe. You must be all together and each one of you holding one token." She handed it back to him. "But you may not have to use this if I can get out of here."

Trevor gave the token to his mother, then reached for the ball in Ms. Harrison's lap and opened it straight away, pulling out the last one. "This is Captain Zreyas' token, and I'm going to make sure he gets it."

He pocketed it and went to the window to check out what was happening outside. What he saw scared him. "Oh, this isn't good."

The two women scrambled to the double windows to see what he was talking about, as he watched droves of the Charred coming out of the woods. There had to be another portal. They seemed to come from Ayya's live oak wood area.

"If dad uses his device, would it get the whole area between the house and the woods, Mom?"

"Unfortunately, probably not if they don't know it needs to be that large. Your father won't want to hurt that many people."

His mind struggled with this whole violent world right now, but something resolved in his mind. "Which one would you want? Killing a few thousand people or the whole earth by the time those things get done with us?” asked Trevor, having a hard time believing those things used to be an actual flesh and blood species, like the captain.

Trevor opened the window as Ms. Harrison said, “You have a good point, Trevor. War is never a good situation for safety; unfortunately, it’s more of a question of how little or how many you want to kill for the best outcome.”

“What do you think you are doing, son?” his mother’s voice was full of alarm, reaching out to grab him. “I just got you back to health.”

With unquestioning determination, he looked back at his mother. “I’m going to get this token to Captain Zreyas.”

“What?” His mother grabbed his shoulder and twisted him around.

In his mind, if Captain Zreyas died, there was no hope for them, anyway. “They have no interest in me. Unless either of you can run faster than me, there is no choice. They need to know about the extra Charred so they can set the—”

“We have to hurry. Trevor, when you get there,” interrupted Ms. Harrison with urgency in her voice. “Tell the captain to give us permission to use the node. I can use it to get back and then get your mother to safety once I return and am whole again. Then you and your father can use the token together. It will work without the third if she is already out. All my senses tell me you will never make it if you have to come back, and we are running out of time to get you there.”

He scrambled out of the window, then turned to look at his mother, who he could tell was in pure terror about him going. “I love you, Mom. I’m scared, but I’m determined, and you know how I get when I'm determined."

She quickly nodded without a word. With tears in her eyes, she handed him the triangle token.

Ms. Harrison put a hand on his mom's shoulder and smiled. "I know you will be successful, even if it doesn't seem like you will be. I just have that feeling."

"Don't worry Ms. Harrison and Mom, I know just the way to get there and I'm pretty fast if you don't compare me to Ayya!" Then he had this urge, so he put his fist to his forehead and bowed. "For the Sleeping Phoenix Order!"

41 Token Broken

The Charred that had been pouring out of the portal seemed to slow down. That was a relief to Zreyas as they ran around all the debris from the bombardment from the heartless General. Some friend. He guessed power and position were more important to him than his people. He didn't know how things worked on Earth, though.

Connor pointed. "There it is, but we better go into that mess from the side door that is on the only wall standing right now. It's an outside door to the basement from the east side."

They ran harder than ever once they both glanced back and saw all the Charred closing in slowly, but Connor didn't seem to slow down any. Keeping his family safe was probably a big motivator for speed, Zreyas guessed. "Is this pace fast for you?"

"Nope, but I'm reserving my energy for when we will need it, unless you got another plan."

Zreyas was hanging on to Connor's collar to keep from falling off. "Do you know where that device is?"

"Yes, let's just hope we can get the vault open. Who knows, they might have damaged it."

One of the Charred crawled out of the tunnel that had collapsed just as Zreyas Q-leaped off his ride to the ground.

It was only a couple of meters away and immediately went on the hunt for them. It had half a forearm. Zreyas pulled his bow and nocked the arrow and chose fire.

Zreyas pulled his bow back, Q-leaped around, aimed, shot it, then turned around, Q-leaping again to catch up with Connor.

Then he heard screeches he could swear would pierce his ears. When he looked back, the whole Charred was engulfed in flames, still in pursuit.

"What the ticking-hell? There isn't enough left in these Charred to even call them living incarnations. They are enthralled machines that no longer feel."

"That doesn't sound good," said Connor. "Look, there is where we need to go in the house. Well, what is left of it."

Zreyas pulled his bow again, nocked a steel ball arrow, then mentally told the neutrinos to expand the size as it flew to something large enough to break it apart as brittle as it was. Then he shot it at the torso of the flaming Charred.

The body of the Charred shattered, sending flaming fragments everywhere. A couple of them hit both him and Connor. It knocked him down, but he righted himself. But then he saw that Connor's shirt was on fire.

"Ice next time, Captain. Ice!"

"Yeah, mistake!" Zreyas Q-leaped onto Connor's shoulder and patted out his shirt. "Whew!"

— Captain, can you hear me?

Yes, can you hear me?

No answer.

"Tap is trying to contact me but I can't get through to her to let her know I can hear her. I'm going to try my Tap-interface while you run."

"Hang on! Going in!"

Zreyas hung on to the poor man's neck for dear life while he tried to concentrate on his Tap-interface. A blank page opened as he focused on sending her a note. He didn't know how to write yet, but he could read. Zreyas pretended he knew and thought about writing what he wanted to say.

> Tap, I can hear you, but I don't think you can hear me.
> It's me.

He groaned at his lack of skills as he sat up, but concentrated on sending it off to her. Sure enough, it disappeared. When he looked ahead, he almost knocked himself out, hitting the top of the door frame as Connor when through.

As Zreyas flew off Connor's shoulder, he grabbed the single hair braid on his back. Connor dipped back momentarily with the sudden pull and weight on the back of his head.

As Zreyas swung out he pulled himself back up. "Your hair is good rope!"

Connor chuckled. "You can thank my wife for that."

"Why? It's your hair."

"It's the chemicals she gives me."

That confused Zreyas, "Chemicals make hair?" As he threw his leg over Connor's shoulder, he saw what was ahead of them. There was their first problem—debris blocking their way.

"Uh, oh." Connor tried hard to move it, but there was too much weight on top of it. The house above had been three stories, so there was no telling when it might shift and collapse further.

"Where is this vault you spoke of?"

"It's not far at all. Once in, we take a right, down some stairs, then another right. Both are immediate tight turns. Ironically, it is almost under us."

"Dad! Wait!" a winded voice came in the distance.

He and Connor jerked their heads around, knowing who that was. Zreyas Q-leaped to the top of the outer storm door steps and Trevor was running as hard as he could with seven Charred right behind him.

His mood suddenly turned darker and ground his words out. "Oh, hell-ticking-no." He pulled his bow and rapidly fired as many steel blunt arrows as he could. All of them shattered but one, apparently a recently acquired Charred, not yet completely gone.

An idea came to him... and he realized that his heart might one day kill him, but that was better than dying the way he would have if he had not found Rhom.

He pulled back and turned on his frequency filter. Then willed the arrow to be neutrinic but at a frequency that wasn't extreme to kill or make him deathly sick. Maybe he could give him a chance before he killed him. Just as the new Charred was about to grab for Trevor, he let the arrow go, hitting him in the shoulder rather than a vital area.

The arrow stuck, and the Charred went down.

Connor went out to meet his son. As Connor brought Trevor back, he listened to the conversation and watched the downed charred. The brittle parts seemed to fall away, revealing the raw, oozing flesh.

Zreyas realized he might have made a mistake. That person would suffer more. He ran out to the body lying there. The first thing he thought to say was, "I'm saying the aplop-o-gies, charred one. I will put you out of your misery. I tried to help you, but I failed and made things worse for you."

He pulled out his knife, just as the ex-Janquar's eyes turned up to him.

Barely understanding him, the now fleshy Charred struggled to utter, "My Com-mander Z-zrey-as." Then Zreyas saw his eyes fill ever so slightly. "I... am... free."

"Easy, friend."

The member of his old line gasped a few times, before saying a breathy struggled, "Peace-tok." Then the old Janquar let out his last breath.

Zreyas' breath hurt as he inhaled, his heavy heart painful. He put his fist to his forehead and bowed.

"Captain Zreyas, I've got something important to tell you." Trevor's voice was urgent, more like an adult than a little kid. He supposed wars like this would do that to a child.

He looked around and saw the droves of Charred pouring down the road and around the buildings like liquid, then more coming from the woods. They hadn't spotted him yet, though, he didn't think.

"Ticking-portals." Then he Q-leaped back toward the entrance they had been at before.

Connor was trying to move debris as Trevor tried to catch his breath.

"Captain... I have something that will get us out of here, but Ms. Harrison said you have to give us access to the challenge node you claimed. Here..." Trevor handed him a token with purple and yellow color and symbols on it.

"How did you—"

"Long story, but glad to tell you later, Captain. We don't have much time and if Ms. Harrison can't get out using her token, she won't be able to save Mom."

It all started making sense to him now. He pulled up his Tap interface with the intention of sending a message to both Tap and Aqum, just in case. Saying it both in his mind and pretending to write again, he said,

> By order of Zreyas of the Atra, give my crew, Rhom, Rtu, and the Sadlers' access to the claimed node of purple and yellow... now! It's still me.

As soon as he said it in his mind, the words shimmered and left. "Thank you, Trevor, for risking your life to save some of us. I'm—"

"Captain Zreyas, I don't mean to interrupt but I have another one, but it's for Dad and I. We can get out of here now." Trevor held up the triangle shaped one. It looked like three tokens stuck together and it shimmered.

"Looks like the message I put through got to the right people. We can use the tokens. Let me see that."

As Connor poked his head out carefully, Zreyas could see his body shudder. "Better hurry at whatever we decide to do because they are making their way here, combing the entire area."

Zreyas held his hand out as Trevor gave him the token cluster. "It's too bad they are not separate. It would have been nice to have that freedom. No wonder Dulce needed the access so Rtu could get your mother. That must cost a lot of balance, but we likely have plenty on our side after all this."

Then Zreyas noticed a flipping and turning fractal spot in the center. He immediately thought about Tulyata, even though all the visages seemed to use them for communication. The energy signature that had been imprinted in his mind, no, in his soul... went out to the symbols to give the thankings to whoever did this for them.

The tokens broke free from each other. All three of them exchanged glances with eyes as big as saucers.

Trevor jumped up and down in excitement. "I love this stuff! Nice magic, Captain!"

"Even though I don't understand it all, it's not magic Trevor, it's science."

Connor's face lit up and reached out to take a token after Trevor reached for his.

Zreyas put his token in his palm and watched it disappear as he told the others to do the same. Then he instructed them on how to pull it back out to use it and talked about the rules for utilizing it.

"So what's the plan, Captain Zreyas? I hope Mom and Ms. Harrison got out."

"Let's get to that vault so we can get my device... but I don't know how. I've tried to get to the vault, but those spaces are way too small for me."

"Dad, I can get in there. It's what kids do, get into places they shouldn't be in."

"No way I'm letting you out of my sight!"

"Dad, now is not the time to be overprotective. We don't have that luxury with the charcoal bricks on the way."

Connor grunted as he sighed. "You are right, son. It's just hard for a parent to let go, especially in danger." He nodded. "If we don't kill that portal and—"

"Oh, Captain Zreyas! I almost forgot, it looks like there is a portal in the woods now too, so the device has to be set for the maximum area to take it out too. *Whew*, glad I didn't forget that."

Connor got a look in his face like Rhom gets when he goes off into that science calculating world he goes into. Zreyas just stared at Connor, mouth slightly agape, waiting for the calculations.

"He gets like that... a lot. When he does that, I know I am going to get to go to work with him soon so he can teach me all about it." Then his face wilted.

"Don't worry, Trevor, you will live in a facility soon that you can learn all you want to learn with your dad."

Trevor's expression lit up and a big grin stretched across his face. "I think I'm going to love this new life, even if Ayya isn't around."

"We can blow both portals, but we will have to put the device on the other side of the house. The problem is the debris, and the Charred, sitting on top of us."

"Well, one thing at a time. We got to get the device first. Does Trevor have the ability to open the vault?"

"I do!"

"What?" Connor was suddenly more fatherly again than a scientist.

"Well, Dad, what did I just say about doing what kids do and getting into things they shouldn't, hmm?"

They all chuckled, despite the dire circumstances.

Then Zreyas thought about why the Charred had not yet come for them. They had to know where they were. They have been ahead at least a step the entire time through this, and using the quantum beyond the challenge. He could shield his mind, but—an idea came to him.

"This might sound difficult, but before we talk about anything else, consciously visualize a shield around your mind, giving no one permission to enter or listen to your thoughts, not even Ayya, just in case she is in trouble, too. Never take her protection, or ours, for granted. That dark visage uses the quantum."

They nodded. Then their faces morphed into a variety of expressions, both looking like they were about to take a shit.

Zreyas scrunched his face up on one side, wondering if that was how he looked when he did that. "Look, it's not that hard... just state what you want and know it is there."

Trevor got an expression that mouthed the word 'Oh!', nodding his head. "Got it!"

"Same."

He made sure he shielded his own mind, then said, "Now I need you to do something for me, Trevor. If *I* do it, it won't be believable to the Dark One, because that ticking-bandhula knows I use the quantum. You will be doing your secret agent work but safely."

Zreyas watched Trevor's expression grow more excited. "This is what I want you to do. Think of a place in the opposite direction from where we are—a place you know that your mother would go to. When you are ready, *UN*-shield your mind and think about how your mother is running with Dulce to that place for safety. Think about how you hope they make it as if they are doing it now. Then, immediately, shield your mind again before you think about anything else."

"Oh, great idea, Captain." Then Connor turned to Trevor. "Your mother goes to the bridge club at the community center a mile from here... use that one... It's more realistic and would make sense why she would go there."

"See, Dad, there is hope for you yet! I'll do that one."

"Wait, let me finish so we can all be doing what we need to do at the same time." Zreyas opened his mouth to explain what he had in mind when Connor suddenly grunted and a few drops of blood splattered over Trevor's face.

"Dad!"

Connor steadied himself against the wall, working his way down into the basement to steady himself as Trevor ran up to help him. "Well... <grunt>... that... was stupid... of me."

Zreyas' heart sunk as he saw Connor with a Janquar arrow sticking through his shoulder and an archer standing on the debris of the house nearby, nocking another arrow.

"Get down!" he ordered, as he pulled his own bow, nocking an ice arrow to freeze the Charred before trying to shatter it. That Charred archer's skills must be declining, or they would have killed Connor. Janquar never miss. They don't take the shot at all if there is a chance they won't hit their target spot on.

As he aimed, he moved up to show himself so the focus would be off Connor and on to him. "Change of plan. Connor, use your token and Trevor can crawl into the spaces out of sight of the Charred till I can get in there. Trevor can help me find and use the device... Hurry!"

He could hear Trevor helping ease his father down on the floor at the bottom of the steps, just barely around the corner. Then he did as he was told and crawled into the spaces between the debris. "Don't worry, Dad, you taught me well, and I got Captain Zreyas with me."

Connor nodded with sweat running down his face, holding his arm.

As he drew his bow to capacity, he gave instructions. "Now open your hand and think about going to the new challenge node, your new home. The token should appear in your hand and it will transport you there. If not, we are all dead because they don't work."

— It will Captain. Freckles used his, and Cerys is safe on the ship.

As Zreyas let the arrow go, hitting the Charred archer spot on at the forehead, he relayed what Tap had just told him. His target shattered and smoked from the cold.

Sighs of relief came from Connor and Trevor.

"I sure hope mom and Mrs. Harrison get to the community center safe. They don't run too good," said Trevor.

Zreyas couldn't help but grin. "Well done, Trevor." Then he looked around to make sure no one else saw him. He used his frequency site and was relieved no one else was in the immediate area to see him, but something wasn't quite right. Things felt more off to him than the normal Charred chaos.

Zreyas sheathed his bow and scampered down the steps.

Connor nodded to him without a word, with a clear message in his expression that he was concerned, but supported him as the captain in his new life. He opened his hand. "Take care of Trevor. He's my hero." He grinned as he fragmented and disappeared.

Zreyas felt relief that someone on the other side would tend to his wounds. Someone had to be there, or the tokens wouldn't have existed. *Thank you Tap for that timely communication.*

— You are welcome, Captain. There was something distorting the quantum field near your area on Earth. We made some adjustments and decoded the—

You don't have to explain the details. I'm not there yet about this science stuff. He guessed the purple and yellow node was in a safe place, and also wondered if the little arrangement he made with Aqum before the talks, just in case activated or they got to the node some other way. Either way, he couldn't think about it now.

"Okay Trevor, let's go. Lead the way, but be careful and watch for dust falling. It's a sign of something that is loose."

To his credit, Trevor said almost in a whispered tone, "Yes, Captain. O-neg is on it. Follow me."

Trevor carefully moved through the debris, but Zreyas wasn't taking any chances. He watched attentively ahead of him for possible collapse signs as he started asking Tap questions. *Tap, is Rhom there on the ship?*

— No, Captain.

She didn't say anything else, so that either meant she was clueless about what had happened or it was something she couldn't talk about for some reason. Either way, his hope waned that he was alive somewhere. *What is relevant to me in this situation here, that you can tell me? The Charred seem to be holding back for some reason. Do you know why?*

— Yes, Captain, I do. I'm glad you asked. There are three portals to that dark realm the nagodara came from and where the visage Ijin now dwells, as you know.

He didn't know about the third one, but he would not interrupt her. Zreyas helped Trevor right himself after tripping on a beam under him, clearly growing tired.

— They are pouring a greenish liquid with dark red tones into the old tunnel room right through the portal.

Tap's voice faded as Trevor pointed. "We are almost there, Captain. I can see part of it now."

Sure enough, there was a corner of what looked like a thick, molded metal wall with a door.

— … and it is smoking, Captain. But it isn't fire.

"Good work, little hero of the Order. Lead on."

Trevor smiled like the sun and nodded. "Yes, Captain."

That seemed to renew his energy a little, and he scrambled forward.

In a few seconds, they arrived, and both of them worked to free up the debris in front of the door. He realized the debris used to be shelves with tombs on it. He wasn't sure what Earth called them.

"Why did you have shelves in front—"

"To hide it, Captain. Dad made the door to look and function like shelves. There are some important things in there from my dad's work that he didn't want the governments to use for bad things."

"Oh, very strategic... and wise." Zreyas crossed his arms and asked, "Time to open it, Trevor."

Trevor walked up to the heavy door. He put his hand on the round dial. "Oh, no..."

"What is wrong?"

"The dial won't move, so I can't unlock it!"

Zreyas immediately sat on his heels in a squat to think. "What is the door made of?"

"It's impenetrable except for torch or a specific acid that get past the coating that acids can't penetrate."

"How can a torch—"

— Captain, he's not talking about a torch like you are used to. It's a more modern torch that streams fire in a very hot thin stream, designed to cut or smelt metals.

Thank you Tap.

Trevor's face looked concerned. "Captain, you okay?"

"Oh, yes. I didn't know what type of torch you were talking about, and Tap corrected my thinking and explained it."

"Man, Tap seems far out."

"She is definitely far out... many universes away."

"No Captain, I didn't mean that kind of 'far out.'"

"I still have a lot to learn about words, I guess."

"I *like* you!"

"I like me, too... most of the time. You are a good... human science hero." Zreyas stood and pulled one of his swords off his back, making Trevor raise an eyebrow.

"Captain, that will not cut the door open."

Zreyas ignored the comment in full concentration as he thought, *My neutrino friends... turn this weapon into a*

— blow torch, Captain

... blow torch.

The sword shimmered and morphed in his hands to a cylinder of some sort, with a metal neck and tube at one end. The weight balance difference almost made him drop it.

"I know how to use one, Captain. Make it a little bigger and I'll do it for you."

Before it fully finished morphing, he thought to make it the size a human would use.

Trevor took it from him before it got too awkward for Zreyas to manage, since it was about as tall as he was or more.

... Then Zreyas smelled the smoke Tap spoke about, and all the words she had said earlier about the green liquid came flooding back into his mind.

The color description...

The smoky vapor...

"Oh, *no.* The acid of the nagodara... no *wonder* they are in no hurry to get at us! And they shot Connor to push us back in the doorway. I wondered why they hit him in the shoulder."

— Good deduction, Captain.

"Trevor... we need to hurry... this place will flood soon with acid, and the vapor from it will kill us long before the liquid will!"

42 The Quantum Destroyer

ּ‌ *Zreyas*

Trevor's eyes grew wide, but somehow kept his composure. He turned, pulled a receded device from the cylinder and turned a knob, making it hiss. He clicked the other thing in his hand and it sparked, making a blue flame shoot out. Zreyas couldn't help but drop his jaw in fascination.

"The artisans would love that thing. Work your magic, little hero."

Trevor turned with a big grin and bright expression long enough to say, "It's not magic, Captain. It's science."

Those words made his chest immediately crack. His eyes filled and was grateful the child couldn't see him right now. Rhom's words coming through this boy made him realize how much he missed the old man.

As he watched Trevor, fascinated, he couldn't understand why he had his head half-cocked sideways, not really looking at what he was doing.

The smell was getting stronger, so he turned to see if there was anything that might give them more time, but he knew that even if he stacked shit up around them, it wouldn't be liquid or vapor tight, and it would eat right through. He didn't see anything melting or collapsing, so he figured they had at least a little time.

Then he saw some piled-up cloths and a sink nearby, almost covered up with debris. He Q-leaped over and turned the water on, glad Tap had taught him about plumbing while he was in his quarters. He turned it on with the cloths under it and he soaked them as much as he could before the water ran out. All those explosions must have messed up the pipes, he reasoned.

Zreyas tore a piece off using his knife big enough that he could wrap it around his head to cover his nose and mouth, then told Trevor, "Here, put this around your face so you won't breathe in the fumes. We used to use this when we had to go into fires during—well, never mind."

Trevor immediately put the torch down and did as he was told. "Yes, Captain Zreyas, thank you." Then he hurried to pick the torch back up, then moved to the third place he had been working on. "It's almost done."

"Good, we don't have much time. We can't let the Charred, and anything from that realm, ruin this planet more than they already have."

"I'm so... *mad* at them," Trevor said as he worked, still looking half sideways.

Zreyas curbed his curiosity to ask why he did that because he didn't want to distract him. Just then, he heard a thunk and watched the door start to fall toward them.

"Woah!" Trevor moved back so fast he fell backwards.

He Q-leaped forward over Trevor, and as he appeared sideways, he used his legs to kick it in the opposite direction before it went too far over for his weight, then leaped back.

But the door was so heavy it only stalled it a moment.

Aggravated, Zreyas said, "Why does everything..."

He Q-leaped and kicked the door again.

"... have to be so..."

He Q-leaped back to see the door wobble slightly.

"Ticking-hard!?"

Then Trevor whizzed past him and he shoved his back against the door, pushing hard.

"That's it, Trevor!" Zreyas Q-leaped once more, kicked the door as hard as he could with as much velocity as he could muster without hurting himself.

That did it. Both the door and Trevor toppled into the vault as he thought about how he hoped the device wasn't under that door now.

Trevor looked up with a grin, propping up on his elbows. "We ticking did it!"

Zreyas almost laughed at him using his own language, but then Trevor's expression morphed into pure wide-eyed fear as he pointed behind Zreyas. "Look!"

Zreyas whirled around to see the vapor seeping through all the debris. "Shit! Trevor, where is that device? Get it and show me how to use it."

The boy scrambled up, looking truly scared for the first time since all this started. He apparently knew exactly where it was because he went over to another door that was much smaller and turned the dial back and forth. *Now is not the time for silly questions, Zrey.*

— It's called a safe, Captain. The dial has a mechanism inside that has to have three or more exact turns in different directions to unlock the mechanism to open the door.

Giving you the thankings, Tap.

Trevor looked back quick before turning to open the door. He reached in and grabbed the only thing in the safe, then turned around.

That was going to be an arm-full for Zreyas. Normally it wouldn't have been a big deal to work around, but all the debris, acid, and fumes were huge problems.

"Captain Zreyas..."

Zreyas Q-leaped onto the table next to him to watch.

"... there are three settings... here, here, and here."

He turned on his engineering filter and his eyes grew wide at how small an intricate a lot of the pieces were, yet most of it was... space in the middle, almost like it had an inner compartment. It was round and each dial or button were in the same cluster in the shape of a triangle.

Trevor spent the next minute explaining the device. Then once Zreyas had the idea, he told him to get up on the table. He did as he was told. And set the device on the table as well.

"Turn on the range part while I look at it through my various vision filters and how far it is reaching."

Once Trevor did as he was instructed, Zreyas changed his views several times and finally figured out which one he needed. He even saw the signatures of the portals coming from the other realm. He did a little sizing up and calculated that he would have to go toward the Charred across the acid to reach all three.

"Ticking-hell."

The look on Trevor's face was one of total understanding and sadness. The kid knew.

"It's okay, Trevor. We have plenty more adventures to have together, just like I promised at the talks. I just have to do some hard stuff right now, and it's time for you to meet up with your family. I need you to give everyone the information that happened here, but make sure you are in a secure place first and have everyone shield their minds before you do. Can you do that for me?"

Trevor nodded and straightened his back. "Yes, Captain Zreyas, I promise!"

"Good, now open your hand and think of going to the new challenge node and new home."

The boy smiled and held out his hand, and the token appeared. It wasn't long and Trevor dissipated and was gone.

— Wise of you, Captain.

I couldn't let the boy die here.

— Captain, you can shrink that down by placing it into your dimensional pocket in your armor, don't forget.

"Giving you the thankings for reminding me," he said out loud as Zreyas slid two sliders on the front of his chest armor. Two straps with diodes flashed at the ends. He touched the device with the two diodes, and it disappeared into his pocket.

Zreyas wasted no time and Q-leaped higher and closer to the surface without showing himself.

— Captain, Rtu suggests you use your weapons and transmute them into a portable earth drill so you can dig through the earth upward, then level off to keep the acid from you longer.

Give me an image of it so I understand it.

— Yes Captain, here you go. Oh, and Rtu said to set it to use the displacement setting and he would take care of the earth so it wouldn't leave a trail at the surface.

The machine had a point and corkscrew-like head. His hands would fit inside and it had long belts. He wasn't really sure what they were.

"Explain this to me. I don't want to end up in a situation like I did when I was on Tarq. If it wasn't for Silence, I wouldn't be here now."

After Tap explained the device, he morphed the bow into the device, making it big enough he could stand in the tunnel after it was dug, just in case he had to run quick.

He angled the extremely heavy device upward against the wall and turned it on. Zreyas almost fell on his ass when it almost got away from him.

Zreyas started again, he braced himself and was glad he still had a Janquar's strength in his little body. Once he got the hang of it, the tunnel progress went well.

He angled up at first for a bit, then leveled off just as Rtu had instructed. He headed toward his marked destination, but things seemed to go way too smooth though. Something didn't feel right.

— Captain, are you thinking you might need to get out of there?

Yes, something doesn't feel right. Can you ask Aqum if I left and came back after checking the time line? Would there be a better time to set this thing to explode?

Zreyas turned on his auras for the challenge and there was a lot of red, which meant there was little he could influence.

— Captain, Aqum advises you are better off staying where you are, but alter your course.

Suddenly, something vibrated behind him and he felt the ground around him shift. He poured on the power and strength into digging. And went straight up about two meters from the surface and then turned down... straight down.

Zreyas tried formulating plans as he went. If they went after him, they would have a straight drop. He dug down to the point where the dirt got more wet.

The captain stopped and dug around to make a small little pit filled with water. Then he Q-leaped high with the point of the drill stuck into the wall and turned it on again.

He didn't take something into consideration though, he had no leverage to push against, so he did several small Q-leaps into the earth until he finally got the drill going, and not falling.

After he could stand, he stopped and looked back. The room was a couple of meters down. If acid or something poured or dropped in, at least it would buy him a little more time.

Zreyas turned around, got his bearings again, and started muttering to himself about how he was always the one that had to do ticking-shit like this. After he thought about it a moment, he really didn't want to have others do this either, and his reaction was purely out of fear.

He needed more small crew members and was going to ask Tap how she thought they could do it. She had mentioned it once when he was on Tarq. Some of the Janquar wanted to be small and do what he did. This was one of those times that his uniqueness was lonely.

Tap, they know where I am, don't they?

— Yes, Captain. I think so, because they are all gathering around where you are on top of the ground, and they have long poles. I think they plan on trap—

Yeah, yeah, I got it. At least—

Zreyas heard a faint skittering. Then he continued the rest of his sentence. *I'm where I can set off the device and take out at least two portals, if not all three.*

He pulled the device out, set it down, and set the range to max. Taking a deep breath, feeling bad for anyone that might still be alive in the area that weren't Charred.

Tap, Trevor said that this thing operated on the science of how stars became what he called white dwarfs. Do you think I could remotely detonate it if I put a charge... like lightening arrow to hit in the vicinity?

— I'm— — sure, Cap—n.

Uh, oh. Trevor said that somehow his father figured out a way to stop the process and quickly reverse it so that the pressure would build so fast that it would create an exponential explosion. I'm just not sure I want to be around for that shotgun bang.

A pole violently crashed through into the tunnel between him and the drill, making Zreyas feel like he almost jumped out of his skin. His sight wavered slightly at the surprise. He assumed he almost instinctively went into the quantum or something.

What alarmed him was that the pole was coated with a green coating of some sort, and it smelled sickeningly sweet. Instinctively, he knew it wasn't *just* paint. He hurried to set the device and prepared to stay where he was to set it off. Trevor said Connor named it The Quantum Destroyer, and he guessed it had a new meaning now.

Loud skittering sounds assailed his ears, and the noise was definitely echoing in from where he had been through that tunnel. He turned on his heat signature filter and saw nothing but distortion. But even through that, there were no moving heat signatures.

This is... weird. I better get out of here fast.

He thought about how his heart was still calming down from the recent jolt when that pole had slammed down through the ground. The sensation of jumping out of his skin gave him an idea, and he quickly made sure his mind was shielded.

He thought back to the lightning strike event at Ayya's grandmother's house and how the form impersonating Jackie had almost killed him... well; it *did* kill him. But he had experienced and learned about quantum mirroring then with the help of who he thought was Tulyata's guidance while he was in the Q-leap.

Zreyas put the device back into the dimensional pocket in his armor, then used his hands to dig to the other side of the pole to get to the opposite side, far enough that he had plenty of room to stand and place the device. He turned the drill back into his weapon. After putting it back in place, he hurried to pack the dirt behind him.

He knew he couldn't use the token now because the rule was, he couldn't travel while being targeted, or in immediate danger. Neither one of those requirements checked off. Somehow, they knew exactly where he was.

He realized he wasn't the only person with advanced technology.

Just as he had gotten the dirt packed and adjusted his dark vision, he heard digging in the dirt behind him distantly. Then he heard it coming from yet another direction.

As he looked around, using his heat signature filter for living beings, all he saw were random distortions.

He turned the temperature range up.

... Nothing.

Then he tried to adjust it down.

His jaw dropped and his whole body froze.

All around him were thousands of what looked like general shapes of ants with shells and a tail. He took a step back in reaction.

The things sped up.

His mind reeled at his worst creature nightmare coming to pass since he had been small—insects overwhelming him. He froze.

To his surprise, the creatures slowed down and then stopped. The signatures of their bodies slowly bent back and forth as if they were looking for him. Sound... sound is how they targeted things, or... vibration. If he had to guess, it was the ladder.

Zreyas did an experiment. He barely whispered, "For science, old man." The creatures didn't move. Then he did it again, louder in a normal voice. Again, they didn't budge.

Carefully, he placed his hand on the dirt wall, then twisted his palm as he pushed in gently. Sure enough, the creatures started skittering fast toward him. He couldn't help but wonder why they didn't turn and run toward each other, because they also made noise and vibrations.

He figured as long as he moved, they would close in. Then, with alarm, he realized the group in the tunnel didn't have to dig, because he had dug it for them. He was in big trouble. *Think, Zrey. Think!*

He risked the noise and squatted and sat down on his heel to think. *Zrey, you aren't thinking, you should have Q-leaped into the position. Maybe it would have made less vi—*

A message blinked in his Tap-interface. He opened it and it was a note from Aqum. That puzzled him. Then he remembered messaging Aqum about the tokens. Maybe that's probably how Aqum knew how to message him.

> Rtu suggests doing a little more experimenting. Use your chemical makeup vision to look at the pole. We think they are using a chemical that will make some sort of creature frenzy when they get close to it. Be careful. We won't communicate again.

Okay, that ticking sucks like two piles of mag-shit on the eyes, he thought to himself. Something must be up because that didn't sound like Aqum at all. He pulled up the chemical view and saw the chemical make-up, but had no clue what it meant. *Useless!*

Tap and Aqum should have known he wouldn't understand that. And why did Aqum message him and not Tap?

He messaged back and told Tap and Aqum to not message him again unless he was about to die, and that it was ticking messed up to waste his critical time with something he wouldn't understand.

Zreyas was seething now, realizing he just wasted his own time. His anger was about to blow. As he looked around, he noticed the creatures were skittering alarmingly fast. And he realized too late just how much he vibrated while he was angry. It was so significant that the pile of dirt he had left behind him partially collapsed enough to see those creatures climbing over each other in the pit he had dug earlier.

43 Reflecting Reflectors

ריריר *Zreyas* ריריר

He didn't know what to do, so he went with what was immediate... using his anger. It would give him away for sure, but it would also buy him some time to set down the device and go with the first ticking-half-assed-thought-out plan.

The *first* thing he was going to do was take his anger out on the damn ticking-creatures that were about to feast on him. He might go out by feeding the masses, but he was going to make his mark on them all.

He couldn't think of anyone but Rhom right now and how the loss felt. It was like re-cutting his raw insides all over again. It ticking-pissed him the hell off at how they forced Rhom to make a choice to save Connor or himself.

He knew it wouldn't do any good, but he let himself rant to get it out of his system anyway, so he could think.

"To top it all off, I had just started a brand-new life with my chosen family, and the Dark One saw fit to rip a large, bloody hole in it."

Pacing in a circle, he waved his hands around like he was swatting insects. "The ticking-LFO's yan is so dark and low frequency now that he no longer has a ticking-soul anymore. Zrey, Zrey, Zrey... look at what you could have become, and still could if you are not careful."

All this made him angrier than he had been since the commander all but killed Aaru at the Viduri ritual.

Get it together, Zrey. You will not abandon your new family and friends just because you are feeling the sorries for yourself and having a child-fit.

He took in a deep breath and waited as the tears formed from the anger. His throat was so full from holding it all back, he almost choked and couldn't breathe.

Zreyas heard something break through the dirt behind him, then a few seconds after that the creatures as big as his foot started pouring up out of the pit like water toward him.

As he watched the little shelled mag-shits scramble toward him, he realized what was causing the distortion in his view. The shells were reflecting energy, temperature, and vibration.

Terror gripped him as he realized his roar probably wouldn't bother them. But the floodgates opened before he could think of an alternative.

As his war aura erupted, everything within range flew back, broke apart, fell, or became projectiles.

But something happened that not only shocked him, but felt like it would rip him apart. All of his frequencies that he sent out in his roar that hit the bugs reflected back, some of it hitting the ceilings and walls.

Zreyas would have knocked himself backward, but he hadn't directed his aura, so from the feel of what had just come back to hit him, it was as if all the energy that hit him came from everywhere the bugs were.

As he grunted, trying to get his breath, he realized that was kind of how they tracked him, by both feel and reflection, maybe. He didn't know; but there was one thing he knew, and that was he just kicked his own ticking-anal-gy!

Had he known that was what was going to happen, he would have accepted it in, and channeled it back... "Whoa..." As he got up, some of the dirt had caved in. It actually surprised him more of it didn't. Then an idea came as he watched the insects charge in.

He stood and breathed in as he filled his compartment and let out his war aura while opening himself to accept it all back.

Sure enough, it knocked everything away from him again and part of it reflected back from the strange insects were. He accepted it in again to his compartment.

This would buy him a few seconds' time to get the device set and ready to go. *Oh, that's right, I already set it up. I just need to place it and push the button. Get it together, Zrey, you are a little stressed.*

Sending out the war aura again at a pace that would give him a few seconds and push them back, he repeated the process. It was working beautifully, except for one thing—the ceiling was collapsing. But he again noticed that when he let the undirected war aura out, it pushed everything around him back up and away from him, too.

So, he sent the war aura out more often to the point he finally got it to an almost constant even exchange.

Then he had an idea. He wondered if he could just do the war aura from inside and not have to get his body quite so involved, so he could actually do things while he let it out.

Before he could try it, poles violently slammed down around him in a circle. The gaps weren't large enough for him to fit through, but... they were plenty big enough for the creatures to crawl through.

That was when he realized the poles were reflectors, too. They had known all this was going to happen all along.

Then the dangerous part crept into the crevices of his mind—the ability to handle the reflections was amazing, but those reflective poles were round and they were causing many odd refractions between all the poles. Either the reflections came back inconsistently, making it hard to even fill his compartment, or they didn't come back at all.

It literally incapacitated him other than arm movements, so he planned to stop. He knew the dirt above him would come down on him or they would kill him with another pole soon enough, so he had to do something fast.

He pulled out the device, reset the delay to one, and held it close to him. Then another ticking-half-anal-oozing-mag-shit-plan idea came.

Zreyas filled his compartment, factoring in the bombardment he was encountering from himself, aiming for the spot he originally wanted to Q-leap to.

He squatted, put his fist over the button, then bent over so the collapse would cause his body to press the button under the weight of the earth.

Namdlo, Selkerf, dna Ataylut. I'm sending the lovings to you. For the Order of the Sleeping Phoenix!

Then he did two things simultaneously—he stopped the aura and took in all the reflections that came back from the previous roars, and... he Q-leaped out.

He knew if he came out of that Q-leap too soon; he was a dead Zrey, no matter which side of the leap he was on because of the explosion.

There was one thing he didn't factor in, though. And that was the quantum itself and who might be right there waiting. The quantum here was a nasty greenish dominated colored place with sick yellow and purple mixed in. Was he in the quantum?

Then he saw them... *legions* of demon-like Charred. Or where they demons with charred mixed in? He was losing his sense of self here. Then he saw it... the large one with the red eyes and inky mist sliding in and out of them that seemed to settle on the sea of demon-charred, like mist on a lake.

This visage Ijin made a deal with, or possessed, a very large demon-like creature. That brought his senses back. He must have Q-leaped right through a new portal to that nagodara realm.

— 1 1 1 1 Adjust...

Zreyas looked around for the energy signature of his Q-leap like he had seen before at Ayya's grandmother's house. But what he saw was parts of it were warping. He reasoned it was because they knew he would do this and put the portal there at the right time.

He looked where he should have landed, but nothing was there.

— 1 1 1 1 Adjust...

Adjust to... oh yeah, the Q-leap. Then he felt a song, in more ways than one. Was it the Dark Ijin's song? No. This was too high of a frequency... but he wasn't sure, because the song was more complicated and realized it was his own... older song.

It was like that because his life conditioning had distorted it before.

— 1 1 1 1

Then Zreyas answered, *1 1 1 1.*

Though he had no form here, he turned his awareness toward the song he was hearing. Now, he was sure it was his own song, but indeed different than he remembered.

Then he paid attention to the same all-encompassing guidance he had felt before when he had been killed at Ayya's grandmother's house.

Zreyas faced himself at the end of the jump, though he still couldn't see his body. He reflected the song back with a more accurate word representation that still made sense to him...

During my journeys through illusion and fear,
I watch myself in the eye of the storm.
I now know it...
I now feel it...
The love and guidance are there.

He felt a resonance as it reflected back to him and realized he had just met part of his original self for the first time, but in a different place.

Zreyas changed his goal for his Q-mirror to where his song reflection was coming from, and in the form he knew he needed to be in to survive.

The scales of his quantum mirror, resembling the ones Tulyata had, came into view clearly.

— 1 1 1 1 Good...

Zreyas decided to only focus on his destination. He remembered he had made the mistake before of looking back to this body that had been dying, so he focused ahead.

A clear picture came into his mind of where he would go, though the place didn't quite seem familiar. It wasn't his ship—it was more like... the sky.

As he saw himself dissipate in the quantum from being there too long, his fear felt more like a death sentence. He watched himself this time, though in the eye of that storm his song talked about.

It's okay, Zrey. Then he heard words he knew, but it was as if he was just now remembering something he learned long ago.

— There is something amazing just around the corner, just watch for it.

It seemed to put things in perspective, and the fear no longer took him over.

Then he remembered his ship and all his friends. He decided he wanted something else more than succumbing to the fear, anyway. There was something important to do, and he wanted to see it through.

As he put himself at his destination, he realized that his body on the other side of the quantum mirror was being scattered by the poles, so not all of him was in the quantum yet. He didn't think they had known that any of this would happen, but it was definitely something that would kill him if he left it behind.

Zreyas looked back, but not the same way he had done before. He hummed his present song to call it all back to him.

He patiently waited for the rest of his energy to come when it was freed. With a pleasant shock, he realized that parts of his energy were coming back from many places, times, and spaces, not just what he had left behind moments ago.

As soon as the last part of himself arrived, he watched his body in the quantum mirror. The ground above it came down on him and he watched himself press the button.

His heart cracked for him there, and he sent a thought to him, *giving the thankings to you for your sacrifice.*

Then he turned and focused—making sure he was all gathered in the quantum.

The light was so bright compared to the quantum; it blinded him temporarily. He quickly realized it was likely not the differences in the lighting as much as the light represented the frequency of the dimension he was in.

He saw no sun or physical place, so that confirmed his hunch in his mind.

Surrounding him were soft silhouettes of shapes that resembled forms similar to Silence, but of all sizes. However, there were no faces or details. But there was something he did notice... they had arrays of wreathed golden horns, just like how he used to form his own at the Janquar nation.

He thought of Aaru, but nothing there felt like him. Oh, that's right, he was now with Ayya on a new path. He could see they were in a new battle, with and against each other in the same incarnated body.

A gentle but commanding voice echoed. "You are not ready to come here. Use your token. We are watching, and are grateful you are one of us."

Zreyas looked down at his hand, remembering he had something to do. He looked back up to the one that had the most beautiful golden glimmering silhouette and sent out a communication. *Are you the Atra?*

— Use the token, Zreyas, you are dying here in that body.

The voice seemed to echo from everywhere, almost like it was part of everything there.

He didn't use his voice but still sent a communication somehow. He wasn't sure how he did it. *Sending you the thankings for helping me.*

— We are sending you the lovings, as you say in your unique way. We are always watching.

As he used his token and dissipated, he heard slow echoes of two words follow him through the quantum:

— Contact

— Tulyata.

Zreyas knew what it felt like to go through a challenge node, but this one felt different. He felt himself enter the node, but it surprised him when nothing appeared in front of him, only to be transported out again. Something about that seemed familiar, though.

Then the welcoming feel of the blue and cyan node came, and he materialized in surroundings, he remembered.

Standing in front of him were Silence and Resolute, like noble sitting statues, on guard, and facing him.

Silence was growing fast and looked regal. His wings were in full now, and his feline muscle structure was strong. That tuft of hair on the top of his head still made him want to chuckle. But right now, with the way he was sitting still, it looked more like a royal headdress.

Resolute was just as regal, but in her own way. She was intimidating with her soot black fur and strong facial structure. The extremely thin white stripes were so brilliant compared to the black, it almost looked like her form was cracking and light was coming through. But her face was the picture of strength and intimidation.

He looked down at their feet and realized both of them still had plenty to grow. It was good to see his fur friends after what he had just been through.

To his right side was Rtu, and an oscillating rainbow-colored hologram of Tap.

Then he noticed Cerys, Connor, and Trevor with three creatures about his own size looking like miniature Screh come through the door.

Zreyas jumped as Rtu threw up his hands and screamed out, "Little buddy! You made it!"

Then Resolute slightly crouched and launched herself at him. All he saw was black. The next thing he felt was knife-like licks scraping up his body and rumbling purrs vibrating through him.

44 Uh, Son...

"I'm glad to see you, too, but can you sand down that tongue of yours, Resolute? It's deadly! I need you to go with me. That tongue would pierce even a Janquar warrior's hide!"

Resolute started pouncing in several places, excited to hear what she had just heard.

"Now you've gone and done it, Mother. She will be impossible now." He paused, then said, "It is good to see you again."

Silence approached him and rubbed his face against Zreyas. Then they pressed their foreheads together.

Zreyas did the same. "It's good to see you too, my friend. I'm giving you the thankings for all you are doing to help me."

"I love you, Mother. There is no hurry, but I need to talk with you when you have time."

"We will make that happen as soon as we can."

"Captain Zreyas, you got out of there in only one piece!" Forgetting himself, Trevor ran up and picked

Zreyas up and squeezed him tightly and gave him a kiss on the cheek. As he hugged him again.

Zreyas felt the kid's soft face on his, then his chest condensed as the boy squeezed him. *Here we ticking-go again. What is it about these wet embracings?*

"Captain, when I left, I thought I would never see you again. It was pretty grim back there!" Trevor squeezed him even tighter and rocked back and forth. "I kept thinking about how that green stuff was going to melt you."

Zreyas must have shown he was about to explode because Connor touched his son's shoulder. "Uh, son. I think you might want to put the... *Captain...* down. He's not a doll. He is a war hero and will probably pound your head in if you keep that up." Connor winked at Zreyas apologetically.

Trevor almost dropped him, but he put him down.

Zreyas straightened himself and checked his weapons, feeling awkward.

Rtu was grinning from ear to ear.

"Well, I wouldn't pound your head in, but I might string your eyes on a rope for experiments."

Trevor gasped, eyes going wide, backing up.

"Ha! I'm giving you the anal-gies." Then he winked.

Trevor immediately laughed with him.

It took a second or two before Connor and Rtu remembered the context of the word earlier that day, but they started laughing too, finally.

"Between you and Ayya, I'm getting something I'm not used to—the lovings-huggings mushy-moo affections. It's good training."

Cerys grinned. "It's good to see you again alive, whole, and still sane from being tossed about like a G.I. Joe doll, Captain!"

After he let out a relieved sigh, he looked up at all of them and his eyes wandered, looking for Tap. She was no longer there. "It is good to be home with my people... and even some new people I don't know yet."

Rtu spoke up. "Captain, if you would like, why don't we all go to the common room and have a seat? You can eat while we update you and do some introductions."

"That sounds good. I'm starved."

As soon as the words exited his mouth, Resolute came up behind Zreyas and shoved her head under him, flipping him over her head, and landing on the back of her neck on his stomach.

"G.I. Joe!" exclaimed Trevor.

Zreyas gripped her fur to get his bearings as she started walking him through the corridor, with everyone laughing behind him.

As he righted himself, he thought, *Why does everyone have the urge to toss me around? Oh well, a casualty of the likings, I guess.*

Rtu chuckled out, "Cree will be mad you took his job, Res."

"Not this time. That made me 'Ha'!" said Cree.

Once they arrived in the common room, they brought food to him.

Rtu started the introductions of the extra crew members, then updated Zreyas on what had transpired with the Screh.

Zreyas calculated what they had done as he put the end of his fork to his cheek. The entire room went silent. Then he put his fork down on the table and sat back.

"Katja, I think you are more than ready to lead your tribe, but I also know what it is like to be thrown into something like that without preparation. You have my support and listenings if you need advice. I think our alliance will help all of us for a long time. And I like you are my size! You can't be that bad!" Zreyas laughed.

Katja made this unique squeaking chitter that made Zreyas feel a fascination for. Though she had arms and legs, her shape was more like a shapely eel with fur.

She finally replied. "Captain Zreyas, I don't *need* your support."

The other two Screh looked at her with faces of like 'really? You are going there?'"

She reminded Zreyas of a Janquar warrior, and without a thought, his intimidation aura erupted toward her. Then he leaned forward and smiled grimly. "I'm informing you I will be direct in my talk with you. If you don't like it, leave. If you are okay with it, then we might have a future as allies. To you I will say this...

"Suit yourself, but I have made that mistake as well, and paid a steep price for it. None of us, including you, wouldn't be here if Rtu and Rhom hadn't advised me otherwise many times."

The entire room went dead silent.

He cocked his head and felt himself narrow his eyes even further than they already were, leaning closer. "If you would like your tribe to fail, you are starting well. But you should not be in power if that is what you want. Your pride and insecurings will be your downfall."

For a brief moment, Zreyas thought he saw surprise in her expressive eyes before they narrowed with indignation.

The captain thought to get yet another thing straight now before it was too late. He learned in his years to recognize leadership struggles, and Katja was showing signs of it already. "You are the one that signed up to be here because you wanted to wander. Learn to take the supportings and likings as members of the teams of choice do here, or get out. You are no longer a leader here."

Zreyas stood up straight, never leaving her eyes. "You are... dismissed." Then he used the order's salute and bowed to her.

She did the same, though her face was the picture of fluxuating expressions of anger, shame, and guilt.

To complete the dismissal, he turned to Rtu and looked at him with scrutiny. "I think you did good work on our behalf, Freckles. Giving you the thankings for that. I'm not sure what I would have done had I been in your situation. When we are finished here, I would like to speak with you alone in my quarters before I get some sleep."

Zreyas considered what he had just said, then jumped down off the table. He turned to look back up and realized he had gotten up out of the chair and somehow ended up on the table. In the middle of his contemplation on that whole thing, he distantly continued. "In fact, I'm exhausted and am going to go right now."

He gave the order's salute to everyone. They returned it.

Leaving the still silent room, he knew he might have been a little too abrasive with Katja, but he felt strongly about what he had said. Fact was, he liked the Screh, but he didn't like her yet.

As they walked, Rtu behind him, he realized it was because she reminded him of his father and brother. Living like wedges had been cut out of their asses, always trying to prove something. He wasn't that different, but he wasn't their kind of extreme.

He had questions about her, as well as other things. Rtu was humming behind him, but his dark mood didn't want to hear it. The losses set in from the brief war on

Earth, and he was tired—that didn't make for a good conversation attitude. *Calm down, Zrey.*

Once they got into his quarters, he Q-leaped up to the counter where his armor stand was. He started taking off his armor.

After Rtu entered and the door closed behind him, Tap's hologram appeared beside him.

After Zreyas got his chest piece off and lowered it onto the stand, he turned and looked at them both, wanting to explode with all kinds of emotions.

Rtu's face was the picture of seriousness.

"I'm informing you two that I'm angry, tired, and grieving. Grieving for losses, but also shattered trust."

Trying to keep from exploding, he distracted himself by taking off another piece of armor, his gauntlets being next.

Once he put those down, he whirled on Rtu and pointed at both of them. "You both lied to me by omission! I've seen you when you lost Tulyata, and there is no way your brother is dead. Where is Rhom?"

"Well, I knew this was coming. Little buddy, he really isn't with us anymore."

Zreyas' mood darkened to the point it felt painful and his eyes narrowed. Then he shifted his scowl to Tap.

— This is an Aqum interruption — We wish to speak with Zreyas of the Atra in private before the captain does something…

Stupid? Go ahead, I'm listening.

Zreyas sighed and took the rest of his armor off as Aqum spoke with him mentally.

— We wish to inform you they had no choice but to abstain from speaking openly about Rhom. — We are saying with much sorrow — If they tell you, the new dark visage, Ijin will win the war. Because no matter how much you shield your mind, you use the quantum so naturally that your awareness leaks.

He turned to look at the two in the room and sighed. *So, what you are saying is that I'm a danger to everyone so they have to keep information from me?*

Zreyas' chest cracked even as Aqum said his next words.

— We are saying with sorrow — Yes. At least regarding Rhom. But we confirm he is no longer with us.

Thinking back on what had happened on Earth, he knew the enemy knew way more than they should have. Now, he knew why. It was dumb luck he got out of there.

He wanted to explode, and he felt his eyes water, but then the anger rose. Zreyas just watched the anger as he asked Aqum, *How can I lead these people then when I don't have all the information for strategy? And how do I even know you are telling me the truth?*

There was a pause, then Aqum finally replied.

— We thank you for everything you have done for all of us so far, Zreyas. But this order has come from almost three thousand varSas ago. Your talent and circumstances had been foreseen and precautions put into place.

Zreyas was angry for many reasons, and he knew his emotions weren't flat to make any sound decision. "I've changed my mind. My emotions are not even, and I want you both to get out of my room and out of my head. Rtu, you have the helm, again. I need sleep."

Both of their faces wilted with dejection, and both of them turned and left. He felt Tap leave him inside, like she had closed a door. Then he realized it wasn't her closing the door, it was him closing it on her. Potential didn't close doors on a person, the person closed the doors on potential. For now, it would be okay. He needed to feel like he had space, but at least he was aware of it.

He jumped down from the table normally and walked over to his bed as he wondered what he would do now.

How could he lead people with critical information missing because he couldn't be trusted not to leak it?

Right now, he was so tired. As he laid down in his bed, he said to himself, "Well, Zrey, at least you got the blue out of the Nation and now they have the potential to grow stronger before Ayya is out of her protection time."

Water leaked from his eyes to the point they sealed. It was just as well. His head seemed to swim gently as he thought, *Well, I'll get them through the gate, and to the new planet. They can take it from there.*

Then maybe he would take Tap to the Order of History to find out about the Heart of Odium and the mothers of the Janquar like Rhom had asked him to do. He would fulfill his promise, then disappear so he wouldn't have anything to leak. There was no shame in that... it was still helping. The crew wouldn't like it, but they liked Rtu.

Zreyas knew there was a lot of fear and hurt ego mixed in his thoughts after all he had done. But it was how he was thinking.

Too bad.

He had done most all that work and took the risks, and he only made things worse for them. Maybe when he got away from all this, he would find a way to contact Tulyata. But without Rhom...

Missing Rhom crashed in him so hard and fast that he gasped. He cried himself to sleep silently, away from eyes and judgment.

◙◙◙ *Rtu* ◙◙◙

Tap sounded almost frantic. "Master Rtu, he might not make it back to us. He has shut the door on me, too. We are almost separate now."

Tap's hologram turned toward Aqum's. "Are you sure this was wise, Aqum?"

"Yeah, something seems off about all this." Rtu sat down with a sigh so he could think.

As bad as things seemed, Rtu couldn't help but chuckle, because he sat down to think and Zreyas sat on his heels to think. His little buddy had a similar habit and it comforted him in an odd way.

But that comfort didn't help the frustration.

Rtu threw his hand down to the arm of the chair and grunted, making the bridge crew start a little. "I want to ask the same question: where is my brother? Du-ude I feel you, Tap. It's like a door has been closed and I can't reach him. Did he really die? Or is this another one of those 'keep from you for your own good' things? We need Zreyas' in-between-the-spaces thinking right now."

— We would like to inquire — What do you mean… spaces?

45 Nested Discovery

Rtu

Rtu blinked...

Panic rose, and he immediately enacted his visage power, shielded himself to hide his intentions, and put a shield around Zreyas, just in case. Then Rtu said he needed to take care of some visagely business and warped a part of himself out and to his own dimension. He was getting rather proficient at splitting himself, and noticed it was as immediate as he thought about it this time.

The two holograms of Tap and Aqum paid no attention to him, which was disturbing, but convenient.

He created an invisible bubble dimension high over Tarq near the cave Zreyas had entered to find the rest of the blue. Then he transported the ship's challenge node to the dimension positioned, then tipped it sideways so that any that transported through it would fall to their death.

As he did so, he noticed Tarq was all but desolation now. Zreyas would be heartbroken, and so was he. There was very little greenery. Even other continents on the planet were not doing well. He had never seen a species wipe out the balance of a planet so fast.

Anger raised its head, feeling it drag his core down, and he felt the warrior in him stand up within himself. He loved everything, but his little buddy absolutely loved that planet, and that seemed to make it worse. Understanding why he never liked to get involved directly with incarnates came flooding in, and memories of heartbreak came back in his early time as a visage. But he loved his little buddy so much, he knew this time it had been worth it, especially given the circumstances.

They were all fighting for the multiverse now, and he was royally pissed off at the moment. Right now, that was good. The weather immediately grew nasty on Tarq with his anger, with almost zero visibility through rain and blowing debris.

Du-ude, calm yourself down, or you might do something that you regret, again, he told himself.

Aqum had integrated with Tap, which meant that was how they knew every little move Zreyas made or planned. But Zreyas instinctively repelled Tap in the later part of that battle on Earth. That was the only reason he escaped that planet. After doing some checking as a full visage, Zreyas had shielded his mind, and there were no 'leaks'.

Aqum had been monitoring Tap and when he told her to leave him alone, he couldn't get any information on what the captain was doing.

Rtu paced, then thought to put his armor on. The most vital part of himself was there, not on the ship. He wasn't paranoid, but he wasn't taking any chances, either.

Where was Rhom? He hadn't wanted to give false hope by saying he thought Rhom was alive, especially if the Dark One had him, who had apparently elevated himself by force to attain visage status. He faintly felt his brother but couldn't locate him.

Rtu nested his personal dimension inside of two more, then opened up and called out to Samsara. After a moment, he felt her respond and the invitation access opened for her to enter.

Sitting down in a chair, he sighed hard. It sure was taking her a long time to get there, at least for a visage. But one never knew when a visage would show, even though he *was* one—at least, he thought he was. He wasn't really sure anymore. The events of the last month really made him second guess that. Well, if nothing else, it was just a title to describe what he did in his existence.

A soft, radiant light filling the room interrupted his thoughts. She apparently had a surprise for him, because there were silhouettes of two people, their faces obscured by the bright light of her flames behind them. But he hadn't given others access.

Rtu stood quick, readying himself for the unexpected, but waited.

"Peace, Great Warrior and creator. They are within me. Might I ask that they have access to our discussion? It is safe and I promise, in Tulyata's name, they are not of the Dark Ijin or associated with it."

Sighing and feeling the tingling of his stress leave, Rtu sighed. "You should have just said before you came... wait, never mind. I understand why you didn't. I give them access to our talks."

Both entities within Samsara surfaced through the Sleeping Phoenix's body. The first one he identified right away *wasn't* a stranger.

Rtu's eyes went wide. A sharp elation ripped through him and his eyes immediately flooded. He let out a half crying laugh at the relief of seeing his brother. He couldn't believe it, but there he was.

Rhom ran toward him and they both hugged each other. He picked Rhom up and squeezed him. "Rhom, we have been in a state thinking they had killed you. I still felt you, but it was so faint that I couldn't even be sure, or locate where you were. And Zreyas' grief is beyond messy, though he hasn't really had a chan—"

"There—there, brother. It's all right. There was a reason we had to do that. Everything is all right. If it wasn't for Samsara, I would have been Ijin fodder. She protected me. I'm glad to see you. It was hard to watch you all grieve for me. I wanted to tell you, especially since we had been through a big separation before, which had been very difficult."

"Boy, was it! But this time was worse... yet easier, in a way. I've grown up a little, so I didn't go off the deep end, but it didn't feel any easier inside. Du-ude I was freakin' out!"

The brothers hugged again.

Rtu looked at the golden fiery visage and said, "Thank you, Samsara for protecting Rhom."

She inclined her head, but before she could say anything, if she was going to at all, Rhom spoke up

"She protected me until the challenge council whisked me away to be Ayya and Lanna's caretaker. I can't say that I mind. I love Lanna and Ayya. It's sad though, when they come out of protection, they will have to assume new identities, and Lanna is in grief due to losing her extended family. Their family was told they died in the explosion that the Commander launched on Connor and Cerys' home."

Seeing his brother and being able to hug him made his body finally let out all the stress of leadership go, even though there was sad news.

Tears flowed from his eyes, and he started sobbing. "This is getting... *<sniff>*... to be... *<sniff>*... too much. I'm not sure I got what it takes to be a visage anymore, bro. I'm a bundle of nerves, and finding the old warrior in me surfacing!"

After Rhom coaxed him to calm down, he did so, apologizing.

Samsara shook out the fiery feathers of her form and settled down in a curled-up position on the floor of the expansive balcony. Her face and energy were the epitome of calm. "Don't be so hard on yourself, noble warrior and creator of the ages. We will fill you in now. Don't worry, Rhom and I will explain.

"My right hand will witness for the Order of History, *not* for the challenge council. You completely secluded us from the challenge council or any of the participants, except the four of us here. That was why I agreed to come. It was wise of you to nest the dimensions so deeply. Just in case, I added another around yours."

Rtu nodded, then focused on Samsara and the Soksheat standing in front of him and bowed his head.

He recognized it as the one that had been there when Samsara was born, witnessing Tulyata's powers given to her. The Soksheat species dedicated their lives to the Order of History, typically. After breeding age, they metamorphosed into an androgynous version of the species naturally with an impenetrable integrity. In addition, after their transformation, they never referred to themselves as him or her ever again, because it wasn't accurate. Their integrity wouldn't allow it. Now they were serving the visage, Samsara.

Rhom changed from Paul's body to his normal visage form. Rtu felt comforted to see his true appearance. His brother always seemed to know what he needed. Then he spoke. He seemed to have a glow about him he never noticed before.

"Brother, my heart goes out to you and your struggles at being thrown into something of more leadership and making the tough decisions you have had to make. I think you have done well. There is nothing you could have foreseen or done to prevent the Aqum impostor from doing what they did. And yes, I think it is an imposter, not Aqum gone rogue."

Rhom knew Rtu was about to ask a lot of questions because he held his hand up to stop any interruptions and continued. "That said, my concern is for Zreyas. He now blames himself for the problems that have occurred on Earth with Ayya, Lanna, the danger his crew is in, etc."

Samsara cocked her head. "And yet, we can't tell him now about Rhom or the impostor because the fake Aqum is integrated with Tap... and as you know, Tap is Zreyas as much as Zreyas is to Tap. If we do, they will find out too soon that we know."

"Thankfully, brother, Tap was wise enough to give it limited access. My guess is that she knows about the fake one by now, but can't do anything without Zreyas' command. We think they are trying to break Zreyas so they can gain control of Tap and him both."

Rtu plopped down in his chair and sighed. "Now, I know how Zreyas feels, making all these commanding decisions and why he didn't want leadership. I have a new respect for my little buddy."

He spent the next several minutes explaining what he ran into that tipped him off, what he did with the node, and how he came here to call Samsara.

"If I couldn't get hold of you, my plan was to set a trap for the fake one somehow... like telling him we were moving it to a new location, but I hadn't got any further than that. I haven't come up with the reason that would be convincing. Come to think of it, my desperate attempt at protecting the ship and crew by relocating the node probably tipped the fake one off I knew about the intrusion."

"We don't think it did, brother, because Samsara checked on the one that was Aqum. The impostor is like an intelligence that was implanted... like a skin by using a hack, not integrated into the node system itself."

"Whew! That's good to know. But—"

"Aqum said that whoever is inside that hologram got there by using the U.I. appearance interface program that temporarily shut out the real Aqum from communicating. That interface program is a separate module, and that is what it really had control of. They regained control of the core engine of that module, but the impostor cut off the connection to update the node's U.I. and its appearance."

Samsara added, "They just chose to not update the appearance because it would have tipped you all off that something wasn't quite right earlier than when the council shut it down during the attack. We think the actual council knew what was going on just before the assault on them."

"So, what you are telling me is that Tap has a bug... a nasty one, that is holding both Tap and Zreyas hostage out there in the middle of a timeless space. And Zreyas thinks he has doomed the world because of his 'leaking' and..."

Rtu stopped to tune into his little buddy. One thing for sure was he was not doing well at the moment, and it made him gasp at what he was thinking about doing. His jaw slightly dropped. His perceived responsibility at all the events, from what Aqum told him, was soul crushing. He could only look at his brother empathizing with Zreyas.

Rhom's expression was sad, but it had an edge of gravity. "It's quite the corner to be shoved into, isn't it? But at least he isn't defensive. At least he is planning to keep promises and doing what he thinks is best for the crew, even if it would be the worst thing for them. He can only go by what he is told, and that was quite the blow attacking every part of who he is at once, directly and indirectly."

Rtu clenched his fists and had to will himself to calm down. "It would take a vile oriented person to do such a thing. Though I am still sending out the love of a creator and visage, it makes me angry."

"I'm with you there. I'm angry indeed. Samsara, do you have any suggestions?"

Samsara looked straight at Rtu. "You, dear friend, are the only one that can do anything without breaking the challenge council's rules. While we have time before the council releases Ayya from protection, I would like to remind you that her father was sincere in his change and is indeed accessible through the challenge.

"In addition, if you want to inform Zreyas of what is going on, you will need to find another way to communicate with him other than your visage way that he understands." Samsara laid her head down and seemed to go to sleep.

"Hmm... another way to communicate. Any suggestions, Rhom? I only have one way to communicate, and that is through my normal visagely-mojo."

"Same here, brother. But maybe..."

"We can—"

"Communicate through—"

"Someone else!" they both said together, laughing at completing each other's sentences again for the first time in a long time.

Samsara even laughed contentedly, still looking like she was curled up asleep. "Now, you two are thinking. Who do you know that communicates differently, other than the quantum?" she prompted. Rtu could tell she was doing what his mother did... that knowing prompt.

Rhom scratched just over his right ear. "Hey, Silence uses his song of the Atraictlic Zizzira Apya."

Waving hands in front of his face a moment, Rtu then said, "Du-ude, that is a mouth-full that would twist my tongue so bad I wouldn't be able to talk for a varSa! But you have a point. I was thinking of a note... like as in an old-fashioned note on paper, but the thoughts required for that are still putting things out in the quantum."

"But the songs he uses go through the quantum to get to him. I've watched the signatures before."

Rtu clapped his hands together in revelation. "Wa-ait, what about Resolute? She doesn't use the quantum *at all*. She is afraid of it because of where she came from and doesn't want to risk it. Of course, we can communicate with Resolute, but they would find out through Tap with that fake Aqum attached to her."

"Good thinking, brother. Silence can somehow communicate with her, though. They said it was Resolute's outward way of communication, but I don't even know what that entails because I suspect it has something to do with Zizzira capabilities and whatever Resolute, being a new species, uses. Neither one of us created either of them as they are now."

"Du-ude, but everything in existence uses the quantum, even a rock. Resolute must just use it in a way that isn't detectable to anyone yet. For now, that is on our side, at least."

Samsara let out a long, 'hm-mm.' "Why not use your visage talents of dimensional balance to create a space to do a transfer of communication?"

Both of the twins exchanged glances and said, "Wha-at?"

"Do you yet have a collar for either of them?"

"Rhom and I made them each minimal armor that had some protections built in, like our armor, but we never gave it to them. We got... distracted."

"I see where you are going with this Samsara. Well done! We could give them the armor under the pretense that they were about to go with Zreyas and his scouts somewhere. And we could put a-a..."

Rhom trailed off into that world he went to when he started inventing or calculating in that science mind of his. This was one time he didn't mind it. He had been by himself way too long for his taste and having help was welcome.

After a few minutes, Rhom finally lifted a finger. "I got it. We could make a special 'pocket' of holding like you made for me that one time when I was a Viduri."

Rtu felt his eyebrow lift, following his brother's thinking. "Go on, I'm liking this!"

"Well, why can't we just make it to hold two breathing incarnates in a dimension? In a nested, breathable dimension. Call in Silence here and put him in it. Update him on what is going on. Then have Resolute's armor put on—"

"That won't work," Rtu said, shaking his head. "We need to include Resolute because trust me brother, after spending a lot of time with her, she is extremely intelligent and intuitive. It doesn't seem right to only treat Silence as the intelligent one. But if we brought *both* here... explained things to them, *then* put Silence in the pocket and then put Resolute's armor on—"

"Yes, yes! That would work!" Rhom's excitement was almost boyish. "Resolute would just have to communicate with him somehow. Right now, Zreyas is in his quarters, and Tap has access to that room too; after all, that ship is her body. But Aqum is a problem, plus, Resolute can't just go in there, the captain's room has top security."

Rtu insisted on sitting around a table to have a good meal as he told them his ideas. He didn't need to eat as a visage, but it was a family thing to do that he loved. Of course, he would have dessert first.

He shoved a fork full of cheesecake in his mouth, then held the fork out, waving it around as he thought and chewed. "Maybe we use a dimension with my signature around Resolute, or hold resolute and go in invisible, drop her off, and leave."

The ideas kept pouring in as he used his fork to cut another bite of his dessert. "Maybe something as simple as a note on her collar with his name on it that says, 'Captain, follow me' would be effective. I know, I know, too many ideas."

Rhom went into thinking mode again, judging from his expression.

For himself, he was growing more concerned for Zreyas, as he thought about how to make the pocket dimension as he ate, since Rhom was thinking.

Then he thought about the other worldly portal on Earth and got an idea. Maybe he could make the dimension extend out like blowing a bubble, expanded outside of the pocket far enough to grab Zreyas and pull him into the collar dimension. Then they could have the conversation while Resolute went where they would need to go to help get them out of their mess, or at least for the next step.

It sounded complicated to him the more he thought through it. Then he interrupted Rhom's thought and Samsara's nap and told them of his ideas.

They all agreed to it, then fine-tuned the plan together.

46 Guilty as Charged

ריריר *Zreyas* ריריר

Zreyas woke from a fitful sleep in the dim lighting of his quarters. Oddly enough, the room comforted him. Zreyas was feeling at home there; it wasn't so much the roominess or luxury, but the peace he got from being there alone and in the silence. The surrounding emulation of laying in his cave on Tarq, which he loved so much, probably factored into it a lot.

The lesson he had received as he had watched the old blind warrior answering Aaru's questions about why he didn't want to die came to mind. It has been about making a choice to go toward what he wanted more than smashing his face into the stone and die.

This wasn't the first time this lesson had come forward to guide him, and he was sure it wouldn't be the last.

Zreyas jerked up to a sitting position when particles started forming near his bed.

In the darker area of the room, the figure looked a bit menacing. It wasn't human or Janquar.

As the figure padded forward toward him, Zreyas put a hand to his chest and sighed at who it was. "Oh, hi, Resolute. At first I—"

Zreyas Q-leaped up to where his weapons were and pulled his two swords. "No one can get in here without my consent except Rhom, Rtu, and Tap. Who are you?"

Resolute, or at least whoever looked like her, had armor on that he had never seen before.

Zreyas immediately thought about his 'leaking' into the quantum. He shielded his mind as much as he could.

"You better say something now or I'll rip you to shreds! I'm in no mood for it."

The dark figure sat down, straight and proud, the epitome of royal stature. Then she turned her head sideways in an extremely vulnerable position, revealing something on her neck that flipped and glittered like fractal patterns.

That got his attention.

Zreyas cocked his head as he watched the churning gold rhomboids flip and move in waves. His heart leaped at the possibility that Rhom was okay. Rtu enjoyed doing it in pictures, but Rhom had a way of doing it like a blank canvas with waves of flipping, and then there was Tulyata.

Only three people could do that kind of thing that he knew of, and two of them were dead. Well, one of them wasn't but only existed in the quantum. He knew there were more visages, but he doubted any of them could create high-frequency fractals like that.

Zreyas Q-leaped down by his bed and laid one of his swords down on it. Resolute never flinched.

A purring rumble emitted from Resolute's throat, almost like a song or speech. This was getting weird, and

Zreyas' sword hand was sweating. He gripped his hilt firmer.

That was when he noticed her eye watching him. Her looking at him wasn't what made his breath catch, but the tear running down across her fur was. The look on her face was pure empathy. He felt it and it took his breath away.

"Resolute?"

She started a rumbling in her throat, and she opened her mouth. The saliva stretched between her sharp teeth, but she never moved her head. Then she let out garbled growls and purrs.

Zreyas walked up to her, who was getting so large she was almost twice his height at the shoulder now. He dropped his sword and rubbed her front leg and chest.

"You can move. I know it's you now."

She did, doing a series of nuzzles that eventually knocked him over. They did a little gentle playing on the floor. As they rolled around, he could tell she was extra careful not to crush him.

Then Zreyas thought, sat up, and looked at her. "Are you or someone else in trouble? How did you get in here? Not that I'm complaining."

She laid in front of him, head up, then she turned her head to the side again, just as she had done before.

He could see her collar well now that she was up close. The fractals on her collar activated. They seemed to go around in a circular clockwise rotation except in the very center. It reminded him of the three tokens stuck together.

Zreyas reached out and touched the center and his surroundings got blurry, and the familiar particles from teleportation appeared.

When he finished, he saw a strange cyan and purple swirling background but there was no floor, though he was standing on something.

There was one other thing he noticed. Everything echoed, even his breathing echoed slightly. It wasn't obnoxious, but it was strange. What had he gotten himself into this time?

Off in the distance, Silence was walking toward him.

"Silence?"

"Hello, Mother." Silence walked close and sat down.

"What are you and Resolute up to? Where are we?" As he spoke, he felt the vibrations of his voice. They gently rumbled through him. It almost tickled.

"I can understand your confusion, Mother. I'm here to tell you in safety that you do not leak."

Shocked, Zreyas immediately looked down, putting one hand down to feel his bits.

Silence let out a soft laugh that sounded more than a little odd, especially with the slight echoing. "Not that kind of leaking, Mother."

"Oh! Well that's good, now what do—" Realization dawned on him what Silence was really talking about. "Oh! Do you mean me leaking into the quantum and giving away our every move to the big ticking-LFO?"

Silence gave a gentle nod. "I'm relieved you understand, Mother. I have hope for you yet. Now, I don't have to say my mother is moonstruck."

Zreyas felt his head and shoulders wilt in a little indignation and his eyes narrowed. "Did you just insult me?"

"Yes, Mother. I'm glad it was for fun though, rather than it being fact."

He parted his lips to say something, but he decided to just ask, "What about my... leaking?"

"You have been the victim of the nasty infection of the Ijin, Mother. We don't know how closely tied, though. But whoever attacked the Council of Challenges, there are still parts of the attack that are not under control, apparently."

"So how did I become this... victim?"

"Aqum, Mother. We think, or at least hope, Aqum is alive, but someone took over as the U.I. Intelligence for their Appearance program thing."

The more he listened to Silence, the more his jaw dropped, and the darker his mood got. But relief also crept in.

"I don't understand technology almost as much as you, Mother. But since they integrated the Aqum impostor with Tap, we couldn't come to you directly because you are her and vice versa."

Zreyas nodded in sudden understanding. He couldn't help it. The relief that he didn't do anything to hurt their efforts felt as if he was so light that he would float away any minute.

"The Rhom and Rtu ones called me to their dimension with Resolute."

As Silence kept talking, Zreyas wasn't sure why his mind wasn't getting why his body was so excited and relieved.

"The Samsara one and her witness were there, too. They collaborated and enacted a plan to awaken you to the situation, and, of course, Resolute and I were more than happy to help. We love you."

Zreyas could hardly think in the shock. "Wait..." Hope soared in this chest. "You said Rhom..."

"Mother, a bit slow, are you? I just said Rhom and Rtu."

Zreyas fixed his gaze on Silence. "So-o Rhom is *really* safe?"

Silence cocked his head, making that fanned tuft of hair animate. That put Zreyas in hysterical laughing from both the comical look and the relief that Rhom was alive and well.

He broke out in actions he had never done before, but his body just did it. Zreyas threw his hands in the air, moving them back and forth in front of him as his feet twisted on the heels and balls of his feet, moving himself to the right. Then he wiggled his ass and then made his feet move him to the left.

Silence's eyes grew wide and cocked his head. The look on his face was so funny to Zreyas with that animated hair that he lost all sense of composure. He laughed harder.

Silence cocked his head the other way, surprised and curious.

Zreyas laughed so hard he finally had to sit down because his eyes sealed from the laughing tears.

"I am giving you the big lovings for giving me this news. I am relieved."

"Yes, Mother, I am too. But I'm not sure relieved is the right word you need for yourself in this reaction."

"Ha!"

"Anyway, Mother, you were about to shatter our efforts and all the while you were thinking you would be doing something to help by halting the leaking that wasn't actually happening at all."

"How did they find out what was going on with Aqum?"

"The Rtu one said that the hologram of Aqum asked about what 'spaces' meant."

"Well, that would do it. The real Aqum would definitely know what spaces were." Zreyas looked around at the endless view of... two-toned nothing and flapped his arms down once. "So, how are we going to get the bad Aqum out of Tap?"

Silence laid down, head upright, still proud and royal, yet almost comical because of his rogue hair. Zreyas couldn't help but grin.

"Well, Mother, you will have to do something you don't enjoy doing."

"What?!" Zreyas eyes narrowed suspiciously cocking his head. "What do I need to do that I don't like to do?"

"Pretend, Mother."

"What's that really mean? Explain it."

"Be something you are not. You must shield your mind and act like you don't know any of this and act like you were an hour ago, so they will think you are not a threat."

Lifting an eyebrow, he thought about what Silence had told him. "Ticking-hell... you know I'm not good at being a fake Zrey, right?"

"Oh, I don't know, Mother. You act senseless enough at times. And for most of your life, you spent it being something you weren't."

"Hey! Now, you are being rude. I've changed from living that way, and even back then, I thought I was doing the best I could to be me."

"I enjoy being rude, Mother. It is how you are. I learned from the best! All you have to do is think you are doing the best you can to be something you are not anymore, temporarily, to save us all, Mother."

He growled audibly, and with the echo in the place they were in, it made it sound otherworldly. His mood grew a little dark at the thought of having to undo himself for a time.

"There you go, Mother. Perfect, you are doing the senseless thing again. It's perfect for the fake Zreyas' mood. Well, it's not really fake right now, though. Hmm."

Zreyas scrubbed his face with his hands vigorously, letting out a growled, "Aau-urg. All right, all right, I got it. What else is part of the plan?"

"That's the main thing for you, Mother. Just do what you do best."

Zreyas slowly opened his mouth as he looked up with total confusion assaulting his head and he heard himself say, "Let me guess, act un-smart, or whatever that word was you said."

Silence nodded, but there was a hint of a smirk on his face.

"Look, I don't know what's gotten into you lately, but I don't like you treating me like I'm less than you. I have my struggles, but I don't deserve to be treated like that!"

Silence's eyes brightened. "Now there is my dear Mother and captain that I've dedicated my whole incarnation to."

Then his friend moved forward on his belly and nuzzled him, almost knocking him over. "Oh, I love you, Mother. You had to be a little afraid you were going to let yourself grow low."

Zreyas reached out to pet Silence's cheek feathers and felt the Zizzirian signature song from him rumble through his clicking beak and throat as he touched his forehead to his.

"Don't worry. I have you, so I doubt I could ever do that again. I'm giving you the lovings for being who you are. But for you, and all the others, I'll act like it."

Then what felt like the incarnation part of him came out through his words, and it felt like a young child still learning. "You are everything to me, Mother."

It reminded him so much of Aaru. Part of him was wise, and part of him was just learning life. It seemed beautiful to Zreyas. It almost made him leak the good kind of water.

Finally, he said, "I'm glad we have had a little time to be with each other one on one. Giving you the thankings for all your help and heart."

Silence pulled back gently, revealing that his eyes had been leaking. He laid down and used the knuckles on each paw joint to wipe his eyes clean, then shook his head.

It was all Zreyas could do not to laugh at that part. That tuft of hair was so comical when he did that. It was like something electrified that tuft and each hair had a life of its own.

He cleared his throat. "So, what is everyone else going to do?"

"Oh, that is the good part, Mother. The Rtu one is going to talk to Tap in the code the Rhom one had set up as a back entrance to Tap's... whatever they called it, I don't remember."

"It's okay, go on..."

"Well, they are going to fake talk and say they are going to move the challenge node to Tarq, where the Janquar would least expect it because poor Zreyas was quitting. They hope it will keep them from chasing the ship and try to take over the node for at least a short time."

"Oh, I see... and of course, Aqum will listen in."

"Yes, Mother. And the Rtu one will tell Aqum they need to go with the node to keep it safe. There is only one problem though, the weather at gate thirty-seven."

"Yeah, it's not showing up, is it?"

"Not yet, Mother, but the Samsara said that the cycle was about to turn around full."

"Whatever that means... wait... What is Rhom doing?"

"He is the caretaker of Ayya and Lanna, Mother."

Zreyas smiled the largest smile he had managed in a while. "I'm glad he is their caretaker, and I hope they do the marrying thing, or at least act like they are. I was doing some reading, and know what that means, ha!"

"The Samsara one said that if she hadn't made him disappear that all would have been lost because the Janquar would have gotten him in the rubble and he would have lived with no good mind."

"So, they would have taken him over."

"Yes, Mother. And the Rhom one knew ahead of time it would all happen. The Samsara one and the Rhom one planned it while you were in that cave room the little Trevor one made. They merged temporarily as protective transport out of there, and now is in an altered appearance of his true form."

"So *that's* why she wouldn't respond. And the caretakers are visages. This is serious business for the Council to do that. This war is turning out to be a lot more complicated than what I'm used to. How can I learn tactics in this kind of war if they don't communicate? Maybe all of this could have been prevented if they had just told me."

"Oh, that reminds me, Mother... the Rhom one would like to speak to you."

"Where is he?"

"He can't come here or he will lose his caretaker status and another visage will take over, and visages vary, so he doesn't want to take a chance."

"Oh, yes, I understand. But he went to Rtu's dimension."

"Ask him about it, Mother."

Silence turned his head to his left, revealing another fractal button just like what was on Resolute, but with a different pattern than the one on hers.

Zreyas pressed a finger to it and a bright light shined right into his face, causing Zreyas to duck and flinch.

"I apologize, my boy. Just move a little and the neutrinos won't bombard your eyes. They are doing me a favor, just like when they brought me through Samsara to meet with Rtu."

Zreyas did as he was told and when he turned around, an image of the old man in his familiar visage form was standing there, lifelike. He rubbed his watering eyes dry and dropped his hands down.

He had such mixed feelings about seeing Rhom again, yet anger surfacing. "Well, good to see you are alive. But you should have trusted me to tell me what was going on with you. Why don't you all communicate with me?"

"We didn't exactly have a lot of time to speak to communicate. But I communicated."

"Yeah, that look you gave me one second before it all happened. I thought we were family. How did you and Samsara talk but you couldn't talk with me? How can I lead with any kind of strategy when I'm crippled by the lack of communication!?"

Rhom started to say something, but he cut him off immediately, feeling the anger rise from the pain he was feeling inside from all the useless grief. "You said you would commit to being with me on the crew, and now you go off being a caretaker for them because you are in the lovings with Lanna?"

"My boy, I understand why you feel the way you do. My heart broke when I had to leave you hanging like that. But now you know, and I communicated my own messages, but you weren't hearing or seeing them because of the distractions. And the communications you saw didn't register.

"You did a fine job of keeping us safe, and that took a lot of focus. I think if you think back, you will pick up on when those communications happened. Would you like to hear something about communication that will help you with not only your friends and crew, but also your enemies?"

Zreyas took a deep, angry breath, trying to calm himself down. All he could do was nod his head because he didn't want his time with Rhom to be filled with lashing out at him in anger. He had no idea when he would get to see him again.

He knew Rhom understood him, but he didn't want to take advantage of that and take his anger out on him. If he said he communicated, then he did, he told himself.

"My boy... you are not alone in being frustrated with the illusion of the lack of communication. Fact is, incarnates complain all the time about the lack of it or too much of it. Typically, it is when they don't get the communication they *want,* or expect, when they complain about it the most.

"But it is always there, my boy. The problem is... it lacks clarity on the sending and/or receiving ends. They are not aware of what they are doing. And during those times when the communication is crystal clear, sometimes the person receiving it is not ready for it, or distracted with their own perceptions and focus."

Zreyas wished he would shut up because his mood was quickly darkening. "Oh, that makes sense, but it really doesn't make me feel better. In fact, it makes me angrier that you tell me this so that you put what you did on me only."

"Understandable. Had I been in your position, I might feel the same way. I ask for your forgiveness."

Knowing there was no way he could hold a grudge against the old man, he just countered. "Yeah, yeah, ticking-hell, I send the forgivings of you. You know I send the lovings. But the wave of anger is not gone... it gave me the anal-gy-hurtings because I didn't understand."

Rhom looked confused a moment, then his face appeared like he suddenly understood something distantly. Then he chuckled. "I see you are still stretching words you don't understand quite fully."

"No time for the schoolings, old man. I want to be angry with you at least a few more seconds."

The two laughed, then Rhom continued. "I would be worried if you weren't hurt, though it wasn't my intention, my boy."

Still feeling resentful, he said, "Well, giving you the thankings that you all worked together to help get word to me. I haven't had time to update you on my teleportation back. I need to contact Tulyata sooner rather than later."

That seemed to stun Rhom, which was disturbing. He guessed with him being in a form and being distracted, his visagely-mojo lost focus on that.

Then he looked up to Rhom again, feeling hopelessness assail him. "What am I going to do without you here, Rhom? We just lost the most adept person we have for science and quantum."

Rhom cocked his head in empathy, with tears forming in his eyes. "I want to be there too, but I didn't know what else to do. I had to protect Ayya."

"Yeah, yeah, I get it." Zreyas sniffed to suck down the reaction he wanted to lash out with. It was time to be captain now, but then he couldn't help it. "How quick you let go of family, old man. I feel the sorries for Lanna and Ayya when the time comes that you leave them."

Resentment surfaced, and he blurted out with deadly calm anger, "Yet another loss for the Order, and I know how they will feel."

"My boy, I wish I could say I was perfect. As much as everyone thinks I should be, I'm not. I'm just like any other incarnate. I've made grave mistakes in the past, and I am probably overcompensating to not make another mistake like it. If you knew my past, then you would understand."

Dead quiet permeated the room for a few moments.

"Sending you the thankings for that, and I don't care about your past. Now, how do I get out of here? I got a lot of faking to do."

"My boy, I—"

"I'm not your *boy*! I'm just an acquaint-lance! Or whatever that word is." His chest cracked wide open as soon as he said it. His fists clenched as he looked down, trying to contain his anger.

He didn't want to hurt him with words, but he was sick of terms that were about making him less than others—sick like ticking-hell of loss and spending his life being pursued like a rat, attacked, and being a dumping ground.

"Zreyas, I will always love you, dear brother. I respect you more than you will ever know. You have taught me more than I could ever have taught you."

Zreyas thought for a moment. He had learned something in the quantum that was valuable for this kind of situation, but for the life of him, he couldn't remember what the details of it were right now.

Frustrated, he decided to forget Rhom, the betrayer. Then the captain dropped to sit on his heels to think. "Can we re-use this dimension? Or was it a one-time use?"

"It was our intention to leave it. It's up to you whether you use it again. It's nothing more than an enhanced dimensional pocket in Resolute's armor. Silence has one, but it does not support life. It is for items. Rtu made both of them. I just did the key part to activate both."

"Is there anything else I should know about these dimensions?"

"The dimension you are in now is under the protection of Resolute's Aura, in addition to being nested. She has what we call a dead, or null, aura, because of her origin. Her aura isn't *really* dead, it's just the name we gave it. It's also why she is so dense."

"O-oh. That is interesting." Zreyas stood and said evenly, yet he felt sincere, "Sending the thankings to you all for the help and getting word to me."

Then he thought about not wanting any regrets. "I'm informing you, Rhom, I'm angry, but also feel betrayed. The dark potential-me statue in the hall of waves called you a betrayer. Was it because of this, or was it because of something else?"

47 Oblique Confession

Zreyas

"Honestly, Captain Zreyas..." Rhom sighed slightly. "It might have been both, due to it being one of your potentials, though my intention in either case was not to betray. The Dark One inhabited that statue as well because of your potential, so it could have been why you called me that."

Rhom sighed, looking at him with a grief-laced expression. "Sometimes, though, we learn from the past and let it go, while others, especially family, won't. They won't let you grow in their minds because of many potential reasons. They want to keep you in that old way, either out of fear, or because they see they haven't progressed and want company."

The anger erupted, and he did everything in his power to not let out a horrible war aura, clenching his fists. "Well, I don't care about the past! I wasn't even around to see it. I mean, look at mine! But I am free to be angry and process things when they come up, so if you don't like it, you can get the ticking-hell away from me.

"You are everything to me, and I owe you more than my life, but don't sling your shit at me to hold because you made a choice that you feel guilty about. This guilt just means you did something against who you are." Zreyas sighed. "Someone wise once told me that."

Rhom was silent. He seemed extra human right now, though, more than a visage. Then he realized he was in human form, not his visage form.

"You are a human now, having human feelings. You aren't the Vidurian High Seer or a visage anymore, Rhom. So don't try to be something you aren't right now. Just be Lanna's husband and Ayya's father for the time you have. Just ticking-protect them and do your job as a caretaker so I can do mine."

He looked around, then he turned to Silence, head still turned sideways.

"How do we get out of here?"

"I love you, my boy, no matter the form I'm in." Then Rhom flickered out of view.

"Wise words, Mother, even in your anger. And to get out of here, all you have to do is think about where you were before you came in. The balance of this dimension is you must exit within ten meters of where Resolute is."

The implications of the potential strategies of that excited his brain. Then he nodded and thought about where he was before, within ten meters of Res.

The particles of teleportation came and went just like a breeze. When he landed, he immediately turned toward Resolute, who was now looking down at him.

Zreyas shielded his mind extra tight, Q-leaped to his dressing area, and dressed in his armor and weapons, because there was no way he could sleep no matter how tired he was. He gave the two a slight wink. "So now, I have to be... ekaf."

Both Silence and Resolute exchanged glances and, after only a moment, nodded—both had slight... grins?

Attempting to sound a little more loud than normal when he spoke, he said, "I plan to leave the challenge node behind where no one will find it, because it will be hidden right in plain view of the Janquar Nation Camp."

He let the anger simmer inside him about this Ijin and all the damage it had caused and stormed out of his room, Silence and Resolute in tow.

꣓ꣃ꣓ ꣓ꣃ꣓

About an hour later, as he walked down the hall past the common room, he noticed his dark mood made all the Janquar do their best to avoid him. He even noticed the walls of the ship turned slightly darker.

Zreyas opened comms to the ship. "This is Captain Zreyas. My mood is dark and I'm angry, so expect the ship to reflect that. It's one of those ticking-mag-shit-eating days. It's not toward any of you on this ship. I'm taking action to fix something I have been told that I'd done inadvertently to put us in danger. Apparently, I have jeopardized you because I'm told I leak into the quantum. Work hard and be ready."

Then he made a series of chirps like Cree had made outside the cave on Tarq, but hopefully disguised within the growls he let out.

"Captain Zreyas out."

Zreyas hoped like ticking-hell that Cree understood.

He walked into the command deck and immediately noticed the fake Aqum saying something to Tap. Her hologram was dark blood red and her head had little horns sprouting.

She turned and said, "Hello, my Captain."

Rtu turned around in the captain's seat.

"How nice of you to acknowledge me," he said darkly.

"You are relieved from acting captain, Master Rtu. I have a plan and I need to talk to all three of you. Everyone else, out!"

All the blue staff got up and scrambled out of the command deck as quickly as they could.

Over the course of the next hour, he informed them about his plan to put the challenge node inside the cave the blue hid in, both out of sight and in plain view. But that would mean that Aqum would have to go with it. Then, when things settled, they would come back for it to put it in the new base of operations.

"Aqum, do you agree with this? And are you sure you are not being monitored? This whole thing hinges on you and your secrecy. We are all doomed if this gets out."

Aqum's hologram turned the color of a glowing blood-red the more Zreyas talked.

"And we can't leave *any* part of you here because Tap is quantum based and they will know straight away. Tell me now because I'm not in a ticking-mood for soft-footing around anymore."

Rtu looked nervous and said, "If we can just... get the weather to change for the path through. It should be here soon, according to Tap's readings. So, if you want to do this, we better get Aqum in that node asap. I've opened the dimensional key up. Now, Tap just needs to do her part in opening her dimension."

"Right, Master Rtu. Captain?"

"Aqum? Are you going to do this or not?"

Aqum let out a drawn-out dark sounding, — Yes-s — Then, as if it caught itself, changed its expression. — Yes! That sounds like the perfect plan! No one would ever guess that will be where you hide it. I mean… We think it should be safe. We are excited about this plan.

Well, that last sentence at least sounded genuine.

"Good, and when this is all over and Aqum does this right, then I think we can trust the entity enough to give them full access to you, Tap."

"What?! Captain! Are you—"

"Once this is done, I'll leave and Rtu will command the ship. I can't have myself leaking out information that will hurt our cause."

"But, Captain!" exclaimed Tap.

"I don't want to hear any more about it! You —will— serve Rtu when I'm gone!"

Tap's hologram turned even darker.

"Aqum, after we retrieve the node safely, and when we are ready for it, then, and only then, will I give you dual control with Tap. I know you have been loyal, but we are under dire circumstances and I would say this to anyone, even Rtu. I think you will understand why I say to you if you show any mistake or foul play, then I will make sure I kill you in the worst way possible before we all die."

— Oh, don't worry, we will make sure it stays safe and leave no trace. That nasty Ijin will never know I was here.

Tap looked at Aqum with a suspicious expression, eyes narrowed. "You are speaki—"

"Let's get Aqum transferred and checked into the node," interrupted Zreyas. "Then scan for any traces Aqum might have inadvertently left behind on the ship. Even one mistake will kill us all and put our allies in danger too. As long as we have at least one leader in the challenge, it continues, and we have over three by now. But if I'm leaking, so is Tap."

He was glad that he could at least tell partial truths. This fake thing was not something he liked to do even when he had been with the Janquar. He didn't have to be fake there. Zreyas could be any way he liked except with the Commander and the Emperor.

One thing bothered him, and it was treating Tap like that. He noticed a message blinking, and he dismissed it. It was probably a furious message from Tap.

Once everything went into motion, and Zreyas started overseeing Rtu, Tap, and Aqum, he remembered he had done that once before and almost got all the blue killed because he wouldn't listen to her.

So, he took the time to open up the messages. He wasn't sure who sent it. There was no origin or signature, and when he opened it, all it said was...

… spaces…

Zreyas scratched his cheek, trying to figure out—

Cree ran into the room and gave him a salute. "Captain, I'm here to help. I got your message loud and clear."

He closed his message and made sure he shielded his mind again, not wanting to let his guard down.

Sounding as dark as he could, he responded as he stared straight at him. "Well, of course you did. Everyone got the announcement."

Cree cocked his head and stared straight back at him. There was understanding in those eyes. His right eye almost imperceptibly twitched along with a few pulses of the gullet of his throat.

He thought about those little slight movements almost no one would ever notice, and he realized that those gullet movements would be the same as if he were to do those signal chirping sounds. He returned the slight communication.

Cree nodded. "Yes, Captain, how dull of me. You weren't calling me. I just assumed. I'll go back to working with the men."

"Once you get them settled and ready for the weather, come back and find me."

"Yes, Captain!" Cree gave him one last understanding-eyed look and started running through the corridor.

Had he just entered the blue's communication world? Rhom's words in the little dimension came flooding back into his mind. His heart wanted to melt, but he had to keep up the... ticking-ekaf plan.

He walked into the busy engine room. He pulled up the map of the ship and called over Silence and Resolute. There was no need to call them. They were there already and had been since he left his room. They just always seemed to stand quietly behind him on each side.

Zreyas had been noticing a pattern. Silence was always to his right and Resolute to his left, yet they never spoke about it.

"Silence, lead me to the engine room," and then Zreyas twitched his left hand in pure whim with his mind on communication.

The next thing he knew was he was being flipped over Resolute's head and riding down the corridor, following Silence.

— You are learning, Mother. I'm glad.

Me too... Daughter... me too. Ha!

The engine room was bustling with activity. It was silent almost all the time, yet he saw communication. It was like learning a new spoken language.

"Captain, what can I do for you? Chief Engineer Right, waiting for orders."

"You are doing fine, Chief Right. Keep going, I just came down to check on communication and if things were properly being prepared for the weather coming." Then he made the gullet motions, but not so obvious.

Right understood by the look in his eyes, then he did a series of motions, but said, "Yes, Captain. Things are going well, and we are ready for the… weather."

He gave the Chief Engineer a slight grin and nod. Then Zreyas squeezed his knees inward to let Resolute know he was ready.

Zreyas nodded to Silence. *Let's get to the Challenge node,* he thought to him.

48 Your Turn!

Zreyas

"Hello, little buddy! Are you ready to put the big plan into place?"

Zreyas swallowed hard, hoping his acting of the fakeness was good enough to fool the ticking LFO. "I just hope my leaking doesn't mess this up."

— We say with brightness that we will do our best to ensure you don't mess this up, Zreyas.

That definitely wasn't the real Aqum, because they didn't say the Atra part in his mind. He did his best to contain his anger.

As he did all this, he watched Aqum in his peripheral vision. He was glad that Tap had attached that hologram thing on the impostor because there was no way it could hide what it was feeling.

Katja walked into the room with a stern, warrior-like glare and gait. Zreyas found her fascinating to watch. The way nature made her body—strong, yet incredibly smooth and agile.

"Katja, if I wasn't leaving, I would have asked you to teach me some of your fighting style." Zreyas converted all his inner armor to full physical protection on a whim. "I like the way you move, it shows—"

<metal slide> <clink> Katja had her curved weapon to his throat standing on Resolute's head.

Rtu gasped and lowered his stance slightly.

Silence immediately went into a predatory stance.

Resolute never even jerked. She stood solid and unwavering.

Zreyas raised his left eyebrow without flinching. He had known somehow she would do that. He guessed by their mating rituals and eating them afterwards, their race didn't tolerate males much. Then again, maybe they did, and he just didn't understand the culture enough yet. "And this predictable action says what?"

Katja grinned menacingly and ground out her words. "You might be worthy to teach a little—too bad you are a *weak* and *spineless* male to walk away from your people."

He intentionally erupted a long war aura for show, putting an invisible shield on himself where Katja was, and let it move around each side of Katja, not wanting to hurt her.

Laughing hard, pointing her blade at him, then sheathing it. "You think that pitiful roar of yours is devastating, don't you?" She laughed again sardonically. "I used to have respect for you and these Janquar blue. I break my contract because I made a contract with another Zreyas!"

"Hey! Don't talk to the captain like that!" Cree yelled as he walked into the room, fists drawn.

Zreyas wilted his whole body, dejected at having Cree see that. He simply said in a soft dejected voice, "I release you from your contract, if that is what you wish."

"Good! I'll just let myself out!"

Zreyas watched her leave the room. "Screen up."

Tap manifested a security camera, and they watched her go into the airlock. When the external door opened, Katja's beautiful colorful body expanded into a gigantic version of herself as it adjusted to no atmosphere. It literally took his breath away, despite the sadness that sunk into his gut.

He hoped he could speak with the Great Grandmother to smooth things over after all this was done.

Zreyas growled, then said to Aqum, "Are you sure you want to do this? I don't want another quitter in the plan."

— Aqum is saying with excited words we dedicate us to make sure this node hides in the cave, Zreyas.

"Well, time for you to move into the node then," said Rtu. "I'm looking forward to the node looking colorful again! When you aren't in it, it's all grey and bleh, and my visage blood needs color!"

Still sitting on Resolute, Zreyas pulled his right leg up to sit slightly sideways to his left to get a better view since the node was on that side.

Aqum's hologram moved toward the node and dissipated as it integrated back into it.

The node again filled with color and the blue and cyan symbols came to life.

"Good! Now Tap, make sure that Aqum didn't leave any residuals. We don't want them to discover where the node really is. I'll check for grey spots on the node while you do that." Rtu walked to the node and began examining it.

Zreyas could tell he was using his visage mojo, as he called it.

"Aqum, as soon as we get you settled in, we will install a monitor so you can communicate with us and still hang out," Rtu said as he diligently looked at the node for possible grey spots.

— We would love that, Master Rtu.

"Captain, I don't detect any residual Aqum remnants. I think Aqum got all of himself in there. Master Rtu?"

Zreyas noticed Rtu had been looking at a single area for a while now. Something was amiss.

Rtu looked at Zreyas in a way that almost looked like a message. "Good, because if Aqum split himself, it would kill the soul and would cease to exist. Fragmented like that, no one can stay incarnated."

After another few seconds, Rtu nodded, then turned around. "I thought I saw a grey spot, but it must have filtered through after Aqum got settled."

— Yes, we are all in. We are ready now.

Cocking his head, Zreyas asked, "Does everything feel right to you, Aqum? I mean, if there is something we need to fix before we plant you down there, it would be easier to do it here."

— We are saying everything is perfect, Zreyas. We are ready to go.

"Okay, here comes the visagely-mojo to move you and get you settled. But I need to have a ride with you so I can make sure everything is okay physically. Then I will come back, get the equipment to install the communication screen for you, then return. Sound good?"

Everyone nodded.

Then Aqum lost his Aqum way of speaking yet still said in a computerized voice. — Oh yes, hurry. This will be good for our side.

That almost made Zreyas chuckle. But instead, he agreed with the ticking-mag-shit impostor. Then again, he was being an impostor now, too.

Rtu stood in the node, waved a hand for show with a big grin. "Time to go!" And with that, the node dissipated.

Everyone sighed in relief.

As Zreyas opened his palm, he nodded to Cree.

Cree announced in comms, "Next step, operation Side Track... three... two... one... *go!*"

As Cree counted, the token appeared and Resolute looked up at him sideways and blinked in affirmation.

Particles of teleportation came and went. They saw the colors of the purple and yellow node just briefly. Then they whipped away in teleportation again, landing inside the original portal console room inside the challenge. But they hadn't landed in front of the Earth portal. They appeared in front of the *second* platform spot in the walkway where a portal had been absent before.

As Resolute bolted toward the console and return node, Zreyas looked back and grinned at seeing both portals side by side. It was something he and the real Aqum worked out a good while ago in case something bad happened. No one being inside that room was a good sign.

Resolute stepped inside the return challenge node and Zreyas smiled.

When the teleportation particles dissipated, he saw nothing but blue sky and puffy white clouds, with Silence orbiting around the node suspended in the sky.

"Welcome to our sky view, Captain!" Trevor said, looking down at him with a bright smile. "I'm doing a job here!" Trevor grinned and held up the odd-looking ball-shaped device in his hand.

"And I'm just here watching to make sure I do nothing but watch... for the moment," said Cerys.

Connor patted his shoulder proudly. "And a mighty fine one at that, Son."

Zreyas grinned. "So, any attacks yet?"

Switch saluted. "Captain, nothing yet. I'm surprised, because they saw the node."

Connor harrumphed. "Maybe Aqum already told them about putting the node in the cave. After all we have been through, this is eerie."

Zreyas couldn't help but mumble, "Saying the agrees with you there."

"Captain, by the way, we all know you don't leak," said Switch. "Cree sent out a communication when you gave him that sign."

"I didn't realize I gave out that kind of information with just a couple of twitches."

"Captain, we have been watching your every move and word for a while now, and we are masters of signaling with body language. It's our language. You told him everything, at least in general. We figured out the rest."

"I need to take lessons from the blue."

A little stunned at what Switch had just told him, he looked down at the ground. There was no longer any plant life and it would have looked sterile had it not been for the remnants of dead life.

Trevor was intent on looking around for whatever it was he was supposed to be looking for. "Cree said he was going to teach you, Captain."

— Captain, things are going well and I wanted to tell you I triple-checked and there is no fake Aqum on the ship… and the fake ship is the only thing that has remnants.

Well, that is good. Giving you the thankings for being on top of that. Wait, wha-at?—

A whistling sound began, and it was quickly getting louder.

"Now, Trevor!" Connor yelled, but Trevor was already on it, and in mid-throw.

Trevor threw the device hard. It flew until… it didn't. It activated when it hit the invisible barrier of the bubbled dimension that had to be clear for balances.

The device released a beautiful iridescent shield that followed around the border of the round dimension. It reminded him of the time that Rhom cried so hard in his own dimension he had to route the water and it ran up the invisible walls. This was different, but it was just as beautiful in a way because it meant protection.

Part of the balance of putting that node out here was that someone had to be in danger along with the node itself, if he had to guess. Then he re-considered that thought.

Nope, that wasn't it. Not everything had to be about balances anymore. And the people out here didn't give a mag's-shitting-anal-gy about it. They were fighting for life, doing what they loved doing, from the largest of us all to the smallest.

Zreyas looked at all their faces and it moved him so much that he felt his chest crack. He wiped an eye, inspired by them all. They were *living*, although they were also probably scared like he was. They lived for something they believed in and what was right for them.

The job they were doing was what they chose. They could be who they were as individuals, yet they still followed direction and helped each other out, even if it wasn't what they wanted to do every moment. This is what they were all fighting for, not just a person's life to save the Vidurian Tantra.

Though he had grown to give the lovings to Ayya, this wasn't just about her, this was about the new age Rhom talked about and Samsara was told about when she was born.

As he watched the iridescent shield spread, he realized that, for him, the sparkling barrier and their faces were going to be a symbol in his mind of the start of the new age. It was going to be rough, but worthwhile for the multiverse.

Just as the shield was in full force, whatever it was that was hurling toward them hit it, followed by several more.

Cheers erupted from them all, even from Silence, who was hovering right by the real node.

Trevor pointed toward where the cave was. "Your turn, Dad!"

"Righto! That it is. What a pleasure this destruction will be."

Connor reached back over his shoulder and pulled around a weapon that he had never seen before. The opening was large at the end.

<ka-thunk> When he shot it, it sounded odd. They all went quiet as they watched it sail. He felt a hand on his shoulder. It was Trevor as he watched his father's shot land.

The entire rock formation over the cave system entrance blew up and there was a chain effect of collapse they could see happen across the land where the tunnel system ran.

More cheers erupted as the bombardment on them continued. He didn't think any of them cared if the shield failed and they got hit or not. Today was a victory... at least so far.

It was for him, anyway. He didn't have to lie in his real-life form... he did all the deception in a challenge form. He knew it really didn't matter, but he had to separate it in his mind, somehow, because he just didn't want to go back where he had been while living in the Janquar Nation.

"Mother, are you ready? The Rtu said the weather was in."

— Captain, Freckles is ready to move you all to the ship. And, Captain, I apologize for all I have done that might have hurt you because of the impostor. When you put distance between us, it hurt so deep that I thought I lost my soul. But I'm glad you did, or we would have all been doomed.

I gave a lot of missings to you too; he thought to her, feeling more than a little awkward. *It wasn't the same not seeing my potential and talking to it. It was a dreary place with no hope, and I don't want to go there again. I'm... giving you the lovings, Tap.*

Then Zreyas saw a half corporeal image of Samsara fly across the sky watching him. She gave a nod.

Something caught his eye to his right. A swarm of Screh slither-glided through the air at a rapid speed toward the Janquar. They were making the most haunting sounds he had ever heard. He guessed they were war cries, communication, or both.

Then one of them diverted and raced toward them. He recognized her as the heir of the Great Grandmother Sheejee.

Sheeja waved a speared weapon above her head. "Captain! Katja has a message for you... She will train you and she wants you to train her. No hard feelings about the desertion—it was part of the show. The one named Cree gave her the update! But she said she wouldn't apologize. And from me, I give you much respect, even if you *are* little!" She winked at him.

Zreyas pulled his bow and put it over his head in return, and an Order salute with the other fist. "We are good! Now, it's your turn to have fun!"

She nodded with a grin. "With pleasure! Now it's time for deliverance!" Then she streamlined her body and weapons and swam through the air at a pace that surprised him toward the Janquar Nation.

Then he heard the old man in his mind.

— You are open enough to hear me now. Well done, Zreyas.

Old man, I would rather you called me what you used to call me. I'm sending you the ap—

— No need, my boy. I understood. Now, the hard part comes, but I'm always with you. I made you a promise and I will keep it.

He smiled. *I made several promises to you too, old man. And I'm going to keep them too.*

Zreyas wiped his eyes and took a deep breath, feeling the gratefuls so much that it made his eyes leak. Then he shouted what he thought might be the most significant question he would ever ask them for a long time. "Everyone ready?"

In unison, everyone cheered a resounding, "Yes, Captain!"

"Then let's go *home*. Your turn, Rtu!"

THE END

Epilogue – Sneak Peek

Zreyas

The teleportation from a visage was different from a challenge node's. It had a waterfall sound; the ride was a sweeping jolt, had an element of bliss about it, and he welcomed it.

As soon as they all landed in place, the room suddenly got very crowded. He saw most of the crew, including Freckles, Cree, Tracker, and the Sadlers.

"Welcome aboard the real UN-infected Tap, Captain," said Rtu, grinning.

Zreyas smiled and greeted them, told them it was good to see them, but more chat would have to come later.

The first thing Zreyas noticed were three miniature Screh a little taller than he was. Katja, and the two behind her, raised a fist to him in celebration.

When they all smiled and nodded, they looked through the screen view of the outside airlock and saw the weather had indeed come in.

Zreyas followed their gaze, then gave his first order. "Places everyone! We are not done yet, and we don't know what is ahead. Let's celebrate as we go."

Before he knew it, Cree scooped him up and ran down the corridor. Zreyas didn't have the heart to tell him he could just Q-leap there now since he knew the ship layout so well. Sometimes it was worth it to have someone feel useful in a time when they didn't feel like they had much skill.

Rtu, Resolute, and Silence were chattering behind him about things he had not been privy to while he was gone. One thing he knew for sure—he was glad he wasn't having to take care of every little thing anymore.

"Cree," Zreyas said softly as he bounced on his friend's shoulder while running, trying to hold on to his bald head. Cree was running ultra-fast and bumpy today.

"Yes, Captain?"

"You never told me what you wanted to do other than be an adviser for me. Weren't you the one that wanted to learn to use the quantum and maybe grow small? I don't think your primary job should be to just wait around and wait till I need a ride."

"I do a lot, Captain. Remember, you still kept me in power to lead the crew along with Tracker as my second."

Zreyas ducked right before his head hit a doorway as they went through. "Okay, as long as you have the happies with it. It's probably why I don't have to manage every little thing anymore. Giving you the thankings for what you and Tracker do."

As soon as they got to the bridge, Zreyas got ready to Q-leap to his station when Cree said, "Captain, I would like to learn more about using the quantum and grow small, though."

"Me too, Captain," said Tracker, standing at a new station.

Rtu spoke up next. "Captain, Tap found a way to use Tracker's skills for the ship. She did a thing so they could work together and translate them to be utilized in space. She made a station just for him. We are still discovering new ways to track and he is also helping with diagnostics. It seems there are a lot of diagnostic skills involved in tracking in nature, and they translate well into space environments too."

Zreyas couldn't help but feel his body lift in pride for them as they discovered all those things and then got something put in place to work with it. "That is pheno-mi-tastic! Well done! Tracker, are you pleased with all this extra work? If so, is it too much with all your other duties?"

"Captain, I'm more than happy doing what I'm doing and it isn't too much. If it gets that way, I'll let you know."

"Good. And I'm glad you have the happies with your new purpose in our team of choice."

Tracker gave him a proud smile, then got back to business. "Your two advisers being able to use the quantum at least a little would be nice. It would give us a better understanding, and new options, of how to help you too."

Cree agreed with an emphatic nod. "Yes, we don't understand your new world, so it is difficult sometimes to advise or understand what your... limitations and advantages are."

Zreyas looked through the large command deck windows that were from ceiling to floor. "So far, the only limitation I have is my way of thinking. Well, a couple other things too, like having the full strength of a Janquar but not having the size fulcrum to use it well in a lot of situations."

He looked at Rtu, and he noticed two things: one—everyone was way too serious, and two—Tap was nowhere to be seen or heard.

"Whew! I'm glad you are back, little buddy. I now have a full appreciation of what you have to do as a leader."

"You are not out of the woods yet, Freckles. You know I have a way of putting the pain on you in some way."

"Tap, why are you hiding? It's time to celebrate."

"I'm here, Captain." Tap didn't show herself. "Do I need to answer that question?

"Yes, you do."

— Captain, I almost killed us all being something other than a machine A.I. I don't want it to happen again.

Well then, I suppose I should just commit suicide then.

— Why, Captain?

According to your logic, which is not logical, then I should kill myself, because I've made horrible mistakes. I even wanted to cut off a visage's head under the influence of the dark one.

"Well, Master Rtu, it looks like you will need to take over command again."

"What? Why?!"

"I have to kill myself."

"Du-ude, that's not funny."

"No, it ticking-isn't. But according to Tap's logic, and she is my potential, that is what I must do... the equal to what she is doing because she thinks she put us all in danger because she didn't see the problem with Aqum until too late. Her first mistake and she is ready to throw in the gauntlet."

The entire room went silent.

"If she does that, then my potential, perfect or flawed, is no more. We are all dead anyway. I might as well get it over-with and we can die together on our own terms."

Rtu looked into his eyes and cocked his head. Then a light came on in Rtu's eyes, apparently getting what he was up to. "Yeah, little buddy. I mean, look what I did to my mother. I guess I should do the perma-death too."

"Uh, Captain," Cree said nervously. "As your advis—"

"No, Cree," interrupted Zreyas. "When you limit potential, it's a slow death, anyway. Let's just get it over-with."

Zreyas shielded his mind from Tap to drive the point home, and he was serious about getting this taken care of. "Yes, we should follow Tap's example. It's what you wanted, isn't it, Tap? Let's just all cower in fear because we might make a mistake."

— Mother, are you sure you want to do this?

If we can't fix this now, we are all ticking-dead, Silence.

Rtu laughed nervously and plopped down into his chair. Apparently, Tap had made a chair just for him so he could 'think'. "How do you want to die, Captain?"

"I think I will just go out the airlock to be with our allies that have worked so hard to bargain and fight for us. That is where I want to be, with those that believed in teams of choice and freedom, willing to risk their lives."

Tap's hologram came into view, looking green. That was a step in the right direction.

Then she responded evenly and robotic. "I see what you are doing, Captain. It showed me the flaw in my logic."

"I'm not sure you get it yet, Tap. You sound very flat and robotic."

"Yeah, Tap," added Rtu. "You are hiding behind a Robotic A.I., just like the fake Aqum did."

Tap fluctuated through several colors in her hologram, then disappeared.

"Well, we failed to help Tap, Rtu. That sets things in stone."

She phased back into view again—a blue color this time. Then she said with as much feeling as he had ever heard her speak with. "Captain, *please* don't kill yourself. That would be the worst outcome. I see your logic now... really. I'm asking forgiveness for giving up on... me and hurting you. I forget I'm just learning to be-e..."

"Alive?"

"Yes, Captain, alive."

"I give you the forgivings." Zreyas grunted, then turned toward Rtu, putting on a serious expression. "I see you have a thinking chair, Freckles. Has your ticking-ass got an activation button in the seat for your brain?"

They exchanged glances. The room's occupants looked horrified at the exchange, and everyone held their breath.

Rtu and Zreyas both busted out laughing.

Rtu said in between howls, "You've been...

<laughing>

"around the..."

<laughing harder>

"old man..."

<roaring laughter>

"... too long!" Rtu slid out of the chair and onto the floor, not able to do shit.

That was too much for Zreyas, and he laughed harder than he had ever laughed before. Normally he would have jumped on Rtu and rode his laughing belly, but he wasn't quite ready to show that much of himself to his crew.

But, by this time, the entire room was doing their own form of laughing, even Tap. One of his crew just held his chest and sat down. He guessed it was more out of relief that he wasn't going to kill himself than anything else.

It was the first time they had shown anything that wasn't official, and they all needed that comic relief.

Once everyone finished laughing, Zreyas turned on his energetic frequency vision and looked out the window. The energy of the channel for gate thirty-seven, with the weather coming in, was breath-taking. Gentle, energetic wafts of iridescent energy swarmed around leisurely within the channel.

Then he turned more toward the channel of gate forty of which Rtu had already taken them through. It still amazed him, though the energy signatures were different. When he turned his vision layer off, he didn't see the channels at all.

Zreyas found it fascinating to see what he normally couldn't see, but he found it more pheno to know it was all there when he used his normal vision. It helped his awareness of tactics and strategy in life, he realized. It was like he could observe it without seeing it.

Without turning around, he said with command in his voice, "Status of our readiness to continue our journey?"

To his surprise, many voices didn't sound at once. As if they had been practicing some sort of order, Chief Engineer Right said, "Everything is ready, Captain. On your word, we will disembark."

"Navigation systems are ready and the way looks clear, Captain," reported Tracker.

"Mother, Resolute and I are in our places by your side and ready."

"I'm in my button pushing chair. Everything looks good to me, Little Buddy."

That made him grin hearing that. He stayed where he was because he wanted his crew to have the satisfaction and experience of taking care of everything themselves.

Then finally, Tap said, "Captain, all things on the list are checked, we are all ready."

Zreyas opened the comms, feeling celebratory, and he wanted to pass it on to inform his team of choice. "Captain Zreyas here." He felt the total energy of the ship quiet down, almost as if it were focused. "I want you all to know I couldn't be prouder of a group of chosen family."

Remembering Rhom's words about how he would change the ship just by how he was feeling, he really wanted his crew to know how sincere he was.

He laid his open palms against the window to connect with the ship consciously and allowed the ship to show just how he felt visually to each one of them.

He heard several gasps in the room, then he continued.

"We have lost many that we give the lovings to. We might have left a few behind so they could live their life purposes, but never forget their energy signatures are with us still…

"All our trials helped get us to where we are now. Remember, we are all choosing a new life and a new home. Welcome to the new members from Earth and of the Screh. Show them they are important and it doesn't matter what we all look like. We all know what it is like to be persecuted because we are different. Teach each other and get to know how valuable each one is.

"My family of choice… We are home already. Though we don't need a building, let's go build a structure to house part of our family so we can save the rest of the multiverse. Then they have a chance to discover what we have. And one more thing… So we can get ready to kick that mag-shit-eating bandhulian-LFO-Ijin's anal-gy-ass! Captain Out."

Zreyas didn't need to turn the comms on to hear the entire crew, no matter where they were cheering as they disembarked. He thought Tap might have had something to do with it. He heard comments as well about the ship and how beautiful it was.

Then he felt a hand on his shoulder.

Rtu stood there grinning with tears in his eyes. "I know I don't need to tell you we have a long way to go, little buddy, but thank you for being who you are and what you are doing." He sniffed, then said, "And I'm proud to be part of your family."

Then Rtu jerked as Resolute moved between them and sat down with a series of purring growl sounds like she was saying something.

Silence sat down on the other side of him. "Mother, she said, and I quote:

> 'I will go back to the depths of that ticking-realm of festering-ass-licking-vile-torment if it is what it takes to keep you safe and fight for you or your family, because you saved me. You and Silence are my family.'

"And yes, she used the word 'ticking'. It seems you are teaching well her the... expressive and useless accentuating words and their uses and application, Mother."

Everyone laughed and Resolute gave Zreyas the largest and most painful lick she had ever given him.

The Back Matter

Glossary of Terms

All definitions are related to this story. Some definitions are fiction, some may have full or partial real-world application but may, or may not, be applied in a fictional way.

Atra - <redacted>

Aramzu - An ocean creature similar to Earth's stingray, but with a larger mouth and the teeth to match. The barbs on its tail are much larger and more deadly.

Bandhula - 1. Bastard 2. An attendant in a harlot's chamber.

Brumble – The closest creature to a bee on Earth, yet its average size as an adult would be between 6-8 inches and red and black in color.

Dina - Earth equivalent of the term, day.

Festering - The process of conditioning one's self to a lower frequency. It can also apply to doing or being something you are not, without awareness of it. It manifests physically in the body as deterioration.

Garavu - A deadly slither that resembles Earth's Cobra, but significantly more predatory. Unlike the cobra on earth, however, they ravenously eat much quicker, and the garavu's throat has hooked serrated, bone blades with poison ducts. They slice the prey as it moves down through the body to enable faster digestion. The bone blades also prevent them from sliding back out.

Incarnates / you incarnates - Slang term of the deities referring to someone that is incarnated.

Kamyami - I love you

Kuravy - Eagle-like predator. Description in the story text.

Lutari - A giant arachnid creature that has a leg span of a meter wide (approx. 39 inches) as an average adult. It bears two fangs that are 7.5 centimeters long (approx. 3 inches). It doesn't make webs like the smaller arachnids on Earth—it hunts and builds nests in small caves or crevices in rock. Its venom is potent and uses its fangs to liquefy its prey from the inside. The lutari can carry quite a bit of weight back to its nest. A lutari can suck dry of everything but the fur in something the size of one of Earth's rabbits in an hour. Their downfall is they can't see very well at all. They use the hair on their body to detect things close to them. A Lutari also has a dulled smelling sense that helps them find prey. (Apparently Zreyas stopped in for the night in a young lutari's sleeping spot.)

Mag - A parasitic insect that thrives on low frequency species, like the Janquar. Its body is jelly-like. No matter how it spreads, or its shape, it can't attach itself to the host. The chemical make-up of the secretions of the body slowly eats away at the skin, though. The mag secretes its feces, creating a crust that attaches itself to the skin of its host. Its weak hair-like legs take a long time to attach to its host, however. It isn't until there is a firm grip of its feces that it is more stable to stay on the host, and eventually burying itself under it. The mag eats away the flesh and its feces replace the host's skin completely. It infiltrates the inner tissues, eventually rendering the victim unable to move because of its solidity of the feces. The host eventually dies a long and painful death. Depending on the host's health and lifespan of race they are, their death could take between 50 to 250 varSas (years). The feces material is so hard, it takes high technology to crack or cut it. It is often taken from victims after death to use for prefabricated armor, or used with other materials to make high grade and incredibly difficult to crack technology for space technology tools and ships.

Mag-shit - An insult, referring to the feces of the mag that attach to a host's skin and gradually kill them. (see the term, *Mag for more detail*)

Neutrinic-gleam - Building blocks of the Viduri made from neutrinos in a condensed form.

Nagodara - These creatures are pure decay and darkness. They are the fetus stolen from entities that become demons. It is a mammal, sort of in that the back part of it is like a large long-haired oily looking rat. The mouth and stomach are lined with rows of teeth that rotate opposite the rows next to them. At the corners of the mouth fin wings with three bones with knuckles. Made for wafting mucus from the stomach and the dark mist from the open slit eyes at enemies that do extreme and quick decay damage. The center of the three bones in the fins are shafts for extending clawed thin and spindly hands like working branches of bone. The nails at the end are needles of pure toxic syringe-like nails. They slide out when it brings prey into its mouth, especially in the inverted state. The creature eats its prey alive or dead by sliding its inverted mouth, teeth exposed back over its body, pulls the creature in and then folds its mouth back over the body and grinding it up with its rows of teeth in its mouth and stomach. When it dies, it stops working when the soul of the person / creature deactivates the decay.

RSi - Singer of ancient songs.

Sana jana - old man

Screh – The Screh are quantum skilled and family oriented massive-sized species divided into smaller nomadic groups. The grandmother of all leads them. Young males leave to join new families when they are of breeding age, at 999 varSas of age.

They have a serpentine body with thick, fine hair and tough skin with two arms and legs that are powerfully strong. They also use their powerful tails in combat.

The females have wider hips and head that betray the typical serpentine shaped body. The males are smaller until the breeding ritual, with an extra set of arms and legs for holding the female and fighting during the mating ritual. Only during mating are they stronger than the females. Once they have mated with all the females, they are killed and eaten most of the time to preserve their line's strength. In space, it is difficult to find food. The males take pride in this, but they don't go down easy.

They have a nation-wide quantum communication skill they can invoke in times of trouble, the Tookna-Connection

Extra Facts:

- Their bodies do not need to breathe and are adapted to space and it is unknown how they sustain their bodies. Yet once they achieve a certain age, they can adapt to atmosphere but shrink to 1/100th their normal size.
- They will happily take on opponents far larger than themselves.
- The Screh have a scent gland that produces a very pungent odor in atmosphere if they are angered, aroused, or afraid (which is extremely rare).
- They are very difficult to kill, but successful breeding is rare because of deaths during their mating ritual.

Shinit - A meerkat-like species much larger than the species found on Earth. Found on many planets in the multiverse.

Slither - A family of creatures similar to an Earth's species called 'snake'.

Soksheat - The Soksheat are a bi-pedal species with an elongated head that curves back with a flare at the tip. They are born with vibrant colors and patterns, unique to their personality and yan. This is important for their mating rituals.

After they mate with the right partner that resonates with their true patterned self for a period of eleven years, their body metamorphosizes into an androgynous version of the species naturally. Their character is still unique but gives way to *impenetrable* integrity.

Because of this integrity, the Soksheat, after breeding age, typically dedicate their lives to the Order of History in order to benefit all of life in many ways. Most of them record events and manage the archives, but some are a little more... special and carry out other services in unique circumstances.

Sol - A time period of one day

Torana - Arch; portal; arched doorway.

varSa - One rotation around the sun. In Earth terminology, this would be equivalent to the word 'year.'

Vyagga - Freckles

Yan - Intention and spirit of someone's actions and its energetic frequency association.

Acknowledgments

I would like to thank my Patreon supporters at the time of this book's release. They are all individually valued, no matter what the contribution.

I would also like to thank Jennifer Meyer for her wonderful beta reading that went above and beyond. She gave the gift of candid and detailed feedback and comradery.

Keep in Touch

Scan the QR code with your smartphone

If you would like to support an indie author that cares about the community, visit **ishKiia's Patreon**:

https://www.patreon.com/ishKiiaPaige

The Sleeping Phoenix **Facebook Page:**

https://www.facebook.com/IshKiia-Paige-The-Sleeping-Phoenix-Series-107707978352041/

You can subscribe to **ishKiia's personal newsletter. NOTE:** She does this personally and promises to never sell or use your information except for this newsletter.

https://www.subscribepage.com/s9y6m0

Finally, if you would like to find out about all of ishKiia's Services, wander on down to her **website**.

https://ishkiiapaige.com